After the Fall

Also by Judith Kelman

Judith Kelman

After

THE fALL

After the Fall

g. p. putnam's sons

new york

G. P. Putnam's Sons
Publishers Since 1838
a member of
Penguin Putnam Inc.
375 Hudson Street
New York, NY 10014

Library of Congress Cataloging-in-Publication Data

Kelman, Judith.
After the fall / by Judith Kelman.
p.   cm.
ISBN 0-399-14511-7
I. Title.
PS3561.E39727A69 1999   98–56133 CIP
813'.54—dc21

Printed in the United States of America

1   3   5   7   9   10   8   6   4   2

Book design by Junie Lee

/01
ICN

acknowledgments

I am exceedingly grateful as always for the support of my outstanding agent and friend Peter Lampack. Thanks also to Sandy Blanton and Ren Soeiro of the Lampack Agency for their able and willing assistance. I'm delighted to be back in the capable hands of my friend and favorite editor Natalee Rosenstein and her dedicated colleagues at Putnam Berkley.

For their generous input and assistance, thanks to Monte Radler, Assistant State's Attorney for the Stamford/Norwalk Judicial District at Stamford, defense attorney Mickey Sherman, Lieutenant Louis A. DeCarlo of the Stamford Police Department, Dr. Nora Brockner, and Anne Ziff. Special thanks to my brilliant young legal consultant, Matt Kelman, who works for hugs.

For Ivan, light-years more wonderful than any continuing character I could have imagined.

Disposing of the remains.

The act held a teasing hope of finality. Consigned to neglect and the elements, maybe the stubborn memories would decay. Years had passed, a sea of days, and still the horror crouched like an enemy in ambush. The most innocent echo, a sight, a sound, could cause the past to leap out and strike with stunning ferocity.

Just last week it had happened again. Jess was in the kitchen fogged in by the aftermath of a restless night and a lazy bout of early-morning lovemaking. Vague-eyed, swaddled in her blue terry robe and fuzzy slippers, she'd sat sipping at a mug of the muscular French-roast coffee Charlie had left steeping in the pot. Flipping through the local paper, she'd collided with the sour visage of the state's star witness, glaring up at her from the obituary page. The appended article described him as an adoring father and devoted husband, not to mention successful, charitable, community-minded, and deeply religious. His life had been rewritten with astonishing speed, as if the sordid facts had been scratched on a Magic Slate.

Then, death often had that powerful detergent effect. Sins were expiated, frailties purged. Even the filthiest soul could emerge from eternity's rinse cycle sparkling clean and stain-free. Even his.

Still, Jess held an indelible image of that creep on the witness stand. She could still see the rabid froth on his lip as he spat his damning testimony. "I shall never forget that night as long as I live," he rasped. "Past midnight, a noise from outside woke me up. Looking out the bedroom window, I saw the defendant's red Mustang in the driveway. The door flung open, and my baby pushed out, shaking and crying. She was running from that animal after he—"

"Objection, Your Honor!"

"Sustained!"

Charlie punched his spade through the ground's brittle crust. Grimly, he dug, hacking in ruthless rhythm. The hole gaped like a fresh wound in the leaf-spattered earth. Jess half expected to see blood seeping at the edges, pain sparks piercing the dense predawn mist.

Her gaze strayed to the box, her mind to its gruesome contents. Despite its large, ungainly size, the crate had seemed oddly light when she and Charlie ferried it up from the cellar late last night. But then, there was nothing substantial inside. Blind hatred, ugliness, lies.

Charlie groaned as the shovel clashed against a rock. Kneeling, he brushed away the surface soil, baring the peak of a skull-shaped boulder. A maze of rushing aquifers ran beneath the land, thrusting forth a giant crop of stones. Planting anything, tulip bulbs to dark secrets, risked the need for major excavation.

"Maybe we should try a different spot," Jess urged.

Perspiration streamed down Charlie's proud-boned cheeks, spreading in dark patches on the collar of his plaid flannel shirt. He set his jaw. "Has to be here, Jessie. We agreed."

She could not muster a reasonable argument. The decision honored a sacred family tradition. Years back, their beloved Bubbles, a rangy mutt with a saintly patience and Beelzebub breath, had died of kidney failure. After several careful explanations, their son Danny, then a gangly seven-year-old, had seemed prepared for the burial. But when they gathered in the yard beside the book carton coffin and the freshly turned earth, the child had dissolved. Despite their best efforts to still his wrenching sobs, a full ten minutes had passed before the little boy calmed enough to explain, on syncopated tics of woe, what was wrong.

They were about to lower the box containing Bubbles's ashes beside a maple tree, he whimpered. Obviously, the dog belonged near the *dogwood*. The look on his gap-toothed face had said it all: How could grown-ups be so dumb and insensitive? What on earth was wrong with these people he thought he'd come to know? Who could a kid trust if his parents didn't have the least idea?

After that, Jess and Charlie always took great care to consign deceased pets and other objects of their children's grief to appropriate burial sites. Max's asphyxiated firefly had been laid to rest under the burning bush. Molly's Barbie, mangled in a tragic lawn mower mishap, took her repose beneath the maidenhair ferns. And Yenta, the Suzy Parker of cockatoos, slept at the base of the phone pole. Clearly, the contents of this box and the ocean of tears it had inspired belonged in the circle of weeping willows beside the pond.

Charlie tunneled beside the stone and wedged his shovel blade beneath it. Straining against the handle, he slowly worked the obstacle free. Low grunts escaped him, and his face flamed with a livid rash of exertion.

"Easy, hon." Jess pictured her husband clutching his chest and keeling over. Events had aged him fast and visibly. The puckish glint in his green eyes had dimmed, and his aristocratic features had taken on a hard, humorless cast. His lanky form, once impervious to sloth and dietary madness, had sprouted soft spots: chin pooch, love handles, the straining promise of a gut.

A week ago, Jess had been brushing her teeth while Charlie showered. Peering across the room, she'd been shocked by his nude reflection in the steamy glass. He looked sapped, verging on sickly. She was reminded of her father in the year before he died. He had thinned from robust to rail thin, and then his bones had risen up under tissue paper flesh so you could picture the skeleton he was destined soon to become.

Jess's heart had gone cold. She could not bear to lose Charlie, especially now when they had struggled so hard to pick up the broken shards of their marriage and piece it back into some recognizable shape. She had made an unspoken vow, right then, to steer him toward a long-overdue checkup—but try steering a mule.

Charlie struggled with the stone, rocking and shifting until the surrounding gap loomed wide enough for him to reach down and gain solid purchase. Poised in a weight lifter's bent knee stance, he wrestled the boulder from the hole. Cords of tension bulged in his neck, and his nostrils flared like an angry bull's with the strain to pull a breath.

"Charlie, please. Let me help you at least."

"Stop, Jess. I've got it."

She fumed in silence. Trying to reason with him would be a waste of perfectly good words. Charlie had always laid claim to outsized physical tasks, even though, as an academic, his normal exercise was limited to juggling theories and wrestling with hard-edged ideas. Unknowns and emotional minefields were Jess's department. He took the rocks; she got the hard places. Some steps in their two-decade dance were bound never to change.

Charlie drew back, bowed and trembling under the stone's unwieldy heft. His work boot tramped through a leaf pile with a sound like snapping bones. Jess bit her lip to still the strident voice of doom. Fool man could suffer a stroke, hernia, slipped disk, God only knew. "Don't come running to me if you put yourself in a coma, Charles Magill."

The ground quaked as he dropped the giant rock. With sharp, shallow strokes, he squared the corners and leveled the base of the hole. "That should do it."

The box rested on a makeshift sling of ropes beneath the trailing skirt of a willow. Charlie grasped the frayed ends on his side and Jess stooped to claim hers. Wordlessly, they maneuvered the crate to the center of the hole and eased it down.

Taking up the spade again, Charlie tossed displaced dirt across the dusty crown of the box. Soon, a plump earthen mound blanketed the hole. He trampled across it, tamping the soil and marking it with the waffle print of his soles; then he bent to smooth away the tracks.

As she knelt to help him, Jess felt the prickling play of eyes at the back of her neck. There followed the sharp report of a snapped twig and a flurry at the hedgerow that shielded their house from the street.

Jess froze. During the trial, intrusions like this had been commonplace. Brash reporters had crouched in the bushes and spied from parked vans with binoculars. Some of the boldest had stolen close enough to peer through their windows, ogling them like specimens on a slide. One ambitious parasite had gone so far as to corner Max as he was waiting for the school bus and attempt to pry family secrets from the guileless child in exchange for the promise of a TV appearance. Curious ghouls would sneak up during the night to rifle through their trash. But things had long since returned to an outward semblance of normalcy.

Their narrow North Stamford cul-de-sac was always deserted until the special school bus came for Pauly Haskel at six forty-five. That's why she and Charlie had picked this ungodly hour. But rotten luck must have served up a restless insomniac or someone stealing home after a very late night out.

Jess's heart seized. They would have to exhume the crate. They couldn't risk even the off chance that the nosy observer, whoever it was, might return and retrieve it. The box held the entire record of the case: newspaper pieces, transcripts of court proceedings, hate mail, scattered letters of support. Much of it had been made public, but they had managed to withhold certain crucial elements, despite the frantic scavenging of the press. No one had seen the report on the private psychiatric assessment they had gotten on their attorney's advice. And no one must ever see the most damning thing: the confession. Danny had made them promise not to destroy these things, but Jess should have followed her instincts and done so anyway.

Charlie was still smoothing the ground. Jess grasped his wrist and whispered, "Listen."

Soon came another crackling sound from the hedgerow. "Who's there?" Jess demanded. She expected whoever it was to flee in embarrassment, probably rush home to spread the news of more strange, suspicious doings at the Magills'.

Instead, a large crow burst from the tangled shrubbery. The creature perched for a beat on the slender branch of an elm, eyed them with bold curiosity, then flared his capelike wings and swooped skyward. They watched as he soared in ever-widening arcs, shrank to a distant speck, then vanished.

"It's done," Charlie breathed.

Jess ached to believe him, but she knew it was not true. It would never be done, not completely.

The wind whipped, raining leaves over the burial spot. Charlie swabbed his brow with the sleeve of his flannel shirt, brushed his palms, and looped an arm around her waist. Their blended image stained the pond's wrinkled face as they turned away and slowly started home.

Jess Magill was staring down the barrel of a steel-eyed, snub-nosed weapon of lethal force. Her name was Dolores Wainscott, and though she'd been custom-crafted by Dr. Herman Delgado, plastic surgeon to scores of Barbie impersonators and the terminally young, she did not come equipped with a silencer or a safety.

"How was the vacation, Jess? Was France *très bien?*" Dolores asked.

"Fine."

"Food must have been *fantastique* from the look of you, *chérie.* You must have put on, what? Ten, fifteen pounds?"

"Come in, Dolores. Have a seat."

The pert nose twitched. "Actually, it's not all bad on you—the extra pork. Smooths out some of the jowls and wrinkles."

Dolores strutted across the office, spiked pumps spanking the hardwood floor. Her signature jasmine scent wafted behind like a vapor trail. Flinging aside a teddy bear, she staked her habitual place on the brown leather couch. She braided her liposuctioned legs at the knee and ankle and tossed her raven mane like a bullfighter's cape. "I have to tell you it was damned inconvenient for me to come in this afternoon, Jessica. What's the big emergency? Overdue phone bill?"

"I'll be with you in just a minute, Dolores."

"You want a loan, ask for a loan. You need to fill your time slots, say so. Of all people, you'd think a shrink would know how to say what's on her mind. I'm so sick of your silly evasive games, I swear it."

Jess leafed absently through the case file, waiting for her nerves to stop snapping like rubber bands. After a dozen years as a psychotherapist, she had come to view herself as largely shatterproof and shock-resistant, at least where patients were concerned. Between her practice in downtown Stamford, Connecticut, and her earlier work at Glenhaven, a psychiatric hospital in neighboring Greenwich, she had seen most every kind of case in the clinical book. And having survived, more or less intact, a forty-year stint as the daughter of Pearl Lefferman, she was no stranger to corrosive, erratic behavior. But training and experience were a flimsy shield against this particular client.

Dolores presented a gruesome stew of affective, narcissistic, and obsessive-compulsive disorders, spiced by a generous pinch of substance abuse. She had no limits, no boundaries, and no civilized restraints.

During treatment, she had bragged about lodging false accusations of child abuse against a friend who crossed her and hurling hot oil at a neighbor's mewling cat. Proudly, she'd claimed credit for the fiscal and emotional undoing of two ex-husbands and the functional castration of several disappointing suitors. The woman had a talent for retribution and no tolerance, whatsoever, for disappointment.

Still, despite—or perhaps as part of—her craziness, she maintained a pristine, modish facade. There was never a misplaced hair or a smudge in her mask-like makeup. Every item in her considerable wardrobe was expensive, precisely tailored, and accessorized right down to to the bleached, bonded teeth. Despite the sweltering heat, she looked astringent cool in a lime-green silk ensemble with a matching Kelly bag and chunky gold jewelry. Dolores Wainscott was a designer maniac. Think Charles Manson as a lady who lunched.

Jess battled a strong urge to flee. Dealing with Dolores was a thankless proposition in the best of times, and this was anything but. The week of stultifying temperatures since their return from France had her energies lolling in emergency reserve. Her office, a two-room suite on the second floor of a converted Victorian house in downtown Stamford, offered abundant charm but spare comforts. Globs of paint glued the ancient windows to the sills. The insulation had long since fallen around the building's ankles like underpants with stretched-out elastic. An ancient ceiling fan hobbled in listless circles. The air conditioner, fueled by a feeble electrical system, whined and issued a watery sigh.

Perspiration had plastered Jess's cream cotton blouse to her back, and her beige linen skirt had the look of a crumpled lunch bag. Her curly copper hair had been whipped to a wiry froth by the humidity, and her feet, accustomed to the freedom of sandals and lazy sight-seeing strolls along the Seine, throbbed with a deep percussive ache. She didn't need the mirror to tell her the rest of the rotten news. In heat like this, her pallid skin took on a ghastly green cast, and her hazel eyes sank in dusky troughs.

The sooner she got this lousy business over with, the sooner she could go home. She imagined peeling off her sodden clothes and doffing the tourniquet panty hose. She wanted to curl up with a good book and her head in the freezer.

"We need to talk, Dolores," Jess began.

"You mean *I* need to talk and *you* need to charge me two bucks a minute for the privilege."

"There is no charge for today. I asked to see you so we could discuss your treatment future."

"Meaning what?"

"I believe it's in your best interest to find another counselor."

"Let me get this straight. You're *firing* me? You're telling me I flunked *therapy*?"

"We haven't been able to work together effectively. You know that."

Sparks of rage lit the flinty eyes. "That's because you hate me, Jess, because you're jealous of what I am and what I have. How professional. Can't wait to tell the folks who hand out the shrink licenses. Bet they'll be fascinated."

"Sometimes the therapeutic relationship simply doesn't work out, Dolores. It's not a personal thing."

"Not personal, my butt. You'd like to see me dead, wouldn't you? Maybe I should suck down some Valium and vodka and make you really happy. I'll be sure to give you full credit in the note."

Jess proffered the list she'd prepared. "You can call any of these referring agencies for a recommendation." She could not bring herself to name specific therapists. That would be akin to slipping a scorpion in a colleague's shoe.

"If that's the way you want it, fine. Frankly, you never were any damned good. Truth is I only kept coming because I felt sorry for you." With a contemptuous sniff, she strutted toward the door. On the way, she shredded the referrals and rained the scraps like confetti over Jess's desk. "You can keep your damned advice."

Dolores slammed out with a jarring concussion and her footfalls faded down the stairs. From below came the creaky whine of the screen door, followed by the roar of a car engine from the lot behind the house. Peering out, Jess spied Dolores's sleek black Mercedes angling toward Summer Street, tires spinning, churning up a grainy haze of dust.

Melting with relief, Jess dumped the Wainscott file in the drawer marked "Inactive." The encounter had gone far better than she'd dared to hope. How many useless hours had she spent rehearsing what she would say, steeling herself against the expected fury of a Dolores scorned? Jess had worried and talked so much about the case, Charlie had accused her of bringing Dolores along on their trip.

From now on, Jess planned to pack far lighter.

She collected the files she needed to review that night and locked the rest in the squat gunmetal cabinet beside the desk. She was eager to get home. Reentering the real world after the long August vacation always gave her a case of the emotional bends. She loved getting away with Charlie and the kids. Shed of school and work and standard obligations and general angst, they had time to get reacquainted. Jess always marveled at how much the children had changed from the previous summer. The shifts in their attitudes and abilities dazzled her, not to mention scaring her to death.

This year, coming back had been harder than ever. Postponing her return to work for a week had not done much to cushion the blow. Family life, as they knew it, was poised to undergo radical change. Danny, their eldest, was starting his last year of high school. His desk was piled with the college catalogues and applications he'd sent for last spring. Jess could feel him pulling away, folding his emotional tents like a stalwart pioneer. This was right. He was ready. Somehow Jess—sane, grounded, self-aware soul that she was—would deal.

The younger kids were growing with horrifying speed as well. Thirteen-year-old Molly had begun to resemble an adolescent, at least in her moods, which pitched and whirled with the dizzying unpredictability of a mechanical bull. Even Max, their little hellion, was developing the visible bones and the odors that presaged an invasion of rampaging hormones. Sooner than Jess could bear to consider, all of them would be grown and gone. But then, that was the inexplicable point. You had kids to let them go.

It was nearing six p.m. when Jess left the deserted building. Oily fumes hovered over the rush hour traffic snaking down Summer Street toward the Turnpike. Ninety-degree-plus temperatures, coupled with drenching humidity and a ponderous shroud of pollution, made it hard to move and impossible to draw a decent breath. Higher reasoning was altogether out of the question. Jess imagined her brain cells lying around like overheated dogs, prostrate and panting in her skull.

As she trudged up the drive to the parking lot, she fished through her cluttered straw tote for the key. Her purse yielded two fat envelopes full of freshly developed pictures, ticket stubs from the Louvre, a wrinkled postcard depicting prehistoric cave paintings at Les Eyzies, and a scatter of sand from the beach at the seaside resort of La Rochelle. Jess ached to be back there, lulled by lapping waves, bone-melting sunshine, and Max's shrilled delight as he buried his bossy big sister to the neck or splashed his know-it-all big brother in the face. Sheer bliss.

The car lock was searing hot. Opening the door unleashed a blast of fiery air. Jess reached in gingerly and turned on the engine. She flipped the temperature to maximum cool. As she stood again, she caught a strong whiff of jasmine and gin.

Wheeling quickly, she faced Dolores Wainscott. The hard eyes were menacing slits, neck arched like a malevolent cobra. Her gleaming black Mercedes idled at the base of the drive, belching exhaust.

Panic squeezed Jess's intestines. "What is it, Dolores?"

"I don't take this kind of crap from anyone, especially not a pudgy frump like you," she hissed.

"I told you, this isn't personal. You'll be better off working with somebody else. That's all."

"You'll be sorrier than you can imagine, lady. Sorry you were born."

Jess evicted the fear from her voice. "I hear that you're angry. But threatening me is not a useful exercise."

"I'll show you what's a *useful exercise,* you dumb, arrogant twit." The shrink-wrapped face flamed with rage and alcohol. "You're nothing. I'll ruin your goddamned practice and your perfect little family and your stupid little life."

"I need to go now, Dolores. Kindly move your car."

The plumped lips retracted in a vicious smirk. "Don't believe me? I've got everything I need on your precious Charlie and the kids. So cute, aren't they? Nothing I like better than to squash something cute."

Jess faced her down. "That's *enough,* Dolores."

"You've been warned, Jessie-poo. Now you get the real thing." Turning on her bug-feeler heels, she tottered to the Mercedes. She slammed the door, gunned the engine, and sped off in a choking swirl of dust.

Jess slipped into the cool cab of the Volvo and shifted into reverse. She frowned at her pale, shaken image in the rearview mirror. *Silly girl,* she chided herself. That tantrum was a small price to pay for a Dolores-free existence.

The taunting threats resounded in her mind. Jess tried to buffer them with soothing reason. It was nothing. Meaningless. Only words.

Her family would be fine.

Approaching the Bull's Head strip mall, Jess spotted Ray, the brawny, mustachioed owner of the fish market, loping toward his pickup in the lot. A few sharp raps on the horn caught his attention. Unabashed pleading got him to pluck out his key ring and reopen the store.

Jess planned to make sole *beau geste* tonight, and she was determined to let nothing interfere, including the fact that the dish was nonexistent. The name had popped into her head this morning as she reluctantly left for the office. Charlie had set out before dawn for an early-morning faculty session at Yale. The kids were still asleep, savoring the final crumbs of their summer break before the start of school the day after tomorrow.

Jess had decided to concoct something quintessentially French, *avec beurre,* arterial plaque be damned. Anything to extend the vacation mood for a few precious hours. After dinner, they could moon over the latest pictures from the trip that Jess had retrieved from the photo shop that morning. They could laugh at the image of Max staring bug-eyed at the topless bathers, while Danny, flushed scarlet and afflicted with a sudden stammer, feigned nonchalance. They could practice their fledgling French, play their favorite game of opposites. The opposite of *mon frère Danny* is *cool,* Molly liked to taunt. To which, Danny would reply, with maddening detachment, that the opposite of *confidence* is *jalousie.* When they'd last played on the ferry at Entre Deux Mers, Max had eagerly reported that he'd figured out a really good one: the opposite of *sûr* must be Grandma Pearl's favorite word, *tsuris,* which was Yiddish for troubles. Pearl collected those, along with unreasonable grudges and blind biases, as if they might someday be worth a fortune.

"What'll it be, Mrs. Magill?" asked Ray.

Jess eyed the gleaming fillets in their snow-filled cases. Whole trout, mussels, bluepoint oysters, mounds of shrimp. Even dead, they looked perkier than she felt.

Four varieties of sole and a flounder vied for her vote. Sole *beau geste* called for the slim, nearly transparent slices in the first case, she decided. But before she could get the order out, a wizened little woman with a dahlia poof of yellow hair bustled in, breathless. She cast a hopeful look in Jess's direction. "I'm in a rush, dear. Do you mind?"

"No, fine. Go ahead."

Her fuchsia lips drew into a pensive seam. "How much grey sole do I need for two West Highland white terriers?" she asked Ray.

"Depends," he said evenly. "What are you serving with it?"

"Veggies. A starch. The usual."

"Half a pound, then. Unless they're big eaters." Not a flicker of amusement crossed Ray's face. Like Jess, the man had clearly seen it all.

Jess settled for two pounds of lemon sole at half the cost of the grey sole. Ray packed them with a bag of shaved ice in deference to the heat. At the neighboring market, she trolled the congested aisles for other *beau geste* ingredients and accompaniments: wild mushrooms, shallots, new potatoes, chicken stock, fresh tarragon, asparagus, a crisp baguette. She chose the shortest checkout line, which naturally placed her behind a woman armed with several untagged items, a balky Visa card, and a fistful of coupons.

By the time Jess slid her parcels into the trunk, it was after seven. The kids would be ravenous. With luck, she could make it home in twenty minutes. But as she peered at the dashboard clock, calculating how long it would take to get dinner on the table, she spied a flaming warning light. The temperature gauge had risen to the danger zone. Steam ghosts levitated from the hood in a clear display of serious overheating.

Jess pulled to the shoulder and dialed the auto club on her cell phone. Dispatch promised to send someone out within the hour.

While she waited, the sky massed with plump charcoal clouds. Soupy darkness descended, and there was a growl of distant thunder. Soon, the first fat drops splattered on the windshield.

The storm rose in rapid crescendo. Lightning flared, followed by huge percussive bursts. Pins of rain struck with the sound of raucous applause. The wipers swayed like hula girls on speed, but the pelting downpour and dense condensation shrank visibility to a wish.

Cars all around limped to the shoulder to wait out the worst of the downpour. From the frantic busy-service signal on the phone, many were also trying, as she was, to call ahead and warn of an indeterminate delay.

On the fourth try, she got through. Molly answered with her usual heartwarming enthusiasm. "Oh, it's you."

"Yes, sweetheart. Sorry to disappoint you. I need to speak to Dad."

Max's elephantine stomping up the stairs followed Molly's banshee yell. When Charlie was in his study, musing about some deep philosophical conundrum, nothing short of a nuclear strike or Max-quality nagging could divert his attention.

Soon, through a haze of static, Charlie's smooth, earnest voice came on the line. "What's up, honey? You okay?"

"Fine, but I'm stuck down at Bull's Head. The car overheated, and I'm waiting for triple A. The kids should have something to eat in the meantime. Maybe ask Danny to make his world-famous pizza bagels."

"No can do. He went out."

"Where? When? Why? With whom?"

"Somewhere, an hour ago, with a bunch of kids. Something doing at school, I think he said."

"Who drove?"

"Danny did."

Jess tapped a nervous cadence on the dash. Charlie's car was a '65 red Mustang convertible, low mileage, lovingly restored. It also happened to be a cop magnet with an automatic, built-in antisanity device. Given that machine and a stretch of open road, even cautious Jess was prone to stomp the accelerator and entertain range-riding fantasies. "I thought we agreed he was only allowed to drive the Volvo."

"Come on, Jess. I was glad he wanted to take the car. We talked about how he's been acting a little gun-shy about driving lately, remember?"

"I'd rather have him gun-shy than hurt."

"Relax. He'll be fine."

"So will my ulcers."

"I'll have a nice drink waiting when you get here. How's that?"

"Make it Maalox," she grumped. "Here comes Elmer's Exxon. See you soon as they get me straightened out."

The rain had slowed to a mere torrent. A wiry kid in a Yankee cap and navy windbreaker slumped from the cab of the truck. Jess popped the hood, and he poked through the car's oily innards. Moments later, he motioned for her to roll down the window.

"Have to tow you to the shop, ma'am. 'Fraid you got a busted radiator hose."

"Can't you put in some water for now? I can take it in tomorrow."

An emphatic shake of his head sent droplets spraying from the long, stringy hair. "You ride with the hose broke like that, the engine's gonna seize right up on you. Could be she already has."

The gas station perched at the juncture of High Ridge Road and Vine. When the wrecker pulled in, lights flashing, a grizzled old man with grocery bag skin and a cross-bite lumbered out to greet them. "That's Pops," the kid said. "He'll fix you right up."

In a dim bay redolent of axle grease and Old Spice, Pops raised the car on a hydraulic lift and ducked beneath to assess the damage.

"How bad?" Jess asked.

"Have to run some tests before I know for sure. Might as well wait inside where it's cool. We got snacks and a soda machine. Plus, there's Maggie who handles the register. Magpie, we call her. She'll be more than glad to oblige if your ears need bending. If they don't, we sell those wax earplugs. Work like a charm."

In the cramped station, Jess fed her frustrations a York peppermint patty and a Reese's peanut butter cup, while Maggie the Magpie, a scrawny, wall-eyed woman, exercised her loose-hinged jaw. "If there's one thing I can't figure for the life of me, it's men. Older they get, the younger they want their honeys. Last week this really old guy comes in with a little girl, looked about twelve, and he's all over her like ticks on a hound. Smooching her, pinching her butt. 'That's my pretty baby,' he says. 'That's Daddy's little love.' I mean, what the hell is that?"

Given her professional training, Jess could have offered a comprehensive answer, but she sized up Maggie the Magpie as a dedicated talking machine. Most likely, the ears were strictly ornamental.

An hour later the mechanic shuffled in, wiping his knobby hands on a rag. "Seems you're in luck. No serious harm done. Have to send someone for a replacement hose, though. We're fresh out of that size."

"How long will that take?"

"Shouldn't be too bad. Rusty can go soon as he gets back from supper. Lucky thing you caught the problem quick," said Pops. "Way that hose was sliced, the radiator bled nearly bone dry."

"Sliced?"

"Clean through." He slashed the air to illustrate the point. "Probably one of those spoiled brats with too much time and money to burn whose notion of fun is making trouble."

Fuming, Jess thought of Dolores. Of course, she had no proof. Anyway, accusing that beast would give her the attention she craved. The only sensible response was to ignore her.

Jess paced the station, muttering under her breath, ignoring Dolores Wainscott with ferocious intensity. Rusty took his sweet time returning from supper and going out again to pick up the hose. Pops installed the length of rubber tube in creaky slow motion.

It was after ten when Jess finally phoned to tell Charlie she was on the way home. "Is Danny back yet?" she asked.

"No. But I made the kids dinner and read to Max. Power was out for a while, so he and Mol hit the sack early. They're fine."

"What are you trying to tell me, Charlie? Having two out of three kids safe is enough?"

"No. I'm trying to tell you that having one out of two parents crazy is more than enough."

"So you think I'm overreacting horribly."

"Not at all, honey. I think you're do it very, very well."

Jess enjoyed a laugh at her own expense, and a swell of affection for this man who tolerated her absurdity with such good humor and goodwill. She had learned to fret at the doughy knees of Pearl Lefferman, master of the game. Jess's mother could divine the dark cloud in every silver lining. She had predicted twelve of the last two disasters and erected bomb shelters against them all.

Jess would never forget the time when she was nine. She'd been invited to a friend's birthday party down the block. The scheduled start of the event happened to coincide with a partial solar eclipse, and Pearl, certain that her little girl would look at the sun and go blind, forced her to walk to the party with an egg carton over her head. "Twelve dozen Grade A, extra-large," the box read. Pearl had watched with unblinking vigilance until Jess was ensconced in the neighbor's house.

For years after that, Jess had suffered the pointed torments of her peers. They'd dubbed her egghead and extra-large and accused her of being a big fat yolk. That Halloween, a group of boys had pelted her with eggs. "There's your brother, egghead," one hooted. "Here comes your cracked cousin from Detroit."

Having borne Pearl's suffocation, Jess took great pains not to overprotect her own kids. She carried the worries inside, sparking cruel electric pulses in her gut. As she drove north, her thoughts kept skidding to some perilous back road. She pictured Danny losing control on a patch of slick, oily pavement, hurtling headlong toward the precipitous edge.

In this case she had rational cause for concern, and so did Danny. His recent reluctance to take the wheel was more than understandable. In the six months since he got his license, he had been in two accidents. Both had been minor, and neither was technically his fault. But seventeen-year-olds, even sound, grounded ones like this kid, had an uncanny knack for attracting road calamities.

Ryan Harrison loomed as a haunting example. Last summer, Danny's long-time pal and general good kid went out for a pizza one night when his parents were away for the weekend. Half an hour later, a passing motorist spied his mangled Acura in a ravine abutting the North Stamford reservoir.

The paramedics sped to the scene in record time. Everything flowed with flawless timing: expert consults, state-of-the-art diagnostics, rapid Medevac to the trauma center at Yale–New Haven. If only Ryan's spinal cord had not been crushed. If only his brain had not been bumped around in his skull like a squash ball. If only . . .

Every time Jess saw him now, skewed in his wheelchair, struggling to remember, to speak, to move about, she couldn't help but think that it could have been her kid. One blip of bad luck or bad judgment could change the course of a life forever, set it irrevocably on a path full of tortuous dips and turns.

She pulled into the drive abutting their sprawling house. Architecturally, the place combined elements of the classic Tudor, Georgian, and Federal styles, with a hefty measure of contemporary White Elephant. The original core of the building had served as the carriage house for a mid-nineteenth-century gentleman's farm, which, as Jess understood it, meant the primary crop was spoiled children. Over the years, a dozen owners had patched on a series of ill-conceived additions. The net effect was long on quirkiness and short on sense, which suited her disturbingly well. There was also a lovely surfeit of space, which they could not have afforded in a saner dwelling. The garage was empty. Danny was not home yet.

Prozac, their golden retriever, was laid out like a furry welcome mat near the door. She cracked a rheumy eye, waved her tail like a listless flag of surrender, and issued a broad, squeaky yawn.

Prozac was the ultimate watchdog. Watching was what she did best. She was the sort of dog a burglar couldn't help but love, welcoming, friendly, and eager to share. She also came equipped with all the perfect pet accessories: large sympathetic ears, huge capacity garbage disposal, and boundless unconditional love. True, she had her little quirks. Laid back, verging on comatose though she was, she'd refused to dine from a standard dog bowl ever since the unfortunate time a dog-sitter had spent a week feeding her from Jess's best china plates. The dog's preferred pattern was the Queen Anne Royal Doulton that Charlie had inherited from his Great-aunt Louise, but Prozac would deign to use the Spode Blue Medallion, an ironstone set that was virtually indestructible, as Jess generally insisted. A cloth napkin helped to sell the deal.

Jess found Charlie asleep on the leather couch in his study under an avalanche of journals and position papers. How adorable he looked, her darling boy amid his playthings. Last June, he was recruited as a consultant to the Manhattan-based Hutchings Institute for Bioethics. Added to his research and teaching load at Yale, the work left almost no time for frivolities like breathing. Jess missed the precious little leisure they used to have, but Charlie loved dissecting the mess that often arose when science raced mindlessly ahead of morality and the law. His cogent, practical side was custom-made for dealing with the most daunting questions. What were the civil rights of a frozen embryo? Did the ovum donor or the surrogate mother have primary claim to a child? If a person eliminated an unwanted clone, would the usual homicide statutes apply? Who knew best: Uncle Sam or Mother Nature?

Charlie mumbled in his sleep and sipped the air. The reading lamp spotlighted his aristocratic profile. A rumpled shirt and salted-whisker stubble gave him that ever-so-chic urban vagrant look. Riding a wave of affection, Jess smoothed back an errant pewter wave and kissed his brow.

They had been together since freshman year at Cornell, and after twenty years, Jess could describe herself as a highly satisfied customer. True, he had his fair share of annoying little traits. He left the toilet seat up with maddening irregularity, so once in a while, in the middle of the night, she found herself immersed like a tea bag in the bowl. He had the money sense of an adolescent and a tin ear for the subtle harmonies of family politics. But he was smart, funny, wise, constant, supportive, and sexy as hell. Jess adored his absentminded-professor side and his not-so-inner child. He remained an irresistible amalgam of tenth-generation WASP stoical reserve and passionate sixties social-liberal dove, sort of a Mayflower child.

"Mm belumbin," he dithered. "Verum dur."

"Honey? Did Danny call?"

Slowly, he creaked awake like an engine in need of oil. "Nope. Haven't heard from him."

"God. I hope he's all right."

Charlie gawked as if Jess were speaking in tongues. "What time is it?"

"Ten-thirty."

"I thought he's not due in until midnight."

"You try holding your breath for an hour and a half. I want that kid here *now.*"

"What you need, my love, is a distraction." He drew Jess over him like a quilt. She melted against his muzzy warmth and the press of his rising erection. His deep, probing kiss reduced her to a puddle of goo.

"For your pleasure this evening, madame, we're offering several succulent additions to the usual menu." He whispered several impertinent suggestions in her ear. Jess's body stood in full agreement, but her brain kept bouncing back to Danny and the car. She stroked his fuzzy cheek, then drew away. "Sorry, honey. I'd like to, but I'm too worried right now."

"That's okay, sweetheart. Go be neurotic. Enjoy yourself."

"I'll be back."

With a shrug, Charlie snuggled between the *Journal of Contemporary Social Philosophy* and a two-pound treatise on anonymity in sperm banking. He was snoring lightly before Jess hit the door.

She stole down the hall to check on the younger kids. Max, their eight-year-old, slept on his back in plaid boxer shorts, nothing on top. The child had spiky buff-colored hair and squash-blossom features lifted from a Peanuts cartoon. His nose was stuffed, and through his gaping lips, Jess could predict continued prosperity for Dr. Luft, the family orthodontist. Killer, a rare, ferocious breed of teddy bear, nestled in the crook of a bare, skinny arm.

Next door, Molly was burrowed beneath a hill of pillows and a white ruffled sheet. Her lithe form barely raised a bump in the bedclothes. Poor Mol was the sole surviving tomboy in a sea of curvy seventh-grade nymphets. That she was smart, cute, and blessed with a quirky, creative mind offered slim comfort. At that age, conformity was all. No bust, no glory.

Danny's room was at the end of the hall. Jess paused to marvel at the pristine space, a monument to her son's natural sense of order. His tennis trophies stood in metered rows, every racket-wielding arm pointed in the identical direction. His bookshelves were lined with actual books, unlike Jess's, which tended to sprout odd paper scraps and knickknacks and assorted unmentionable debris.

Her mind kept swerving back to Dolores Wainscott's threats. Jess flashed to a terrifying image of Dolores in her Mercedes, driving Danny off the road.

Please, don't let anything happen to that kid.

Pearl had schooled Jess in the fine art of protective superstition. If you failed to fret about a potential disaster, it was far more likely to happen. If you spoke of good fortune above a prudent whisper, some malevolent spirit was bound to hear and wrench the luck away. In Yiddish this was known as giving oneself a *kineahora,* an act almost as rash as leaving the house with a wet head. As an educated woman, Jess knew far better than to believe such nonsense. But what if it was true?

Downstairs, she poured an iced herbal tea and stared out the kitchen window. The air hung limp and heavy. Wispy clouds veiled a gibbous moon. Its hazy reflection rode the ebony surface of the pond. Through the glass came the woolly hum of tree locusts. Only that, and a ponderous hush.

The clock ticked relentlessly toward midnight. Danny often argued against the curfew, but he accepted Jess's honest explanation that it was for her sake, not his. From birth, their firstborn had been a paint-by-the-numbers kid: healthy, smart, rational, the kind you couldn't foul up without a concerted effort.

So where was he?

The kitchen was a mess. Jess cleaned and straightened when she was aggravated, and the past few months had been strikingly crisis-free. Now, she attacked the disorder, putting away, throwing out, sorting and stacking.

Eleven-thirty. Eleven forty-five. There was still no reassuring sound of tires on the driveway. True, he was not due home until twelve, but her neurosis had a time clock of its own. Jess pictured Danny sprawled behind the wheel in a ravine, bleeding and unconscious, spine snapped like a desiccated twig. She imagined speeding ambulances, sirens, shocked faces, and screams.

Midnight. Ten past. Quarter after . . .

She nested the pots according to size, type, age, and composition. With military precision, she aligned the dishes, glasses, and flatware. The drawers were freed of coins, matchbooks, paper clips, old lottery tickets, and expired coupons. Green, fuzzy things and all objects of unknown age or provenance were banished from the refrigerator. Nothing left to do but alphabetize the spice rack, lower than she had been known to sink in the worst of times.

Basil, bay leaf, cinnamon, coriander, cumin . . .

Nearing one, panic goaded her to call the police. The officer who answered assured her there had been no reported incidents involving a red Mustang or a teenage boy.

"Thanks."

"Listen, ma'am. If you're afraid your boy's in some kind of trouble, I'd be glad to put out the word."

"No. Nothing like that. I'm sure he'll be here any minute."

"You sure? Kids today."

"Absolutely. Forget I called. Please."

Jess hung up more worried than before. The last thing she wanted was some hotheaded cop tracking her son, maybe spooking him into a dangerous maneuver on the rain-slicked roads.

Come on, Danny. Jess wanted him home, right then—immediately. She needed to see him safe and unhurt, so she could wring his inconsiderate neck.

Rosemary, saffron, sage, tarragon, thyme . . .

Finally, misty lights pierced the darkness. Outside, a door smacked. Rapid footsteps struck the walk.

Jess's neck went hot as she strode to the foyer to meet him, stepping over Prozac on the way. "Do you have any idea how late it is, young man? I've been worried sick."

She was revving up for a really satisfying fit of righteous indignation, but the sight of her son, pale and vague-eyed, cooled her pique. A bloody abrasion poked through a rip at the knee of his jeans, and a seeping scratch flared at his hairline.

"What happened, honey? Are you all right?"

"I slipped on some muck. No big deal."

"Come. I'll clean it up."

He perched on the battered cane stool beside the breakfast bar, designated treatment site for boo-boos of the spirit or flesh. Jess flashed back to the countless times she or Charlie had stood like this, ministering to one of the kids. She pictured Danny at three, plump little legs dangling in midair, when he broke his wrist falling off the jungle gym in nursery school. No swelling and the joint moved well, but he'd reported solemnly that it felt like a really mean monster was biting his arm.

How small and vulnerable he'd seemed then. How Jessica had ached to shield him from life's ugly bumps and vicissitudes, but she understood only too well how kids could grow warped and stunted in the shade of parents who hovered too close.

Danny twined his muscled calves around the uprights. His size 11 cross-trainers were planted on the floor like bridge stanchions. Jess doused his wounds with disinfectant and dressed them with sterile gauze. He exuded a dark, ripe smell that made her oddly uneasy. "Where exactly was this muck you slipped on?"

"School. They had a welcome thing for the incoming freshmen."

"How was it?"

"Blueglass and McWilliams spoke for about nine hours each, and then Nyborg the Cyborg played a full set of elevator music. Afterward, the choristers sang a rousing medley of songs to snore by, and last, but definitely least, the boosters served stale brownies and green, I kid you not, *green* bug juice. Plus, it was hot as hell in the gym. I bet you right now prospective freshmen all over town are begging their parents to send them anywhere but Stamford High. Including Sing Sing."

"And afterward?"

He shrugged and averted his gaze. It was a gesture Jess had dubbed the teenage two-step. "Hung out with some kids. Usual stuff."

"You forgot the part about giving your mother an ulcer."

"I had to drop Ryan off way on the other side of town, Mom. Plus, I had to break down his manual chair and take the wheels off to fit it in the Mustang's trunk. Was I supposed to risk my neck speeding for a stupid curfew?"

"No, you were supposed to use better judgment and come directly home from school when you saw it was getting late. And you were supposed to call if you were going to be late for the stupid curfew."

"You're right. I'm sorry."

Jess bit back the smile. "Stop being so damned reasonable, Danny Magill. I have a right to stew for a while without that kind of interference."

"Sure, Mom. Go for it. Stew."

Her smile dissolved. Her son still had a clammy look of shock. "Sure you're feeling all right? Not nauseous?"

"No."

"Stomach, head? Anything hurt? You're sure?"

"Positive, Mom. I'm fine."

He was better than fine, but Jess resisted the urge to say so. No point asking for trouble.

THREE

S ex is a seriously good thing. The rules are flexible. No costly lessons or special equipment are required. Anyone can play.

Only a few studies have documented the countless benefits of a healthy lust life, but Jess could attest. As rumor had it, sex did wonders for the complexion. It also cast a rosy glow on the disposition, reduced pain and stress, relieved anxiety, and improved sleep patterns. Failing that, one could find far more enjoyment in an episode of insomnia. When Jessica and Charlie were unable to sleep, they used the time wisely and well.

"You up, Jess?"

"Yes, honey. You?"

"Very much so. Feel."

She did; he was. Which happened to be a lovely coincidence, since Jess had been lying awake for the past twenty minutes, longing for just such a diversion.

Jessica and Charlie had always enjoyed frequent, enthusiastic, inventive lovemaking. They shared the logical conviction that if the body were meant to be treated as a temple, it would not be designed like an amusement park.

"It's way past your bedtime, little girl," Charlie leered.

"Oh yeah? What are you going to do about it?"

"I'm afraid I'm going to have to punish you."

She gaped in horror. "Torture, you mean?"

"Yup."

"Oh goody."

Jess rolled onto her stomach. Charlie ran his tongue along the exquisitely sensitive spot at the back of her knees. Higher he climbed, tickling, probing. She moaned, savoring a warm, liquid rush.

"You know the punishment for making noise like that—more torture," he said.

"No, please stop. In about an hour."

He nuzzled between her thighs. Stroked with slow, teasing passes. Lifted her to the brink of release. Entered and moved her beyond.

Afterward, they assumed their cozy postcoital pose. Charlie was a custom fit, better than her father's cozy old club chair. Headrest, back support, leg cushion, heated, adjustable. There was even built-in music, if you didn't mind the monotone. "I have a confession to make, Charles Alton Stansworth Magill the Fourth."

"Which is?"

"I'm in love with you, hugely."

"Shocking."

"Actually, it is after all these years. We're supposed to be bored and annoyed with each other by now. If not positively hostile."

"Now she tells me."

At a hush, she added, "Seriously, Charlie. Sometimes I think how lucky we are, and it scares the hell out of me."

"Sounds like true Leffermanian logic."

Jess clutched her throat in horror. "If I'm turning into my mother, the only humane thing to do is shoot me."

"You know I'd do anything for you, Jess. But jail is not for the likes of me."

"Now you sound like you're turning into your *father.*"

"Maybe we should shoot each other."

They spent the next hour rambling and giggling like two punchy kids on a sleepover. Then, sated and drowsy, limbs twined, they fell asleep.

Jess dreamed she was in a room filled with small human bones: femurs and ribs, piles of vertebrae, matchstick digits, tiny skulls.

Max and Danny were the same age, both about five, and she could hear them playing and battling beyond the wall.

"Stupid, it's my turn."

"No—mine."

"Give me that. I'm not fooling."

"Touch it, and I'll kill you."

There was no door, so Jess could not reach them. Her pleas for reason reverberated in the bone room, but failed to pass through to the boys. Jess could hear them perfectly, but in the warped logic of dreams, her words bounced off the wall and hit the floor like more desiccated bones.

The argument heated, and their chirpy voices thickened and dropped to deep bass snarls.

"You're dead, you little creep. Toast."

"You wouldn't dare."

The scream pierced her heart. From the desperate timbre, she knew one of the boys had been seriously hurt.

"Danny? Max?"

Between wretched sobs, she heard, *"You did it. I can't believe you."*

"Stop kidding around, Danny. And stop bleeding all over like that. Mom'll be furious."

Danny, no!

The scene shifted. Danny, grown instantly to a gangly teenager, was racing across a snow-choked field toward the car, raining crimson droplets like a macabre sprinkler. He slipped behind the wheel of a rusted wreck and gunned the engine. Dizzy with pain, he sped toward a distant sign that flashed, *EMERGENCY, EMERGENCY.*

Watching from an impossible distance, Jess spied an ambulance speeding directly at him. Bearing down—closer.

Stop, Danny. Look!

Charlie jolted up beside her. "What's that?"

"I had the most god-awful dream, Charlie. Danny was—"

"Wait, Jess. Listen."

From downstairs came harsh, insistent thumping. A voice boomed: "Police. Open up!"

Charlie scowled. "What the hell?"

"I called before to see if they'd had any reports of kids in accidents. I suppose they got the number from a caller-ID and came by to check that he got home safely. Your tax dollar too hard at work." Jess pulled on her white piqué robe. Charlie slipped into his rumpled work shirt and khaki pants, not bothering with underwear.

The noise struck Jess's sleep-slogged brain like a jackhammer. "Open up!"

Charlie jogged down the stairs. "We're coming, damn it. Hold your horses."

He opened the door to a blast of light, wailing sirens, crackling bursts from a two-way radio. A trio of patrol cars lined their drive, cap lights flaming. Prozac loped over, surveyed the scene, and smiled in her fashion. Grand human drama never failed to amuse her.

Two grim-faced cops in uniform stood in the vaporous pools of light cast by the porch lamps. "I'm Sergeant Huppert," said the older, taller man. "This is Officer McPhadden. You Daniel Magill?" he asked Charlie.

"Danny's our son."

"Is he in?"

"Yes, and he's fine. You didn't need to come," Jess said.

"We have a warrant for Daniel's arrest, ma'am."

"For what?"

Huppert produced a warrant. Scanning the text, Charlie went pale.

"What is it?

Wordlessly, he passed the document to Jess. While she read, he draped a protective arm across her back. His grip tightened when she reached the impossible wording of the charge. Jess blinked to bring the words in focus. She honestly could not make sense of them.

"Sexual assault in the first degree? I don't understand."

"Your boy's been accused of rape," Huppert said.

"That's ridiculous. Who said such a thing?"

"The complainant is underage, ma'am. I'm not at liberty to reveal her identity at this time."

"Look. This is obviously a mistake." Charlie tried to sound calm and commanding, but there was an edge of desperate stridency to his tone.

Jess clutched his hand. He felt reassuringly real, a patch of solid ground in this sea of madness.

"It's no mistake, sir. Now, either lead us to your boy, or we'll have to go find him on our own," McPhadden said.

Prozac caught the cop's menacing tone. She sniffed his leg and took a long appraising lick at his hand. Backing off, she sneezed to express her severe disapproval.

From overhead came a jarring thud, then a flurry of footsteps.

"Son of a bitch is trying to bolt," said Huppert. The cops charged upstairs, guns leveled. Jessica and Charlie raced up behind them. By the time they reached the landing, the two officers were closing in on Max's room.

"Stop!" Jess shrieked in horror. "Don't."

McPhadden was about to charge inside when a heavy-lidded Max appeared in the doorway. His face was flushed and branded with folds from the pillowcase. Killer, the teddy, was clutched to his bony chest. "Mommy?"

Circling the brawny cop, Jess drew the little boy to her. He smelled of sleep and coconut shampoo. "What's wrong, sweetie?"

"I fell out of bed," he whined. "How come they're here?"

"It's nothing, big guy," Charlie soothed. "Go back to sleep."

Max drifted into his room, wagging Killer's furry arm over his shoulder. Prozac trotted behind him, seeking refuge from the fray. "Night, you guys," Max yawned.

"Danny's room is this way." Jess drew the robe tighter as she led the cops to his door. There, she turned to the sergeant. "Let me wake him, please."

"Sorry, ma'am," Huppert said. "Procedures."

"You'll scare him to death," Charlie said. "He's just a kid."

"I understand, sir. But we'll have to ask you folks to wait out here."

The pair burst into the room and flipped on the lights. Danny bolted up, mouth agape, eyes bulging at the sight of the strangers, the uniforms, the guns.

"Daniel Magill?"

"Yes. What do you want?"

"We have a warrant for your arrest, Magill. You'll have to come with us. Get up."

He kicked off the covers and stood. With the bandaged knee and the terror in his eyes, he looked like a scared little boy.

"Hands on your head."

"Why? What did I do?"

"They're saying you raped someone, Danny," Jess told him hoarsely. The impossible words caught in her throat.

His jaw dropped. "No. You don't understand. It wasn't like that."

"Don't say anything, son," Charlie urged.

On a chair near the closet was a neat pile of folded clothing. "Are these the things you wore tonight?"

"Yes."

McPhadden dumped the T-shirt, denim shorts, boat mocs, and Jockey briefs in a plastic bag. Next, he poked through the hamper in the bathroom. He checked the closet and rifled the dresser drawers.

"You can't do that without a warrant," Charlie protested.

"It's perfectly legal, sir. Personal items can be confiscated at the time of arrest. We'll come back with a warrant if we need to search further."

Finished, the detective pulled a shirt and jeans from the closet. "Get dressed." He hovered at Danny's side while he wrestled on his clothes. The teenager's moves were stiff and clumsy, starched with fear.

Huppert tugged a page from his pocket and read the Miranda warnings. Then he cuffed Danny's wrists and herded him out of the room.

"Wait." The boy reddened, chafing against the constraints. "I'm telling you, I didn't do anything wrong."

"Easy, honey," Jess soothed. "We'll get this straightened out."

"Let's go, Magill," said Huppert.

The cops prodded him downstairs and out the door.

Jess hurried after them. "Wait. We're going with you."

"I'm afraid that's against regulations, ma'am," McPhadden said. "He'll be booked downtown, and then bond will be set. Shouldn't take more than a couple of hours."

The cops led Danny into the dark, dreary night. McPhadden sat the boy in the rear of the cruiser.

Jessica and Charlie stood on the porch, watching until the cruisers turned off their winding road and the haze of their receding taillights evaporated. Charlie broke the stilted silence. "We'd better get busy."

Jess shivered as she shut the night outside. Despite the heat, the house thrummed with a dark, expectant chill.

Will Huppert's headache was outgrowing his skull, throbbing in sync with the blaring whoop of sirens. He pressed his brow with the heel of his hand to squelch the strident ache. The Magill kid was really getting to him. Maybe he'd file a workmen's comp claim: total patience failure caused by one six-foot, smart-ass pain in the butt.

The trouble with kids these days was cop shows. Cop shows, lawyer shows, Grisham movies, and Court TV. The little creep should be wetting his pants and screaming for his mother. Instead, he kept carrying on about his rights, ranting about his innocence. He wanted a lawyer. He wanted his freedom. One call and his accuser would cave in. He was entitled to the call, he railed.

"You can't just arrest someone like this, for no reason," he whined in irate delirium. "I didn't do this. Can't you see? It's like listening to someone saying I have two heads."

Huppert shot McPhadden a weary look. "Right, Magill. And both heads have the right to remain silent."

For a blessed instant, the boy went still. Huppert drew a bead on him in the rearview mirror. The suspect was a strapping specimen with a proud-boned face capped by dark shaggy hair, but at the moment, he had the air of a petulant six-year-old. He sat with his cheek pressed to the glass, pale eyes staring blankly at the road. The cuffed hands hung limp in his lap. Kid looked genuinely stunned to be confronted by a consequence.

That was another trouble with teenagers today. They'd cut their teeth on negotiable plastic. Buy now; pay later. Or pay never, if you happened to be so inclined. They considered it fine to float through life on a cushy mound of debt. When the time came, Saint Pete probably took American Express and frequent-flyer miles. If all else failed, you could always file for moral bankruptcy. Say three Hail Marys and start again clean.

The Stamford Police Department occupied a beige-trimmed brick box on Bedford Street. Off-duty cruisers, angled like repeating commas, lined the street in front. Old Glory slumped beside a tepid orb of light at the building's entrance.

Huppert circled through the gate-controlled lot to the sally port at the rear. The steel security door closed with a harsh clank behind them.

The kid lurched from the car as if he'd been hobbled and cast in leg irons, not simply handcuffed. McPhadden grabbed his elbow and worked him like a bad shopping cart. "March, Prince Charming. No one here's going to carry you."

Suspects were processed in a series of rooms at the rear of the jail. From the sally port, they passed through the intoximeter room, where alleged DUIs were challenged to walk the dark line that spanned the center of the floor. Here, Breathalyzers and blood tests were administered to the city's two-legged, four-wheeled lethal weapons.

A squat patrolman named Martinez patted Danny down. The kid's ID bracelet and class ring were logged in and locked in a blue property safe. A device called the Digital Biometrics Tenprinter recorded his inkless prints. From the glass pad, they would be zapped electronically to a state data bank, then relayed to the national FBI print bank for a run of prior offenses and outstanding warrants. The machine spat out copies for the department and the prosecutor's office. Everything nice and neat.

A digital camera captured his mug shot. The teenager took the procedure like a rain of blows. Huppert figured he was accustomed to being snapped with a trophy, not as one.

The trouble with this particular kid was an excess of goods. Everything good had been handed to him for free: genes, looks, smarts, talent, opportunity, an avalanche of stuff. His room was a monument to excess: big hog computer, high-end stereo, TV, and VCR, closet full of pricey clothes and sporting goods. No wonder he was prone to toss a tantrum if he didn't get his way. He was nothing but a spoiled overgrown baby. But instead of holding his breath until he turned blue, he grabbed what he wanted. In this case, that happened to be zipped inside a sweet young lady's jeans.

Unfortunately, his guilt had slim bearing on the probable outcome. The Magill kid had all the necessary advantages: powerful family connections, bucks, appeal, a ninety-mile-an-hour serve. Big-gun lawyers would be hired, favors called, screws turned to ensure that he got nothing worse than a knuckle rap. No matter how often Huppert witnessed this brand of fix, it sparked his fuse, especially since the Storrow case.

Three years ago, twins named Rob and Billy Storrow had gotten their hands on a batch of Rohypnol, a street drug designed to zap unsuspecting lovelies into convenient unconsciousness. The twosome lured a young neighbor girl to their house, fed her spiked lemonade, and took turns invading her with a variety of body parts and household objects.

The victim had no memory of the events, so she was unable to serve as a credible witness, but nonetheless, the case appeared to be as solid as they came. There was unassailable forensic evidence, witnesses who saw the girl enter the house, a witness who saw one of the Storrow boys dragging a girl-sized, sheet-wrapped bundle into the woods behind the house. A classmate was prepared to testify that Rob Storrow had bragged about having some rape drug and planning to make good use of it. Several kids had come forward with tales of the twins' violent outbursts and brutal behavior. Ten months and a mountain of hard work later, the case had reached a predictable conclusion: *dismissed*.

The Storrow kids' father was a high-stakes real estate developer, flush and connected. People like that could afford to have everything altered to suit their needs.

The only punishment meted out in the Storrow case had been Huppert's. In granting a defense motion to dismiss, the judge had cited sloppy police work. Huppert's credibility had taken the fall. He was handed lame, thankless assignments, passed over for recognition and promotion. It had taken three years of hard scrambling for him to climb back to square one, and he had no intention of sliding down again. This time, he would give Lady Justice a hand, help her pin the tail on the right donkey.

Martinez pulled forms from a row of cubbyholes in the Windex-blue desk. He reread the prisoner's Miranda rights and had the kid sign to attest that he had received them. The patrolman hurled questions in a mechanical monotone, like balls from a practice machine. "Age, name, Social Security number? Occupation? Address? Phone? Date and place of birth? Any priors? Surgeries? Distinguishing marks? Disabilities? Allergies? Medications? Height? Weight? Married or single?"

Magill's halting responses warmed Huppert's heart. The kid was out of his element, foundering. Perfect.

Finished with the preliminaries, Huppert led him through the jailer's command center, where Rick Parmenter, the officer in charge, manned the desk. To his right, five stacked monitors were trained on the male and female cellblocks, the gray-walled holding cell, the Howard Johnson–colored processing rooms, and the black-foam-padded interview room. A small safe bolted to the floor held bail bonds.

Huppert trailed the kid's gaze to a red-lettered warning sign on the wall. *Suicide Alert,* it read. *White males, aged 22 or less, arrested for intoxication, first three hours critical. Be alert.* There was hope for a speedy, convenient conclusion to this case, he thought. The Magill kid was obviously intoxicated with himself.

If Huppert had his way, kids like this one would be turned loose in a room equipped with knives and guns and poisons and vicious animals like themselves. Huppert believed in prisoners' rights as much as the next guy. He would give Magill the right to choose the method of his own destruction. Imagine what cost and trouble that would save the taxpayers. The sole glitch was that the plan would reduce the number of clients available to the attorneys. Those parasites with portfolio would have to find some other way to keep their trophy wives in mink.

Since the department did not provide a self-destruction space, Huppert threw the kid in the tank for a half hour to cool his heels. He made sure he had just the right roommate, one guaranteed to shake the kid up and leave him even more vulnerable to idle threats and empty promises.

After that, Huppert ushered Magill into the "interview" room. Loaded words like "interrogation" had been dropped in an attempt to bolster department image. Gone too were the one-way mirrors that allowed squirming prisoners to be observed. Scratch that. They weren't "prisoners," they were "guests." Their comfort, rights, and safety were paramount. Any time now, Huppert expected the jail cells to be fitted with little soaps and turndown service, mints on the pillows at night. Maybe HBO.

A honeycomb of black soundproofing material lined the walls, assuring total privacy. Narrow beige blinds blocked the windows. A county map was suspended from the ceiling. Opposite was a blackboard scrawled with the legend "Dream, believe, achieve." A wood veneer conference table ringed by steel-cased chairs occupied most of the space.

"Let's have a little talk, Danny boy. Off the record. Just you and me."

"I don't know. Maybe I should wait for my parents."

"Seems to me you talk just fine on your own, buddy. I read you loud and clear."

"Can't it wait?"

Huppert threw up his hands. "When am I going to learn? Trying to help a guy out gets me nowhere. Let's go, Magill. I'll drop you back in the holding cell, then go tell the judge you've refused to cooperate."

"Okay, fine if you want to talk. Let's talk."

"Good answer. First, let me get a couple of snapshots they forgot to take out back." Huppert took pictures of the bruises on the kid's knee and forehead. "How'd you get those boo-boos, Danny."

"I slipped on some mud."

"Sure you did. Perfectly logical. So how are you feeling? Comfortable?"

"I'm okay."

"Need anything? Snack maybe? A soda?"

"Nothing, thanks."

"Okay then. I'm going to give you a chance to tell your side of the story. All we know is what the girl said. And believe me, you wouldn't want us to go by that."

"What did she say, exactly?"

"Usual story. You know."

"I don't know anything."

"Let me explain then. A criminal case is like any business. Most of the work goes on behind the scenes. People talk, make deals, get things moving. The girl says whatever's necessary to make her case. If you tell me what really happened, I can put in a good word for you with Judge Harrigan. Coincidentally, he's an old pal of mine. We watch ball games together, hang out with the wives. If I have something solid to offer him, we can get this business cleared up before it goes any further."

"You mean drop the charges? Everything gets erased? Is that possible?"

Huppert snapped his fingers to demonstrate the simplicity of the task. "Now is the hour, Danny boy. Once the lawyers get involved, everything is strictly on the record and by the books. A year down the road, maybe two, you could still be waiting for your case to come up. Meanwhile, your college hopes are screwed, your senior year gets flushed, you're nowhere. Bright, talented boy like you should be out having fun. Thinking about the future."

"I didn't do anything wrong, Sergeant. You have to believe me."

Huppert nodded in eager assent. "Just gave the girl what she wanted. Am I right?"

The kid perked up like a thirsty plant doused with water. "There was a freshman orientation thing at school. Lisa said she needed to talk to me. She asked if we could get away somewhere, just the two of us."

Huppert shifted in his seat. "And then what?"

"I dropped my friend Ryan off at home and drove to Lisa's. We were sitting in the car, and I asked what was up. She had this really strange look on her face like she was in some kind of a trance. She didn't say anything, just started kissing me. Then she put my hand under her shirt. It was weird. We've been friends for a long time, but that's all."

"What did she do? Change her mind in the middle?"

"No. Nothing like that."

"Must have been something pretty awful for you to rough her up that way."

"Rough her up? What are you talking about?"

"It's all right here in the hospital report." Huppert drew a folded sheet of paper from the pocket of his shirt. "Two busted ribs. Contusions and lacerations. Not going to go down real well with a jury."

The kid made a sound like a sucking chest wound.

"I want to hear your side, Danny. I'm sure you have a perfectly reasonable explanation. Maybe she was a tease. Or maybe she made fun of you. Something like that could set any guy off. Perfectly understandable."

His face went the pale blue of skimmed milk. "This can't be happening."

"Go ahead, son," said Huppert. "Get it off your chest. What did that little slut do?" Huppert almost had him. He sensed the wobble in the boy's resolve. But before he had a chance to spill, the phone rang.

A bondsman was at the desk. Soon bail would be posted and the kid would walk. His parents would sign on a high-powered lawyer who would choreograph the kid's every move. This was Huppert's last chance at an open-field run. As he passed the equipment cart, he slipped a tiny recorder in his pocket.

He perched on the table, so the kid was caught in his looming shadow. "That was the boss, Magill. He's afraid I'm going soft on you, wants you down in lockup so no one will accuse us of playing favorites. Now or never, Danny boy. You tell me what went down, the whole truth, and I'll do what I can to help you. Otherwise, the future looks like this: first degree sex assault is a B felony. A jury sees the hospital report, listens to that traumatized little girl, you're going in for fifteen, twenty years. They'll be lined up to bend you over. Used to be bad enough, but today the jails are lousy with that nasty virus. One mistake and you've bought yourself a death sentence. Real pity." Deftly, he slid a hand in his pocket and hit the record button.

Little creep hung his head. Sobs of grief bubbled up from the dark of his soul. Huppert waited, cheering mutely, for him to hang himself on a rope of words. But again, the phone rang. The kid's parents were making noise, demanding his release. Their lawyer was on the way, and things would get even hotter. The desk sergeant doubted he could hold them off much longer.

Huppert had the little scum. He couldn't bear the thought of letting him spit the hook. No way.

Playing by the book had gotten him nowhere. Time for plan B. Huppert knew the art of not so gentle persuasion. He turned the recorder off and spent the next ten minutes cracking the kid along his seams where the breaks would not show.

Finally, Magill looked up. His limpid blues pooled with sorrow. Huppert hit the record button again. Every golden word was captured on the tape. He had the kid write out his statement and sign it for good measure. In this business you couldn't be too careful.

Crisis in prospect brought out the irrational worst in Jess, but faced with a truly grave situation, she went dead calm and meticulous. She swiped an errant tear, tightened the belt on her robe, and drew a resolute breath. Her mind filled with rank-ordered lists: who to call, what to do, myriad details that had to be attended to at once.

First things first. She strode purposefully to the phone and speed-dialed Libby Amory. Jess's dearest friend had everything the current situation required: common sense, intelligence, a good and generous heart, and a law degree. Libby's practice was domestic relations, or, as she liked to put it, homemade torts. But she would be able to recommend the best person to help them clear up this mess quickly.

The two women had met in Lamaze class when Jess was pregnant with Danny. Libby had been acting as a birthing coach to her kid sister, Eve, whose navy pilot husband was stationed in Korea. That was quintessential Libby, always there to pick up the slack, or when need be, the pieces.

"It's Jess, Lib. Sorry to wake you."

"You did me a favor, pal. I was dreaming that Alan was still out burning the stripes off my Visa card. It was so real I'm actually shaking. What's up?"

Libby could make light of anything, including the shopaholic ex-husband who had left her nest egg in Humpty-Dumpty condition. Three years after the divorce, stray creditors were still coming forward, trying to get her to make good on his copious bad debts. Libby liked to quip that she'd made a disastrous investment in a bum steer.

"Danny's been arrested," Jess told her. "Some girl is accusing him of sexual assault."

"Right, and I'm the Easter Bunny."

"I know, Lib. Talk about nightmares. They're holding him downtown."

"Are they out of their minds? Of all the kids in the universe, Danny's the last one who would ever do such a thing."

"That didn't stop them from coming to the house like a pack of storm troopers and dragging him away. We've got to get him home, Lib. We need to post bond and find a defense lawyer."

"No problem. I can help you with both."

"Also, I know it's a huge favor to ask, but I hate to leave Molly and Max alone. If they woke up and found us gone, they wouldn't know what to think."

"I'm on the way. Meanwhile, I'll make some calls from the car, get things rolling. How much cash have you got in the house?"

"Couple of hundred, maybe less."

"With a mother like Pearl? I'm astonished. Blossom always warned me never to be caught without clean underwear, plenty of mad money, and her preferred form of birth control: a pill to hold between your knees. Luckily, I've got a little stash dear Alan didn't know about. The bondsman might take a credit card, but I'll bring it in case."

"You're the best, Lib. What would I do without you?"

Jess hung up and went in search of Charlie. She found him at Danny's desk, hunched over the computer, sporting a look of single-minded intent. The normally pristine room was a wreck. All the drawers were agape, spilling their contents. Piles of books lay open on the floor amid a scatter of papers. Prozac sprawled among them, up to her floppy ears in work.

Charlie tapped the keys, then scowled at the monitor.

"What on earth are you doing?" Jess said.

"You heard the detective. As soon as they can get one, you can bet they'll come back with a warrant and search through Danny's things. I'm just making sure there's nothing here they'd be better off not finding."

"Like what?"

"Like this." Charlie sucked air through his teeth. "Look."

He was on-line, reeling through their son's bookmarked web sites. In the past year, Danny had shown avid interest in exploring the Internet, joining chat groups, doing hours of what he'd termed "research" on-line. Jess had never been one to snoop, and her instinct, even now, was to respect her son's privacy. When she was a little girl, her mother had removed the locks from the bedroom and bathroom doors. Pearl had considered nothing sacred, except her unlimited right to know. She'd thought nothing of peering through keyholes or listening in when Jess was on the phone. Later, she would confront Jess with the purloined confidences. *What do you mean, you're fed up with my nagging, Jessica Lynn Lefferman? What kind of a way is that for a girl to talk about her mother?*

"What possible difference does it make what Danny looks at on-line?" Jess asked.

The screen flamed with lurid scenes of caricature studs and balloon-breasted women, naked save for studded leather belts. There were numerous triple-X-rated sites, hawking ecstasy for a low hourly rate plus tax (Visa and MasterCard gladly accepted). One offered teaser clips of videos for sale. Jess scanned the titles: *Bedman and Throbbin, Forrest Hump, Citizen Pain.*

Charlie moved down the bookmark list, deleting every item with even a hint of sexual reference. "Jesus Christ, Jessie. What's with him?"

"He's curious about sex. All kids are. It's normal."

Charlie brought up a site devoted to sadomasochism. The home page featured a woman bound in broad restraints, cowering in the shadow of a massive hooded creature wielding a whip. "This isn't normal. It's brutal, vicious stuff."

"Maybe so. But it doesn't mean anything. He's got bookmarks about all sorts of things. Look. There's one on skin diseases of movie stars. Does that mean Danny's into dermatology?"

Charlie turned to face her. "He hasn't been arrested for removing moles, Jess."

"This is Danny we're talking about. Not some stranger. Are you honestly suggesting that you believe that sweet, thoughtful, terrific kid is capable of forcing himself on a girl?"

Charlie's lips pressed in grim resolve. "Doesn't matter what I think. The law is about perception, assumption, and fear. Ultimately, all that matters is how the case looks to a judge and jury. Evidence of interest in things like this could make Danny look guilty."

Jess held up a hand. "Stop, Charlie. This thing is miles from a judge-and-jury situation. God knows why this girl, whoever she is, made up such a story. Maybe she has a crush on Danny and got angry because he didn't reciprocate. Or maybe she made it up to get attention. Talk show syndrome, I call it. I see it all the time. Some kids think it's cool to claim they've been abused or molested or that Mommy's a prostitute or their parents do drugs. Anything to take center stage."

"A trial will certainly put her there."

A hideous thought occurred to her. "Maybe Dolores Wainscott is behind all this."

"Sounds a bit far-fetched, don't you think?"

"I wouldn't put anything past that woman. She warned about getting back at me through you and the kids."

"Planting convincing evidence in a rape case would seem a little much, even for Dolores."

"Who says they have convincing evidence? It could be nothing more than some girl's word. Maybe Dolores hired someone to lie. Crazy as it sounds, I bet that's exactly what this is."

"I'm not willing to bank on that, Jess." Charlie turned back to face the computer. After he finished deleting the offensive bookmarks, he scrolled through Danny's e-mail files. "Christ, look at this."

A subdirectory labeled "Hot stuff" held hundreds of messages. The teenager had amassed a colorful collection of on-line pen pals: swingers, fetishists, perverts of every imaginable persuasion.

"Charming company the boy's keeping," he said.

"Most of them are probably other kids like Danny, having a great old time pretending to be those things," Jess said. "It's nothing but words, Charlie. Innocent mischief."

Jess saw this as a contemporary spin on the phony phone call. Caller-ID and call blocking had quashed that innocent, if annoying, form of fun. Naturally, kids would invent fresh new ways to play practical jokes. Charlie held a finger on the control key and targeted an entire directory for extinction.

"There are ways to lock a kid out of this stuff, Jess. We should have done that."

Jess resented the implicit slap. Somehow, when she was not looking, she'd been appointed executive in charge of routine parental supervision. She got to carry the ball; Charlie jeered when she fumbled. "Danny's going to college in a year. He's not a little boy anymore," she said, with more defensiveness than she cared to admit.

"Obviously not." He kept eliminating files. *Highlight, delete.*

"He's a good kid, Charlie. He doesn't need us to play cop or censor."

In response, he continued doing exactly that.

Heartsick, Jess began restoring the drawers to their customary order: stacks of shirts, boxer shorts, tennis whites, socks turned in neat bundles. She made tidy piles of Danny's papers and restored his books as he normally kept them, sorted by subject and size.

"This feels wrong, Charlie. Plus, it could backfire. What if the police have a way to tell what you've removed? It's like running from the scene of a crime. They'll think Danny had something to hide."

He was still zapping files, eliminating most of what the boy had chosen to save. Even innocuous-looking things were expunged. Charlie was on a search-and-destroy campaign. "I'm going to wipe them with a program called Norton Utilities. It overwrites the files so they can't be recovered. No one will know."

"Danny will."

"He'll get over it. After we get this cleared up, he can start a whole new smut collection."

"Think how this is going to make him feel. Danny needs to know that we believe in him, that we support him without reservation. Especially now."

He puffed his exasperation. "Save the touchy-feely crap, Jessie. Danny's treading water. He needs us to pull him out, not toss him an anchor."

A haze of oncoming headlights shone through the window. Jess pushed in the last of the drawers. "That's Libby. I asked her to come and stay with Max and Molly while we go downtown."

There was a rap at the door. A pause, then another round of tapping. Prozac hauled herself up like a sunken ship, shook off the bonds of sleep, and ambled down to welcome the latest late-night arrival. Charlie huddled closer to the screen, erasing more files.

"Enough, Charlie." Libby had a key. She would let herself in if Jess didn't answer the knock. "Please stop. This could be illegal for all we know. It's not fair to get Libby involved."

Charlie shot her a sharp, angry look. "Forget fair, Jess. Fairness has nothing to do with a thing like this."

Jess's breath caught when the door to the booking room swung out. But instead of Danny, an oily, emaciated man stumbled through. He staggered across the lobby, then pushed out into the steamy night, admitting air rank and heavy as laundry exhaust.

Next came a sallow tough with three brow rings and a calico do-rag. He postured for his welcoming committee, a buxom girl in a tube top and two jittery thugs. "Whassup, homes?" He slapped the row of raised palms. "What it is!"

For the third time, Charlie questioned the officer at the desk, a small, dour man with wire-rim glasses. He glanced up from his crossword puzzle and sighed. "I'm sure he'll be coming along anytime now."

"Sure he's coming. So is Christmas," Charlie muttered not quite beneath his breath.

"Shh," Jess urged. They had slipped down a rabbit hole to a place of alien rules and responses. Who knew what might make this nightmare worse?

The door opened again, drawing all eyes to a towering creature with opalescent nails, a pink Dynel wig, spike-heeled pumps, a silver miniskirt, and a spandex bustier with actual fishbowls for cups. Tropical specimens swam amid the tinted stones and undulating greenery.

"Well, hello there," crooned the drag queen expansively. Everything waggled as she walked: hips, hands, fish, tongues. "How you all doing this fine evening? Having fun?"

She dipped into the mock cleavage behind the bowls and plucked out a fistful of gilt-edged business cards. She passed them out, pressing one on the cop at the desk and another on the tough with the brow rings. "Come on down to the Purple Passion and see me real soon, cute stuff. We'll show you what fun is. You hear?"

The kid recoiled as if she'd tossed him a bucket of fetid slop.

With a broad grin, she flapped away the slight. "It's a fine place, sweet lips. You'll see. Tell them Aquaria sent you and get a free Muff Dive." Coyly, she added, "That's a drink, honey. Specialty of the house."

A passing detective herded her along. "Better move it, Queeria, unless you're angling for a permanent stay."

A neon tetra darted to the center of the left fishbowl and perched in nipple position, mouth pursed, whipping its luminous tail. "Did I hear you say angling? Why, that would qualify as a genuine pun. Didn't know you had it in you, Officer baby. Thought you had your sense of humor surgically removed." She pointed to his tight lips. "Why else would you have that ugly scar?"

"In or out, Dr. Strangelove. I'll count to three."

"That high? Hoo-wee. You better watch you don't get yourself a nosebleed."

A mottled flush stained the cop's scruffy cheeks. "Don't start with me. I'll toss your twisted ass in the can and lose the key."

"You know, you should get mad more often, Sergeant cupcake. Look what nice roses it puts in your cheeks."

He called out to the man at the desk. "Get this pile of garbage out of here, Tommy. It's stinking up the joint."

The cop at the phones picked one up.

Aquaria tossed up her hands in mock horror. "All right. Okay, sweetheart. No need to make a fuss. I'm leaving. Got to get home and take care of my little fishies anyway. Sweet babies need their rest after all this commotion."

Near Charlie and Jess, the drag queen came to an abrupt halt. The water sloshed, jolting the fish like an undersea volcano. She stroked the bowl until the currents ceased. Then she peered up again and flapped lashes long enough to stir a breeze. "Must be your boy I saw in there. Looks just like his daddy." She handed Jess a card. "I could tell you a thing or two about that boy, if you'd like to hear. Anytime you want, just stop by."

A hard silence settled when she left. Jess kept peering at her watch. What could be causing this endless, grinding delay? She could not bear to stand around like this, doing nothing. The cops could be subjecting Danny to strong-arm interrogation, pressuring him to confess. "Libby's lawyer friend should be here by now. I think I'll call and find out what's going on."

As she started toward the bank of pay phones, a perky brunette breezed in from the street. The crisp navy suit and white blouse gave her the look of a flight attendant. She stopped for a moment at the desk, then headed for Charlie and Jess. "Mr. and Mrs. Magill? Glad I caught you. I'm June Gold from Gus Grantham's office. Mr. Grantham is out of town. Due back first thing tomorrow. He asked me to come down and make sure things are in order. Your son hasn't been released?"

"Anytime now, they keep telling us," Charlie said.

"Let me see what I can do." She had further words with the desk sergeant. With a strident buzz, the security lock released to admit her. Minutes later, she emerged with Danny in tow.

Jess drew her son in a hug and caught the smell of nervous sweat and stale cigarettes. He felt stiff and wooden in her arms. Stepping back, she had a long, hard look at him. "Oh, sweetie. Are you okay?"

"I'm fine."

The scratch at his temple had lost its fiery wrath. Otherwise, she spied no signs of fresh hurt or abuse. The arrest, this crazy night, had not left a mark on him, at least any visible one. He still had the rumpled air of a small child wrenched from sleep. He was still her beautiful kid, still her Danny.

Charlie turned to the lawyer. "We're grateful to you, Ms. Gold. Are we free to go now?"

"Absolutely. Get some rest. Danny's arraignment is scheduled for tomorrow afternoon. The office will contact you before then to set things up."

"Is there anything we need to do in the meantime?" Charlie asked.

"Wait until you hear from us. That's all." With a pointed look at Danny, she added, "I'd avoid talking about this with anyone. You never know what might come back to haunt you."

"Do we know yet who made the complaint?" asked Jess.

"I think I have it in my notes," said the lawyer. "Yes, here it is."

Jess's blood ran cold as she listened to the name. There was no end to the nasty surprises.

So you go to the bridge and nab that ugly troll. Then, you raid the Seven Dwarfs' place and bring in that dirty rat Bashful. You got that, Tucci? I think they're both in cahoots with the Wicked Wolf and that badass Lamb Chop."

"Yeah, Chief. Sure," Tucci muttered. He tried to pay attention to what his boss was saying, but his mind had gone over the wall.

"Good. Then you jump down, turn around, pick a bale of cotton. That work for you?"

"Excuse me?"

Chief Kenneth Klonsky slammed his desk with a ponderous copy of the Connecticut Penal Code. "No, Detective. I don't excuse you, and I don't get what's going on with you. When Lou Silver briefed me, he raved like you were the Second Coming. Tucci this, Tucci that. And then you get your puss smeared all over the local press like you're the Second Coming of John Wayne. Well, you might have pulled the wool over some people's eyes, but my vision's twenty-twenty. In the three weeks since I came on board, all I've seen you do is yawn and fart, and you're not even all that good at those. I get the feeling you think you can sit back and ride that hotshot reputation of yours. Well, here's news. You get paid to *work* here, in case that's slipped your little mind. If I wanted a great big goombah paperweight, I'd get one that didn't cost me pension bene-fits and a health plan."

Tucci snapped alert at that. The last thing he could afford to lose right now was his medical insurance. "You're right. I've had a lot on my mind lately. Don't worry. I'll get it in gear."

Klonsky started tapping with a fury on the desk. Tucci made it as "Hey You, Get Off of My Cloud," by Mick and the Stones. He'd always been a whiz at *Name That Tune*.

"You will, or you'll find yourself shagging golf balls like old man Silver down in some Nearer-My-God-to-Thee condo complex for the terminally washed up. I don't carry dead weight. Never have, never will. You read me, Detective?"

"Loud and clear."

"First thing I do on a new watch is clean up. Any trash I see goes directly to the dump. That way, the rot doesn't spread."

Klonsky leaned back in his throne-sized mock-leather chair and wove his ropy hands behind his neck. "While we're having this little heart-to-heart, let me lay out all my cards. I don't buy excuses, no matter how cheap or well packaged they happen to be. I don't want to hear about the pregnant girlfriend or the slut daughter or the frigid wife. Rumor has it you're going through a rough patch, but I don't care. Don't show me yours, and I won't show you mine. I'm not interested in your overdrawn checking account or your aching hemorrhoids or your general disillusionment with life. If you've been boozing or drugging, quit. If you've lost your edge, sharpen up. This is your last, hear me, *last* chance to get it right."

Klonsky slid a binder across the desk. As he caught the file, Tucci met the chief's frosty stare. He took in the leather-clad block of bones that passed for Klonsky's face. Hitler mustache, cropped Fascist hair. Molten hatred filled the aching void in his chest.

Then, flipping through the particulars of the case, Tucci went numb again. "Can I ask why you're pulling this from Will Huppert?"

"Sure you can ask. You just did."

"It would help to know," he persisted. Hot-potato cases and the ones that reeked had a way of getting passed from hand to hand.

"Call it artistic differences."

Tucci nudged the folder back across the desk. "Sorry, Chief. I've got a conflict. I knew the kid's father growing up. We weren't exactly what you'd call friends."

"I'm not asking you to take anyone to the prom, Tucci. I'm *telling* you to investigate a sexual assault charge."

"That's not all. My daughter goes to school with both the plaintiff and the accused. Having me on the case could be really rough on her." The words stuck in his throat: *my daughter.*

Klonsky shoved the folder back across the desk. "That would be in the category of *your* problem, Detective. Unless your precious princess happens to be on this squad, selling smack, or under indictment on a B or better felony, I couldn't care less about her."

"But—"

"The only butt on the line here is yours, Tucci. Your two choices are yes or yes." He started tapping again. "The Party's Over . . ."

"Yes, then."

"Good answer. Now, get a move on. Who are you riding with these days?" Klonsky checked the duty roster and frowned. "Says here your partner is Mike Samuels? Who's that?"

"Short guy, tough. Looks a little like a pit bull. Everyone calls him Mule. You must have noticed him, Chief. He's the one always sits right in the front row at morning lineup and asks the dumbest questions. Remember?" Tucci held his breath, awaiting the chief's response.

Fortunately, Klonsky was not the type to cop to ignorance in any form. "Sure I do. Problem is there are so many jackasses around here you all start to run together in my head. Where is this guy Samuels? Why isn't he here?"

"He's out tying up a few loose ends in that can-factory robbery investigation. Nobody ties things up like Mule."

"I'm not going through this twice. You bring him up to speed."

"Yes, Chief."

"That's *my* speed, not yours."

"Don't worry. It's under control."

In fact, the situation was anything but. Six months ago, Tucci's partner had fired at a silver flash in the chaotic heat of a drug bust. Instead of the loaded gun he'd imagined, the reflection had beamed off a metallic ribbon in the hair of a three-year-old girl. Mule had been exonerated after a thorough departmental investigation, but so far, he had not come close to letting himself off the painful hook.

Tucci felt for the guy, who'd been his friend and partner for half a dozen years. He'd been covering, hoping Mule would get his head untwisted and come back to work. The guy had to haul himself out of that sewer of despair, come clean, and get moving. He had a wife and three kids to take care of, for Chrissakes. Tucci was godfather to two of the little ones. He wasn't going to stand by and let Mule wreck his life over one irreparable mistake.

Tucci raked through his wiry hair and caught a whiff of rancid oil. He couldn't remember the last time he'd washed it. Forget the mop, he couldn't remember when he'd last made love to his wife or called his mother or had an appetite or gotten two back-to-back hours of sleep. Since Gina took sick, he'd turned into a human tenement. The more run-down and seedy he got, the less energy he had to tackle a fix-up.

"Is that all, Chief?"

"Bring me a nice, fat, ironclad pile of evidence against this budding deviant, and maybe, just maybe, I'll consider keeping you on the payroll."

On the payroll, on the insurance roll, clutching every last straw. "Okay, Chief, I'm all over it."

"You'd better be. I'm talking high-quality stuff—pattern of similar behavior, solid forensics, the works. You don't go after someone named Magill around here without very, very big guns. Turns out the kid's grandparents own a few little things in this state, including half the capitol and the governor."

"I know."

"From what I've seen, all you *know* is how to take up space. Now haul your lazy butt out of here and show me different."

Tucci reined in his runaway temper. Telling Klonsky off was a luxury beyond his current means. His daughter's future was at stake. And that future hung by a slim and fraying thread.

Somewhere, three months ago, Gina had picked up some rotten bug. Kid may have cut herself, eaten something bad, gotten zapped at the dentist, caught it changing a diaper on a baby-sitting job, who knew? The doc had explained that these days, deadly, resistant strains of bacteria were popping up all over the place. You had to count yourself lucky if you happened to stay well.

Gina's luck had gone from lousy to don't-ask. The germ she'd caught was a rare new extra-stubborn breed. It refused to respond to IV antibiotics, immune boosters, alternative therapies, angry tirades, threats. Damned germ kept changing stripes, pulling dirty tricks, slithering out of reach like a seasoned con man. Meanwhile, his daughter's organs rebelled against the chemical assault. First her kidneys failed, so she had to be placed on temporary dialysis. Then her liver enzymes soared so far off the charts there was talk of a transplant. At one point, the bug had caused terrifying seizures.

Tucci would never forget that night. He was working a homicide, putting in eighty-to-one-hundred-hour weeks. When he finally dragged home after two a.m, he found Marie crouching over Gina in the bathroom. Gina was thrashing wildly, eyes rolled up in her head, limbs flailing, burbling in her throat like a plugged drain.

And that was not the end of it, nor the worst. The treatments made the symptoms look pleasant. Poor kid suffered night sweats, hallucinations, septic shock. She became agitated and disoriented. She'd lost so much weight and hair she resembled a freshly hatched bird, frightening in her fragility, barely there.

Tucci had taken to wincing each time the phone rang. Good news seemed to have lost their number. Just when they thought things couldn't sink any lower, the bottom fell out yet again. Another disheartening report. Another battle with the insurance parasites. Blood values worse. New, improved kinds of damage they hadn't considered. He couldn't bear to think where or how the slide might end.

Back in the squad room, Tucci found Will Huppert perched on a chair tossing souvenir beer mugs, cheesecake photos, paperweights, sports banners, and other rejectables into an overflowing carton on the floor.

"What's up, Hup? Spring cleaning?"

"I've had it, Tooch." He tapped his throat. "Up to here. Time to stop beating my head against it and cash out."

Panic squeezed Tucci's guts. "Are you telling me Klonsky canned you?"

Hup snorted. "Not hardly. I've got a three-quarters pension coming. I work a couple of private gigs, do a little investing, I come out ahead in a stroll. I don't have to put up with his crap or anyone's."

"Retiring, honest?"

"I've done my time. Enough's enough."

"Enough's too much. Wish I could join you."

"You'll get there." Huppert threw in the last of the books and clambered down with a grunt.

"Mind filling me in on the Magill case?" Tucci asked.

Huppert's look went dark. "Everything's in the report."

"I'm talking impressions, Hup. Did the kid come across as guilty to you?"

"As sin."

"Too bad you couldn't get a statement out of him."

"No sweat. Thing's solid. Doc found semen, blood traces, the works on the girl. Plus, the victim is one of those fresh-faced perpetual-virgin types. Couldn't be better."

"Yes it could, Hup. It could be on someone else's head."

"Things are tough all over." Huppert dumped the contents of his desk drawer into another box: paper clips, pocket change, trick dice, hard candy, business cards, a twenty-year accumulation of hair, lint, and fingernail clippings.

Leaving headquarters, Tucci ran the gauntlet of guilty looks and averted gazes. Having his kind of trouble was like walking around with your fly open. People turned away, felt uneasy, couldn't find the words. Only Patty McNees, who played mugger bait as a bag lady decoy, had the stones to face him squarely. "Hey, Joey love. How's Gina doing?"

Tucci wanted to hug her, gap-toothed smile, grungy rags and all. "Best she can."

"Anything I can do?"

"Nothing anyone can do but wait and pray."

"Got that covered. Meantime, you guys need anything, anything at all, just holler."

"I will, Pats. Thanks. Means a lot."

Andy Gordon, head of vice, cleared his throat. "We're all pulling for your girl, Tooch."

"Yeah, Gordo. Thanks."

Outside the station house, he slammed head-on into a crushing wall of heat. Last night's rain had done nothing to break the string of nasty scorchers. Weather like this was great for business, or lousy, depending on how you kept score. What better way to beat the heat than to bump off a nice cool convenience store or score a nice new air-conditioned car? What better way could there be to cool a simmering temper than to simply let go? Murders, assaults, wife beatings, drive-by shootings, rapes, all had a way of climbing with the mercury.

Worse, Gina, in her weakened state, could not handle the heat at all. She was trapped in the air-conditioned den, depressed and defeated, too weak to do anything but watch whatever trash came at her from the tube. Her entire summer break had been filled with dismal treatments, disappointments, pain. Now it looked as if the new school year was going to start without her. Who knew when she'd be well enough to get back to class? Poor kid was dying to be done with this mess, to return to normal, see her friends again.

Not dying, no.

Tucci thrust his hands in his pockets and trained his eyes on the ground. He was determined to keep a low profile. Bringing yourself to God's attention was a dumb, dangerous idea. He had witnessed more than enough human misery to handicap the odds. You were far more likely to be singled out for a barge of grief than smooth sailing.

That reminded Tucci of the Magill case, which reminded him of the box Chief Klonsky had put him in, which made him even madder at the world. Both the Magill kid and the girl he'd allegedly raped were part of the popular bunch at school that Gina would trade a limb to join. She'd always been a sweet, solid kid, busy helping out at home, working odd jobs, volunteering, hitting the books—not the type to draw big social attention. But she still had the standard yearning to be accepted and liked. His working on the case was bound to upset her, big-time. It was a lose-lose proposition. No matter what the outcome with Magill, emotions would run high. Sides would be taken, hard lines drawn. No doubt some of the bad feelings would slop over onto Gina, who had already suffered more than anyone's fair share of loneliness and isolation. Most of her dopey friends had lost interest and drifted away. For the few who still took the time to call once in a while, drop by on a rare occasion, this might make things worse. But Tucci couldn't see a choice.

His only reasonable response was to get the chief what he wanted and be done with it. Sticking it to the kid's old man would be an incidental bonus. Tucci would never forget how Charlie Magill and his silver spoon bunch had treated his mama all those years ago. Now, by chance, he had a way to settle that ancient score.

Tucci's old man used to say that the measure of a man's wealth was the size of his family. As he turned at the mailbox, marked with an ornate *B* for Beningson, Tucci had a different idea. You could guess a guy's net worth by the length of his driveway. If you could go from zero to full speed without hitting the house, you were dealing with a major pile of bucks. At least, that was true if you could do it in a motor vehicle. Given the shape he was in, Tucci could hit full stride, panting, on the average welcome mat.

He wheeled his ash-gray Chevy through a lush bower of evergreens. With a twinge of guilt, Tucci pictured his own yard, weed-choked, overgrown, and fried to a dismal sea of hay. Given the recent drought, this place had to have an underground sprinkler system plus the Mayo Clinic of lawn doctors. And forget garden-variety gardeners. Tucci pictured an army of compulsives armed with cuticle nippers down on their knees, trimming the individual blades twice a week. Plucking strays. Touching up unsightly roots. Cooing encouragement.

The house, an imposing colonial, perched beside the looping brick-chevron drive. As Tucci pulled up, the double doors drew silently agape, and a man's silhouette bloomed behind the screen. Tucci swerved around and parked on a minor downslope. The Chevy had needed a new battery for the past couple of months, but as part of his general no-maintenance program, he had not gotten around to taking it to the department's auto shop for a replacement. No matter that the shop was fifty feet from headquarters and all necessary repairs to his boat were made for free. Making and keeping the appointment felt like two too many things to do. These days, it took a rolling start to get the engine to turn over: the car's and his.

Striding up the walk, Tucci caught a better look at the victim's father. Gray hair and silver aviator specs broke the monotony of skin burnished to the rich hue of butterscotch syrup. A sky-blue knit shirt and gold Rolex showcased forearms blown to Popeye proportions. He had a trim waist and abs flat as a landing strip. Clearly, the lawn was not the only thing around here subject to regular, high-quality upkeep.

The man squinted at Tucci's ID. Twice, he measured the photo against the

face. Satisfied at last, he stepped aside. "I'm Leo Beningson. We've been expecting you, Detective. Please come in."

The house had the hushed, cool feel of a rainforest. Tucci listened in vain for
the rush and hum of machinery, voices, any signs of life; the entire place
sounded as if it had been sprayed with a giant cloud of WD-40. Beningson led
him past a string of formal rooms, decorated to forbidding perfection.

"Lisa is resting in the den. As you can imagine, all this has been a terrible
strain on her."

"I can imagine." He'd spent most of the night imagining, thinking it could
have been his kid.

At least, Gina did not feel violated and betrayed. In that, at least, she was
better off than some. Tucci felt like a creep for digging a nugget of pleasure out
of someone else's pain. But there it was.

Lisa Beningson lay on the chintz couch in a shrimplike curl. Tucci's notes
put her at sixteen and change, but she could have passed for twelve with the
small upturned nose and heart-shaped face. Sun-streaked hair spilled over her
dainty shoulders. Beside her sat a chunky stylish blonde in a cinnamon silk
pantsuit that set off a bumper crop of freckles. The mother had large brown
eyes. A stiff smile hung over her visible sorrow like a picture set to camouflage
a safe.

"Detective Tucci, meet my wife, Sandra. And this is Lisa. Sit up, Lisa dear,"
Beningson said gently. "This officer will be investigating your case. I mentioned
that he'd be stopping by."

Pain twisted the girl's face as she sat and smoothed her prim white robe. The
lace collar was buttoned to the throat, and the hem grazed the tops of her blue
leather scuffs. "I go to school with a girl named Gina Tucci. Are you related?"
Her voice was a high-pitched, forceless fluff.

"It's a common name," said Tucci as he sank into a cloud bank masquerad-
ing as a chair. He wanted to keep this as far from home as he could.

"You need to tell the detective what happened last night, sweetheart,"
Beningson said.

"Do I have to, Daddy? I'm so tired."

"I understand. But you do, honey. It's necessary."

"Here, baby. This'll perk you up." Mrs. Beningson poured a glass of lemonade from the ceramic pitcher beside the heaping plate of homemade cookies on
the coffee table. "Would you care for some, Detective?"

"That's okay. I'm fine."

"Have some. Nice and cool." She offered a tour of the cookies. "Those are
mocha chip, these are peanut butter, and the little ones are Linzer tortes with
the most delicious raspberry filling. Sinful."

Mrs. Beningson pressed a frosted glass and several cookies on everyone. She smoothed her daughter's hair and brushed an invisible crumb from the corner of her mouth. "Go on, Detective."

Tucci focused on the girl. "I'd like you to tell me everything you can remember, Lisa, starting with when you first saw Danny Magill last night."

"I already told the doctor and that lady from rape crisis. Can't you ask them?"

"It's better if I hear from you directly."

She crossed her arms and clutched her sides as if the situation threatened to pull her apart. "I don't want to talk about it anymore. Please don't make me."

"This is important, sweetheart," Beningson said.

The kid trained her melting gaze on Tucci. "I really don't feel well. Can't we please do this another time?"

He shrugged. "I suppose I can come back."

Beningson turned to the girl. The anguish in his eyes matched hers. "I know this is difficult, sweetheart, but putting it off is not the answer. Let's get it over with."

She nodded meekly.

"Good girl," Beningson said. He nodded at Tucci as his wife worked soothing circles on their daughter's back.

"Where did you first see Danny Magill last night?" Tucci asked. "Did you two go out together?"

"No." Lisa stared at her lap. Her slim fingers tortured the skirt of her robe. "I went with my friend Ali Weisberg to a back-to-school rally in the gym. She was supposed to drive me home, but she has this huge crush on this guy Brian Carmody, and he asked her to go out for a bite afterward. Ali said I could come along, but I felt funny so I told her to go ahead without me."

She drew a shuddery breath. "I needed a ride, so I asked Big Mac."

"Who?" Tucci asked.

"Big Mac. That's what they call Danny Magill."

Beningson's face flamed. "That animal is six foot two inches tall, two hundred pounds or more. Just look at the size of this child he attacked. She's five feet tall. Size two." His gravel voice quaked with rage. "They should string that kid up. They should fix him so he can never hurt another beautiful girl like our Lisa. I want that boy castrated, Detective. Nothing less will satisfy me."

"Daddy, please."

"Stop, Leo," said his wife. "Shh."

"He'll get what's coming to him. You can count on that."

Lisa doubled over, clutching her stomach with a groan.

"Please, Leo. Look at how you're upsetting her," said Mrs. Beningson.

Her husband's jaw twitched. "All right. I'm sorry. I didn't mean that."

Tucci gave the situation time to settle. "Go on, Lisa," he said. "You asked Danny Magill for a ride, and then . . ."

"He had to drop this kid Ryan Harrison off at home first. Ryan was in a bad car accident last year and he's pretty messed up. A lot of the kids find it hard to handle, but Danny's been really good to him."

Mrs. Beningson refilled Tucci's glass in a jangling concerto of ice cubes and sloshing lemonade.

"What happened after Danny dropped Ryan off?" Tucci prompted.

"He drove me here. I started to get out of the car, but he stopped me."

Tucci interrupted gently. "Did he drive directly here from Ryan's?"

"Yes."

"And parked right out front? On the driveway?"

She nodded.

"Strange that he wouldn't stop somewhere more isolated, where he was less likely to be caught or seen. Any idea why he'd choose to assault you here?"

Lisa's face warped with pain. "You'd have to ask Danny that, Sergeant. I only know what happened."

"What did he do to stop you when you tried to get out of the car?"

In demonstration, she gripped her left wrist and clutched above her knee. " 'Wait,' he said. Then he leaned over and kissed me really hard on the mouth. Then, he was all over me, pinning me down, tearing at my clothes. I didn't understand what was going on at first. It happened so fast."

Tucci thought of his own kid, attacked by a similar nasty germ, though much smaller. "What did you do then?"

"I begged him to stop, but he wouldn't. He held my arms and legs, so I couldn't move. I heard his zipper go down, and then he started pushing at me." Her cheeks went hot with the memory, and her lip quivered.

"Did you scream, Lisa? Try to fight him?"

"I don't know," she cried.

"What did you do?"

"I can't remember."

"I want you to try."

"I can't. Please, can't we stop?" She bowed her head and wept in mute pulses. "Please."

Mrs. Beningson scooped the girl in a hug, tenting her in vibrant silk and freckled flesh.

"You told us your screaming and struggling made him furious," Beningson urged. "You said that was when he started to hit you. Remember?"

Sniffling, she muttered, "I want to forget it, Daddy. Don't you understand?"

"I do, but you need to tell the detective what happened, sweetheart. You want that boy punished, don't you?"

Lisa nodded numbly. Her eyes clouded with the memory. "I was shouting, 'No, stop.' He told me to shut up. Then, he started hitting me. Punching all over." Her sobs grew to great heaving bursts. "Please don't make me talk about it anymore—please!"

Beningson's arms were crossed. The clawed fingers dug into his flesh so hard that bloodless circles bloomed on the bulging muscles. "I woke up and saw them from my bedroom window. Lisa got out of the car and tried to break free, but he wouldn't let her go. If I'd had a gun, that boy would be scattered all over the driveway right now. Lucky for him he took off before I had the chance to get downstairs. I could have murdered the little bastard with my bare hands."

Lisa's hands flew to her ears. "Stop, Daddy. Don't," she sobbed. "Please, please, I can't stand this anymore."

Tucci stood. "I've got what I need for now. You were a big help, Lisa. Thanks. You too, Mr. and Mrs. Beningson."

Leo Beningson saw him to the door. "We want to be on hand for all proceedings, Detective. I trust someone will keep us informed."

"You'll hear from the prosecutor's office, but there's no need to put Lisa through all that. She'll have plenty to deal with if this thing goes to trial."

"Oh, it will, Detective. No question about it."

The glaring sun stabbed Tucci's eyes as he exited the air-cooled cocoon. No sign of a break in the crushing heat. Before Beningson had a chance to close the door, he turned back in afterthought. "If you need anything, give me a call."

"All we need is a conviction."

"That's what we're after, sir."

Tucci gave the house a final once-over. He had a nagging sense of unfinished business, but he could not give it a name.

His head was at home with his wife and daughter. Gina was scheduled for more tests at the hospital today. He'd planned to give Marie a break and take her himself, but now he was too busy with this damned case.

The major burden of their daughter's sickness had fallen squarely on Marie. She'd had to take a leave from the catering business she'd built from scratch and loved with fierce proprietary pride. She'd been shut in with Gina all summer, sharing the misery.

Marie had never been one to complain. Whatever happened, no matter how unfair things got, her unfailing response was good-natured acceptance. Tucci would be grateful for some ranting indictments, a juicy tantrum or two, anything to blunt the screaming guilt.

But Marie's unreasonably good nature was not the worst thing. Worst of all was standing by helpless while some invisible microbe trampled their lives and leveled their sweet little girl.

If only their battle was more like the one the Beningsons faced. Their adversary was a strapping, big-shot jock. You could wrap your mind around a kid like that and squeeze. You could aim your hatred at him and fire away, volley after satisfying volley. You could savor the satisfaction of his public humiliation and punishment. It would be Tucci's pleasure to help these people enjoy that minor consolation.

Tucci checked his watch, slipped off the emergency brake, and wheeled down the drive, pumping the clutch and accelerator until the engine caught. He turned out past the ornate mailbox, and headed for town. He could not wait to hear what his next appointment had to say.

The law firm of Grantham & Greene perched above a row of stores on New Canaan's main commercial strip. The town, with its bright clapboard churches, charming little shops, and grand, pristine homes, seemed trapped in a Norman Rockwell time warp, but Grantham's firm was a model of modern efficiency.

A closed-circuit camera caught the Magills at the street entry and they were buzzed through. At the landing, a bespectacled young woman in a calf-length floral dress welcomed them and offered refreshments, including the hazelnut decaf that suffused the area with a sweet earthy scent. "Mr. Grantham will be right with you," she said. "Make yourselves comfortable." The room contained half a dozen plump gray chairs and two leather love seats. A large antique trunk in the center of the space was strewn with current magazines and a volume entitled *America's Best Attorneys*. A leather bookmark held the page where both of the firm's name partners were listed.

An older woman in a suit appeared, to record necessary information. Moments later, a slender redhead appeared. She ushered them to Grantham's office at the end of a long, narrow hall.

Grantham led with a mighty handshake and a practiced smile. "Dr. and Mrs. Magill. Danny. Come in." He was a large, imposing man, resplendent in a pin-striped navy suit, a white-on-white shirt, and an Hermès tie and matching pocket silk. He had thick chestnut hair, a commanding voice, and the rugged good looks of a film heavy.

Dark wooden shelves crammed with leather-bound sets of lawbooks lined the walls. Bow windows afforded a view of the courtyard garden. The desk was an outsized antique, carved mahogany inset with tulipwood. That and a matching serpentine sideboard stood in stark contrast to a free-form chrome and smoked glass conference table.

Grantham claimed the head of the table opposite Danny and smiled. "I'll have to beg your indulgence. I just flew in from a conference, so I haven't had time to fully review your case." The folder in front of him was marked with Danny's name.

"These things generally come down to her word versus his. Our job is to make his word hold water and to poke as many holes as we can in hers. You know this girl well, Danny?"

"Yes."

"How long have you known her?"

"Forever."

Jess was still reeling from the shocking identity of Danny's accuser. Lisa Beningson had been Danny's classmate and friend since early elementary school. Countless times, the girl had come to the house to play or work on school projects or hang out. When Danny was unavailable, she was the top choice to baby-sit for Molly and Max, and she'd been the most effective tutor they had found to unravel the riddle of Max's multiplication allergy. For some unknown reason, the little guy had developed a mental block about the subject. Lisa had concocted catchy tunes that finally drilled the times tables through his stubborn skull.

Jess had always found her to be a delightful kid, sweet and considerate. But given this absurd accusation, it was clear that somewhere, somehow, she had gotten derailed. Jess saw it in her practice all the time, especially in adolescents, who made up more than half of her client list. Some kids simply could not handle the flood of pubescent hormones. They were swept away by inner weakness or compelling external force. They yielded to stifling self-doubt or confusion. They broke from the terror of failure or success. Desperate to ease the pain, they clutched whatever offered even the slimmest hope of relief or redemption: gangs, mind-numbing drugs, sex binges, starvation, crazy risk. Her son was an innocent bystander, struck by Lisa's runaway emotions.

"How would you describe Lisa, Danny?" Grantham asked. "Would you say she's the hysterical type?"

He frowned. "I never thought so."

"Does she make things up? Has she always been a liar?"

"She's not. I mean, she never did anything like this before. Makes no sense."

"These things rarely do." Grantham flipped through the file again. "You're saying the sex was consensual?"

The boy flushed. "It was her idea. I never even thought of her that way. Why would she turn it around? I don't get it."

"Happens. Could be a simple matter of interpretation. Her yes really meant no. Or she changed her mind after the fact. Buyer's remorse, so to speak. I've seen it plenty of times."

"So you think there's a good chance Danny will be exonerated?" asked Jess. *Exonerated.* She liked the sound of the word, the smooth, exuberant feel of it on her tongue.

"Absolutely. The prosecutor has the burden of proof. I'm going to dig around before the arraignment and find out what, if anything, they have in the way of corroborating evidence."

"What could they possibly have?" Charlie said.

"My guess is, nothing," Grantham said.

"Then won't they throw the case out?" asked Jess.

"The court will be reluctant to dismiss until there's been a thorough investigation. This is a sensitive area, especially when the plaintiff is so young," the lawyer said. He turned to Danny. "Where'd you get that scratch on your forehead?"

"I fell. It's nothing."

Grantham frowned appraisingly at the bruise. "I thought your friendly neighborhood policeman might have given you a love tap."

"No. Nothing like that. It was muddy near the school. I slipped."

The lawyer fixed him with a hard, appraising stare. "All right. Here's your first assignment. I'll need you to make a list of people who might be willing to talk about what a prince you are. Employers, teachers, clergy, neighbors. The more prominent and holy, the better."

"That's easy," said Jess. "Everyone knows what a good kid Danny is."

"You never know how people might react to a situation like this, Mrs. Magill," Grantham warned. "I'd suggest you hope for the best and prepare for some big disappointments."

Any member could call a meeting of the Magill family council at any time, as long as the subject was of interest to them all. The group had been convened last by Charlie to announce that he had been asked to offer the keynote address at a forthcoming bioethics symposium in Paris. The value of his first-class ticket plus honorarium would cover five coach seats and most of the cost of an extended family excursion through the countryside in France.

The news had converted the kids into instant Francophiles. Molly, who had spent most of a year growing her curly blond hair into a massive mall-chick mane, resolved to clip her tresses in a chic Parisian do. Danny had logged onto the Internet and emerged from his room hours later armed with reams of information and impressive expertise. They should stay on the Rive Gauche, he suggested, preferably in the 6e Arrondissement, where they would be in easy walking distance of the Louvre, the left bank of the Seine with its famous bookstalls, and Notre Dame.

Max had suggested that they all assume French names, and Charlie, who loved to play with words, had seized the challenge. In recognition of all the hot dogs he had cooked on the grill, he would go by Charlemagne, King of the Franks. Funny, histrionic Molly would be named for the comic French dramatist Molière. Danny, good buddy to all and a longtime enthusiast of Three Musketeers bars, would be called d'Artagnan. Max's *nom* would be Maximilien, first name of Robespierre, who, like Max, had been the architect of a long and memorable reign of terror. Stumped for a fitting appellation for Jess, Charlie had settled on *Gésiers,* claiming he liked the sound but had no idea what, if anything, it meant. Weeks later, in a bistro in the charming town of Sarlat, she'd discovered that the translation for her French *nom* was gizzards.

All of that seemed to exist across a monstrous chasm of time. Right now, her *gésiers* were tied in knots. Too jumpy to sit, she kept adding to the collection of foods on the breakfast table: coffee cake, cereals, bagels and cream cheese, muffins and jams, cookies, juice, and fruit.

Charlie and Prozac ambled in from their regular morning constitutional. The soupy heat had Charlie huffing. The dog's tail swished like a diva's fluttering fan.

Bless Charlie—nothing interfered with his precious routines. Faced with imminent nuclear holocaust, he would no doubt peruse the morning papers, down a mugful of coffee, pour another as he always did, and take caffeine and Prozac for a walk.

"Ready?" he asked.

"I told them ten o'clock."

On the hour, Molly padded in barefoot wearing cutoffs and a scruffy sleeveless shirt. Max, anticipating auspicious news, had a dotted necktie looped around his neck. He looked like a baby Chippendale dancer with his bare chest and droopy plaid boxer shorts. He set out a tented paper sheet hand-lettered with his particular interpretation of his French name, "Max a Million." Jess waited for questions about their nocturnal invasion by the law, but the child made no mention of it. Most likely, he had taken it for what it was, part of a bad dream.

"What's the big news?" Molly asked.

"Bet we're going away again," said Max. "Am I right?"

"We'll explain as soon as Danny gets here," Jess said.

Charlie scowled at the clock. "Where is he?"

"I'm sure he'll be right down, honey. It's only ten after." Jess had answered the phone fifteen minutes ago when Emma Goldstone returned Danny's early-morning call. Emma, a freshman at Yale, was Danny's prime tennis rival, surrogate big sister, and closest confidante. She was a decent, sensible, solid kid who put her outstanding brain to excellent use. Having Emma in any picture improved the focus. At the sound of her voice, some of Danny's brittle tension had dissolved.

Charlie paced and sputtered, railing at the time. Jess was unaccustomed to seeing him so unnerved. He came from the sort of stiff-lipped stock whose emotions were pulled taut and tucked in with hospital corners. But now he was trailing loose ends like lethal live wires. Five minutes later, he strode to the hall and bellowed up the stairs, "Everyone's waiting, Danny. Get down here—*now!*"

"Jeez. What's with Dad?" Molly said.

"Someone's in trouble," Max predicted. "Hope it isn't me."

Jess heard Danny on the stairs. Charlie's words were muffled, but she caught the bitter sharpness in his tone. So did Molly, who drew up her knees and caged her chest with slim, protective arms. Even Prozac sported a rare look of unease. Humans were animals after all, and even the tamest animals had been known to turn vicious under extreme stress. Max alone ignored the gathering storm, anointing a bagel with cream cheese and strawberry jam.

Danny slumped into his chair, feet splayed. His face was fixed in grim resolve. "Okay, I'm here."

"Good of you to deign to grace us with your presence."

"Sorry if I'm late."

"Not if—you *are* late."

"What's that, Dad? Another felony?"

Charlie poured more coffee and stood at the sink. Steamy vapors rose around his head, as if his anger had peaked to a boil.

"Please, honey. Sit," Jess coaxed.

"Let me be, Jess."

Molly cupped her ears in horror. "If you guys are getting divorced, I don't want to hear about it."

Jess soothed, "No, sweetie. It's nothing like that."

"Then how come everyone's so mad?"

In level tones and the mildest possible words, Jess explained what had happened. Lisa Beningson had accused Danny of hurting her, which of course, he had not. Lisa was confused. Something had made her mix up the lie with reality. Or this could be a horribly misguided attempt to remedy some painful problem in her life. The police had no choice but to make an arrest and investigate her claim, but very soon they would determine Danny's innocence, and all of this would be behind them. Meantime, they had to try to be extra patient with one another, she said with a weighty look in Charlie's direction. Things were bound to be tense at times.

"Lisa's really nice," Max observed from behind a sugary red mustache. "Too bad she's nuts."

Molly propped her chin on her hand. "This is awful. What does she say you did, Danny? Beat her up?"

"Worse. Much worse," Danny said.

"The charge is sexual assault," said Charlie. "She's accused Danny of rape."

Max's eyes stretched to circles of awe. "That's what happened to this girl on *NYPD Blue.*"

"When on earth did you see a show like that?" Jess asked.

"At Timmy's. Remember when he had that sleepover for his birthday?"

The event had occurred late last spring, and Jess recalled it well. Though this had been Max's first pajama party, she had dropped him off without a twinge of concern. Surely a night spent at Timmy Greene's house would be well supervised and crammed with wholesome fun. After all, Timmy was the son of Reverend Greene, minister of the Methodist church, and his wife, Lorraine, a white-glove and hat type who was director of the Sunday school and president of the garden club. Now it emerged that Reverend and Mrs. Greene had retired early, leaving a dozen eight-year-olds to their dubious devices. The children had watched lurid cop shows and gorged themselves on junk.

"Timmy barfed three times," Max declared. "It was great."

"You're such a lame-o, Max. This is very serious," Molly huffed in grand thespian style. "What happens next, Danny? Will you have to go to jail?"

"The cops already took him last night," Max said. "I saw them. He had on handcuffs and everything."

Molly gasped. "Is that true? My God, Danny. How did you stand it? Was it awful?"

"Laugh a minute," Danny said. "Place was beyond disgusting. Full of lunatics and drunks. One guy threw up in the water fountain. Max would have loved it."

"This is horrible. When will they figure out that Lisa is messed up?" asked Molly.

"Soon," said Jess.

"But how will they *know*?"

"They have ways to get at the truth. Try not to worry, sweetie. It's going to be all right."

Molly's eyes sparked. "What if it's not? What if they believe Lisa?"

"That's not going to happen," Jess assured. She shot a pleading look at Charlie. *Speak.*

"We'll get through this," he said finally. Rising, he added, "If that's all, I've got some errands to run."

"Wait," said Jess. "Are you guys okay? Do you have any questions?"

"I just don't get it," Molly said. "Why would Lisa lie like that?"

"How should I know? Ask her," Danny said.

"Makes no sense."

"I told you," said Jess. "She's confused for some reason. It happens."

Max chewed in round reflective arcs. "Could it happen to me, Mommy?"

"No, honey. Your mind is perfectly fine."

"Is Prozac's?"

The dog was splayed beneath Max's chair, where the precipitation probability for a crumb shower was one hundred percent. "Yes, baby. I can pretty much guarantee that Prozac is not going off the deep end anytime soon."

"What about Molly? She's nuts about that actor guy."

"God, Max, you are such a little dope," Molly said.

"Am not."

"Are so."

"Stop," Jess muttered in forceless reflex. In truth, their squabbling was a welcome distraction. Max's curiosity threatened to draw them down a path she could not bear to take. Every mind had perilous twists and dark recesses. Given the wrong mix of perception and circumstance, it was impossible to predict how anyone might behave.

Jess had seen this in her practice, time and again. She had lived it herself when she was Danny's age, and her beloved father got sick. They thought it was a cold at first, then the flu. Every day, he dragged himself to the store where he'd worked for twenty years selling major appliances. He ignored the odd pains and crushing fatigue. Then, late one afternoon near quitting time, he collapsed in the bathroom. A customer found him on the floor, bleeding profusely from a head wound.

He was diagnosed with pancreatic cancer and given three months to live. As Jess watched him slip away, her stolid veneer had cracked in a million sharp, forbidding shards. From inside burst a torrent of emotion, fear and fury raging beyond her control.

Jess knew that she was to blame. Her father was dying because of her. That hideous awareness had reduced her to a shiver of desperate guilt. In her agony she had lashed out, done terrible, unspeakable things. People lost their way. It happened.

"I'm going downtown," Charlie said. "I can drop you at Amy's if you like, Mol."

She scampered after him. "Good deal, Dad. It's too hot to walk. 'Bye, you guys. Try not to worry, Danny. Best thing is not to think about it."

"Sure, right." Danny pushed away from the table. "Mind if I go upstairs?"

"Not at all. Go get some rest, honey. You need it," said Jess.

"Emma's driving down. If I fall asleep, wake me when she gets here, okay?"

"Of course. I'm glad she's coming to see you. That's good."

"Nothing's good, Mom. Not anymore."

After the others had left, Max formed a jam-capped cream cheese mountain on another bagel half. "Know what happened to that guy on *NYPD Blue*? They found him not guilty."

"I'm glad to hear it, Maxy."

The little boy's mouth warped in distaste. "No, it was bad, Mommy. First thing, soon as he got out, he went and did the same thing to this other girl. She was bleeding all over. It was gross."

ELEVEN

The best explanation of detective work Tucci had ever seen was an essay Gina wrote in seventh grade. The assignment had been to describe your father's or mother's career. Gina had summed his up in a word, saying that her daddy dug for a living. She had gone on to make him sound like a cross between an urban archaeologist and a bone-hoarding dog.

Reading that A+ paper, Tucci had enjoyed a big puff of pride. Kid was smart and to the point. He could not have put it nearly as well himself.

Detecting was a dig in every sense of the word. At the start of a case, you surveyed the surface, made your best guess, sniffed around. You went deeper, layer by layer, sometimes hitting rock, sometimes pay dirt, until the bones of the truth or its closest possible relation were laid bare.

Speed was critical. Pushing too far too fast risked trampled opportunities or lethal collapse. If you moved too slowly, facts and clarity could be eroded. In this case, dragging his feet would also leave him hanging out to dry. Klonsky wanted tied ends and solid answers, fast. He was expected to beat the chief's clock. Good luck.

Tucci found it helped to work from a list. In this case his list was outrageously long and growing all the time. He had to interview friends, neighbors, teachers, relatives, old girlfriends, teammates, classmates, rivals, idols, anyone who might shed some light, especially the negative kind, on Danny Magill.

And that was just for starters.

He'd need to baby-sit the Beningson girl for the duration. Lisa was a vulnerable kid in a vulnerable place and this was a very vulnerable situation. She would be pressured from all sides to question and doubt herself. Innocent victims brought out the worst in some people. Many clung to a perch of false security by presuming that the damaged party was to blame. Others distanced themselves, as if random violence, like lightning strikes, could be avoided. Victims of sex crimes had it far worse than most. Beneath the usual publicly stated sensible view that innocent victims were just that often lay the nasty supposition that the girl must have done something to provoke the attack. The fault had to be her long, dark eyelashes or the short skirt or big boobs or clear inviting smile. She must have been dumb enough to be in the wrong place at the wrong time with the wrong person. In any event, she owned the bad judgment and its consequences. If the victim had not provoked the attack, if such events were truly random, then no one was immune, and that was too dangerous a fact to leave lying around. So they wrapped it in layers and layers of nice soothing, anxiety-reducing bullshit. Lisa Beningson would be a victim of that as well.

Tucci had to keep an eye on the rest of the family too. The old man loomed as a particular problem. From the appearance of the lawn and the house, it was clear that Leo Beningson had precious little tolerance for imperfection. His wife looked to be second in command, at best. She would do what he said. So would Lisa. As this thing played out, Daddy might decide at any time that the best idea was to turn the tainted soil and start again fresh. That would be the end of the case, and Tucci.

While he was watching all those bases, Tucci had to keep one eye on home plate. Cops made mistakes, same as the next guy. But their errors could set a killer free or buy some poor innocent schnook a date with the lethal injection machine. He could not risk screwups in the evidence chain or assessment. Given what hung on this case, Tucci planned to make sure everything was signed, sealed, and delivered without a hitch. No cookie crumbs in the semen samples or coffee drips in the blood. Nothing mysteriously lost or mislabeled or carelessly destroyed. He would do everything in his meager power to ensure against embarrassing surprises. That meant riding herd on the field forensic guys and the lab and the property department.

The list did not end there. Tucci was fast running out of fingers and toes, not to mention steam.

Experts. Add that to the wish list. The better he shored up the case against Magill, the happier he'd be.

He slugged down the bitter remains of his third cup of coffee. Got nothing for his troubles but a sour stomach. Seemed as if his battery was too far gone for a jump start. The java failed to arouse so much as a decent case of jangling nerves.

The list was spreading, consuming his desk like the Blob. No way he could handle all this alone.

He stopped at the Dunkin' Donuts on Strawberry Hill for a couple of cream-filled, a chocolate cruller, a multicolored sprinkle, and a French twist. On second thought he took a dozen doughnut holes for the little ones and a fat-free, sugar-free, taste-free muffin for Frannie, whose physical ideal was a broomstick with ears.

Mule's house was on Virgil Street at Stamford's south end, in a mongrel neighborhood of modest homes and two-bit businesses. Tucci's partner lived half a block down from the Italian social club that had been a home-away-from-home for Tucci's old man before he died. It was still a favorite haunt for Tucci's uncles and other *paesani* from the old country, who would gather several times a week to complain in Italian, play bocci, watch soccer games, and drink homemade wine that went down with the subtlety of a depth charge.

As Tucci rolled up the street, he spotted his Uncle Pasquale parked in front of the club on a folding chair, sallow face tipped to the sun. Pete, as he was sometimes called, had been married for fifty-plus years to Aunt Graziela, who made the Wicked Witch of the West look like Mary Poppins. The poor guy had survived half a century of wedded blitz by staying away as much as possible. Mostly he hid out in the past. The guy loved to go on and on about the old country, the good old days. Tucci liked him well enough to put up with his endless repetition, but he had no time for rambling reminiscences right now. He tapped his watch by way of explanation and drove by.

Upturned tricycles and scraggly tomato plants littered Mule's yard. Hand and garden tools were scattered on the porch, though from the look of the place, they had not seen much use in some time. Moldy streaks and rust blots stained the siding. Paint peeled from the shutters, and several roof tiles were missing or displaced. Giant weeds choked the flower beds.

Frannie stepped out to greet him. She sported a weary smile and toted a small boy on each slender hip. Fine lines fanned from her warm brown eyes, and a few wiry gray hairs were sprinkled through her long chestnut hair. Otherwise, she looked barely older than Gina.

"Good to see you, Joe. It's been too long."

"Good see Doe," aped the two-year-old. He squirmed free of his mother's grasp and rushed Tucci like a guided missile.

"Whoa, Nicky boy. Easy."

His three-year-old brother followed suit, hurtling headlong for Tucci's leg.

"Incoming! Hit the trenches. Duck!" Tucci bellowed.

He scooped up the little guys. They squirmed in his grasp like hooked fish. Tucci set them down and propelled them lightly toward the toy pile.

"I need to speak to your mom now, guys." He turned to Frannie. "How's our boy?"

She sighed. "See for yourself."

Tucci followed her inside. The house smelled of lemon oil, and fresh vacuum tracks striped the carpet, but there was no keeping up with the jumble of toys and spills and cracker bits. The biggest crumb was sprawled on the couch, sucking at a beer, watching a talk show. "Daughters who steal their mothers' boyfriends" was the topic for today. The stage was packed with the standard-issue idiot exhibitionists, eager to air their deepest secrets and filthiest laundry on national TV.

Tucci stood over Mule in the gloom. "You've really got me worried, pal. I got to tell you."

"Nothing wrong with daytime TV, Tooch. It's American as processed cheese."

"It *is* processed cheese. But I'm not talking about that. What's worrying me is the beer. Ice Lite, for Chrissakes. The main ingredient in that stuff is rat spit."

Mule rubbed his grizzly face. "Just the thing for that oh so kissable breath."

As soon as Tucci set down the doughnut boxes, the little guys swarmed over them like greedy ants. Frannie swiped at the seeking hands and spirited the box up out of their reach. "Not now, gentlemen. After lunch."

Zach, the oldest boy, accepted the prohibition with a long-suffering sigh. He had come to understand that parents were designed to thwart and frustrate. They were the cross your average five-year-old was forced to bear.

Three-year-old Georgie chose to battle the situation with logic. "I already had lunch."

"That was yesterday," Frannie said.

"Yesterday counts," he insisted.

"Only for yesterday."

"I'm still full."

"Then you don't need sweets."

"Yes I do. I'm hungry for doughnuts. Look." He raised his T-shirt and displayed his belly like a miniature Lyndon Johnson.

Little Nick was warming up to a full-blown tantrum.

"Sorry, I didn't know they were loaded," Tucci said.

Frannie sighed. "With three little kids in the house, most things are. It was sweet of you, Joe. Thanks."

"Nicky need doughnut," the little one wailed. "Need doughnut NOW!"

"What Nicky needs now is a nap," Frannie said. "Come on, you guys. Daddy has to talk to Uncle Joe alone."

Mule took another pull at his beer, crumpled the can, and dropped it under the coffee table, where three other crushed empties languished in a pizza box.

"Sit, Tooch. Take a load off."

"That's what I came for. Getting you back on the job would take a big load off right now."

"I'm working on it, Tooch." He plucked a fresh brew from a six-pack stashed under the couch. "Honest."

"You're working on something. Question is what?"

Mule spewed air like a bad tire. "Give me a break, will you? Bad enough I have to hear that crap all day from Frannie. Lighten up, Joe. Have a brewski."

"So happens I'm on duty, Mule. Which, by the way, so are you. Look, I've given you plenty of breaks. It's been months. I can't keep carrying you forever."

"Okay. I hear you. Give me a couple more weeks. That's all I need." The last brew had pushed him to the fuzzy side of the sobriety line, so his tongue sounded furry and fat.

Tucci wrenched the can from Mule's fist. The foam sloshed over, splattering his partner's startled face. "I don't have a couple of weeks. In a couple of weeks I could be history. You hear me, Mule? If I go down, you sink with me. That's how it is."

Samuels sat up and blotted his face with a crumpled napkin. The dousing had stalled his drunken slide. "Don't you think I know that? I want to help you, Tooch. Honest I do. I just can't right now. I'm not ready."

"Then get ready. You've got three little kids, for God sakes. You've got no right to act like one."

"I'm trying. I'm doing the best I can."

"It's not good enough."

"*I'm* not good enough, Tooch. That's the problem."

Tucci looked his partner hard in the eye. The spark, the edge, the hardheaded determination that had earned Samuels his nickname, had been replaced by flabby defeat.

"Look, Mule. I've got to bring this case home quickly, and I can't go it alone. Either you're up and running or you're out. Make up your mind."

"Give me a little more time. That's all I'm asking."

Tucci tossed down a copy of the file. "This is what we're working. First degree sex assault. Find time between *Geraldo* and *The Young and the Ridiculous* to look it over. See what you think. Maybe get some ideas. A couple of days are all I'm going to give you, Mule. I can't afford any more."

Mule clutched his hand. His face shone with sloppy emotion. "Thanks, Tooch. You won't be sorry, buddy. I won't let you down. You'll see."

"No, you won't, Mule. I'm not going to let you."

Tucci popped his head into the kitchen, where Frannie was feeding her mini-monsters lunch. He showed his empty palms.

She sighed. "Thanks for trying, Joe. Give my love to Gina and Marie."

"Hang in there, kiddo. You guys, behave. Mind your mama, you hear? Especially you, Nicky boy." He picked up the baby and gave him a quick air-plane ride. The child screeched and giggled wildly, then upchucked down the front of Tucci's shirt.

"Hey, Joe. I'm so sorry." Frannie mopped the mess with a wad of paper toweling. "Let me run up and get you one of Mike's shirts."

"Forget it. I've got a spare in the car."

Mule was back in the zone, staring at the talk show. He didn't blink as Tucci passed on his way to the door.

"Get it together, partner," Tucci murmured under his breath. "I only got so many hands."

As Tucci's car neared the social club, his Uncle Pasquale sprang into the street. Tucci swerved hard and stomped the brakes, missing the old man by inches.

"What the hell are you doing?" he yelped.

Pasquale shuffled to the window. "You too busy to say *buon giorno,* Giuseppe? In my day a boy showed his elders a little respect."

"*Mi dispiace.* Sorry, Uncle Pete. I'm busy with a very important case."

"What kinda case?"

"Rape. Victim is a sixteen-year-old. Kid who did it thinks he owns the world."

"*Ma stronzino,*" he spat.

"Yes, he's a scumbag. That's why I want to put him away. So it's good seeing you, Zitello Pasquale. Give my love to the little woman."

He rolled his rheumy eyes. *"La moglie infernale."* The wife from hell.

Tucci considered the conversation over, but the old man stood blocking his way. "I got to go, Uncle Pete. Honest."

"Let me help you with this case of yours."

"That's nice, Unc. Thanks anyhow."

"I never told anyone, Joey. But I worked undercover in the war. Top-secret intelligence. I know how to find things out. Give me a chance. You'll see."

"No can do, Unc. I got to go by the rules."

The hoarse voice broke with angry static. "Don't give me rules. Cops use outsiders all the time."

"Informants, witnesses. Not volunteers."

"You think I'm a stupid old man. Good for *niente.*"

"That's not true, Pete. You're good for lots of things."

He swatted away the lie. "I'll show you different, Giuseppe. I'll show you what an old man can do. I'll find out about this case of yours. I'll help whether you like me to or not."

"Sure. You bet."

"You're on, Giuseppe. When I win, you kiss my *culo* in Macy's window."

"Right, Uncle Pete. See you around."

L eaving the bank, Jess spied Mary Murray threading her Lexus into a space at the far end of the crowded lot. Fond of Mary though she was, Jess turned away and slipped into Genovese Drugs to avoid her. They had not spoken since before the Magills left for France, and Jess was not equipped to face the inevitable game of catch-up. *What's new? How's Charlie? How are the kids?*

What was she supposed to say? Same old, same old. Oh, except for the felony charge.

With any luck, no one would ever need to hear about the arrest. At seventeen, Danny was eligible for youthful offender status. Grantham intended to apply for that favorable treatment at the arraignment this afternoon. If the judge agreed to grant the YO, court proceedings would be closed to the press and public and the results of a trial, if it came to that, would be sealed. Hopefully, there would be a prompt dismissal.

Jess could not consider any other outcome, though she and Charlie were scrambling to build a dike against all eventualities. Charlie was at home helping Danny compile a list of people who would likely be willing to speak on his behalf. Jess had come to collect more tangible backing.

The envelope lay in her hand like a brick. Inside was a cashier's check in the amount of seventy-five thousand dollars, payable to the law firm of Grantham & Greene.

Gus Grantham had demanded that staggering sum as a retainer. If he brought the case to a rapid, positive conclusion, all unspent sums would be refunded. If not, marshaling an effective defense for Danny would require enormous work. The lawyer would need to interview witnesses, examine prosecution evidence, and collect compelling data to rebut any potential damage. During the preliminary phases, there would be numerous motions to file, pleadings to prepare and argue, hearings, conferences, on and on.

If the case went all the way to trial, Grantham had warned them to expect considerable additional costs for experts, exhibits, and consultants. Surely they would want their son to have every conceivable advantage: jury analysts, an image adviser, a spokesperson to manage public spin. Modern jurisprudence took a page from Cecil B. DeMille and another from P. T. Barnum. Everything had to be perfectly cast, costumed, scripted, choreographed, and rehearsed.

Once Jess stopped reeling from the financial shock, she was struck by the bitter irony. Recent expenses and indulgences had left them cash-poor. Applying for a loan would take time they did not have. Charlie would never consent to seek financial help from his parents; the emotional interest they'd charge would be more than he could bear to pay. Jess's folks had everything tied up in superconservative long-term investments. Their only immediate means to raise Grantham's fee was to cash out Danny's college fund. Heartsick, Jess remembered how they had built the account, bit by bit, over the years, depositing gifts, small windfalls, extra sums in honor of special occasions and achievements.

They had always viewed the kids' college funds as sacrosanct. Otherwise, Charlie was not inclined to save. Jess, reared in the Chicken Little School of Perpetual Apprehension, believed in socking money away for a rainy day. Charlie's answer was to stock up on trench coats and umbrellas.

Growing up, he'd been treated to a banquet of privileges and the flimsy delusion that unlimited largesse would be available to him for life. As a young boy, his head had been filled with images of trust funds and investment funds and a huge prospective inheritance. He'd never considered that the fiscal rug might be pulled out from under him. Then he'd committed the unpardonable sin of independent thought.

Charlie's father, Charles senior, had wanted his only child to center his life around the quest for the almighty buck. Charlie had opted instead for a career in medicine. Worse, he'd eschewed a lucrative practice for academia and research.

Senior answered his son's unthinkable insolence by cutting off his funds and disinheriting him. Charlie had run up considerable debt putting himself through medical school. Paying off the loans had taken them most of a decade. After that, something always seemed to come up that kept them treading water with their heads just above the solvency line: illnesses, home repairs, appliance mutinies, necessary celebrations, irresistible opportunities.

And now this.

Jess peered through the broad glass storefront. The air thrummed with a dense acrid haze. Puddles of molten tar pocked the blacktop, which gave off a ripe oleaginous stench. Mary's car was still across the lot.

Killing time, Jess strolled the aisles. She picked up a package of washable markers and construction paper for Max and several spiral notebooks for Molly. For Danny she got a box of floppy diskettes and a ream of printer paper. Charlie's favorite Pentel pencils were on sale, so she took two packages and an extra box of leads. She added other sale items to the cart: panty hose, moisturizer, and shampoo. In the drug aisle, she dropped in a bottle of aspirin, antacids, Band-Aids, disinfectant spray, cotton balls, gauze. On second thought, she went back for antihistamine for Molly's hay fever and an over-the-counter sleep aid for herself. All the products she found on the shelf sounded so benign: Nytol, Sominex, Sleep-EZ. What she needed now was extra-strength Sledgehammer in caplet form. Or perhaps, Liquid Coma.

Finally, she hit the snack aisle, where she tossed in Twizzlers, Danish Butter Cookies, Reese's Pieces, and Three Musketeers. Normally, she tried to keep down the supply of sugary temptations. She had vowed to diet off the extra pounds she'd piled on in France. But desperate times called for desperate pleasures. These were bunker supplies. This was war.

Everything conspired to remind her of saner, happier times. The drugstore was a virtual museum of life cycles: contraceptives, pregnancy aids, baby things, nursing supplies, disposable diapers, toys, games, greeting cards, school supplies, books and magazines, acne creams, datebooks, makeup, colognes, contraceptives.

Jess wheeled her haul to the checkout counter. As the clerk scanned her purchases, she spotted Mary leaving the lot. The Lexus paused at the traffic light on High Ridge, then swerved onto the northbound parkway entrance ramp.

Having avoided that uneasy encounter, Jess bumped through the revolving door and hurried to the side of the lot, where the Volvo occupied an evaporating pool of shade. She flipped up the hatch and deposited her bundles in the trunk. As she slid onto the scorching driver's seat, she took a quick mental inventory. She had three plastic shopping bags, her straw tote, and the car keys. Frantically, she looked in her purse and fished through her pockets. No check.

She left the car running in front of the drugstore and raced inside. The moon-faced manager regarded her with ill-concealed irritation. No, he had not seen any stray envelopes and none had been turned in. Jess was welcome to fill out a report if she liked.

Jess retraced her steps. She did not relish having to explain the loss of a seventy-five-thousand-dollar check. It could take days for the bank to stop payment and issue a replacement. In the meantime, Gus Grantham might refuse to proceed with Danny's defense. In true Leffermanian tradition Jess's direst imagination slipped into overdrive, escalating the incident from a dumb error into a world class-catastrophe.

Until they could straighten out the mess, Danny's fate might be entrusted to some twelve-year-old trainee from the public defender's office who knew about as much as Max did about the law. Little Lawyer Fauntleroy would foul up the case in some unthinkable, disastrous way and Danny would be found guilty.

Her heart flapped like the wings of a frantic bird. Jess made a hurried circuit of the aisles, panic nipping at her heels. She scanned the shelves and crouched to peer underneath where the envelope might have slid out of sight. She questioned everyone—clerks, customers.

She imagined Danny sentenced to the maximum for the offense, serving twenty years because of her stupidity. By the time he got out, Danny would be close to her age. She pictured him gray and grizzled, his handsome face etched with deep hard lines as if he'd been assaulted with a linoleum knife. Her sweet, lovely son could lose his chance at a career, home, wife and kids, a normal life. He could be subjected to unthinkable assaults and indignities. His thirsty intellect and sweet, giving heart would be squeezed into dry wrinkled pits. All that. All because of her.

She was fast running out of places to look. What if someone had taken the check and cashed it? A cashier's check was as good as hard currency. What if they lost the money for good?

She turned into the magazine aisle, and there, poking forth from the current issue of *Better Homes and Gardens,* was the envelope. Jess stuffed it deep in her purse, eyed the acoustical tile ceiling, and offered a silent prayer of thanks.

As she exited the store, her bubble of relief broke at the sight of Carla Levitan, closing in like a ravenous shark. Her three daughters trailed behind. Ilona, the oldest, was in her second year at NYU film school. Bettyann was a year behind Danny, and Dee was Molly's age, though she could have passed for Molly's mother with her glum face and lumpy stoop-shouldered frame. Bringing up the rear was Mel Levitan, a shmoo-shaped accountant with a voice like Alvin the chipmunk's. Dressed in tennis whites, he resembled a giant bowling pin.

The Levitans were a cookie-cutter family, so alike in form and face that Charlie referred to them as the Levittowns, after the Long Island community of identical postwar tract houses. They had close-set squinty eyes and cropped curly hair. They were all plump and neckless, with simian arms and generous centers of gravity.

"Look, everyone," Carla gushed. "It's Jess Magill. How are you doing? Are you okay?"

"Fine. Hi, Mel. Girls."

Carla was a black-belt busybody. She had a knack for tossing people off guard with her rude, nervy questions. Even though Jess had come to expect outrageous probing from Carla, she took care to steel herself. The last time they met, Carla had had the temerity to ask how Danny had scored on his SATs. Jess had countered with her standard challenge, "Why do you want to know?"

Jess cast a wistful eye at the roadway, but there was no simple way to escape. Carla and company surrounded her like a thick-hipped fence.

"Excuse me. I have to run," Jess said.

Carla ticked her tongue. "Such a hectic, crazy time. I can imagine."

"Right, exactly. Bye now."

Nobody moved. As Jess sought a path through the fleshy cordon, Carla said, "I have to tell you, I was shocked, Jess. You could have knocked me over."

"Shocked by what?"

"Why, your Danny's arrest of course." She hooked fleshy arms around Ilona and Dee, drawing them close. "Danny Magill of all people. Who'd think he was capable of such a thing?"

"He isn't," Jess railed. "It's an accusation, Carla. That's *all!*"

"Whoa," said Carla, tamping the air. "Look, Jess. I understand how upset you must be. It's like when they found Bettyann's scoliosis and told us she'd need to wear a brace. Maybe have surgery. When bad things happen to your kids, you don't know whether to scream or shoot yourself."

Jess wanted to recommend the latter, but she kept still. Her head ached. If Carla knew, everyone did or would soon. "How did you hear?"

"This is a small town, Jess. Did you honestly think you could keep a thing like this under wraps?"

"Who told you, Carla?"

"It was in this morning's paper. I still have mine if you need any extras. Just give me a call and I'll drop it off."

Tucci rolled over the crest of the hill, perched on the downslope, and set the emergency brake. By his watch, an old Timex you would not want to set your watch by, he was almost fifteen minutes late. Given the timepiece, it could be five or ten minutes worse than that. Trotting heavily down Cove Road, huffing hard, he prayed that his contact had not given up and left. An overheated car, stalled in the middle of Summer Street, had hobbled downtown traffic for nearly half an hour. Once the jam broke, his cranky overheated bomb had bucked along like a mechanical bull, refusing to do better than a brain-jangling twenty miles per hour.

He did not want to blow this chance. From the uncertainty in her voice, this informant was on the edge. She had important information about the Beningson case, she'd said, but she did not trust discussing it on the phone. She'd refused to come to headquarters where she might be spotted. If Tucci wanted to hear what she knew about the rape, he should meet her at the picnic tables near the Cove Island Park concession stand.

Dispatch had relayed the call to his house first thing this morning. The ring had roused him from a deep, disorienting sleep on the floor in Gina's room. Poor kid had been up most of the night, cursed with hiccups that rocked her scrawny frame and reduced her to a puddle of exhaustion.

The caller had described herself as dark-haired, average height, on the slim side. No one at any of the picnic tables came close to fitting that bill. His eye lit on a cluster of kids, a young woman dandling a squalling infant, an amorous couple conducting exploratory tonsillectomies, two men hunched over a backgammon game, a homeless man picking his blackened toes.

Tucci widened his scope. Beyond the picnic area sprawled a jogging track. A kid on Rollerblades whipped by, followed by a meandering pair on recumbent bicycles. A choking haze blanketed the beach, where a plump woman fanned her florid bosom and watched her kids romp in the frothy surf. Another woman, tanned to the hue and texture of tree bark, lay reading a tabloid on a folding chaise. A group of girls in bikinis rested on a giant beach towel with their tops untied and their young breasts oozing from beneath like melted marshmallows.

Tucci could not even muster any interest in the sprawl of nubile flesh. He had the sinking sense that he had blown a critical opportunity. A surprising number of cases were solved or cemented by canaries. Tracking clues, fancy footwork, and forensics all had their place in detective work. But often, the answer came by simple word of beak. Criminals bragged. Conspirators ratted each other out. Witnesses came forward out of spite or conviction or fear.

It was also true what they said about birds of a feather congealing. The city's scum tended to slog around in the same squalid circles. They heard rumors, knew things. Whatever went down went around. Plenty believed that a few bucks were more than sufficient reason to sell out a relative or friend. Tucci didn't know whether this one was singing for her supper or some other cause, but he had hit the ATM for a couple of hundred in crisp new twenties in case. If the tip paid off, even a stiff-ass like Klonsky would be willing to cover the chit. If he got stuck holding the bill, it wouldn't be the worst bet he'd ever lost. Not close.

But now, he might never know.

He kicked the parched ground, raising a gritty cloud. Sweat in the shape of a Rorschach blot stained his rumpled blue chambray shirt. He was in lousy shape and it showed in the way he felt and looked. His mug was the color of wet cement. His gut ranneth over.

He panned the area again, starting with the snack concession. Greasy hot dogs spattered on the grill. Fries bobbled in a roiling sea of oil. The floor was littered with sandy footprints, shell fragments, soiled paper plates, crumpled napkins. The counter kid yawned broadly and flipped a burger that had long since crossed the line from edible junk to charbroiled fossil.

No one new had appeared at the picnic tables. There were no single women on the jogging track or beach. With a heavy sigh, Tucci turned and trudged up the hill toward his car.

As he jiggled the key in the door lock, he felt a hard press at his left kidney. He wheeled around, swinging hard. But instead of an armed assailant, he found an attractive woman splayed on the grassy strip abutting the sidewalk. Her pale skirt was hiked to her thighs, revealing a peek of white lace panties and a long stretch of lathe-turned legs.

"Oh my," she said.

He offered a hand. "Hey, I'm sorry. Are you okay?"

Deftly, she got to her feet and smoothed her skirt. "Mildly humiliated, but otherwise fine. I gather that's not the recommended way to catch a policeman's attention." In response to his perplexed look, she added, "I recognized you from that cover story in the Sunday *Advocate,* Detective. You must have been proud."

Miffed was more like it, but Tucci made a show of polite agreement. The piece, which ran a few weeks ago, had plastered his mug on the front page of the local paper, hailing him as Stamford's top cop. Kip Reilly, the reporter, had meant well. In fact, Kip had written the thing in a misguided attempt to thank Tucci for wrapping up a long-stale homicide case against the junkie who'd offed his cousin in a stickup gone sour. Reilly had never meant for Tucci to take the truckload of teasing that the article had inspired. He could not have known that the piece would propel Tucci to the top of Chief Klonsky's hate list. The reporter had never considered that the press would put Tucci in the spotlight, where the scrutiny and heat were bound to scorch him.

"We spoke this morning," the woman said. "So glad I caught you. I got stuck in a traffic mess downtown."

"No problem. Good to meet you, Miss . . . ?"

"Let's get out of the sun, shall we? I'm sweltering."

She sweltered in a cool, unruffled way. Aside from the grass stain on the rump of her pale linen skirt, there wasn't a chink in her composure. She walked with a crisp finishing school stride, head high. Tucci trailed her back down to the park and out to the snack pavilion. She claimed a bench beneath the shade of a giant maple and set her sunglasses on the picnic table.

"Want anything?" Tucci asked. "Cold drink? Something to eat?"

"All I want is to tell you what I know, Detective. Frankly, since it happened, I haven't been able to think about much else."

"You were right to call and come forward, Miss . . . ?"

"If you don't mind, I'd rather not say." Her eyes dipped behind the dark, lush lashes. "I suppose I owe you an explanation. For the past several years, my husband and I have been having certain difficulties. I came to rely on a dear friend for comfort and support. This man was a great help to me. We became quite close and, recently, we became involved—romantically. But it was a mistake. I felt so foolish and confused. That night, I went to break it off, which is why I happened by the Beningsons' house. This man lives in their neighborhood, and I was on my way home from seeing him when I spotted the car. At first, I thought those kids were simply necking. I drove past, but when I was about a block away, it registered that there was a struggle going on.

"I didn't know what to do. If I'd called the police, I'd have had to explain why I happened to be in the neighborhood. My husband thought I was out with a friend who was recently widowed. She doesn't live anywhere near the Beningson house."

Tucci didn't press for her name. She would be far more valuable as a witness than an anonymous ghost. But he knew how to treat songbirds. You stroked them until they opened up and crooned. Otherwise, they might simply fly away and be lost forever. He could push the question after he learned what she knew.

"I'm afraid I panicked."

"So you went home?"

"No. I couldn't do that. I turned around and drove back. I stopped as close as I could get to the car. The girl spotted me, at least I think she did, but the boy was too, shall we say, involved to notice or care. I'll never forget the look on that poor girl's face. She was so terribly afraid. I revved the engine, hoping to distract him. But he was beyond that. He had this glazed, horrid smile. So sick."

"How did the girl look?"

"Terrified, as I said."

"Anything else?"

"Her clothing had been pulled away. Maybe torn, I can't say for sure."

Tucci pressed on. "Was she hurt, I mean? Did you see any signs of violence?"

She frowned. "I can't honestly say. You'll have to forgive me for being vague, Detective. It was dark, and I was rather distressed at finding myself in such a hideous predicament. You may find this unbelievable, but in nearly fifteen years, I've never so much as looked at another man. This was the first time, and the last. I need to be able to hold my head up and speak the truth."

Tucci did not find her account unbelievable in the least. First times held special appeal and particular peril. Lapsed virgins got pregnant, fledgling burglars got nabbed. Eager rookies had their bellies lined with lead and little girls were leveled by the first rotten bug that happened to come along. That had been Lisa Beningson's misfortune. And his daughter's.

"You can tell the truth," he urged. "And you should. What you were doing in the neighborhood has no bearing on this case. If you agree to testify, I can keep the circumstances strictly under wraps. Arrangements are made to get at the truth without hurting innocent witnesses. Happens all the time."

"Everything could be ruined if this got out. There are children involved. Other difficult complications."

Tucci feared he was on the verge of losing her. "How about making a written statement? I can guarantee you complete anonymity. It won't hold the weight of a corroborating witness willing to go to court, but it will be a huge help in making the charges stick."

Tucci could see the internal fight going on as she considered his request. Her conscience was going ten rounds with her instinct for self-preservation. Her lips pressed in a grim line. "Sorry, Detective. I simply can't take the risk."

"There is no risk. I'll keep your name strictly out of it."

"I told you what I know. What I saw. I'm afraid that's all I can do."

She was slipping through his hands. Tucci had no choice but to squeeze harder. "Telling me is worthless. Without a statement, some backing, I can't take it to the prosecutor, and I can't take it to court."

"I consulted an attorney. He said my corroboration would be helpful to you."

"Well, your attorney's wrong. It's worse than useless," Tucci railed. "Having no witness is one thing. Having one who refuses to do what's right is another."

She bristled. "I didn't come here for a civics lesson."

"If that kid gets off, he's not going to turn into Cary Grant. He'll attack other women."

"You're asking me to earn the A in good citizenship at my family's expense."

"No I'm not. I'm telling you I can keep your name out of it. I can arrange for you to testify in closed session. No press, no publicity. Please, lady. Next time, his victim could be your kid. It could be you."

"I hear you, Detective." She met his gaze. "How can I be certain that my identity will be kept confidential? It would be a total disaster if this got out. My family. His family. So many people would be hurt."

"You have my word. No one is going to be hurt except that rotten kid."

"He deserves to be punished."

Tucci bit back the victory grin. She wasn't in his pocket yet. "Exactly. And you're going to help us put him away where he belongs."

She sucked air through her trim nostrils. "What do you need me to do?"

"I need your name and phone number and the times that would be good for me to call you."

She recoiled. "I don't know, Detective. Maybe this is a mistake." She was pulling away again, ready to turn and bolt.

"Wait," Tucci said. "There's no risk. When I need to reach you, I'll pretend to be from one of the long-distance phone companies, trying to sell you something. If the coast is clear, you buy. If it's not, just say you're not interested. Then, the next time you get a chance, you can call me back. I can always be reached through dispatch. I'll instruct them to put you through anytime."

She shook her head. "That won't work. I can't have my name circulating around the police station."

"No problem. You can go by a code name. How about we call you Miss Muffet?"

Her lips drew in in a small ironic smile. "I wasn't entirely an innocent bystander, Detective. If I had been eating my curds and whey like a good girl, I wouldn't be in this particular fix."

"That's history. All that matters is current events."

She tore the edge from a piece of paper in her purse and wrote the information he had requested. As she stood to leave, she handed the scrap to him. "I'll be hearing from you, then."

"You won't regret this. Believe me. You're doing the right thing."

"I sincerely hope that's true." She turned and walked briskly toward the park exit.

Tucci lagged behind. No point pressing his luck. If they were spotted together by someone she knew, she might revoke her agreement to cooperate. Corroboration in any rape case was as rare as a black swan—maybe rarer—especially from a disinterested observer.

Tucci observed Miss Muffet's confident stride and elegant appearance. She was smart, articulate, consistent, sympathetic, and attentive to detail.

Having a witness like this one was about as good as it got. Klonsky could have his quick, solid conclusion to the case. Tucci's job and his health insurance would be safe. They could concentrate on getting Gina well.

Maybe, when all this was over, they'd take a vacation, just the three of them. Rest up. Enjoy each other. Heal.

Tucci's heart went warm and mushy at the thought. He pushed away the nagging notion that this might all be too good to be true.

FOURTEEN

A Stamford man was arrested and charged with sexual assault in the first degree after an alleged attack in North Stamford last night. Daniel Magill of Coventry Lane was released on a $25,000 bond. The victim's identity has not been divulged.

Those lines appeared in the police blotter, a slim column on the inside back page of the *Stamford Advocate*. Also reported were a domestic violence complaint, two arrests for DUI, a public lewdness charge, and a dog bite story.

The news of Danny's arrest had inspired a flood of calls. When Jess returned from the bank, the phone was blaring yet again. "Jeesh," Max said, charging to the kitchen to answer. "What's going on around here?"

Jess set her purse down and pried off her shoes. Her feet were puffed like brioches from the heat. "Who is it, Maxy?" she asked as she entered the kitchen.

"It's for Mol. It's that geeky kid Caitlin from gymnastics, the one she doesn't like." Back on the phone, he said, "Nope, I don't know when she'll be back. Call her later."

Max's tongue worked like an auger in his cheek as he added the latest name to the message list. Jess scanned the names, all penned in her little boy's loopy hand: clients, neighbors, casual acquaintances, friends. Some of the entries were unrecognizable. Max spelled by the frenetic method. When in doubt, he tossed in extra letters, line drawings, whatever hopped into his grasshopper brain.

The house felt oddly hushed. "Where is everyone?" Jess asked.

"Mol's at Amy's. Dad went out with Prozac. Danny's up in his room with Emma. He says he needs to talk to her alone about stuff that's none of my business, and I should get lost. Want me to interrupt them? I'd be really, really glad to."

"No, honey. That's fine." She was about to ask if he'd eaten, but from the peanut butter smears on the counter and the milk mustache, the answer was obvious. "I need you to ride your bike over to the Pattersons', honey. Carolann is expecting you for a play date."

"Sure you don't want me to stay home and answer the phone some more? It's fun."

"No, sweetie. That's fine." She turned off the ringer and activated the answering machine.

"I'm old enough to stay alone, Mommy. Prozac does, and she's only six."

"As soon as you grow four legs and fur, you can stay alone like Prozac. Now, go wash your face and remember to say please and thank you."

"What for?"

"For everything."

"Even bad stuff?"

"Go."

Jess's heart sank as she scanned the list of callers. She had hoped for a clean and rapid resolution. But the piece in the paper had made this a very public issue. Now, whatever happened, they would have to deal with the fallout. Rumors echoed long after the source of the noise fell mute. Danny would be marked by the accusation. Regardless of the outcome, some people would persist in viewing him as suspect.

The arraignment was scheduled for two o'clock. It was nearly one. With a sigh, Jess sat at the table and dialed Libby Amory.

Jess caught her friend between clients. "Lib? I hate to bother you, but I'm in dire need of a long-distance hug."

"You've got it. Try not to worry, especially about that stupidity in the paper. Tomorrow it'll be yesterday's news."

"People don't forget a thing like this so easily."

"Yes they do. Does the name Weldon mean anything to you?"

"It's vaguely familiar, why?"

"How about Vinnie Venetos?"

"Some name. Sounds like a character from *West Side Story*."

"How quickly they forget," Libby said. "The Venetos kid was accused of vehicular homicide five or six years ago. Early reports claimed he was DUI and hinted at the possibility of cocaine abuse. Turned out the kid had a brain tumor. He'd suffered a seizure and lost control of the car. The case got front-page headlines until the truth came out. Then they printed a minuscule retraction on page twelve."

"That's terrible."

Libby went on. "Bobby Weldon's story was worse. In the late eighties, three victims picked him out of a lineup as the armed robber who'd tied them up, menaced them with an assault rifle, and cleaned out their cash registers. While he was in jail awaiting trial, some guy from New Jersey who was a dead ringer for the Weldon kid robbed two more stores in the identical way. If he hadn't kept up the crime spree, Bobby might still be cooling his heels in a cell for those heists."

"Is this supposed to make me feel good, Libby?"

"Yes, my sweet. The moral of those stories as far as you're concerned is that people have short memories. Those two cases were huge. Banner headlines. A little time goes by, and even a smart, well-informed person like you forgets all about them."

Jess was not blind to the glaring fallacy. "Maybe I have, Counselor, but you haven't."

"That's only because Weldon and Venetos came to me as clients later on." There was a pause, and Lib's secretary, an aspiring actress with the Dr. Seussian name of Corinne Zinn, buzzed through to report that her next client had arrived. Corinne was a smart, personable young woman with a rich, commanding voice.

"Sorry, Jess," Libby said. "My afternoon deposition is about to start and I need to get ready. Collect the file and put on the flak jacket. This couple makes the Hatfields and McCoys look friendly."

"Sounds like fun."

"If nuclear warfare means fun, then it's fun. You guys all set for the arraignment?"

"If scared to death means set, then we're set."

"Nothing to it. Believe me. Legal proceedings are slow, boring, and routine. Most of the time is spent waiting around for the thrilling opportunity to wait around some more. The best advice I can give you is to try to keep things at home as normal as possible until this gets cleared up."

"I'm trying, Lib. Believe me."

"Hold on a second, will you, Jess?"

Corinne's voice marked a percussive thump in the background. Libby sounded harried when she reclaimed the line. "Sorry. Seems we've got a bit of a situation here. Plaintiff and defendant are at each other's throats. I'd better go help break it up. I'll check in with you later."

Jess went upstairs and paused at Danny's door. As she raised her hand to knock, Emma's firm protests rang from inside.

"Enough, Danny. Stop trying to make excuses for her. Why is it you go easy on everyone but yourself?"

"Because it doesn't make sense, that's why. People don't lie for no reason. Something had to set her off."

"Like what?"

Jess imagined Danny hitching his broad shoulders, as if he were trying to shift the weight of the world to a more manageable position. "I honestly don't know, but there had to be something."

Emma blew a long, frustrated breath. "You're the one who's not making any sense, Danny. You act as if you want Lisa to be right."

"I don't, but . . ."

"But what?"

Jess waited out a long, uneasy silence. Danny had no answer. Or gave none. Reluctantly, she knocked.

"It's me, honey. Sorry to bust in on you guys, but we need to leave in a little while."

Emma opened the door. Once coltish and awkward, she had grown into her long, lanky frame. Close-cropped auburn hair framed her fine features and wide-set almond eyes. Astride her model's body, even the ratty T-shirt and worn jeans looked elegant. "That's okay, Mrs. Magill. I need to get back anyway. I've got chem lab at three." She eyed Danny severely. "I don't like people messing with my friend, Danny Magill. You take care of yourself."

"I'll try. I'm ready, Mom."

The teenager sat on the bed in a navy blazer, gray slacks, a white shirt, and a striped tie. His hair was scored with comb tracks and his shoes were polished to a high reflective sheen.

The starched spine and special-occasion uniform propelled Jess back to other momentous days. She recalled Danny's bar mitzvah, his honor society induction, awards dinners, parties, and the junior prom. Until now, all his dress-up events had been celebrations.

"You okay?" she asked.

"Hanging in there."

"Did you have lunch? I'll be glad to make you something."

"I'm not hungry."

"All right. I'll go change."

"So Dad's not coming."

"Of course he is. He's out walking the dog. I'm sure he'll be back any minute."

"I don't think so. He doesn't want any part of me, of this." A sweep of his arm encompassed the sum of his pain.

"That's not true, honey."

"He as much as said so." His voice broke.

Jess sat beside her son and set her hand on his. She was startled anew by the sprawl of his palm and digits. It seemed a mere moment ago that she could tent his tiny baby fingers with vast room to spare. "What happened? You two have a fight?"

He swiped his eyes with his jacket sleeve. "We were working on that list Mr. Grantham asked for. Dad wanted me to put down Mr. Obler as someone who'd vouch for me, and I said Obler was a dork."

"True. But he was a terrific tennis coach, and he had excellent taste in kids. You were a major favorite of his."

"I know. I like the guy. I was only trying to say that he might not make much of an impression in court with his buckteeth and that snorting sound he makes instead of laughing, not to mention the way he dresses like a refugee from *The Dating Game*."

Jess couldn't argue. Ollie Obler was a devout eccentric, who flaunted his considerable peculiarities for dramatic effect. She conjured his sprawl-collared shirts, bell-bottom polyester pants, garish platform shoes, and bushy sideburns. He was quite the character, but as a character witness, he left more than a bit to be desired. What could Charlie be thinking?

"Dad bit my head off. He said I was in no position to put anyone down. Don't be a wise-ass, he told me. With the fix you're in, you'd better be grateful for every bit of help you can get." His jaw went hard and belligerent. "Let him hate me. Let everyone think I'm dirt. I don't care."

"Dad loves you Danny. You know that. He's upset, that's all."

"And I'm not? This is happening to *me*, Mom. Not him."

"Everyone who cares about you is bound to be affected by a thing like this. It's tough stuff. But soon it'll be straightened out and we can work on getting over it."

"I don't think so. It's like a bad accident, Mom. One thing goes wrong, then everything goes sour. You can't get things back the way they were. It just doesn't work."

"I hear that you feel that way, and I can understand why." She ran her palm across his smoothly shaven cheek. "But it's going to be all right. I believe that, Danny. I'm sure of it."

"I'm not sure of anything anymore."

The front door squealed and Charlie's voice boomed up the stairs. "Jess? Danny, you ready? Time to go."

"See? He's here."

Prozac slogged into the room and plopped her muzzle on Danny's lap. He stroked her scruff absently.

"We'll be down in a minute," Jess called to Charlie. She winked at Danny. "Maybe we should put Prozac on the character witness list."

A grudging smile played on his lips. "Sure. Right after Max."

"Come on, Jessie," Charlie bellowed. "This is no time to show up late."

"I said we'll be right down," she snapped. "Get a grip for God sakes."

As soon as the surly words slipped out, she regretted them. The kids were unaccustomed to witnessing discord or anger between them. Since early in the marriage they had always resolved their conflicts in the privacy of their room. Whatever the issue, they'd arrive at some satisfactory compromise, usually sealed with prime-quality lovemaking.

Jess shook her head, dismayed by Charlie's impatience and her unnecessary outburst. She took in Danny's stricken face. "I'm just wound a little tight, honey. It doesn't mean anything."

"Better get ready," he said. He looked away, but not before Jess saw the welling tears.

She hurried to her room and threw on her navy suit, low heels, and a short-sleeved blouse. She ran a brush through her hair and splashed her face with chill water. Glancing at her weary reflection, she repeated the assurance she had offered to her son. "It's going to be fine," she murmured, willing it to be true.

"It has to be fine."

Jess passed through the metal detector first. Inside, the clerk lifted her purse from the conveyer and fingered the mongrel contents with distaste. Charlie followed unimpeded, but Danny set the buzzer off three times. He emptied his pockets of keys and coins and shed the metal-buttoned blazer. The culprit turned out to be his belt buckle, handed down from Jess's father, David, after whom their eldest son had been named. Poor kid sputtered with embarrassment as the line behind them stretched out the courthouse door.

Gus Grantham parted the milling crowd to greet them. "I've arranged a place where we can talk. The clerk will call us when it's time."

He squired them up the stairs and down the right arm of a T-shaped hallway, where knots of people waited and conferred. The building had the look of a shabby schoolhouse. Drab tile and brash fluorescent lights cast a sickly glow over the bored and anxious faces.

Sun spikes pierced the grimy conference room windows. The table was littered with crumbs and wadded candy wrappers. Grantham brushed the debris into a trash can. His broad grin did not waver as he landed the first blow.

"I've talked with the prosecutor and I have to be honest with you, folks. Right now, things do not look promising."

Jess's temper flared. "Why is that? It's Danny's word against Lisa's. You said so yourself."

"Yes, I did. But—"

"Lisa lies, and Danny is forced to defend himself. What kind of justice is that?"

"This is not about what the plaintiff said, Mrs. Magill. Apparently, the girl suffered injuries."

"That's ridiculous," Jess said.

"Bruises, lacerations, two broken ribs." He turned to Danny. "Ever been in trouble for fighting, son? Any history of violence of any sort?"

"No. And I didn't hurt Lisa. I swear I didn't."

"I believe you," the lawyer said. "Let me see your hands, Danny. Turn them over now. . . . Excellent. We'll want professional photographs taken right away. I'll have my office arrange it." With an appraising nod, he said, "What you're looking at is a nice neat bit of reasonable doubt."

"I don't understand," Jess said.

"If Danny inflicted a beating, his hands would be bruised and swollen. We can argue that Lisa's wounds had to come from someone else. Or, they might have been self-inflicted."

"One of those has to be true," Jess insisted. "Danny's the gentlest person I know." Even as she spoke, she flashed back to a rushed trip to the emergency room with Mark Ackerman after Danny smashed his little friend on the head with a hockey stick. And there was the time Greg Bender needed seven stitches because Danny clipped him with a wooden block in nursery school. But those things had happened a zillion years ago when her son was a small explosive bundle of raw response.

"Let's move on to another issue." Grantham said. "I'm confused by something in the intake report, Danny. Maybe you can help clear it up." He riffled through a sheaf of pages. "Here it is. According to a sergeant named William Huppert, you made an incriminating statement. What's strange is that there's no further mention of any such statement or admission. Normally, anything like that would be signed, sealed, taped, and splashed in neon all over the file. Do you have any idea what this means?"

"No. I don't think so."

"If you did say something to this Huppert character, I have to know what it was. The circumstances, everything."

Danny's head trailed an arc of misery. "I don't know. I can't remember."

"What did you tell them, Danny?" Charlie demanded. "Did you admit that you did this thing?"

"Of course he didn't," Jess said.

"I'm asking Danny," Charlie snapped. "What is it? Yes or no?"

Grantham raised a hand like a symphony conductor, seeking a better note. "Try to remember, son. It's important."

"Maybe I said I was sorry. Something like that."

Charlie dropped his face in his hands. "My God."

Grantham rushed in. "Please, Dr. Magill. Jumping to a negative conclusion is not the answer. There are plenty of ways to interpret what Danny said. My guess is he regretted having sex with the girl, especially after it led to a situation like this."

"Why don't we get the facts." Charlie fixed Danny with a dark, challenging stare. "Why did you say you were sorry? What did you mean?"

"I told you I can't remember," the boy groaned. "You have to believe me,

Dad. This cop kept at me and at me. He kept asking question after question. Telling me all these awful, scary things. I was tired, wigged out, frightened half to death. It got so I honestly didn't know what I was saying."

"Why didn't you keep your mouth shut, then? The officers told you whatever you said could be held against you. I heard them, you heard them."

"I screwed up, Dad. I'm sorry. Okay?"

Charlie pounded the table. "No, it's *not* okay, damn it. None of this is okay."

"Leave him alone, Charlie. This is the last thing he needs," Jess urged.

"No, Jess. The last thing he needs is to be coddled." His lips drew in in a tight angry line. "This is no simple screwup."

"I'm sorry," Danny cried. "Or I'm not sorry. What are the right words, Dad? What do you want me to say?"

"The truth would be a good start, if you remember what that is."

Danny deflated. "Jesus Christ."

Jess sat frozen by the exchange, torn between the seductive fury of the storm and an instinct to curl up and hide from it.

"What's done is done," Grantham broke in forcefully. "Let's focus on how to proceed from here. I plan to showcase Danny as a model young man with an unblemished record. I said this doesn't look good, but that's now, before we've done the necessary work. My job is to get this thing dismissed, or worst case, to bring in a not guilty verdict, and I intend to do just that. But I need full, focused cooperation from all of you."

"You'll have that," Jess said.

"I want to know the truth," Charlie persisted. "I need to know. Did you do what Lisa said, Danny? Did you force that girl to—"

"Stop right there." Grantham's look was fierce. "Your son is innocent, Dr. Magill. That is the truth right now in the eyes of the law, and with any luck at all, we're going to keep it that way. I'm presuming you want to see him acquitted."

"Of course I do." Charlie spewed a long, mournful breath. "Forgive me. I'm lost here. I've never been so lost."

Grantham set his jaw. "No one is prepared for a situation like this, Dr. Magill. I'll walk you through it, step by step. But you have to let me take the lead."

"I will." Charlie turned to Danny. "I'm sorry. I'm afraid I'm not doing very well with all this."

"Me neither," Danny said.

The words were right, but Jess could feel the strange, brittle stiffness between them. They had always been close, but since the arrest, they were like old friends who'd just learned that they were on opposing sides of a business deal or a lawsuit or a sexual rivalry.

"I'll need you to agree to certain conditions, Danny," Grantham said. "One.

What I say goes. You follow my instructions, no matter how foolish or insignificant they may seem. Is that understood?"

"Yes sir."

"Good. Number two. You discuss this case with no one unless I give the go-ahead. No exceptions, even your best friend. As far as your folks are concerned, if you talk to them, I don't want to know about it. The police will question everyone. And you never know who they may call to testify. Are you with me?"

"I am."

"Fine. Once we're called, the arraignment will only take a few minutes. We'll waive the reading of the charges and plead not guilty. I'll do the talking. All you need to do is sit still and keep whatever you may be feeling to yourself. Nothing Judge Harrigan hates worse than a smart aleck."

"I understand."

"I don't expect the Beningsons to be there, but they might. If they are, you say nothing and do nothing. Don't even look at them."

He allowed a long pause for effect.

"Okay then." His grin fell away. "Judges and juries take a hard look at the family. It's important that they see you as a close, supportive unit. No matter what pressures you're under, no matter how difficult this gets, you need to think about what kind of impression you're making."

"You needn't worry about that," Charlie said.

There was an insistent thump at the door. A grainy voice announced, "You're next up, Mr. Grantham. Trial room A."

"Thanks, Nate," the lawyer called. "We're on, folks."

Charlie stood beside Danny and smoothed his lapels; then he took Jess's hand. His palm was sweaty. Danny lagged back like a child facing the pediatrician's hypodermic. Her own leg muscles sagged like spent elastic. She sent them frantic signals. *Step. Move. Don't collapse!*

Grantham sported a look of misplaced cheer. "Here we go, folks. So it begins."

Jess's mother stood at the door, fanning herself with a copy of the *Weekly World News*. "Frankfort moose man impaled on own antlers," one headline blared. "Baby smuggled in watermelon cho on seeds," said another. "Angry spouse beats husband to death with 18-pound turtle." Jess's eye drifted to the subhead. "The turtle was not injured in the exchange."

A black and yellow warm-up suit gave Pearl the look of a portly bee. Her ash-blond hair was shaped like a catcher's mitt and lacquered to porcelain stiffness. The scent of sautéed onions hung on her like a fog.

Jess's stepfather, Lou, a kindly soul with the presence of a sigh, lagged three flagstones behind his wife. Dressed in khaki pants and a matching shirt, he blended to near disappearance with the parched lawn. He bore a giant Igloo cooler and a look of abject apology. "Sorry to barge in, Jessie dear. If it's a bad time . . ."

"It's fine, Lou. Hi, Mom. Come in."

"We could come back when it's better for you," Lou offered. "Come, Pearl. They're busy. Let's leave the food and go."

Jess's mother dismissed the idea with a backhand swipe. "Don't be ridiculous. A mother is always welcome."

Lou trailed her in, lugging the weighty cooler. Jess could predict the burnt offerings: desiccated chicken and brisket suitable for rigging yacht sails. Accompanying that would be German potato salad, salami, pickles, seeded rye, and brownies baked to the consistency of paving stones.

Whatever the question, Pearl's answer had always been great quantities of ill-prepared food. Food was not only love, it was salve. In the hands of a skilled ego assassin like Jess's mother, it was also a powerful bludgeon. Jess had been flogged with nourishment and its contradictory implications from early childhood. *Why don't you eat, dear? I made all your favorites. Don't you like them? You really want more? Haven't you put on some weight? If there's one thing I can't stand, it's a fat girl.*

Pearl bustled into the kitchen. Her plump thighs, encased in polished nylon, scratched a rakish rhythm when she walked. "Sit, Lou. You're all flushed. Where are the children, Jessie?"

"Max is playing in the yard. Molly's at a friend's. Danny's upstairs resting."

Pearl sucked air through her teeth. "When I called and Max told me where you were, I almost died. I got so faint and flushed Lou was worried I was having an infarction."

"I was not, Pearl. You've got a heart like a horse."

"Horses don't have heart attacks?"

Charlie glanced up from his paper. "Hello, Lou. Pearl. How are you?"

Pearl sat with a sigh. "How could I be?"

"How was the trip?" Charlie asked. "Did you have much traffic?"

"Took no time," Lou said. "Piece of cake."

"Man drives like a cowboy," noted Pearl. She turned to Jess. "Max told me you were out half the night. Keeping a young boy like that up so late." She ticked her tongue in indictment. "What are you sitting for, Lou? Those things need to go in the icebox. You got a little cold water, Jessie? Or maybe a lemonade? Wait. Don't bother. I'll get it myself."

A grand moan escaped her as she stood. Jess's mother was kvetch-propelled. Her every move was accompanied by a grunt or grimace. "Who wants a sandwich? I brought nice fresh meat and all the fixings."

She was not deterred by the crushing silence. "Pot roast, Jessie?"

"Nothing, Mom. I'm not hungry."

"It's delicious. You'll see." Pearl mounded a bread slice with brisket, slathered on mustard, added potato salad and a pickle slice, and handed her daughter the plate.

"What about Charlie? Can I make him a sandwich, or is he still so picky?" Pearl was master of the third person invisible. She often referred to people in her presence as if they did not exist. This was especially true of gentiles like Charlie and others she viewed as inferior species.

"He's still picky," Charlie remarked dryly. "And he'll take mayonnaise on the brisket he doesn't want."

Pearl fixed Charlie's sandwich with mustard, the way God intended leftover pot roast to be consumed. For Lou, who adored brisket, she fashioned a plate with a minuscule scoop of mashed tuna, a scoop of fat-free cottage cheese, two lettuce leaves, and a wedge of something that bore a passing resemblance to a tomato. "He's got cholesterol," she explained, swatting her husband's hopeful fingers from the meat. "You know what Dr. Gottbaum said, Lou. Red meat is not for you."

"When did he say that?"

"When you weren't listening. Now eat your cottage cheese." She eyed Jess with disdain. "A girl doesn't call her mother at a time like this? I have to hear from the baby?"

Max and Prozac loped in, lured by the phony aromatic promise of the food. "I'm not a baby, Grandma."

"Who said you are?"

"You did."

"Listen to the baby, what a mouth on him," Pearl chuckled. "It's a figure of speech, darling. You're your mother's baby and your mother is my baby. Even when you're an *alte cocker* like me, you'll still be the baby."

"How old are you, Grandma?"

"Thirty-nine plus."

"Plus what?"

"Eat."

Pearl shoved a sandwich in his mouth and beamed at the blowfish bulge of his cheeks. Prozac perched at her knee with an expectant look on her muzzle. By the dog's reckoning, anyone who practiced force-feeding could not be all bad. "Give the baby a glass of juice, Lou," said Pearl. "And feed the poor dog. Look, she's starving."

Danny appeared, rumpled and yawning. He stopped short at the kitchen door. "Hey, Gram, Grandpa Lou. I didn't know you were coming."

Pearl labored to her feet and wrapped him in a crinkly nylon embrace. "How's my sweet boy?"

"I'm okay."

She smoothed the hair back from his forehead. "You look exhausted. Sit. Let me fix you a snack."

"Thanks. I don't want anything."

"You don't know what you want," Pearl informed him. She made him a sandwich, then massed a plate with salami chunks and pickle slices and passed it around. "Here, everyone have some nice hors d'oeuvres."

"I'm still pretty tired. May I be excused?" asked Danny.

"Of course, darling. Go. We'll see you for dinner in a little while."

The teenager beat a rapid retreat. Charlie followed moments later. Lou retired with the paper to the bathroom, his favorite place of refuge from Pearl. Max, never the diplomat, said he was so bored he might as well take a bath.

After he left, Jess turned to Pearl. "I apologize for not calling you about this, Mom. We were hoping it would be over with by now."

Pearl chewed in extravagant rounds, working her pleated lips like a sea anemone. "Salami's delicious, Jessie. Have a piece."

"I'm not hungry."

"For salami, you don't need to be hungry. It's like medicine."

In typical fashion, Pearl refused to discuss the issue at hand. No matter that Danny's arrest loomed like a huge dead elephant in the center of the room. In Pearl's view, dead elephants and other unseemly things deserved to be ignored.

That was how she had handled her husband's cancer. The entire family, including Jess's wonderful dad, had been forced to tiptoe around the enormity of his dying. Speaking of it was sure to bring down the wrath of Pearl, a fate far worse than any terminal disease. Only once, near the end, when he was alone with Jess, had her father dared to remark on his imminent demise. "It's been such a good life, sweetheart. I've been so blessed, especially with you kids, I honestly hate to leave."

Pearl frowned at her watch. "Would you look at that. Almost time for the news. Come."

"Wait, Mom," Jess said. "This is no good. We need to talk about what's happening with Danny."

"Hush," Pearl hissed. *"Die Kinder."* She cocked her head in warning. *Keep your voice down. The children might hear.*

"They know, Mom. Everyone does. It was in this morning's paper."

Pearl's mouth gaped like a sinkhole. "In the paper? The nerve of them! The gall! It's defamation!"

"You mean libel, Mom. But it's not. "

"Nonsense. You should sue the pants off them. You should go right down to that paper and tell them where to get off." She pressed a hand to her bosom, restraining her unruly molecules.

"They're allowed to print news of arrests."

"You defend such a thing? I swear, Jessie, I'll never understand you."

"I don't care about the newspaper, Mom. I care about Danny."

"He's a wonderful boy and that's that. I don't want to discuss it anymore." Skirting an elephant in a ten-by-twelve room was no easy feat, but Pearl was up to it. "How about a brownie? They're absolutely delicious if I do say so myself."

Jess refused to give up that easily. "We've hired a good lawyer. Libby recommended him."

"How is Libby? I haven't seen her in an age."

"Please don't change the subject, Mom. The lawyer is optimistic about the eventual outcome, but it doesn't look as if we can hope for an early dismissal. The judge took a hard line at the arraignment. He refused to treat Danny as a youthful offender, and he set high bail."

"I told you to stop, Jessie. I don't want to hear another word."

"Pretending won't make it go away, Mom. Please let's talk about it."

Pearl stuck her fingers in her ears and whistled an off-key rendition of "Someone's in the Kitchen with Dinah."

"It could take months at least, possibly a year or more, for this case to come to trial. You can't just act as if it isn't happening." Jess couldn't bear to be shut off like this, her feelings trampled into nonexistence.

Pearl threw up her hands. "That's it. You won't listen. I'll leave. Come, Lou," she hollered. "We're leaving."

"Don't do this, Mom. Please."

But Pearl was as headstrong as the tides. In a huff, she collected Lou and the cooler, chanted her farewells, and slammed out.

Jess sank inside. She had always wished for the kind of soft, cushiony mother she'd seen on sitcoms and at friends' houses, a mother you could lean on, a mother capable of buffering life's brutal side. Even now, she ached to race after Pearl, grab her by a stubby ankle, and cling for dear life.

But after forty years, she knew the drill. Her mother would come around in her own good time and offer crumbs of support in the form and size she chose.

Dead weary, she went upstairs and knocked at the door to Charlie's study. No answer, so she turned the knob and slipped inside.

A thick volume lay open before him on the desk. But Charlie sat staring blankly at the wall.

"You okay?" she asked.

"Not really. You?"

"The same."

Jess sat on his lap and wrapped her arms around his neck. She melted into his familiar contours and breathed his comforting scent. "Just when I think things can't get any bleaker, Pearl comes along to prove me wrong."

"You had a fight?"

"Pearl doesn't fight. She hits the detonator."

"Sorry your mother's being herself. Having a little parental support and understanding right now would be useful all around."

"For Danny too, honey. Go talk to him. He needs to hear that you know he's innocent."

"But I don't know that."

Pulling back, she peered into his pale, pained eyes. "What are you saying?"

"Danny's our son, and I love him, Jessie. But that doesn't mean two and two have stopped adding up to four. Danny admits he was alone with Lisa. Next thing she's crying rape and she's sustained serious injuries. Broken ribs, bruises. That hardly sounds self-inflicted."

"You heard Gus Grantham. Someone else could have been responsible."

"Who? Santa Claus?"

"I don't know who. But it wasn't Danny."

His eyes went vague. "I've seen too much craziness to know anything as a certainty, Jessie. And so have you. You *want* to believe Danny couldn't have done this. Maybe you *need* to believe it. But you can't be absolutely, without a doubt, positive about what happened between him and Lisa in that car."

"Yes I can, Charlie. I am, and so is the lawyer."

"Grantham's job is to establish reasonable doubt. I need the truth. I have to know."

"I don't get it, Charlie. Do you want Danny to go to jail? You want his life ruined?"

"No, Jess. I want exactly what you do. I want this never to have happened. I want to go back two days and stay right where we were."

The tides at La Rochelle, France, are among the world's most extreme, dragging the shoreline out ten thousand feet or more from peak to ebb. When the seas had skittered to the horizon, Jess, Charlie, and the kids would gather on the plank terrace at the Hôtel Les Brises. In silence, they would marvel at how the motorboats and sailing vessels that only hours ago had sliced through the currents and embraced the winds now lolled on their sides in the littered sand like wounded beasts.

At low tide, trucks bumped across the shoals to dredge for salvage. Clammers with their pants legs hitched to the knee trolled the sodden beach, scanning for telltale bubbles among the tide pools. Vacationers meandered along, gathering shells and memories to sustain them through the long winter's cold and monotony.

The change occurred with jarring suddenness. The sea was whisked away, lacy hems flying, like a small girl misbehaving at a ball. Its absence spelled opportunity for merchants and scavengers of varied species. But Jess always felt a tug of desolation at the sight, a longing for things to return to their more natural, graceful state.

Danny's arrest had the identical effect on the family. The Magills' buoyant cushion had been wrenched away, leaving each of them mired in cruel uncertainty. Everything looked and felt askew, as if Max, master of the bias shot, were holding the camera.

Jess hoped that this day might bring part of the solution. The start of school meant a return to normal rhythms and routines. The heat wave had been swept away in a wash of crisp, cool wind. Dawn brought gem-blue skies and a sparkle of early frost. Streaks of blush and lemon splashed the greenery.

From outside came a harsh pneumatic wheeze and the scream of brakes. Through the window, Jess spied Max, clad in new jeans and a striped T-shirt, clambering up the steps of the yellow bus that would ferry him to his first day as a third-grader at the Davenport Ridge Elementary School.

Jess had set out to escort him to the bus stop, but the little boy had stopped her with a milk-curdling scowl. "I can go myself, Mommy. I've been doing it for years."

"I know that, Maxy. But I thought since this was the first day, you might like me to walk you out." She had done this every year for all of the kids when they were small. Ritual and tradition were important to children, especially big ones like herself.

Dripping with exasperation, Max sighed. "I keep telling you, I'm not a little kid anymore. Year after next, I'm going to be ten."

With a mixed pang of sorrow and pride, Jess had watched her baby emeritus stride forth like a runt warrior. He had his book bag slung rakishly over one shoulder and his Yankee cap flipped backward, so a spiky clump of hair poked through the crown. He had developed a sense of what was cool and the single-minded zeal to achieve it. Max's fierce independence told Jess everything she needed to know about his developmental state, except how to live through yet another impending adolescence.

Dealing with Molly was more than enough. In the past year Jess's sweet little girl had grown into an alien force, capable of inflicting bruising harm with a single word or look. Before leaving for school this morning, she had expressed her contempt for Jess with one all-encompassing glare. In Molly's view, Jess lacked the capacity to understand any of life's central issues, such as the cosmic importance of blue toenails or the mysterious allure of scrawny movie stars with zits. She saw Jess as a hopeless case, incapable of acceptable speech, action, or dress. Even the way she breathed was a considerable annoyance. No doubt Molly wished she would have the grace to stop.

Jess could remember feeling precisely the same way about Pearl, who had deteriorated from infallible to unbearable seemingly overnight. At Molly's age, Jess's fondest secret wish had been to wake up one morning and find that her mother had inserted her head in the oven and turned on the gas, as she so often promised to do.

How dramatic that would have been. Surely Pearl's suicide by propane would have elevated Jess to that lofty status normally reserved for classmates with extraordinary good looks or select outsized body parts or special talents, like the ability to shake a pom-pom with rhythm and style.

In those days one of her biggest fears had been that Pearl, in her limitless perversity, would choose a more unsightly means of self-annihilation. Sometimes, Jess's mother would step into a lawn-and-leaf bag and draw it to her neck. "With the way everyone treats me around here, I might as well put myself out at the curb and let them haul me to the landfill."

Of course, Jess understood Molly's disdain. Disavowing one's parents was a common clause in every budding child's Declaration of Independence. It was normal, even necessary. Still, ducking the hurled contempt was exhausting and demoralizing, especially now. Children did not understand their power, or perhaps they understood it all too well. Jess shrank a bit with every snide remark. After each scathing encounter, she had to patch the holes that Molly had poked in her ego and pump herself back to normal size. If only the diminishing scorn of a teenage child could be localized to hips and thighs.

Danny had set out over an hour ago. At breakfast he had seemed almost like his old self, precociously wise and in command of the situation. When Jess asked how he felt about going back to school, he'd answered philosophically. "What can I say, Mom? Some of the kids are bound to be jerks. Some of them are jerks when there's nothing going on. But I've got to deal with them sooner or later. May as well get it over with."

Jess had ruffled his hair and forced a tight-lipped smile. She hadn't trusted herself to speak. If she opened her mouth, the fear and fury boiling inside her might erupt. Danny was right to keep it together at a time like this. The least she could do was try to set a similar brave example.

When the worst of the emotion had passed, Jess had offered him the use of her car. Charlie could drop her at the office on his way to work. She'd been dismayed when he refused. He preferred to take the bus, he said. Thanks anyway.

Max's school bus started up with a rush and a whooping sound, turned by laborious degrees, and drifted off the block. Jess loaded the soiled breakfast plates into the dishwasher and sat at the kitchen table with a second cup of coffee and the morning papers. She leafed through the *New York Times,* avoiding the local rag, which might contain some further mention of Danny's arrest.

Grantham had warned that the legal system could take four months to a year or more to bring Danny's case to a conclusion. If she spent that long focusing compulsively on this thing, she'd go crazy. She vowed to strive for normalcy instead, even though she could barely remember how that looked. She recited the steps as if they were some unfamiliar poem she had been assigned to memorize: shower, get dressed, go to the office, work with clients, return home, deal with the kids, eat, sleep, get up and start the cycle again.

She scanned the headlines. As usual, most of the news was a dull shade of bleak: murder, conflict, scandal, and threat of doom. The themes were repeated in section after section: sports, business, society, science, even entertainment. She read three articles without absorbing a word. Her mind was like the neglected coffee in her mug, cold mud capped by an oily, obfuscating film.

A column on the rising chic of heroin as a recreational drug caught her unsteady attention. She slogged through the first paragraph twice, then again, wobbling over every word like a small child learning to ride a two-wheeler.

Charlie came up behind her, pushed her hair aside and nuzzled her neck. "Max got off okay?"

"Like a trooper."

"I take it we're alone then."

Prozac sneezed in mild contradiction, then flopped her muzzle on her paws and drifted off.

"It's strange," Jess said. "Normally, I'm delighted when the kids go back to school, but with all that's going on, it feels strange. Lonely in a way."

His warm breath played against her ear. "I have just the antidote." He nuzzled her again and edged his fingers down her spine.

Jess struggled to still the worries swarming in her brain. She and Charlie had not made love since Daniel's arrest, and she craved that close connection. She pulled long, measured breaths, closed her eyes, and imagined a sunny beach. Bone-melting warmth. Playful waves lapping against the breakwater. She conjured sunset over the sea, drawn in bold streaks of pink, gold, and dusky lavender.

Charlie drew her up and kissed her deeply. Jess's hibernating nerve cells stretched and sprang to life. Tingling currents coursed through her limbs, traversed her chest, and settled in an ache between her legs. She was melting in the feeling, swirling in a pool of sensation, surrendering to the currents. Charlie girded her waist and guided her upstairs.

As they sank onto the bed in a fleshy tangle, she was startled by the squealing plaint of the screen door. There was a blurred rush of footsteps; then the house went bristling still.

Jess clutched Charlie's wrist. "Did you hear that?"

Grantham had warned that a case like Daniel's could arouse nasty passions. Jess imagined some crazed vigilante tearing up the house, terrorizing them, bent on exacting a blood toll for their son's alleged sins.

"Probably the dog. I'll go check."

"Be careful." As she followed him into the hall, Danny came charging up the stairs. Without a word, he burst into his room and slammed the door.

Jess knocked. "Danny, honey? Are you all right?"

From inside came a churn of angry commotion. Entering, Jess and Charlie found their son furiously ripping up the pile of college catalogues and applications he had taken months to amass. He had sorted them in neat stacks for further consideration: tennis schools, state schools, safeties, Ivies, Big Tens. Now they lay in a jumbled heap in the center of the room, covers ripped off, pages torn.

"What's this about?" Jess asked.

"I don't need them anymore. It's over. I'm over."

"Why, honey? What happened?"

"What difference does it make?" He wrenched apart another glossy brochure. "Nobody gives a damn about the truth." He snatched an honor society plaque off the wall and threw it across the room. The award smashed in a crystalline rain. Next, he lifted his regional tennis trophy, a large brass-and-marble statuette with his name engraved at the base.

"Calm down, Danny," Charlie said. "That's enough." He wrested the trophy from the boy's grip and set it on the floor.

"Tell us what happened," said Jess.

"Three security guards came to my first-period math class. They pulled me out of the room and dragged me down to the principal's office. Mr. Resnick told me I've been suspended. My presence in the school would be a serious disruption to the educational process, he said. They're putting me on home instruction. Like I'm some sick, contagious freak."

Jess had served on a number of school committees and town boards with the high school principal. She knew Wayne Resnick to be a reasonable, compassionate man. Why would he handle this situation with such cruel, clumsy force?

"I don't get it. Why didn't he call?" As she spoke, the answer came to her. She had turned off the ringer yesterday and neglected to turn it back on until this morning. She hadn't bothered to check the phone machine, avoiding what she presumed would be a number of unwanted nosy calls. Now, she wondered what other critical messages they might have missed. "I'm so sorry, honey. It's my fault."

"I'll take care of this," Charlie fumed. "They've got no right."

"Maybe you should call Gus Grantham," Jess said. Soaring blood pressure stained his cheeks a hot, ominous pink. Among those of his relatives who had hearts, there was a history of sudden, early death from coronary disease. Three uncles had died that way, two cousins, one his age. Jess had a constant nagging awareness that Charlie could be taken from her without warning.

"I know how to talk," he bristled. "I don't need to pay some expensive mouthpiece."

"You're wasting your time, Dad. They're not going to change their minds."

"We'll see about that."

Charlie stormed out to make the call from his study. Danny sat heavily on the bed. "It's not going to work, Mom. Resnick said it's standard procedure when a student is accused of a serious crime. I won't get to finish my senior year. I won't graduate. Even if I did, what kind of school would take me after a thing like this?" He started to weep.

Jess set her hand on his back and felt the heaving grief. "That's not true, Danny. It's going to be all right."

"No it's not," he sobbed. "Don't you see? They've taken everything."

"I know you feel that way, but it's not true. You'll be found innocent. Things will get back to normal."

He shook his head in despair. "There's nothing left."

Jess kept still until the cries played out and he struggled back in control.

He squared his back and wiped his eyes on his sleeve. "I need to be alone for a while, Mom. You mind?"

"Of course not, honey. I'll be downstairs."

Charlie was still on the phone. From the quivering rage beneath his firm, controlled tone she knew he was not getting the answers he wanted. But then, he was beating his head against a cast-iron rulebook, not to mention a giant wall of fear. Their model child had become a pariah. Suddenly, Danny was viewed as a dangerous, disruptive force. Jess would have laughed at the ridiculous notion if not for the bitter lump lodged in her throat.

The counter on the answering machine read a daunting 23. She pulled a pen and pad from the drawer and pressed play. The tape rewound in a long comical chatter.

The first message was from a neighbor named Eileen Slattery. The Slatterys were childless, not by choice, and Eileen had heaped much of her unrequited maternal affection on Jess's kids, especially Danny. *I heard the news, and I'm completely horrified. What can I do? Who can I call? Let me know.*

Next was a call from Danny's longtime tennis teacher. *Hi. This is Dave Eddy. I just wanted to let you know that I'm thinking about you. Hang in there, Danny.*

Several more calls of support and encouragement followed. Then came a long pause in the tape. Jess was about to fast-forward to the next message when a poison snicker pierced the crackling hush. *This is just the beginning, Jess Magill. You're going to get exactly what you deserve. Whatever happens to that precious son of yours is your fault. Remember that. I warned you.*

Dolores Wainscott. Either she was somehow behind this or the bitch was enjoying it all too well.

Flushed with rage, Jess listened to the rest of messages. There were three calls from Mr. Resnick, trying to warn them about Danny's suspension. If only she had remembered to turn the ringer on again—they could have avoided the nasty scene at school, spared the kid more unnecessary humiliation.

She jotted down the rest of the news. Grantham's office had set up an appointment for Danny to undergo a private psychological evaluation. Three of Jess's patients had phoned, two to commiserate, one to cancel. Friends, neighbors, and casual acquaintances had left messages, along with one or two amateur social critics. Jess took particular note of one anonymous caller who offered Danny relief from eternal damnation in exchange for a one-year subscription to some heavenly-enlightenment magazine. She couldn't help but wonder what bonus came with a two-year subscription.

Libby had called to commiserate. *I heard about the arraignment. Try not to worry about it, Jess. Judges are only human, and some are barely that. Harrigan probably had a fight with his wife this morning. Danny was a convenient place to vent his spleen. Call if you need someone to join you in howling at the moon or whatever. I'm available.*

A draining call from Pearl followed that heartening one. Jess's mother left a rambling message, complete with weather alert and nutrition update. *Jessie darling, they say it's going to be really chilly tomorrow morning, so make sure that everyone wears a sweater and a windbreaker at least. Molly probably needs something heavier. No meat on that girl at all. I was thinking, maybe you should give her a milk shake every day after school like I used to do for your brother Larry. Remember? I'd make him a shake and I'd put in a liquid vitamin with iron, which was fine because it didn't get him constipated. If you give Molly iron, watch to make sure it doesn't stuff her up.*

Pearl's sigh was the shrill of a kettle approaching the boil. *That's how it is with children. You have to watch them all the time. You don't, who knows what can happen? Mothers go to work today, and no one is minding the kids. So naturally, they act up, get in trouble. They're only kids, for heaven's sake. What do they know? Speaking of which, maybe you should take some time off, especially now. You don't make such a fat fortune, after all. The world wouldn't come to a halt if you stopped encouraging people to blame everything bad in their lives on their mothers.*

There was a brief silence. Jess imagined Pearl finding herself out of bruising barbs and pausing to reload. She pictured her mother setting her sights, bracing for the recoil, lining up Jess's shaky confidence in the crosshairs, and preparing to squeeze off a fresh, devastating round.

Pearl chuckled. *Remember how you use to drink Larry's milk shakes when you thought no one was looking. He stayed the same, skinny as a rail, and you gained and gained until I had to shop for you in the chubby department. I'll never forget the comment one salesgirl made when we were there to buy you a dress for the holidays. Look at those arms, she said. They look just like Wiffle bats.*

The rest of the messages played out. A couple of Danny's friends had called, including Ryan, whose voice sounded like an old record played at far too slow a speed. *Hey, Danny. It's me. You'll be all right, bud. You'll see. Give me a call.*

Now Danny was the damaged one, and Ryan, with his bent spine, warped limbs, and trampled synapses, was offering comfort.

Jess switched off the machine and cast around for a better distraction. She wiped the counters and put away place mats and dropped the morning papers in the recycle bin. Next, she leafed through a stack of mail, discarding outdated sale circulars and announcements for past events they had meant to attend. Jess could barely connect to the pleasant jumble their lives had been, a surfeit of obligations and a chronic shortage of time.

Prozac jaunted into the kitchen and nudged her dish, raising a noisy clatter. Turning, she shot Jess a mild look of rebuke. Easygoing though the dog was about most things, she expected regular meal service on the Modified American Plan.

Jess filled her flowered china plate with kibble and scraps and set it on the floor. Prozac took a mouthful, backed into the dining room, and chewed with loud, crunching exuberance. She preferred to take her meals on the Oriental rug. The dog had a dogged sense of elegant entitlement. If this was the echo of some former incarnation, Jess imagined she must have been a privileged aristocrat, not to mention a major pain in the ass.

From overhead came the low thwack of Charlie's voice, still on the phone. There was no sound from Danny's room. Jess ached at the thought of how he must be struggling to make sense of what had become of his life. If only there were some magic kiss or incantation she could invoke to make it better. She had never felt so powerless.

She plodded upstairs and stood staring blankly at the limp row of dresses and suits in her closet. Deciding what to wear to work was beyond her. Even the simplest things seemed too difficult.

If only she could hide for a while. If only she could crawl under the covers and sink in cool, dreamless sleep until the tide rushed in and the world looked right again.

And so—"

With that, Stephanie Hutt fell silent. Moments ago, the girl had been chatting with infectious animation about her plans to join the drama club at Greenwich Academy this fall. She wanted to play Juliet, she confessed, though Suzy Sanders would probably get the part. Suzy was the type who got everything she aimed for, even though she wasn't all that good. Some people made life look easy that way, the girl opined, as if it was done with mirrors.

Jess observed her client's sudden shift in mood. Stephanie wove tense arms across her chest and caught her lip between teeth bound in draconian braces. Her feet skittered beneath the chair and gripped the rails.

Most people rushed to fill conversational holes as if they were hazardous traps. But Jess had been trained to respect silence as a powerful tool. She watched the girl, studying the size and shape of her withdrawal, taking its temperature, noting its power and weight.

This was a loaded stillness, crammed with heat and emotion. You could almost feel the conflict behind it, opposing forces battling to break loose and to remain in careful check.

Five minutes passed. Stephanie squirmed and shifted in the chair, decorously tucking the short print skirt beneath her thighs. She shot a guilty glance at Jess; then dipping from the waist, she pulled an envelope from her purse, a lumpy brown affair that lay at her feet like a fat, sleeping raccoon.

"This is for today," she said, handing over the crumpled envelope. "I can't come anymore. I mean, I don't need to see you anymore. So this will be my last session."

"You can't? Or you don't need to, Stephanie? Which?"

"School starts at the end of next week, and I'll be really busy."

"We've always been able to work around your schedule."

"It's different now." The girl shook her head with vehemence, whipping her high ponytail. "Let's just leave it at that, okay?"

"I think it's better if we talk it out."

The silence descended again, a stifling drape this time. Jess had the sense that she could not have lifted it if she tried. Instead, she decided to wait it out. And wait she did, as the session clock ticked toward a necessary close.

Maybe terminating treatment was the right thing. On the surface, this girl looked so much better than she had when she first came to Jess four years back as a decimated twelve-year-old, marked by the flaming welts of fresh tragedy.

Her father and brother had been riding on a tour bus during a family vacation in Tel Aviv when a terrorist bomb exploded, killing them both instantly. Stephanie, recovering from a stomach bug, had stayed back at the hotel, and her mother had passed on the tour to keep her company.

Though she had not been at the scene, Stephanie had suffered devastating injuries in the attack. She felt guilty for having survived. Like any child, she had wished her big brother dead any number of times. In anger she had also wished for her father's disappearance. Fortunately, few children experience the horror of having those innocent wishes fulfilled.

The things she had not done haunted this poor girl. She believed she should have anticipated the tragedy and found some way to avert it. Why hadn't she insisted that they visit a safer place? Why hadn't she developed some horrible disease, forcing them to cut the trip short?

She was obsessed by the thought that they could have just missed the plane. That would have been so simple, and she'd had it in her power to make that happen.

On the day they left, Stephanie had gone to the Town Center Mall with a friend to shop for last-minute things she needed for the trip. If only she'd forgotten about the time, as she sometimes did. If only she had hung around talking for another half hour or so, trying on outfits at the Gap or having a slice of pizza with Michelle.

Her simple act of childish neglect would have fixed everything. Her father would have gotten sick of waiting in front of the ice cream store, as they had arranged. He would have parked the car in the cavernous lot and come in to look for her.

The mall was a huge place, and it would have taken him forever to track her down. By the time he got through yelling and lecturing her about being an airhead, he'd probably have been so upset he'd have forgotten where he parked. That had happened more than once under much calmer circumstances.

The security guard would have driven them around in his golf cart until they found the family bomb, one of a zillion silver Taurus wagons in the parking lot. By then, her father would have been in such a hot hurry to get home that he would have driven too fast and gotten stopped for speeding. For spite, the cop would've taken extra time writing out the ticket. Stephanie imagined his hand working the pen in long, slow, exaggerated spikes.

Though the incident would have seemed a total mess by anyone's definition, it would have been a miracle in fact. They would have missed the plane. There would have been no trip, no tour bus, no scatter of severed limbs and shattered existences.

Stephanie had once mused that the best miracles were the ones you never knew about, the quiet beats of astonishing good fortune that kept your life chugging along on track. Cancer cells consumed by your own immune system. Averted accidents. Not being in the wrong place at the wrong time. Every day that tragedy did not strike was a silent miracle.

Jess could relate.

As Stephanie constructed the elaborate fantasy, her family, having missed the flight and lost all that money on the nonrefundable tickets, would have decided to forget about the whole vacation and hang around at home.

Of course, everyone would've been furious with her. She would've been grounded for a decade and subjected to an endless barrage of blame and anger, but from where she now sat, that seemed like a rock-bottom bargain price to pay.

But that was not the way it had happened. And no matter how hard she tried to change the past or offer herself in stoical sacrifice, there was no way to trade the hand she'd been dealt for a better one. Only in the past six months had the girl allowed herself to do or think of anything beyond the tragedy. Jess was optimistic, but she was not convinced that Stephanie would continue to progress without further help.

They were almost out of time. Jess's next client was due any minute. She didn't want the session to drift off on a trail of unspoken words.

"Are you sure about this, Stephanie?"

"I'm fine. I don't need a shrink anymore."

"Have you discussed it with your mom?"

"I told you. I'm over it. I didn't kill Jeff and Daddy. It wasn't my fault. I was just blaming myself because I was confused. I get all that now."

The words were smooth, but Jess detected plenty of raw, bumpy emotions underneath. "That's good, but I think you still have some work to do. Why don't I call your mom to come in, and the three of us can talk it over?"

"You can't do that. Promise you won't."

"She has to know, Stephanie. All I'm suggesting is that we talk. No one is going to force you to do anything. I'll leave a message for her at home."

Jess reached for the phone, but the girl lunged from her chair and pressed down the receiver. "My mom already knows. Don't you get it? She won't let me come anymore."

"Why is that?"

The door swung open and Manny Dickler, Jess's next scheduled client, peered inside. Dickler suffered from a crippling fear of heights. Climbing to Jess's second-floor office remained a challenge for him two years into treatment. But Manny kept at it. "Oops, sorry. Am I early?"

"No, Manny. I'm running a bit late. I'll be with you in a few minutes."

"Sure, no problem."

Jess waited until Manny had retreated to the reception room downstairs. "Why doesn't Mom want you to come anymore, Stephanie?"

"Why are you making me tell you?"

"I'm not making you do anything. But I would like to understand."

Angry mischief bloomed behind her eyes. "It's because of what your son did. My mom says you can't be any good if you let your own kid get messed up like that."

"I see."

"But she's wrong. Kids stink. That's the problem. All they do is make trouble and wreck everything. I'm never having kids of my own. Never."

"I want you to ask your mom to find you a different therapist. Quitting treatment is not right for you yet."

The girl's look was chilling. "I mean it. If I ever get pregnant, I'll get it cut out. That's what my mother should have done to me. Then my brother and father might still be alive."

Jess's breath caught. How could she have been so deluded about this kid? Stephanie was still the same terror-stricken twelve-year-old, a flimsy patchwork of guilt, pain, and rage.

"That's what *you* should have done." She leveled an accusing finger at Danny's picture on Jess's desk. "You should have had that kid cut out of you before he was born. He's a filthy, disgusting boy. What he did makes me sick."

The girl charged out of the office. Jessica sat in the thrumming silence she left behind. She tuned to the rasp of the ceiling fan and the groan of the weary compressor. She stared at the dust motes dancing in a cone of strident light beside her desk.

Jess chided herself for being so unnerved. Stephanie was not the first client to defect and this was not the first bucket of icy, raw emotion that had been hurled at her since the arrest. Not the first, and likely not the end of it.

Her next appointment mounted the stairs, clutching the handrail so hard Jess heard the pressured protest of the joists. Manny sat in the place still warm from Stephanie's rage. He smiled meekly and started telling Jess about his month. The weather had kept him from going to buildings downtown and riding the elevators as he had agreed to do. The heat was responsible, he explained with a sheepish grin. Blame it on the weather and the circumstances. Everything had conspired against him, as usual. It simply was not his fault.

In the twenty years since Jess and Charlie's wedding, the elder Magills had been to their home exactly three times. Charlie's parents elected to host their infrequent family gatherings at their exclusive country club in Armonk or on their ten-acre estate in nearby Bedford, New York.

Until now, the sole exception had been the birth of a new Magill. One month to the day after each grandchild was born, Charlie's folks had stopped by to view the latest arrival and deliver a gift, which in all three cases had been a savings account passbook in the infant's name containing an initial deposit of ten thousand dollars. Each time, Senior, as Charlie's father was called, had offered his presence and the largesse with painful stiffness and unease. Clearly, he viewed these as duty calls, best quickly and cleanly dispatched.

Senior was all business all the time, and this morning was no exception. When Jess greeted him at the door, he looked every inch the chairman of the board. Charlie's father was a tall, trim septuagenarian, who was most at home in a dark suit, starched white shirt, club tie bound in a flawless double Windsor, and gleaming custom-crafted brogues. Jess presumed he wore a short-legged version for tennis and a waterproof dark suit and rubber brogues in the shower. Thinning white hair framed his sullen strong-boned face. His chauffeured Bentley idled on the drive.

"Come in," Jess offered. "Charlie will be right down."

"How have you been, Jessica?"

"Lousy, actually."

"Understandable."

Jess led Senior to the dining room, where she had set the table with her best linen cloth and tableware. She had polished her grandmother's silver coffee set and made a quick dash to a bakery in Greenwich for the best local pastries an obscene amount of money could buy. Fresh blooms from the garden graced a slim porcelain vase. As always, Senior's presence inspired her to strive for elegance, dust off her most impressive vocabulary and place it on display. Despite herself, Jess still craved her father-in-law's unattainable approval. It was the same futile, irrational effort she made, again and again, with Pearl. No matter how she reminded herself that she was scrambling up a sand hill, doomed to take a painful topple in the end, she felt compelled to give it one more try.

Senior claimed the head of the table.

"Would you care for some coffee or tea?" Jess asked.

"This is not a social call. Where is Charles? What's holding him up?"

"He's putting the final touches on something. I'm sure he'll just be a few minutes more." Jess thought it prudent to keep the nature of the something to herself. Senior would not be pleased to learn that Charlie was upstairs finishing up the tantrum he'd started to throw as soon as she reported that Senior was on his way.

This is about Danny, Jess. I know it. If that old bastard thinks he can dictate what we do about our son, how we should handle things, he's got another think coming.

Jess, ever the optimist, had suggested that maybe the old man was trying to be supportive for a change. Maybe having heard about Danny's arrest, he was stopping by with an open offer of help. Senior and his wife had been away on a monthlong cruise, and Charlie had decided that the news could wait for their return. But Senior had legions of advisers and informants, who made certain he was not kept out of any interesting loop for long.

His idea of support is squeezing so hard he cuts off your air. I've got the scars to show for it. Remember, this is Senior we're talking about, Jess, not some real person with actual feelings.

She had urged him to relax, to reserve judgment until he heard what his father had to say. Charlie was the one forever advising her not to stew or worry in advance. But all his solid rationality crumbled to dust where his father was concerned. Their relationship had always ridden a shaky substrate of seething resentments. They were like Jess and Pearl, oil and water, Israel and her Arab antagonists. They refused to blend for very long, no matter how you tried to shake them into harmonious coexistence.

"How is Mother Magill?" asked Jess. "I was hoping to see her."

"I shall convey your regards."

"How was the cruise?"

"Long, excessive, and tedious, exactly as advertised. Why Katherine enjoys those things, I shall never understand. It reminds me of Charles's insistence on leaving Choate to attend the public high school. Some people do things out of simple perversity." Senior straightened the razor crease in his trousers and tightened the matching ones on his brow. "I trust Charles knows I'm here."

"I'm sure he does."

"We left the ship and caught an early flight back from Bali specifically so that I could have the opportunity to speak with you and Charles as soon as possible."

Jess seized the excuse to escape the deep freeze. "Let me see what's holding him up. I'll be right back."

Charlie was sprawled on the couch in his study, feet up, head on the armrest, leafing through a journal as if he had nothing in the world to do.

"The natives are getting restless," Jess told him.

"Good. Maybe they'll get restless enough to leave."

"You know Senior. If he has something to say, he's going to say it. You may as well come down and get it over with."

He kept turning pages.

"Please, Charlie. Be reasonable."

He tossed down the journal in disgust. "You should have checked with me before you told him it was all right to come over, Jess. My father is the last thing I need right now."

"He didn't exactly ask."

"Fine then. Tell him I'm busy. Tell him I'll see him the day after Thanksgiving at three o'clock at the club as usual. Then and the Saturday before Mother's birthday and Easter Sunday Eve are more than enough for any mere mortal to stand."

"Remember our deal, my darling. I don't sic Pearl on you, and you don't saddle me with Senior."

He shot her a world-weary look. "That's not fair, Jess. Pearl is self-deploying."

"Your father is here now, Charlie. Deal with him."

Jess drew him up and ushered him downstairs. She made no mention of his deliberately scruffy appearance. In obvious defiance of Senior's rigid formality, Charlie had donned his oldest, rattiest jeans and a stretched-out T-shirt with sweat-stained armpits and a frayed collar band from a seventies Grateful Dead concert. Whisker stubble stained his cheeks, and his hair looked as if he'd styled it with a weed whacker.

The rebellion had no effect. Senior held himself above petty issues like soil, disorder, and his son's feelings. "You know I detest waiting, Charles," the old man groused.

"Nice seeing you too, Father," Charlie said.

Senior planted his interlaced fingers on the embroidered white tablecloth. "Let me come right to the point. As soon as we learned of young Daniel's recent difficulties, Mother and I made arrangements to cut our trip short and come home."

"That wasn't necessary," Charlie said.

"I believe it was. As a theoretician, an academic, you know nothing of matters such as these."

Charlie sniffed. "And you do?"

Senior nodded gravely. "Over the years, several unfortunate incidents have required my involvement with law enforcement personnel and the criminal justice system. Employee thefts, one sizable case of embezzlement, two cases of grand larceny that resulted in lengthy prison terms for the perpetrators."

"How come I never heard about all that intrigue?"

"I chose not to burden you with such matters."

"Right, Father. And I've been involved with four cases of plagiarism, three stolen exam questions, two student political uprisings, and a partridge in a pear tree. The bird was trespassing. They sent him up to the big house for life."

"Your sarcasm is unwelcome and unwarranted, Charles. I have come to offer valuable advice for the benefit of my grandson. You must engage first-quality counsel for Daniel. You need to mount an aggressive, effective defense."

"We have," said Jess. "Augustus Grantham is representing Danny. According to my lawyer friend, he's the best defense attorney in the state."

Senior chuckled. "That's tantamount to lauding someone for being the finest entrepreneur in a high school Junior Achievement club, Jessica. I've discussed Daniel's case with a close acquaintance of mine who happens to be affiliated with the top criminal litigation firm in New York. Sidney Rosenthal is available to represent Daniel, and Sidney is who he should have."

"Thanks anyway. We're pleased with Grantham," said Charlie. "We don't intend to replace him."

"What advantage would Attorney Rosenthal offer?" Jess asked.

"Intelligence, experience, and exhaustive resources. The firm retains all manner of experts and consultants. They have links to the finest research facilities. Their judicial and political connections are superb."

"This is not about connections."

"Everything is, Charles. Connections and quality. How do you suppose certain legal difficulties you had as an adolescent simply disappeared?"

Jess cocked her head. "What difficulties?" After twenty years, she thought she knew everything there was to know about Charlie.

"Ancient history. No big deal."

Angry blotches scaled Senior's neck. "It was only *no big deal* because you had expert counsel, because I was willing to make more than generous restitution to the complainant, because I made it so."

"It was adolescent nonsense."

"Perhaps you wouldn't be so cavalier had I allowed you to suffer the consequences."

"You've always allowed that, Father."

"Maybe Senior is right, Charlie. The least we can do is meet this attorney, see what if anything might be done differently." Jess braced against the storm her unthinkable alliance with Charlie's father was certain to arouse, especially under the current explosive circumstances.

"The only thing we need done differently is less outside interference." Charlie strode from the room. He slammed the door with fury as he left the house. Jess heard the roar of the Mustang's engine, mixed with the purr of the Bentley as Senior's chauffeur backed out to let Charlie pass.

"Thanks anyway," Jess said. "It would seem that Charlie's mind is made up."

"As I see it, this has precious little to do with his mind. Charles is being anything but reasonable and rational in this matter. But then, my son has always preferred defying me to almost anything else." He drew a business card from his wallet and handed it to Jess. "This is the information on Sidney Rosenthal's firm. I implore you, Jessica. Ignore my part in this and do what you honestly believe to be best for Daniel. Convince Charles to view it from that perspective. Somehow, he's able to hear you."

She walked him to the door. "Thanks for stopping by."

He met her gaze, and Jess saw a rare spark of humanity. "Say hello to the children for us. Tell them Mother and I hope to see them soon."

TWENTY

The First Presbyterian Church on Bedford Street resembled a huge brooding whale. On Sunday mornings, congregants streamed through the gaping maw of the giant fish, reenacting Jonah's harrowing journey from rebellion to rude awakening and ultimate redemption.

As Jess recalled the tale, Jonah had suffered from a serious attitude problem. When God asked him for a favor, the foolish man ran off to sea. Understandably, this put the Lord in a foul temper, which he expressed by churning up a cataclysmic storm at sea. When Jonah's fellow seamen realized that his disobedience had brought on the dangerous rotten weather, they tossed him overboard to save themselves.

Instead of drowning Jonah, God had him swallowed by a great fish, the biblical equivalent of grounding a rebellious teenager. Eventually, Jonah got the message, apologized, and the whale vomited him up on dry land.

As a little girl in Sunday school, Jess had found that story terribly disturbing. She was well aware that she had Jonah tendencies. When Pearl called, hollering in that ice pick voice that preceded scathing criticism or extra chores, Jess's instinct had always been to run or hide or both. Often, she would pretend not to hear her mother, a condition she now referred to as Sudden Adolescent Deafness syndrome.

Pearl's wrath made God's look benign. She shrieked and threatened and insulted and belittled and accused until Jess was reduced to a puddle of quivering remorse. Anything would have been preferable to one of Pearl's tirades, including ferocious storms and deliverance on a tide of whale barf.

Jess angled to the curb in front of the church. Midweek, the place had a cold, desolate feel. Dense shadows shrouded the gray slate facade. A funnel of papery leaves swirled across the abandoned parking lot. A solitary workman stabbed stray bits of litter on the lawn.

At first, Jess saw no sign of Danny. Then, scanning again, she spotted him propped against the gnarled trunk of a swamp maple. He sat inert, steeped in a dense swath of shade. Beside him lay a stack of textbooks bound by a thin rubber strap.

Jess rolled down the window. "Hi, honey. Have you been waiting long?"

"Couple of minutes." He hoisted himself up listlessly and made for the Volvo's passenger side.

"Want to drive?" she offered.

For most kids Danny's age, heaven was operating heavy machinery. When he first got his license, he would seize any excuse to get behind the wheel. Drive ten miles for a quart of milk? Certainly. Pick up his sister from a friend's house half a block away? *Let me go for her, Mom. Mol's probably tired after school and everything. She shouldn't have to walk.*

"No thanks. You do it," he said.

When Danny and his friends got together, everyone used to vie for the driver's seat. It was not unusual for ten of them to go to the same place in ten different cars. Jess and Charlie had served up the requisite lectures about preserving resources and cutting costs by carpooling, but she understood that driving would sink to the level of tedious routine soon enough. A major joy of growing up was reveling in fresh freedoms. Jess found it troubling that now he was willing to relinquish even that intoxicating pleasure. This struck her as a bad sign, like a feverish flush or a loss of reasonable appetite.

"You sure?" she persisted.

"You know the way."

"Not exactly, but I have directions. Shouldn't be too hard to find. You can drive, and I'll navigate."

"That's okay." He slipped into the passenger seat and folded his arms, forestalling further discussion.

They headed up High Ridge Road toward the Merritt Parkway. The clinic was in the northern backcountry of nearby Westport. Jess had left forty minutes for the twenty-minute trip. Based on recent events, she was primed to allow for complications.

"How did it go?" she asked.

Daniel deflected the question with a noncommittal shrug.

"Is Persky okay on a one-to-one?"

Mr. Persky taught sophomore English, creative writing, and an honors literature class at the high school, and Danny had taken all three. Now, the man would be working as Danny's home instruction teacher, though their daily sessions would be held at the church, not at home. Jess understood that gruff old Roger Persky had volunteered for the assignment. Given his tenure and position, this was not the sort of task he would be ordered to assume.

That meant Persky was a partisan. He believed in Danny, which placed him high on Jess's shrinking list of good guys. Jess was grateful for his support in particular. Danny's education would be in the hands of a seasoned pro, not some hourly hack who was otherwise unemployed or unemployable.

"What difference does it make?" he challenged. "The whole thing is a joke."

Jess glanced at the book titles: calculus, American history, the complete works of Shakespeare, physics. Obviously, Persky was determined to keep Danny on a par with his classmates. Once the case was settled, he could graduate on time and get on with the life he was meant to have.

"Doesn't look as if Persky is fooling around," she said.

"He's a teaching machine. Wind him up, he'll instruct you."

"Sounds right to me."

The exit loomed sooner than she expected. Jess veered right and bumped over the grassy berm to catch the ramp.

"What the hell was that?" Danny yelped.

"Exactly what it looked like, a poorly conceived and hideously executed automotive maneuver," Jess said evenly. "I screwed up, honey. People do."

"Sorry, Mom. I guess I'm a little edgy about this."

Jess squeezed his hand. "I'd be surprised if you weren't."

"What if they decide I'm crazy?"

"No one thinks that."

"Then why are they giving me these tests?"

"You heard Mr. Grantham. A case like this comes down to your word against Lisa's. If it gets to a jury, they'll have to decide who's lying and who's telling the truth. We have to help them see what kind of person you are, that you're honest and decent and sane."

"I don't want someone digging around in my head."

"I hear you, sweetie. But there's no choice."

His jaw tensed like a bowstring. "Sure there is. I can go someplace. Disappear."

"No you can't. You have to see this through. Running would be the worst thing. It would only make you look guilty."

Five years ago, a local kid charged with rape had done just that. With his parents' help, he'd skipped to South America. At first, many believed the family's cries that he had been mistakenly accused, and applauded the defection. But the tale took a gruesome turn when the teenager was tracked down and shot to death by the alleged victim's boyfriend.

"What difference would it make?" Danny said. "Everyone already thinks I am."

"Then you'll prove them wrong. You can't run from this. Promise me you won't do such a thing."

He spewed a noisy breath. "Relax, Mom. It was only talk."

"Promise me."

"Okay. All right. I promise. Let's face it, I'm not exactly the fugitive type."

Jess forced the tension from her voice. "True. It's pretty hard to imagine anyone with Lefferman genes on the lam."

"Imagine what I'd have to pack to keep Grandma from having one of her infarctions." He enumerated on his fingers. "Extra sweaters, vitamins, gloves and a muffler, a hat, cold remedies, rubber boots, two umbrellas—one for the sun, one for the rain. Emergency snacks. Poison antidote. It can't be easy to lay low with all that baggage."

"Tell me about it."

Enjoying the banter, Jess realized too late that she had missed the required turn. An attempt to correct the mistake landed her on a one-way street aimed in the wrong direction. Getting back on track required a convoluted detour and several consultations with a map.

She chuckled at her own roaring incompetence. "That's screwup number three. Root for me, kiddo. I think I'm on world-record pace."

"Maybe you're just a little bit edgy yourself, Mom."

"I am, Danny. But it's not about you. I don't like what's going on, that's all. It upsets me that you have to deal with this mess. You don't deserve it."

"What if I do?"

Jess's stomach churned as she asked the necessary question. "Meaning?"

"Maybe a person only gets so much good luck. Maybe all the bad things you do get added up, and when you reach a certain number, you get paid back."

"Bad things happen, Danny. People get sick. They get hurt. They get in trouble for things they didn't do. You shouldn't look for a reason to blame yourself."

"There has to be a reason, Mom. Otherwise, nothing makes any sense."

"Sometimes things don't."

"I don't buy that."

A discreet brass plaque on the mailbox distinguished the Shelburne Diagnostic Center from the pristine private houses surrounding it. The plaque and its carefully worded legend, "Shelburne D.C.," had been negotiated several years ago after a protracted zoning battle and a bitter lawsuit by residents fearful that the center would draw dangerous undesirables to their quiet neighborhood and damage property values.

Jess remembered the fight, which had been waged largely in the press. The question came down to the right of people seeking treatment for painful disorders versus the right of other people to keep unsavory issues at long arm's length. The Shelburne case stirred ancient beliefs and biases. Was mental illness a disease or a blight? Did privilege and affluence promise protection from unsightly human conditions? Wasn't there a constitutional right to pursue righteous self-interest? If so, weren't crazy people somehow excluded? And of course there was the age-old question, if not in my backyard, where?

In the end the clinic founders had agreed to maintain this facility for diagnostic and research purposes only and to treat patients at a satellite clinic in downtown Norwalk. Ironically, the controversy surrounding the clinic's opening had attracted a number of top people to the site, which now commanded far more influence and attention than it would have under normal circumstances.

Grantham wanted Danny to be tested here because of the prominence of the Shelburne's chief forensic psychologist. Fortunately, Jess had no direct affiliation with the facility, which might have called the results into question. The specialists were unknown to her personally, though she recognized the names from the volumes in her professional library and countless journal articles. There was David Rosen, highly respected for his work in treating multiple personalities. Ellen Benson was an expert in obsessive-compulsive disorder. Matthew and Ilene Heckerling had devised an effective behavioral approach to addiction therapy that had been adopted in programs around the world.

Janetta Rebold was among the country's foremost forensic assessment specialists. Dr. Rebold tested suspects accused of serious crimes and offered evidence at trial. She had been called to testify in hundreds of cases, including several of the nation's most notorious. Sometimes she spoke for the defense, sometimes for the prosecution, depending upon who engaged her and what she found. Her conclusions were often desperately assailed, but they were rarely impeached. Rebold was as well known for impeccable integrity as she was for her keen, in-depth understanding of which personality factors were likely to predispose someone to commit criminal acts.

Jess had every confidence that the doctor would find Danny to be the solid, good-hearted soul that he was. But as they crossed the marble-floored entrance foyer toward the door marked reception, a nameless anxiety fluttered in her chest.

She entered the front room and paused at the broad mahogany desk. "The name's Magill. We're here to see Dr. Rebold."

The receptionist was a puckish-looking woman in her sixties with a mad froth of curly charcoal hair. "Of course. We're expecting you. I have a few forms I need you to fill out, Daniel." She handed him a clipboard laden with printed pages. "There you go. Soon as you're ready, I'll let the doctor know you're here."

He breezed through the papers in a careless scribble. Normally, his handwriting was ordered and even. Normally, he took great care to formulate answers before he wrote or spoke. Jess wanted to warn him that he should be himself, or rather, that he should be the solid self she had always known, the rational, charming, cooperative kid everybody liked.

She feared that the arrest might have plunged him into a self-destructive spiral. Sometimes, it was easier to dive for the bottom than to risk being pushed there against your will. Giving in could bring some measure of ironic relief. A total failure meant you had lived through the worst and you didn't need to fear it any longer. Jess had seen this in her practice, time and again.

If Danny's head had been twisted that way, he might give the doctor a devastatingly wrong impression. Even the best examiners could be fooled, and that would be a terrible blow right now. A positive report from Dr. Rebold would be a huge boon to their case. If her report was not favorable, Grantham could elect to suppress it, but the prosecution was sure to put Danny through a psychological assessment of their own. Grantham needed ammunition to counter the negatives that were bound to come from the other side. From long, hard experience, Jess knew that everything in this field was a matter of impression and interpretation. Depending on the lens and angle, Danny could be viewed as a model kid or a slick, and highly suspect, façade.

Danny finished the last of the forms and deposited the clipboard on the receptionist's desk. She checked the papers for completion. "Everything looks hunky-dory. I'll let the doctor know you're all set."

While she rang through on the interoffice phone, Jess urged, "Just be yourself, honey."

The psychologist appeared moments later. She was a trim woman in her fifties with ginger hair and piercing jade eyes.

She crossed the room and proffered a pale, graceful hand. "Hello. You must be Daniel."

Jess was relieved when Danny shook the woman's hand instead of biting it.

"Good to meet you both. If you don't mind, I'd like to get started immediately so we won't be rushed. We'll be about an hour and a half, Mrs. Magill. You're welcome to wait or come back."

"Thanks. I'll wait."

Dr. Rebold led Danny through a rear door.

Jess sat nearest the door on the right side of the reception area. She leafed through a year-old copy of *Architectural Digest,* trying to lose herself in the fantasy of spaces laden with objets d'art instead of the dust bunnies and dog hair that often graced their home. But the drone of unintelligible voices from behind the wall kept tugging at her attention. She could not filter any meaningful words through Glenn Gould's rendition of the Goldberg Variations, piped through tiny speakers mounted high on the wall.

Naturally, all attempts would be made to keep the transactions here strictly confidential. Jess had conducted several sound tests at her own office for the same purpose. She'd placed a radio on her desk, turned it to a talk show at normal speaking volume, and stepped outside to make certain that privileged conversations could not be accidentally or deliberately overheard. Next, she had cranked up the sound and repeated the experiment. Voices had a way of rising like steam in the heat of a difficult therapy session. In Jess's office, the noise of the ceiling fan and the heat pump or air conditioner, depending on the season, provided more than adequate conversational cover. Here, Glenn Gould had been recruited for the job. Normally, Jess loved the pianist's brilliant, eccentric style, but today she wanted to slam the lid on his fingers.

She remembered suffering similar unbearable curiosity last spring, while she and Charlie waited in the reception area at the Princeton admissions office. Danny's interview there had been a mere three months ago, though it seemed like a million years now. Jess could barely relate to how totally absorbed they had been with the college admissions process and its seemingly monumental consequences. SAT scores, class rank, decisions about where to apply, had loomed as huge, compelling issues then. But that was before their world spilled out of sane rotation and began doing tumbling runs like a circus clown gone mad. Everything was relative. An invasion of field mice can loom as a huge problem until a dead elephant threatens the sanctity of your home.

The receptionist tried to engage Jess in diversionary conversation. "Do you live nearby, Mrs. Magill?"

"Stamford."

"Lived there long?"

"Twenty years."

"You happen to know people named Davis on Blue Rock?"

Jess smiled apologetically. "It's a big place."

"How about the Jerome Moore family on Vine? He's in auto body. Has a shop near the railroad station."

"Doesn't sound familiar."

"No? He's excellent. Made my Honda look like brand-new after I skidded on an ice patch and front-ended the Dempsey Dumpster behind the A and P. Car looked exactly like an accordion when I took it to Jerome. Thought for sure it was a goner."

Jess was grateful when the phone rang and the receptionist was forced to drop the dead conversational ball. She sat back and leafed through an old issue of *Newsweek*.

In half an hour she'd exhausted the entire inventory of outdated periodicals. She stacked them neatly on the coffee table by title and date. Finished, she paced the small square room, examining the plaques and pictures. She straightened a watercolor seascape and a row of close-up shots of flowers in exuberant bloom. She recognized the foolish root of her actions, the desire to impose rational order in a disordered world. It was a matter of seeking some tiny measure of control when everything appeared to be hurtling headlong toward some unthinkable end. The bigger mess Jess's life became, the more pathologically neat she made her surroundings. Naturally, Pearl was thrilled.

She surveyed the rest of the space. The parquet floor was worn to a dull sheen at the periphery. In a former incarnation, this house had been a gracious private home. Jess imagined small kids playing tag here, pushing toy cars around, running electric trains with sound effects and shrieks of unbridled delight.

Families left an indelible imprint on a house. Decades after they moved out, traces of the former occupants remained. Forgotten objects. Lost pets, secret echoes. Pencil ticks in the doorframes to mark the children's growth. Scars of hard, loving use.

Jess wondered what that meant for her family and their rambling, improbable home. Would they be haunted by the ghosts of this hideous time, no matter how it played out? Could they sneak out in the middle of some moonless night, and somehow leave the experience behind?

She paced the room like a compulsive zoo creature, straightening chairs, tidying pillows and leaflets, swiping at bits of dust. If only there were some way to hurry time along like little kids who can be made to scoot home quickly by the threat of gathering dusk.

"A cleaning service comes in, Mrs. Magill," the receptionist said in all sincerity. "You needn't bother."

"No bother at all."

At last came the scrape of chairs from inside, followed by a flurry of footsteps. Jess moved closer to the door.

Rebold's professional mask revealed nothing. "If you have a minute, Mrs. Magill, I'd like to speak with you."

"Sure. I'll be right back," Jess told Danny.

Rebold's office featured plump upholstered chairs, prints of Winslow Homer landscapes, a rolltop desk, and lush green plants. The room had a self-consciously cozy feel, as if the decorator had been ordered to create the pretense that visitors were welcome. There was a glaring absence of personal touches. No family photographs. No knickknacks. No books except for professional volumes with dense titles and rigid spines.

"How did it go?" Jess asked.

"Daniel's very bright and articulate, as I'm sure you know."

"Thank you. What tests did you give him?"

The psychologist gazed through rimless granny glasses at her notes. "I administered a full battery of standardized instruments, including the Rorschach and MMPI, and of course, I did a comprehensive interview and behavioral assessment."

"What did you find?"

"I'm not prepared to offer any firm conclusions yet. I need to evaluate the results."

"How about preliminary conclusions?"

Rebold hesitated. "In my opinion, your son was not being entirely forthright."

"He's terrified by the situation, that's all. What you're seeing is the strain he is under. Danny did not rape that girl."

"That's for the courts to decide, Mrs. Magill. Not me."

"But your results could push them one way or the other."

Rebold folded her arms and perched against the desk. "I've been asked to observe your son and report the results of those observations. And that's all I intend to do. It is not my job to make assumptions about guilt or innocence."

"What you're doing amounts to exactly the same thing." Jess's tone was climbing to a sharp, dangerous peak. "If you suggest Danny is hiding something, it's as good as an indictment. You can't help send him to jail because of some tests and opinions. All those can be dead wrong. You know that as well as I do."

Rebold waited for the air to clear of fury and unspoken threats. "In my *opinion,* Daniel is suffering serious inner turmoil. It may have something or nothing to do with this case. I'm not prepared to speculate on the reason. I urge you to get to the root of what it might be and get him the help he needs to deal with it. I see him as a young man at some considerable risk."

"Risk of what?"

"Of self-harm."

The psychologist had tossed her a live grenade. Jess was powerless to drop or deflect it. "Danny believes that his future has been stolen. He's feeling hopeless and overwhelmed. Who can blame him?"

"The reason does not reduce the risk," Rebold said.

"I understand that." Jess inhaled, pulling herself back in some semblance of sane control. Having a crazy mother would not help Danny or his cause. "Of course, I'll keep an eye on him."

"Let me add a further caution, Mrs. Magill. When it comes to a situation like this, I doubt that any parent would be capable of dispassionate professional judgment. You are too close to see your son clearly."

"You're wrong, Dr. Rebold. I know Danny. I know what he's capable of and what he isn't."

"Arguing about opinions is always a futile exercise." She glanced at the door, inviting Jess to make use of it on her way out.

Jess hesitated. "May I ask what you are going to say about Danny in your report?"

"I need to evaluate the results before I formulate any conclusions. I'll have the report to Mr. Grantham in about a week."

"You can't know Danny from a bunch of tests. Believe me, Dr. Rebold. He's a kind, compassionate, gentle, loving kid. He would never hurt anyone. Never!"

"Keep an eye on him, Mrs. Magill. Please, remember what I've said."

Entering Stamford High sent Tucci hurtling back through time. He was an ugly stretched-out kid again, a pencil with ears, who would have given his left arm to be anyone else.

He passed a few of his daughter's friends giggling their way down the hall. They all had their hair slicked back to showcase glowing skin and bright, expectant eyes. Their biggest problems were term papers, boyfriends, and clothes. That, and parents who cared too much and insisted on reasonable limits. Tucci hated all of them for their unreasonable good luck. He wanted to wrench their health away like a rich lady's purse, and race it home to his own kid, who deserved it every bit as much or more. Gina would have made better use of it. That should count for something.

"Hey, Mr. Tucci," called one. Her name was Biffany or Leather, he dimly recalled, one of those dumb made-up handles parents hung on babies with no thought to how they would sit later on. Then they wondered why the kid turned out to be a stripper instead of a brain surgeon.

"How's Gina doing? Tell her hi," the girl trilled.

Tucci tucked away his hostility as best he could. "Why don't you call and tell her yourself?"

"That's okay. We don't want to bother her."

"Wouldn't be any bother," he said. "I bet she could squeeze you in between lunch and the hairdresser's."

"Always joking, Mr. T." Biffany flapped her blue-nailed hand. "We'll catch up when she's feeling better."

Tucci shrugged, though he wanted to shake the little twits. They didn't get that all they could catch over the phone was a little gratitude. Why couldn't they put themselves in Gina's place and imagine the aching loneliness? He was dying to suggest that their eyes would work way better if they turned them right side out, tried to see life from somebody else's perch. But kids could only really learn the hard way, by growing up and taking a clear look back. The sad fact was, plenty never got that far.

No one had been a dumber kid than Tucci. What he'd want to be, above all, was like Charlie Magill and his bunch. From the way he saw things back then, those characters had everything that mattered.

Magills had fancy cars and pockets full of discretionary dough and mothers who spoke perfect English without using their hands. Magills belonged to country clubs and went to summer camps and got the opportunity to hate piano lessons. Their parents played bridge and dined out at restaurants and watched color TVs where the faces were people-colored, not orange or green. They smelled of hair spray and expensive aftershave, not garlic and pepperoni like Tucci's folks.

After school, Magills got to hang out around their families' pools or pool tables and rag on the likes of Tucci, while he swept and shlepped and waited on customers in his family's Italian deli in the blue-collar slice of town known as Springdale.

Magills had leisure suits and leisure in which to enjoy them. Sunday mornings they got to sleep in, while Tucci, dressed in ill-fitting hand-me-downs, got his soul washed and detailed at St. Gabriel's RC Church. Father Donovan was a doddering old man with bad allergies, whose rambling remarks about the Devil were punctuated by sneezing fits and great honking blows. Eventually, Tucci even got bored with those.

Once, he stole a quarter and a dime from the poor box and used them to buy a pack of Newports at Kay's Convenience on Long Ridge Road. Dizzy from the mentholated smoke, he'd fallen off the curb and chipped his front tooth so it looked like the top of the Citicorp building. Magills got endless gimmes from God and expensive orthodontia. Tucci's stunt had earned him three Hail Marys, a Dracula smile, and a conscience that nagged him for months.

Farther down the hall, he passed a punk kid he'd arrested a couple of years back on suspicion of dealing dope. From the look of him, business was not so hot, or maybe he'd started sucking up the profits.

"How's it going, Santoro?" Tucci asked.

There was not a glint of recognition in the glazed, droopy eyes. "What can I say, man? It's going."

"Going, gone," Tucci predicted as he passed.

Kids measured things on warped, inaccurate yardsticks. As a teenager, Tucci could not see past shiny packaging and privilege. Magills had dazzled him. They got four-year free rides at fancy private colleges, then came home to family practices and trust funds fat enough to float on comfortably for life. Tuccis were relegated to night school and Christmas club. Four bucks a week rain or shine. You got out what you put in or less. Never more. Not for him.

As for the family firm, his had not been very firm at all. For as long as Tucci could remember, the business was always teetering at the edge. If it wasn't rising rent or ingredient costs, they were plagued by a wobbling economy. They were forever being sideswiped by unexpected competition, first from the fast-food chains that popped up everywhere like chicken pox and later from the spreading plague of megamarkets that provided low-cost convenience foods and irresistible loss leaders. They were never free from the fear that they could sink at any time.

Magills enjoyed a limitless supply of willing buxom girls. Tuccis got unlimited pepperoni ends slapped on slices of two-day-old bread. A regular feast.

But from the clear view of hindsight, Tucci would not change a thing. Once his hormones stopped fizzing so he could hardly hear himself think, he'd come to realize that his folks were plenty rich in all the really important ways. They loved each other and gave everything they could to Tucci and his kid brother, Billy. That included solid values and a sense of justice and the capacity to give and command respect. Tucci had never doubted for an instant that he was wanted and loved. His people were hardworking, decent, the genuine item. Not like Danny Magill and his long line of pure-bullshit thoroughbreds.

Entering Resnick's office, he felt a small thrill of unease. Once during his freshman year, he'd yielded to unreasonable temptation and scratched his name in the fresh blacktop on the basketball court. Naturally, he'd been called in and reamed out by the principal. The guy had called the store and gotten his mother, who'd shown up wailing and praying, still wearing an apron soiled with meat juice and sauce, so that Tucci thought he would surely die of shame. Tucci had been forced to do detention and make restitution, half a buck a week for the rest of his life or eternity, whichever came first.

Of course, Tucci had brought the punishment and humiliation on himself. If only all criminals were dumb and accommodating enough to sign their handiwork. He imagined the van Gogh of vice. Murder by Michelangelo. Dope deals by daVinci.

Resnick greeted him warmly. "Good seeing you, Sergeant. How are things with Gina?"

"Coming along." He didn't bother to say in which direction.

"Good to hear. We're anxious to have her back."

"She can't wait."

"I've arranged for you to meet with several of Dan Magill's teachers as you requested. We've set aside the conference room for as long as you like. If there's anything else you need, let me know."

Resnick's charm would have seemed more in place behind a sales counter or the reception desk at a swanky hotel. Tucci could not picture this soft-spoken, affable man scaring the bejesus out of his little Frankenstein's monsters or Bonnies and Clydes, though from what he'd heard, the principal had no problem rising to the necessary occasion.

"Thanks. That's a big help," Tucci told him.

"We're as eager to clear things up as you are. The situation has been very upsetting for everyone."

Tucci could see why Gina liked the guy. He came across as genuinely involved, not just passing time like a lot of civil service grunts. "How well do you know Danny Magill?"

"Better than most. He's always been active in the school community, hardworking, a genuinely nice young man. I can't tell you how many times I've wished I could have a thousand kids just like him."

"Lucky you don't."

"That's still hard for me to swallow. I'd believe this of almost anyone, Sergeant. But not Danny Magill."

Resnick's office overlooked the courtyard, where clumps of dead-looking kids traded cigarettes and cynical sneers. Most of them sported tattoos and several extra holes in their heads, as if that might help to get anything worthwhile inside. The girls had their bare essentials bandaged with tiny elastic garments, and the boys wore clothes that drooped like wash poised to fall off the line. Their skin had the greenish cast of not so virgin olive oil. They had gumdrop-colored hair cropped like the wings of weird exotic insects. Not even two decades old and they already had the seedy feel of a street you wouldn't want to travel after dark.

"What you see is not always what you get," Tucci observed. "Especially when it comes to teenagers."

Resnick turned from the window. "I suppose. But in this case, I sincerely hope it isn't so. It's kids like Danny who keep you going in this business. Your Gina too. Kids like that make it possible to deal with the rest."

"You mean kids like the Danny Magill you thought you knew."

Resnick plucked a yearbook from the ordered volumes on his bookshelf. The annuals dated all the way back to 1928, the year the building was dedicated. Tucci spotted his own year, class of '71, at the middle of the stack. A pack of ghost memories circled him, taunting.

Senior year he'd fallen in with a pack of losers like himself. They had no ambitions. No pride, nothing. They hung around smoking, talking trash, trading dares. Tucci's mother took to praying for him all the time. Whenever he looked at her, which was as little as possible, she was staring down and muttering in peasant Italian. Mama Lucia donated extra money at collection, bucks they could not afford, as if Tucci's soul had been kidnapped and held for some large, unspecified ransom.

Tucci had gotten over the rebellious phase with the help of his drill sergeant in the Marines, a pit bull named Rudy Reyes who struck the necessary terror in Tucci's heart and taught him the meaning of life-altering humility. But his mama had never quite recovered. Even today, Tucci could see the imprint of his foot on the old lady's bent spine. He was to blame for her sadness, her pain. What happened to Billy was his fault.

If he hadn't been such a lousy little SOB, his parents would never have pushed him toward the recruiting office. Billy, the dumb jerk, had revered Tucci, held him up as a model of something worthwhile. Six months after Tucci enlisted, his kid brother had followed suit. No one had been able to talk him out of it, though everyone, especially Mama, had tried.

For Tucci, a stint in the service was right and necessary. The experience had turned him around, gotten his head screwed on straight again. For Billy, the effects had been far more profound. Some fool in his platoon had inadvertently discharged his rifle while cleaning it. Billy happened to be walking by and caught the bullet in the brain. Friendly fire, they called it. Accidental annihilation. A gentler brand of death.

The yearbook Resnick pulled was from two years back. He consulted the index and opened to the picture of the half-dozen kids who had volunteered to man the peer counseling hotline.

Tucci recognized Danny Magill at the center of the group. Resnick pointed to the strapping young man poised behind him. "That's Ryan Harrison. You've probably heard about him."

Tucci knew all about the accident that had landed the Harrison boy in a chair. When it first happened, Gina had been horribly upset by the news and had talked about it constantly. Over time, the subject had been dropped. But recently his name had started cropping up again with increasing frequency. Gina put herself and Ryan Harrison in the same sorry category. They were homebound, hamstrung. Damaged goods.

"Yeah, I heard. Too bad," Tucci said.

"Let me tell you something that you probably don't know. Mr. Harrison is in his seventies and not well. Has a heart problem, Parkinson's disease. Ryan's mother is not the strongest woman. Both of them were so overwhelmed by the accident they could barely function. Danny Magill sat with Ryan for hours every day while he was in a coma. After he came around, Danny did everything he could to encourage the boy. Most teenagers are much too full of their own needs to devote themselves to a friend that way, especially a friend in that kind of rough shape. Most kids would simply turn away."

Tucci glanced at the picture again. The Magill kid seemed to be smiling up at him. His look was all doe-eyed innocence, but Tucci didn't put much stock in looks. He'd known dozens of kids like this, and every one had been cut from the same lousy mold. Real nice wrapping paper, nothing much to speak of in the box.

Nor was he all that impressed by the tale of Danny's loyalty to his injured friend. Jack the Ripper may have been an Eagle Scout for all he knew. And maybe Hitler called his mother twice a week. Nothing inspired good works like a screaming conscience. Hallmark Cards had built a giant industry on that sorry fact of human nature.

Resnick eyed him sternly. Tucci felt like a kid caught spacing out in class. His first instinct was to fish around for a decent excuse or the answer to some unheard question. Amazing how being in this building sent him back. Next thing, he'd start sticking his hand up when he needed to use the can. Beg for a hall pass.

"If you're ready, I'll show you to the conference room and start sending people in," Resnick said. "Here's the list of the staff members you'll be seeing. There's a little information about each of them, what they teach and such."

"Sounds good."

For the next three hours Tucci got a comprehensive course in Daniel Magill, star student. He was honors this, advanced that, outstanding, unusual, talented, brilliant. Math prize, English award, talent search finalist, blah, blah, blah.

None of this came as a particular surprise. The kid's father had been head of Tucci's class, a giant brain, big shot, popular. But scum.

Charlie Magill and his bunch would swagger into the deli and give Tucci's mama a hard time. Picking on a sweet defenseless lady was their idea of fun.

Lucia Tucci had grown up in a tiny village called Campesino, south of Rome. Though she'd immigrated to America in her teens, her English remained a flimsy tool she rarely used. Words came hard to her, and people easy. She managed to communicate well enough through the universal language of baked ziti and chicken parmigiana. Nearly everyone loved Mama Lucia with her quick smile and generous heart. The only problem she'd ever had was with the stinking Magills.

They would come in and order sandwiches for lunch and try to pay with a bagful of pennies. Or they would toss around a jar of expensive imported balsamic vinegar and pretend not to understand Mama's frantic protests. "No speaka de Italian," they would taunt. "Hey, Butch. Go out for the pass."

Those preppie jerks always made a point of showing up when none of the Tucci men were in the store. The old man went out several times a day to get supplies or to make deliveries. Tucci and his brother spent mornings and early afternoons in school, where they were supposed to be. Magill and his buddies came and went as they pleased, ditching classes, bucking the system, writing their own rules.

They were prep school types, here against their parents' better judgment. Getting booted was no major threat.

So now, Charlie's kid had the same rotten attitude. He figured he could screw up and depend on his old man to fix things the way he always had. But that wasn't going to happen. Not this time.

Next on the list was a math teacher. She was a feisty older woman with sparkling blue eyes, white hair, and a handshake reminiscent of Tucci's drill sergeant's.

"Detective Tucci," she said with a chuckle. "Frankly, Joseph, I would have predicted that you would take a very different path indeed."

Tucci had not recognized the face, but there was no mistaking that voice. It still liquefied his spine. "Mrs. Breen?"

"Yes, Joseph. How nice to see you after all these years. I read the article about you in the newspaper recently, and I must say it reaffirmed my faith in the power of people to change. I was quite proud, actually. But please, don't quote me on that. I've worked long and hard to maintain my reputation."

Her efforts had paid off in spades, as Tucci vividly recalled. Way back in ninth grade, when he had Breen for algebra, Tucci had believed all the rumors about her, even the wildest ones: that she kept failed students in a dungeon beneath her house and made them eat their inadequate test papers. Late at night, it was said, you could hear them screaming if the wind blew just so. According to one story, mean Mrs. Breen kept the finger and toe bones of those who hadn't survived in her desk drawer. Supposedly, she liked to count them in her free time. Made her smile.

"I gather you're here about Danny Magill, Joseph. Dreadful thing."

Tucci raised a hand to stall her. "I know, you're going to tell me that Magill is a fabulous student, a terrific kid, best of breed. Let me save you the trouble, Mrs. Breen. I've already heard it a dozen times today."

"Joseph, Joseph. Some things never change. Here you are leaping to conclusions as always, telling me the meaning of x before you've looked at all the data and done the necessary calculations."

She eyed him harshly. "To be perfectly frank, I dislike Danny Magill, always have. There's something about that boy I don't trust. I've known enough young people to recognize one that's too good, on the surface at least, to be genuine. I, for one, was not at all surprised when these allegations came to light. If you had asked me, without naming names, which of my students might stand accused of a crime like this, I may well have put Danny Magill at the top of the list."

"How come?" Tucci's heart was racing, partly because he was face-to-face with the woman who was queen of mean decades before Leona Helmsley, and partly because she might be able to provide some evidence that the assault on Lisa Beningson was no isolated incident.

Mrs. Breen thought for a minute, the effort twisting her face into its frightful signature scowl. "It's not easy to define. Danny Magill has an arrogance about him, a standoffishness. I think he holds himself above the other students, that he believes he's deserving of whatever he desires. Who but a boy like that would be likely to violate someone?"

"Did you ever see anything, did he ever do anything to make you believe he might?"

"No, as I said, it's an impression."

So mean old Breen was also capable of leaping to unsupportable conclusions. "Thanks for coming in," Tucci told her.

"Always a pleasure, Joseph. Aside from the dungeon, there's nothing I enjoy more than seeing a boy like you turn out well."

A scruffy bearded teacher named O'Sullivan strode in next, swinging his navy canvas briefcase like a club. He claimed the vacant chair opposite Tucci's and planted a pugnacious jaw on his fist. The beard spread over his knuckles, so the hand resembled a shaggy puppet. Tucci was reminded of Señor Wences from the Ed Sullivan show. *'Sall right? 'Sokay. Close de box.*

According to the principal's list, Francis X. O'Sullivan taught eleventh-grade honors English, advised the drama club, directed the writing center, and coached girls' varsity gymnastics. Gina had not been in any of those, so the name was unfamiliar to Tucci. The lead pipe approach, he recognized right away.

"I'm here to tell you that I'm not going to tell you a thing," the teacher snarled.

Tucci nodded, long and slow. "Okay, 'bye."

"My students trust me. I'm not going to violate that trust."

"Look, Mr. O'Sullivan. It's been a long day, a long week, and a really long year. If you have nothing to tell me, do both of us a favor and go away."

O'Sullivan stroked his mangy whiskers. "I don't like cops."

"What's to like?"

"Danny Magill's a good kid. You're making a big mistake going after him."

"I'm not going after him. I'm doing my job. If you want the charges dropped, take it up with the judge or the state's attorney. I bet neither of them could resist a charmer like you."

O'Sullivan pecked at his briefcase with a chewed-down nail, tapping out an angry ditty from Alanis Morissette. "You know about the seal of the confessional, Tucci? You understand the meaning of trust? Confidence is a sacred thing. Kids have to be able to count on something, on someone. I give them that."

Tucci chuckled. He'd thought all the Christ impersonators were on street corners in New York City or upstate in padded cells. He steepled his hands. "Forgive me, Father, for I have sinned. It's been twenty-five years since my last creative writing assignment."

"I'm not kidding around. You think you know it all, but you're wrong. You can't get the right answers if you're asking the wrong questions."

"If there's one thing that drives me nuts it's a riddle, Teach. You ever hear the one that goes, 'Brothers and sisters he has none, but this man's father is his father's son'?"

"That's all I can tell you without crossing an impossible line." He rose in a frustrated huff.

"Can't remember the answer," Tucci said. "That's the thing about riddles, they're just too damned much trouble. Give me straight talk any day."

"You just don't get it, Tucci."

"That's because you're talking in hieroglyphics, O'Sullivan. Babbling Sanskrit. I know a couple of words of English, a little pidgin Sicilian, some church Latin, and enough Yiddish to get by. Try me in one of those, why don't you?"

The English teacher tossed down his briefcase in disgust. It hit the floor with a hard crunch of breaking crockery.

"Son of an F-ing, B-ing P," he railed.

Tucci put a hand to his mouth. "Now I am seriously offended."

O'Sullivan sat again with a loud deflating rush. "You don't have to like me, Officer."

"Lucky thing."

"I'm trying to do the right thing here. That's the truth. The problem is I'm caught in an impossible position."

"And you want me to fix this exactly how?"

"Read my mind. Or find some other way to get to the simple fact, which is that Danny Magill is not a rapist."

Tucci pressed a knuckle into the sore spot at the base of his neck. He'd had more than his fill of this crackpot. "Let me ask you a couple of real easy questions, O'Sullivan. Were you a witness that night? Did you see what went down in that car?"

"Of course not."

"Do you have a crystal ball, then? Or maybe tea leaves?"

"I'm telling you I know."

"And *I'm* telling *you* I don't give a damn about anything but hard facts. If you have any of those, I'm all ears."

His lips shriveled up inside the mangy whiskers. "The truth is the truth."

"And a waste of time is a waste of time. You take care, Mr. O'Sullivan. See you around."

TWENTY-TWO

J ess ran dripping from the shower, glanced warily at the caller-ID, and caught the phone before the machine picked up.

"I've got a break between clients, Jess. If you have a minute, I thought I'd stop by."

"I'd love it, Lib."

"Need anything?"

"Yes, I need to see you. Get here now. Immediately."

As she hung up, Max burst in from the bus stop like a depth charge. There was a jarring slam. Stomped feet. The book bag fell like a sack of stones. Jess heard the pull and thwack of a refrigerator invasion. Then came two shrill reports from Prozac. Red alert. Finally, the little boy bellowed his unnecessary announcement: "I'm home!"

Charlie had left early for an all-day symposium at the Hutchings Institute in New York, Molly was at gymnastics practice, and Danny was at his daily tutoring session at the church. Moments ago, Jess had been alone with Prozac in the rambling old house. Now, Max's arrival made the place seem fully occupied in every sense of the word.

"Hi, sweetie," Jess called. "Be right there."

Another harsh slam echoed through the floor joists. Something dropped. The dog yipped, her canine plea for reason. Max unleashed a horrifying squeal.

Jess hurried to the hall and leaned over the stair rail. Water from her sodden hair dripped to the foyer floor. "Are you all right, Maxy?"

"No, I'm not," he wailed. "Help, Mommy. Please!"

The little boy was a disembodied voice beyond the range of her radarscope. A flood of possible horrors rushed through Jess's mind: blood, broken bones, vital organs impaled.

She raced downstairs, damp feet skidding over risers worn satiny smooth. Pearl's carping voice competed with the hot pulse bashing in her skull. *You leave children alone, they get into trouble.*

Jess found Max rampaging through the refrigerator. The child set a juice carton on its ear, so the sticky liquid began cascading down the porcelain wall.

Jess righted the container and knelt to check out her son. She gripped his bony shoulders and peered into his round, angry eyes. "What's wrong, Maxy? Are you hurt?"

He raked through his spiky hair. "We're out of peanut butter," he whined. "There's nothing to eat."

In a dead calm tone, the dangerous kind, Jess said, "This is hardly what I'd call a big screaming emergency. You got me really, really worried for nothing."

"It's not for nothing, Mom. What am I supposed to do for a snack?"

"You are supposed to make do with what we have. Look, there's cheese, chicken, leftover soup, fruit, bagels, cookies, plenty of stuff. And anyway, you are *not* supposed to carry on about a snack as if it's the end of the world."

"But I *want* peanut butter." The boy planted defiant fists on his hips. "You should have bought an extra jar."

"Your protest is duly noted, sir. If you'd like, you can file a formal grievance with the unreasonable children's union. They will probably suspend my peanut butter purchasing license altogether, but I can deal. Meanwhile, how was school?"

"Dumb and boring. Mrs. Helman is a yucky witch and none of the good kids are in my group."

"Sounds like business as usual. I presume recess stank?"

"Big-time. Freddie Dickler always hogs the ball."

"You forgot the part about hating the food."

"They cook the hamburgers in green water. It's really gross."

"Any other complaints?"

His features scrunched in thought. "Not right now."

"Fine. Since we've covered everything, I'm going up to dry off. Libby's on her way over. If she gets here before I'm ready, please let her in."

The baby face dripped with disgust. "But I'm hungry, Mommy. Starved."

"Then help yourself to something."

Jess trudged back upstairs, bowed by guilty indecision. Maybe Pearl was right. Maybe she was a lousy, neglectful mother. Maybe none of this business with Danny would have happened if she had been watching harder and worrying more. Maybe she should have warned him about friends behaving oddly. Maybe she could have primed him to react to Lisa's advances in a more suspicious way. No one had ever told that kid about the worms that might be lurking in the most tempting apples.

That was her job, wasn't it? A parent was supposed to anticipate the dangers her children might face and find some way to avert them. A really good, diligent parent would fit her son with a full-body condom of Superman proportions, strong enough to ward off speeding bullets and other unanticipated assaults.

Jess had thought she was vigilant enough. Hadn't she always kept syrup of ipecac in the medicine chest in case of accidental poisoning? Hadn't she always been religious about vaccinations and checkups? She had prided herself on being the kind of mom the kids could come to when they were in trouble or doubt. But maybe that pride had been a case of dangerous self-deception.

What if her standards were simply too lax? Take now. Pearl would never have taken a shower when Jess or her brother Larry was home or scheduled to arrive anytime soon. She would have settled for a sensible bath instead, filling the tub before she stepped in, so she could soak in vigilant silence and monitor whatever might be happening or planning to happen in the house.

At the slightest errant noise, Pearl would lunge out of the tub like a flying marlin, fling a towel across her blue-veined flesh, and charge down to break up whatever fun the kids might be having in her absence. Once, she caught Jess and Larry chasing each other around the den with lollipops in their mouths, a behavior Pearl considered every bit as unthinkably reckless as swimming in a shark pool or toe-dancing on the third rail.

Absorbed with rage, she had dropped the towel and stood naked, breasts heaving, stretch-marked gut draped decorously over her groin like a cluster of fig leaves. Jess had seen her mother in all her doughy, jiggling glory a time or two before. Larry walked around with his mouth hanging open for days.

Prozac trotted into the bathroom, shot Jess a baleful look, and sprawled on the cool tile floor. The dog had a genius for avoiding strife, and lately there had been much to avoid.

"Hang in there, pal. This too shall pass."

Max's plaint rose up the stairs again. "Mommy, come quick!"

"What is it now, sweetie?"

"Hurry. It's really, really important."

"I'm getting dressed, Max. I'll be right down."

Maybe firmness was the answer. Jess might well be innocent of criminal neglect and guilty of impersonating a doormat. Much as Charlie detested his father's cruel inflexibility, he had trouble with the fuzzy shades of gray that Jess was willing to tolerate. She saw much of this mommy business as an on-the-job training program. You had to roll with the situation, assess and reassess, make it up as you went along.

Different children had different needs, and effective parents made the necessary adjustments. Danny kept his most difficult feelings to himself, offering them up only after they were fully processed, neatly sorted, and presentable. Molly's psyche had a complex, ever-shifting code. Fear might emerge as anger, anger as silliness, sadness as withdrawal. With that one, it was necessary to read between the lines, seek sensible patterns, make logical assumptions, and always be prepared to be wrong.

Max let everything out. He was an audio book, announcing his every need and desire, loud and clear. The trick with him was balance, not giving in too little or too much.

Again, he shrilled, "I need you, Mom. Right this minute. Now!"

"It can—"

Wait, she was about to say. When the crash came, the word hung suspended between her brain and lips. The concussion shook the house like angry hands. A tremor of fear filled the silent aftermath.

"Oh my God!"

Jess charged downstairs again. She tracked Max's desperate whimpers to the pantry. The child stood clutching his head and moaning, "She's going to kill me. She's going to murder me dead."

Jess frisked her baby boy for injuries. She felt his bones and searched for cuts and blood. Nothing serious appeared to be wrong with him. The same could not be said for their best china and crystal stemware, which was dashed in scraps and shards across the linoleum floor.

Max wrenched free of her grasp and crouched like a flier on a crash-bound plane. "I didn't mean it, Mommy. Don't be mad. Don't hit me. Please!"

Jess had never raised a hand to any of the kids, though this was a more than spankable offense. She could still feel the sting of Pearl's fury on her cheek. Love taps, Pearl used to call the smacks, as if they were a precious gift.

Her voice was taut with rage. "I want you to tell me, *right* now, how you knocked down those shelves."

Two of the long, thick, solid boards that had held the company tableware lay on the floor behind Prozac's fifty-pound kibble sack.

Max emerged from his crouch, as if someone had sounded the all clear. "Stupid things fell down on their own. I just came in here to fill Prozac's bowl, and boom!"

The lie held a flame to Jess's wrath. "I want the truth, Max Magill."

"I told you. The dumb shelves fell off the stupid moron wall. Dad put them up. Blame him. I could have been hurt, you know. Really badly."

"I want you to go to your room and stay there until you're ready to talk with no fibbing."

Max crossed his arms and jammed his fists into his armpits. "That's not fair. I didn't do anything."

Jess was devolving into a toxic pool of maternal frustration. "I am going to count to three, Max. One. . . ."

"Two!"

He stood immobile, hardening in his resolve. Jess understood the stakes. If an eight-year-old defied the fearsome countdown, her parental advantage was history. "Two and a half. I am not fooling around, Max. Go to your room."

The little boy was giggling, getting drunk on his own imagined power. "You can't make me."

"Two and three quarters."

"Hah hah," he taunted. "Hah."

"If you won't go on your own, I'll have to help you." Jess carried him, kicking and squirming, toward the stairs. As she passed through the foyer, the bell chimed. Through the bubbled panel flanking the door, she spied Libby Amory's reassuring face.

"Come on in, Lib. Door's open."

Libby entered with a rush of crisp air. She had an instant softening effect, even in an explosive situation like this. "Hey, you guys. What's going on?"

Max stopped flailing long enough to accept Libby's peck on the cheek. "Mommy's blaming me for something I didn't do," he bleated. "Tell her to stop, Aunt Libby. Please."

"Sorry, champ," she said. "I only handle grown-up couples. My license doesn't cover moms and kids."

"Please, Aunt Lib. You have to save me. Please!"

"You guys go work things out. I'll wait."

Libby's presence boosted Jess from basest doldrums to simple depressive defeat. "Make yourself at home, Lib. I'll be right down."

"Take your time."

When they were halfway up the stairs, the little boy went rigid and unleashed a shattering shriek.

"Calm down, Maxy. Hush."

Her attempts to soothe him only served to ratchet up his fury. His screams grew teeth and fists. The child was a flailing, roiling mass of rage.

"Stop."

He thrust his head back and caught Jess hard under the chin, so that she bit her tongue and tasted blood. She wrestled him to the top of the stairs and into his room. Jess had experienced everything from two-year-old tantrums to Dolores Wainscott–sized fits of unbounded wrath, but nothing had been worse than this.

Max had always been a quirky, unpredictable, short-fused little guy. He and Molly had both inherited Grandma's Pearl's penchant for melodrama and Grandfather Magill's stubborn insistence on having things his way. Both of them required cautious handling, like any armed explosive device. Jess had tripped Max's fuse, set him ticking on the verge.

She held the little boy on her lap, containing him with arms, feet, knees, words, soothing noises, everything she had. He was too big for this, and he spilled down her legs like one of Molly's tent-sized nightshirts. Jess clung fast, offering a wordless reminder that he was safe and loved, no matter what. Still his temper raged like a river that had dashed its banks and could not be set back in containment.

Jess rocked in soothing rhythm and sang his favorite tune from infancy: "Hush, little baby. Don't say a word."

When that had no effect, she took a different tack. "A hundred bottles of beer on the wall, a hundred bottles of beer. If one of those bottles should happen to fall—"

Jess went suddenly, deliberately still. Max unleashed one final yelp; then the metal stiffness drained from his body. Small pulses shook his slender frame, and he started giggling with the same maniacal intensity that he had put into his anger moments ago. "Ninety-nine bottles of beer on the wall," he sputtered, "ninety-nine bottles of beer." Slowly, gradually, he wound down like an old mechanical clock.

Jess eased the child off her lap and looked him hard in the eye. "I know you were scared about breaking those things, and I'm not happy about it. But accidents happen, Max. I know that."

His face was dirt-streaked and striped with tears, and his nose was running. Jess plucked a Kleenex from the box on his nightstand and helped him blow.

"But hear me, Maxy. Lying is *not* okay. When you do something bad, even by accident, you need to admit what happened and take responsibility."

His lip curled. "I can't take responsibility, Mom. That fancy stuff costs a fortune. All I get is one stinking dollar a week for allowance. I don't even have any charge accounts." He was weeping again, revving up for another bout of serious misery. "Not even Visa."

"I don't expect you to replace those things. That's not what I mean by responsibility. Please tell me what happened, so I can understand. Then I'd like to go downstairs and visit with Libby, and you can relax for a while."

"Promise you won't be mad?"

"If you tell the truth, I won't. I promise." She didn't bother to add that his outburst had left her too exhausted to raise a decent pique.

"I thought I saw some peanut butter behind one of those big squiggly glasses you use for wine. Prozac barked like she wanted me to get it, so I did."

Jess sighed like a leaky balloon. Now he was a miniature Son of Sam, following animal instructions. "You did the climbing, Max. You broke those things. Don't try to blame it on the dog."

The grimy face drew into a dare. "How come it's okay for Danny then? How come he gets to blame what he did on Lisa?"

"It's not the same. Danny didn't do what Lisa said."

"You like Danny best. He's your favorite."

"I don't have a favorite. I have three."

Max's scowl set. "All you care about is him and his stupid trial. That's why there isn't any peanut butter."

"I'm afraid you've lost me. What does one thing have to do with the other?"

"The house feels sick, Mommy, that's what I'm saying. Like the whole place has a bad, bad cold and not having peanut butter is the stuffed-up nose. Understand?"

"I can cure this, my child. First thing tomorrow, I'm going to pick up not one but two jars of peanut butter, maybe three."

"That's not going to fix it."

"Why not?"

"Because if you fix the stuffed nose, you'll still have the headache and the cough." He wrapped his arms around Killer the bear. "I'm ready to relax now. Okay?"

"Sure, me too."

Libby was cleaning up the mess, shoveling the tiny fragments into a dustpan, setting the larger chunks of china and glass aside.

"Don't bother, Lib. I'll deal with it later."

"Is Max okay?"

"I think I can safely say that nothing is okay with anybody," Jess said with a rueful smile. She eyed the spill of crockery and glass. "What a mess."

"It's not so bad, Jess. Look. Lots of them can be saved. Do you have any Krazy Glue?"

Jess rummaged through the junk drawer and found a tube. Libby fished two unscathed squiggly glasses from the pantry floor. She extracted a bottle of chilled champagne from among the legal files in her briefcase, popped the cork and poured.

"What's the occasion?" Jess asked.

"We finally got the Hatfields and McCoys to settle."

"Hear, hear."

"Would you believe it's been five years since the complaint was filed? I honestly thought that one would go on forever."

"All things in time, I guess," Jess mused.

They drank to happy conclusions.

Libby plucked several crockery slices from the pile and found a pair that meshed. She drew a slender bead of glue across the edge and pressed them together. While she held the parts, waiting for the bond, she tipped her head toward two other scraps. "Try those."

Soon, they had reconstituted six dinner plates, five salad bowls, four coffee cups with saucers. They rescued a creamer and repaired the gravy boat save for one missing chunk that made the spout look as if it had gone to Dr. Delgado for a nose job.

Libby rubbed some glue from a fingertip and smiled. "You see? It's coming together."

"Over there, Lib. I think those are part of a tray." Jess melded the pieces with a nearly invisible seam. It would be just as strong as before, maybe stronger.

Tucci raised his desk phone and hurled it in the trash.

Patty McNees, shuffling in from a night shift, ticked her tongue. "Easy now, Joey. Whatever that nasty phone did to you, I'm sure it's very sorry."

Tucci shook his head. "I did it to myself, Pats. You are looking at the dumbest wop in the history of wopdom. Shooting me would be a mercy. That's the truth."

She perched on his desk. "Go on. Get it off your chest, love. You'll feel better."

"I had a witness in the Magill case, a goddamned corroborating eyewitness to the rape, and I let her get away." Tucci hung his head in misery. "Bitch gave me a phony name and number. For a day and a half, I kept calling and calling and got no answer. No machine, nothing. But I figured, hey, not everyone has a machine. Or maybe they have one and it's broken. Or maybe they forgot to turn it on. I kept telling myself, be patient, sooner or later there's bound to be somebody home. I must have tried that number two, three million times. Finally, this morning, I get through. Turns out to be a tile-manufacturing company. And moron that I am, I figure I dialed wrong. So I try again, twice more, three times, same answer."

Patty scratched her mangy gray-streaked hair. "Maybe you wrote down the number wrong, Joey. Could be simple as that."

"She wrote it." Tucci fished through the trash around the phone and plucked out the paper scrap. "I checked it out in the reverse directory. It's all a fake. The name, number, everything. She made it up, and I swallowed it whole." He wadded the paper again and executed a neat overhand swisher. He followed with his department ID, his shield, his car keys, house keys, wallet, watch.

Patty clamped his wrist with the blackened fingers that poked through her filthy raveled gloves. Bag lady couture knew no season. Summer and winter alike, she carried her entire decoy wardrobe on her back: dress, sweater, raincoat, gloves, two pairs of threadbare stockings, headscarf, ancient Keds. "All right, that's enough carrying on. I'm off for a long weekend in Atlantic City, and I'm not leaving until I know you're okay. So let's just put on our thinking caps like the nuns used to have us do at St. Agnes School, and work this thing out."

"I already worked it out, but good," Tucci groaned. "I mentioned the witness in a memo to Klonsky. Put it in writing, exactly like you're not supposed to do. When the chief finds out I screwed it up, he'll can my dumb ass in five seconds. What am I going to do about Gina's medical bills then, Pats? I'm having a hard enough time getting them covered through the department plan. No new insurance company is going to take that on."

"So we'll all kick in."

"We're talking the gross national product of Peru, Pats. This thing costs like you can't imagine."

"For the love of God, Joey. Stop whining and think. There must be some way to track that flyaway bird. Did you happen to get a look at her car?"

"No. She met me on foot. Made sure I didn't follow her when she left."

"Were there any monograms on her purse or wallet or key ring, then? Engraved jewelry. Anything like that?"

"Nothing, Pats. *Niente.* I'm toast."

"Don't give me that. The Joe Tucci I know doesn't give up so damned easy. My Joey pulls a rabbit out of the hat every single time, even when the case isn't his. A person goes to my Joey, and guaranteed, he'll help you get to the bottom of whatever it is you're scraping for, even when it looks bleak as hell. Now shut up and think."

She crossed her arms and held Tucci in her fierce, determined sights. He felt powerless to do anything but go back over every detail of his encounter with Miss Muffet. He relived the early-morning phone call and the ride to the park through the maddening traffic. He heard the blare of horns and smelled the suffocating gas fumes. Again, he was in the park, scanning the concession stand with a sinking sense of dread. The traffic delay had made him so late the informant had probably given up and gone home. He was sure he'd missed a crucial opportunity to nail Magill. Remembering, he felt the heaviness in his legs as he plodded up the hill to his car.

Tucci switched to a view of the witness sprawled on the grass after he took her for an armed assailant and knocked her to the grassy strip flanking the sidewalk. He could see the perfect features widened in bemused surprise, the lacy flash of panties, the perfect legs. In surreal slow motion, he played back the way she'd stood, brushed herself off, and led him back down the hill to the park like some society matron trailing her pedigreed pooch on a leash. She'd been all cool self-assurance, even when she was on her butt, even while she sat in the blistering heat and confessed to doing some guy on the side.

Looking back, Tucci spotted several holes in the cozy scenario. The woman had held her gaze sure and steady. She had not acted the least bit afraid of being seen with him. If, as she claimed, she'd been fearful of getting caught, wouldn't she have squirmed and darted her eyes around and acted the part?

Which brought him to another vexing question. Why had she chosen to meet him at a public park in broad daylight on a bright sunny day, where there were bound to be crowds? Made no sense. Nervous informants chose private, anonymous spots. They covered their tracks and did their best to look invisible. This one had strutted around as if she did not have a thing in the world to hide.

"Are you thinking, Joey?"

"I am, Pats. I'm thinking the whole deal stinks and always did. I'm thinking maybe she was a three-dollar bill all along and I was way too anxious to take her for the genuine item."

Another dismal fact occurred to him. The assault had taken place in front of the Beningsons' house, on a driveway screened by shrubbery and confounding shadows. There was no way Miss Muffet could have happened by and observed what was going on inside the Mustang. No way she could have turned around and pulled up beside the car as she'd claimed. That would have meant wheeling into the Beningsons' drive. "Lying bitch."

"So good riddance to her."

"It's not so simple, Pats. What am I supposed to say to Klonsky? Oh, by the way, Chief, you know that corroborating witness I said I had? April Fool."

"No problem, Joey. All you need to do is find her and get her to recant."

"Great idea. Perfect. You're a genius, Pats. How?"

"Think."

Tucci pushed past the hopelessness of the situation. He forced his thoughts back to the park, back to the picnic table. Miss Perfect was across from him again, spilling her phony guts. Can't risk hurting my children, his children. It was my first time ever, never again, blah, blah, blah. Oh all right, if you really tug on my conscience, I'll play ball. As he approached the part where she wrote down her made-up name and fake phone number, Tucci ran the tape in slow motion. He went through it frame by frame, examining Miss Muffet's moves. She had torn the snip of paper from a folded sheet in her purse. Something had been drawn on the other side. He remembered catching a glimpse of color. Tucci dove for the trash can and retrieved the crumpled note. He smoothed it and stared in disappointment at the scratches on the back. There was half of an oval, part of a line beside an upturned half-circle. Beneath that was another loopy shape. A couple of swipes of color, beige, a reddish brown.

"Doodles," he said in disgust.

As he was crumpling the paper again, Patty grabbed it. "Wait, Joey love. Not so fast." She studied the shapes and color blots. Smiled. "So happens I know what this is. Bet you can't guess."

Tucci shook his head miserably. "Sure I can. It's a picture of the fat lady singing. I mean it, Pats. Klonsky is going to skin me for this."

"No, he's not, because you are going to follow this little scrap to that rotten canary. It's part of a makeup chart, Joey. At some salons they give you a diagram like this to take home after the makeup artist designs your new color scheme. All we need to do is find out who did this one for whom, and you've got your bird."

"You mean it?"

"Would I jerk you around, Joey?"

"You're the best, Pats. The ultimate." Tucci wanted to hug her, though he resisted the urge. She was a national treasure, that one, fleas and all. "Where do we start?"

"Shouldn't be hard. There are only a couple of local shops that do this kind of full-service work." She went to the back of the squad room for the phone book.

"Wait," Tucci said. "There may be just a few local shops, but who says she didn't have her makeup done in New York, or Timbuktu for that matter. With the way my luck's been running, that's exactly what she did."

Patty fixed him with a kindly smile. "You may know about lots of things, Joey love, but obviously this isn't one of them. Here's how it goes. When a woman has her makeup done, she buys a mess of new cosmetics. We all know that's the point of the so-called *free* makeup application, but we're a sucker for it nonetheless." She caught him gaping. "Yes, love. That includes me. In fact, since I started dressing this way for work, I've turned into quite the glamour puss when I'm off duty."

"I can imagine," Tucci said.

"No you can't, love. But that's not important except that I know how these things work. Soon as we drop a bundle on new shadows and liners and blushers and creams, we can't wait to try them out at home. Of course, after a couple of days, we realize that we haven't a snowball's chance in hell of looking anything near as good as we did when we left the shop. But that doesn't stop us from dumping all those useless cosmetics in the drawer and getting sucked in again after a while. So the bottom line is, this woman, whoever she is, had her face painted that very day, just before she met you? Think back. Was she all made up, looking perfect, like a porcelain doll?"

Tucci conjured the informant's face. "Exactly."

"Then it was a professional who did that makeup job. And given the timing you describe, it's not likely she strayed too far out of the area before you met her."

"So we let our fingers do the walking," Tucci said.

Patsy squinted at the list of beauty salons and pointed with a filthy finger. "Take your first step here. Then try these."

"Can't you call, Pats?"

"This is your case, love. I've been at mine all night. I'm going home. Then off to Atlantic City."

"Sure, kid. I understand. Thanks." As she slogged out of the squad room, Tucci dialed. "Salon Demoiselles," the receptionist chirped. "Can I help you?"

Tucci cleared the embarrassment from his throat. "You do makeup applications?"

"But of course."

"Do you send the client home with some kind of a chart?"

"No. We do videotape, step by step. State-of-the-art."

He had no better luck at the next two shops he called. The makeup artist at Danielle's Day Spa had been on vacation for the last two weeks. Jean Darcy's did makeup charts on a computer. If the next place did not pan out, Tucci would have to widen his nets. There were dozens of towns in Connecticut and nearby New York that his phony songbird could have visited for her makeover. He was running out of energy and time. Any minute now, Klonsky might call him in for the beheading. He dialed the last name on Patty's list.

"Hair and There," said the chirpy young man who picked up.

By now, Tucci had the question down to a routine. Yes, they had a makeup artist. Mr. Martin was a genius, the young man assured. Every client went home with a detailed diagram on which Mr. Martin indicated precisely which products went where. It was a system Mr. Martin himself had developed, and the clients were universally pleased. "Would you care to make an appointment?"

Tucci twirled his head around, making sure no one was close enough to hear. "I just need to talk to him," he whispered into the receiver.

"Certainly, sir. I'll put you down for a consultation. What would be convenient for you?"

With the way his cheeks were burning, Tucci would definitely not need any blush. "Soon as possible," he rasped.

"Well, looks like this is your lucky day. Mr. Martin has a cancellation in an hour."

Tucci gave his name. His lucky day. Whoopee.

Fifty minutes later, Tucci pulled into the broad lot fronting the salon on High Ridge Road. The shop was overwhelmingly pink. Pink walls, pink roof, pink chimney. Bubble gum door, cotton candy trim, and a sign like a giant splash of Pepto-Bismol.

Inside, the pink was relieved by traces of lavender and mauve. The staff wore shirts the color of baby cheeks and tight black skirts or spandex pants. Many of them had cough-syrup-red or Harlow-blond hair, which to Tucci's eye clashed with the decor. He found words like "decor" and "palette" scampering through his mind. It occurred to him that they needed a contrasting accent color, maybe a splash of something warm.

A willowy blond receptionist challenged him when he tried to slink past the desk. "May I help you?"

"I'm looking for Mr. Martin."

"Ah yes, you must be his two o'clock consultation. Would you care to change into a gown?"

A pair of waiting women turned and smirked. Tucci was dying to show them his Glock, maybe fire a couple of rounds at the pink ceiling for effect, but he restrained himself.

"I'm just here to talk to the guy," he announced. "That's all."

The blonde gave him an indulgent smile. "Mr. Martin will be with you in just a few moments, sir. Can I get you something to drink? We have mineral water, diet soda, decaf cappuccino, herbal tea."

Under the circumstances, Tucci would not have taken anything short of grain alcohol, except maybe liquid nails. "Never touch the stuff."

He waited five, ten minutes on the tufted fuchsia bench beside the door. The stink of dye and hair spray made his head spin. So did the parade of fancy women who kept strutting in and out. If he hadn't known better, he would have sworn it was the same one again and again, rotating through the shop on some looping conveyor belt. They all looked alike to him—chichi costumes, eye-popping jewels. He could not see the difference in how they looked coming and going, except maybe lighter in the purse. Two hundred and up for a cut, three for highlights, sixty for a blow-dry. Trip to the cleaners, no extra charge.

Thank God he didn't have to back a fancy dame like that. Gina and Marie got their cuts from Marie's cousin Ruthie, who charged a tray of Marie's vegetable lasagna or a medium cheesecake. Tucci went every couple of months to Sal the barber in Glenbrook. A trim was ten bucks. For fourteen, he could get a straight-razor shave with hot towel, the monster hairs clipped from his eyebrows, and a fresh crop of corny jokes.

After another five minutes passed, he approached the desk again. "How much longer will he be?"

With pursed lips, the blonde rang inside. "Very well, Mr. Martin will see you now."

She led Tucci through flesh-colored curtains into a square room with mirrored walls and garish lighting. Stylists were stationed every five feet like prison guards, assaulting clients with pistol-shaped dryers and menacing shears.

The blonde paused at the corner station beside a slim young man with dime-slot dimples and a generous smile. A large pink plastic tool kit brimming with pots and brushes sat before him. "Mr. Martin, this is Mr. Tucci."

"Nice to meet you. Have a seat." After the receptionist strolled away, he looked at Tucci appraisingly, then started to tuck a white cloth into the collar of his shirt.

And Tucci plucked it out and set it firmly on the counter. "I'm only here to talk," he proclaimed again in an even louder voice.

Mr. Martin shrugged. "How can I help you, then?"

Tucci flashed his shield. "I need to find a woman who comes here, to ask her something about a case I'm working on. I don't know her name."

"What does she look like?"

"Brown hair. Slim. In good shape, as if she works out. Forty or so years old. Expensive-looking, if you know what I mean."

"That describes about half my list."

"This one's obviously educated. Well-spoken. Comes across as very, very sure of herself."

"I can't say that narrows it down a whole lot."

Tucci pulled out the paper scrap. "She gave me this."

The makeup artist clacked his tongue. "All that work, and someone simply rips it up. So discouraging."

"I know the feeling. Can you tell who it was?"

The young man took the scrap and placed it on the lid of his open case. With deft motions, he began pulling out eye shadows and tubes of color and matching them to the pigments on the diagram. He started with the eyes. "That's Golden Moss shadow with an accent of Ombre Rose and Firefly. The mascara is Forest Brown over Ash, which I've been using a great deal lately—I find it much softer, even on dark-complexioned brunettes. That would seem to be a touch of Crimson Heather, there, on that tiny piece of the cheek I'm able to see."

"Whose colors are they? Can you tell?"

"Hmmm. This is a tough one. So many of my clients use a similar palette. I do like to keep things fairly neutral and as natural as possible. That's my cosmetic philosophy."

Fascinating. Tucci remembered the cosmetic philosophy of Patty McNees. "This client was in for a makeover in the last couple of weeks."

Mr. Martin gave an apologetic shrug. "With the new season and all, I've been incredibly busy. I've been seeing as many as twenty clients a day, six days a week. After a while, I'm afraid they all start to look alike."

Tucci shrugged back. What was the use? "Thanks anyway."

The voice caught him halfway out the door. "Wait."

Tucci turned back. "What?"

Mr. Martin beckoned him with manic enthusiasm. "This is it. Right there. I just noticed that tiny edge turned under. It shows part of the upper lip. Would you just look at that liner with that lipstick! Woodrose over Scarlet Frost. Absolutely atrocious. I'm ashamed to be associated with such an appalling combination, honestly. But one does not argue with this particular client."

"You mean you can tell me who it was?"

"I certainly can. That she-beast is one of a kind." He flipped through his card file and wrote the name, number, and address.

Tucci caged Mr. Martin's hand. "Oh man, you can't imagine what this means to me. Thanks a million."

"My pleasure. Come back anytime."

Her car was backing out as he approached the driveway. Tucci screeched to a halt behind her. She honked the horn like an irate goose. Then, spotting Tucci in her rearview mirror, she sprang from the car and bolted for the house.

Tucci's feet took action before his brain was fully engaged. He chased after the shrew and caught her as she was about to plunge her key in the front-door lock. She flailed in his grasp, struggling with astonishing strength. She was all bone and sinew, fueled by raw, explosive rage. Breaking free, she jammed the key between her index and middle fingers and stabbed the business end toward his eye.

Tucci clamped her wrist and twirled her around with her back to him, so she was bound in the straitjacket of her own limbs. "That's tilt, lady. Game over. You lose."

"Let go of me, you revolting creature. I happen to know Mayor Davisson and Police Commissioner Foster. Neither of them will be amused to hear that you attacked me for no reason. Attacked me sexually, no less. Obviously, you were drunk on the job. Out of your mind. Dangerous."

Tucci wrenched her arms tighter. He wished he had a free hand for the mouth. "You're under arrest."

"For what?" she demanded.

"For being yourself. Plus all the lesser included charges."

"Don't be ridiculous. You let go of me this instant, or I'll have more than your silly little job."

Tucci's knee nestled in the small of her back. It took everything he had to keep from bending her spine back, cracking it like a wishbone. Instead, he recited her rights and cuffed her over the diamond-bezeled Cartier tank watch and the blinding tennis bracelet. She fought him, hissing threats and curses as he walked her toward the cruiser.

Tucci took special care not to break Miss Muffet's nails or mess her makeup. He wanted her to look just so for the mug shots. When he held her head to ease her into the car, she tried to bite him. She tried again when he pulled a seat belt across her and fixed the buckle. Too bad the department didn't issue choke chains and muzzles for situations like this.

But then, cops were rarely called upon to deal with anyone quite this vicious. Normally, they handled garden-variety criminals: armed robbers, pimps, hop-heads, serial killers. Reasonable folk like that.

"You'll be sorry, you dumb son of a bitch. Do you happen to know who you're dealing with?"

"No, but if you hum a few bars, I'll give it a try."

Woman was hissing like a viper, raining spit. "I will ruin you and your pre-cious wife and your darling little girl. Too bad she's so sick, Detective. I gener-ally enjoy a bigger challenge."

"I'll see you get one."

She fell silent. Tucci kept a wary watch on her. He could see her sick mind rolling behind the twirly eyes. She was like something out of a triple-X-rated cartoon.

As he put the car in gear, she snickered. "Okay. Good joke. Now stop right here and let me out."

He kept driving, counting down the distance to the station house. They were four miles away. Three. . . .

A hint of desperation crept into her tone. "I mean it, Detective. This is quite enough. I have things to do. A very busy day."

He swung down Washington Avenue and made a broad looping approach to headquarters. "Going to be busier than you ever imagined," he muttered.

Her sculpted features settled in a petulant scowl. "All right. I'm bored with this. What do I need to do?"

"Admit you lied."

"Okay, fine. I didn't see the rape. I made the whole thing up. I'm a naughty, naughty girl. Now, take me home."

Tucci angled off the road and yanked the brake. He pulled a letter from his pocket and read aloud: "To whom it may concern, this is to certify that my testimony in the matter of the State of Connecticut versus Daniel Magill was given falsely. I hereby retract and recant all statements made by me regarding the aforementioned case. I was not a witness to any alleged actions by any par-ties named in this action. I have no pertinent information regarding the alleged crime."

"I can't exactly do that with my hands behind my back. Can I, Detective?"

Tucci lumbered out, opened the rear door, and unlatched the cuffs.

Most prisoners spend a minute or two rubbing the circulation back into their wrists, enjoying the freedom. This one sprang like a cocked arrow. She was all over him, teeth, nails, poison spit.

Tucci wrestled her down and restrained her. "That's it. I'm taking you in. Right now."

"All right. Let me up and I'll sign your stupid note."

Tucci was enjoying the feel of his weight at the small of her back. He wanted to crush her, but that wouldn't solve his immediate problem.

She got to her feet and brushed herself off and smiled. "There's no reason for us to argue, Detective. We both want the same thing."

"Really? You want to murder yourself also?"

"I'm talking about convicting Danny Magill. Why don't we work together? You supply me with the necessary details, and I play witness for the prosecution. We can put that little creep where he belongs, give his parents what they deserve too. What do you say?"

"Let me get this straight. You're proposing that I help you give false testimony in a felony case, so we can stick it to the Magills."

"I prefer to think of it as performing a public service."

Tucci had never felt such murderous disgust. "Either you sign this retraction, right now, or I'll haul your bony ass to jail. And by the way, I hear the cosmetology services in the can really suck. No styling, no highlights. Can't get a makeup consultation to save your life."

"Save your breath. I don't take threats, especially from foolish little nobodies like you."

"Let's go then. I've had enough of this. I've got things to do. A very busy day."

They were at the car when she grabbed for his pen. She scrawled her name in a sharp, stabbing hand. Then, as she slipped back into the rear of the cruiser, she issued a high-pitched laugh. "Little man honestly thinks he beat me," she trilled. "Poor fool has no idea."

Her laughter came in harsh ugly bursts. The sound felt like a hot rush of acid along Tucci's spine.

Tucci didn't draw a decent breath until he dropped her off in her driveway. As she strode inside, he took full note of her, committed her to memory, and marked her dangerous. She was one of those rare birds whose wings were not clipped by conscience, fear, or public humiliation. Dolores Wainscott made Chief Klonsky look almost reasonable. Tucci would need to keep an even closer watch on his back.

Charlie circled the block, muttering angrily. The striking absence of parking near the courthouse served as an apt warm-up for legal proceedings. Tempers were preheated. Biases were laid raw. The lust for vengeance grew to biblical proportions.

On his fourth circuit, he vied for and lost two precious spaces, one to a police cruiser and one to a woman in a green Volkswagen who waved her jury duty summons like a badge of entitlement as she stole Charlie's rightful spot with her bug. As she strutted down the street, her portly rump wobbling like water balloons under the flowered dress, Charlie's fingers went white on the wheel.

"I'm going to run her over," he said with chilling detachment. "I won't kill her. But I need to crush some bones."

"Cut it out, Charlie," said Jess. "That's not cute."

"A leg would be good. Maybe both. My only concern is her backside. Hitting that would probably be like colliding with an iceberg. Think of it, Danny. Our very own little *Titanic*."

"Come on, Dad. We're going to be late," Danny urged.

"No we won't. Running her down won't take but a minute."

"I'm nervous enough as it is, Dad. Please."

"A little diversion like this will relax you, my son."

He blasted the horn. When the woman turned, he clenched his teeth and stomped the accelerator. The engine roared. A scream formed deep in Jess's chest and stuck there. She braced against the expected burst of speed, the jolt of impact. But nothing happened. There was a silence, followed by Charlie's demonic laugh.

As he spotted her shocked, pale face, his mirth ran out. "The car was in park, Jessie. It was a joke."

Jess refused to join him in the sandbox. Since the start of this, they had fallen dangerously out of sync. They kept stepping on each other's toes, collecting sore spots. She had no strength for this, not now. Plus, she knew all too well what their foolish wrangling did to Danny. Pearl used to scream at Jess's father, calling him no good, lazy, a failure, lashing out with the sharp whip of her perpetual discontent. Jess could still feel the hollow her mother's cruelty to her darling dad used to dig in her chest. The last thing Danny needed was a couple of selfish overgrown kids for parents. As best she could, Jess kept the anger stowed away until they were alone. Hard words and harsher accusations had taken the place of their affection and lovemaking.

Someone was angling out of a spot halfway up the block. Charlie made a jolting U-turn, floored the gas, and nabbed it.

They straggled in uneasy silence down the hill to the courthouse, where a long queue awaited the slow drip through security. Explaining procedures to the uninitiated took time. There were further delays as belongings were searched and bodies probed by the seeking electronic rays from the metal detector. Several people tripped the alarm and had to go back around. A bald man at the front of the line refused to give up his switchblade, causing a protracted argument and a hasty summons of two security guards, who escorted him, red-faced and cursing, out the door.

As she stepped through the metal arch, Jess felt a squeeze deep in her womb, a cramp of dread and something deeper. Years hence, some investigator would likely learn that the machine and this entire place posed a serious health hazard. Heart fractures. Cancer of the spirit. Severe anemia of hope.

By now, the security clerk recognized them and offered a grim little smile. By now, Danny had mastered the necessary nuances. He deposited his grandfather's belt buckle in the mesh basket before passing through the electronic sentinel. That buckle, along with his maroon striped tie and black loafers, had assumed talismanic importance. The kid needed something to hold on to. That was clear.

June Gold was waiting in the lobby to squire them upstairs to the conference room. At first, Jess had taken this for a courtesy. But now, she understood that they would be charged for it. Everything was part of a billable hour. The smile, the casual greeting, the walk. Ten cents a step, she calculated. Fifty cents a word. A buck a grin.

Grantham was poised at the head of the littered table, chatting dramatically on his cell phone. As always, the lawyer was puffed with optimism. Somehow he remained confident despite the inexorable downslide in Danny's case. He was like a coach for a chronically lousy team or a sixty-year-old ingenue still expecting her big break as a Hollywood starlet. Bleak realities had no place in his equation.

After turning down Grantham's request to treat Danny as a youthful offender, Judge Harrigan had refused to revoke or reduce the hefty bail. He had denied the lawyer's motion to suppress any statements Danny might have made early on in the absence of counsel. Last week, he acted unfavorably on their petition to have early court proceedings closed to the public.

Grantham's high drama had failed to move the judge. "I'd like to remind Your Honor of the defendant's tender age and unblemished record. He deserves to be shielded from public scrutiny. This boy stands innocent in the eyes of the law. Your Honor can't possibly justify inviting in prurient onlookers and the parasitic press," the lawyer had argued, with an exaggerated passion that moved Jess to refer to him as Oliver Wendell Schmaltz.

Harrigan had cut off the performance with a thwack of his gavel. "Motion denied!"

Prior to every crushing disappointment, Grantham expressed unwavering certainty that the currents were about to shift their way. The collective defeats had not reduced his baseless confidence in the least.

Jess marveled at how he maintained the starched poise and steady melon-slice smile. Somewhere, he must have learned the tricks they teach beauty pageant contestants. Perhaps there was a law school class in convincing appearances, where legal eaglets learned to balance stacks of books on their heads and slather petroleum jelly on their teeth.

Increasingly, Jess disliked and distrusted the man. When his cheery predictions failed to pan out, Grantham had a ready arsenal of players and situations to blame. Judge Harrigan was a hardnose. The public pendulum had swung impossibly far to the side of alleged victims' rights. People resented solid, good-looking kids, especially brainy jocks like Danny, who inspired jealousy and a mindless urge for revenge. Even judges were not immune to such subconscious forces.

Nothing was ever Grantham's miscalculation or shortfall. Never once did the lawyer question or doubt a single thing that he had or had not done. Jess could picture him at the end of this, scaling their defeated remains in his crocodile loafers, planting his designer flag, and claiming some perverse, personal victory.

Today marked the fourth time they had been summoned to Harrigan's courtroom for some nameless step on the convoluted road toward trial. They were veterans.

Grantham winked to acknowledge their presence, then returned to his call. The tiny flip-phone perched like a cockroach on his face. "Don't give me that, Peterson. I want those charts in my office and ready to go by Thursday latest. . . . No, I cannot reschedule the depositions. They've been postponed twice already, and Warner is threatening my client with contempt. What am I supposed to tell him? 'Sorry, Your Honor, turns out the consultant I hired to do exhibits has this very important golf tournament at his club, so the wheels of justice will just have to come to a grinding halt until the putz putts out.' Sure, Peterson, that will go down real well. . . . That's right. Thursday morning. By ten."

Grantham snapped the phone and slipped it in the pocket of his silver Cerutti suit. He was always quick to flash his fancy labels, anxious to show which drain your hard-earned dollars were going down. He glad-handed Charlie and Danny, then Jess. "Good news, folks. I understand that the state's attorney plans to make some hush-hush announcement today. My guess, he's ready to plea-bargain. So let's talk strategy, shall we? What's our bottom line?"

"We need to understand the possibilities first," said Charlie. "What is he likely to offer?"

"What matters is what we're willing to take, Dr. Magill. My recommendation is probation, worst case. And we may have to agree to toss them some kind of a bone for show. Community service maybe. An electronic monitor or a curfew of some kind for a few months. The point is I don't want our boy doing time. I presume we're all in agreement on that."

Danny did not react. For all the interest he displayed, they might have been discussing municipal bonds instead of his future. Jess watched this with growing concern. At the most critical times, he seemed to pull away, turned in on himself. Dr. Rebold's warnings haunted her. *The boy is at risk.*

"Why should he have to plead guilty at all?" she said. "He didn't do anything."

"I agree with you, Mrs. Magill. But we need to be realistic. If we go to court, there's always the possibility that the jury will find against him."

Jess was sick of his convenient memory lapses. He had a fresh contradictory explanation handy to suit every situation. "You said all we needed to do was establish reasonable doubt."

"Absolutely true. At least, that's how it's supposed to work."

"Then isn't it your job to see that it does?"

She ignored Charlie's stern look that proclaimed she had trampled some sacred line. Naturally Senior's strong objection to Grantham had turned Charlie into an avid supporter. But Jess was determined to keep her focus fixed on results, not politics. She didn't care if the man was a pompous ass, as long as he was a pompous ass who was capable, if it came to that, of winning an acquittal.

"Let me try to explain," Grantham said with exaggerated patience. "Juries are like women in a dress shop. They make emotional decisions and not always wise ones. They can be influenced by the slightest, most irrational forces."

Jess matched his steady smile with one of her own. His contempt for women was his problem, not hers. "Let me see if I understand. You're saying that it doesn't matter whether the lawyer builds a competent case or not."

"Of course it matters. It just isn't a guarantee." For a moment his grin slipped, and Jess caught a glimpse of the insecure bully that was Gus Grantham's inner little boy.

The lawyer flared the front of his jacket, showing his label again, showing exactly what he was made of—stuff. "I'm saying that he shouldn't go to trial if we can get a reasonable deal. It's a crapshoot. You'd be betting the satisfaction of a not guilty verdict against the possible downside of twenty years in prison. I call those odds unacceptable, don't you?"

He spoke to Jess as if she were a slow-witted child. "I call all of this unacceptable," she snapped.

The clerk knocked. "Harrigan's called a ten-minute recess, Mr. Grantham. You're up next."

"Thanks, Nick. Let's go, folks."

Danny pushed out his chair and rose wearily. Grantham gripped him by the scruff and gave an affectionate shake. "This could be the day, Mr. Magill. Let's hope this is the last time you have to look at old Harry Harrigan's nasty puss."

That thought brought a wan smile to the teenager's face. He stood straighter, and a hint of life lightened his listless stride. Danny held that hopeful posture until they stepped through the polished double doors that led to courtroom 2. Then he stopped with a sudden jolt as if he had hit a wall.

Danny and Grantham were in the lead. Jess could not see past them. "What is it?" she asked.

Charlie drew her close, and poured the chilling news in her ear. "The Beningsons are here." He leaned forward and set a reassuring hand on Danny's shoulder. "Go on, son. It's all right."

Danny moved as if his joints were frozen. Grantham marched him down the center aisle like a reluctant groom and planted him in his regular place at the center of the defense table. The lawyer sat beside him, opened his briefcase, and arranged his features in their customary uphill slant.

The assistant state's attorney, Paul Rodell, occupied the center chair on the prosecution side. Rodell was a slim, humorless man with the lockstep heart and soul of a civil servant. To the spectators' gallery, he presented a monk's tonsure rimmed by a horseshoe of fading strawberry curls. A dark brow and brushy red mustache made him look as if he'd been patched together from spare parts. His brown suit hung from his bony frame. Unimpressive as he appeared, Attorney Rodell was a smart, talented, dedicated advocate for the citizens of the state of Connecticut.

Jess and Charlie sat in the third row. The first two were reserved for lawyers and police. Her gaze drifted across the aisle where Lisa hunched between her parents.

The girl's hair was drawn in a ponytail, bound by an ivory clip. She wore a chaste white long-sleeved blouse, buttoned to the throat, and a pleated navy skirt from some designer's parochial school collection. No makeup, not even a trace of color on her lips, though she'd been in the habit since seventh grade of wearing a full complement of the latest fashion shades whenever she came to visit Danny or sit for the younger kids. Molly would listen raptly when the older girl regaled her with the latest beauty news, straight from *Elle* magazine. *The look for fall is what they call forest naturals. Soft greens and brown shades for cheeks, eyes, and lips.* Her unadorned eyes met Jess's for a pained instant, and then fell away.

Leo Beningson shot Jess a murderous look, then whispered something to his wife. She nodded nervously and fiddled with the pastel chiffon scarf that draped the lapels of her ivory suit like a prayer shawl. Sandra Beningson could not bring herself to look at Jess. Small wonder.

Jess could not count the number of meals Lisa had eaten at their table, the number of times they had taken the girl along on family outings. Leo Beningson liked things clean, quiet, and orderly. None of the kids, Lisa included, felt all that comfortable in the house. And how many times had Sandra Beningson looked to Jess for advice? She was a sorry soul, drowning in insecurities. Jess had never failed to listen and offer what solace she could. More than once, she had suggested gently that Sandra seek counseling. But the woman was certain her husband would never allow such a thing. Leo believed that psychotherapy was a sign of weakness, not to mention a waste of time and money. All of life's really important problems could be solved by a talented golf pro or a clever interior decorator.

Jess faced down Leo Beningson and fired off a lethal round of her own. Danny was the victim here, not that lying little wretch. They could dress Lisa up like a junior mother superior as they usually did, they could buy her a jeweled halo from the Tiffany's born-again virgin department, but that did not change the facts.

Having sex had been Lisa's idea. Jess did not doubt that for an instant. Danny had never seen the girl as anything but a pal. Never once, in the thousands of times Jess had watched them together, had he shown even a hint of interest in converting their buddy relationship into anything else.

Lisa was the one who often eyed Danny when she thought no one was looking, the way Prozac would stare lovingly at a steak. Jess had observed how the girl sparked with pain when Danny said he thought Jennifer Slavin was a fox and maybe he'd ask her out. For as long as Jess could remember, Lisa's crush on Danny had seemed like an innocent, sweetly amusing fact of life. She'd never imagined how that innocence could grow twisted and sprout thorns.

Grantham rose and strode to the prosecution table. He gesticulated grandly as he conferred with the assistant state's attorney. Rodell's face betrayed nothing. Grantham's ran the gamut from amusement to dismay and back again.

Jess was trying to read the situation when someone tapped her shoulder.

A rawboned, sallow woman loomed over her on the aisle. "Excuse me, Mrs. Magill. I just wanted to say how impressed I am by your courage."

Jess shrugged. "Thanks."

"If that was my kid, I don't know what I'd do. Probably take a knife to him, where it counts."

Jess turned away, cheeks flaming.

"How do you keep your head up?" the woman went on. "Don't you people have any shame? Any decency?"

"Leave us alone," Charlie rasped. "Or I'll show you exactly what we have."

His menacing tone pushed her back a step. "Well. I can certainly see where he gets it. Like father like son."

A restless flurry presaged the arrival of the judge. Grantham's look was tight as he took his place at the defense table. Rodell drew a folder from an accordion file.

The bailiff, a wizened little man, clasped his hands. "Hear ye, hear ye, all those having business before this court, draw nigh and be heard. The Honorable Harold Harrigan presiding. All rise."

His Honor appeared on cue. Harrigan was a ruddy, broad-browed septuagenarian with a whip of silver hair. Silver-framed glasses perched near the tip of his bulbous nose. Peering over them, he addressed the prosecutor.

"Where are we on this matter, Counselor?"

Rodell stood. "At this juncture, the state sees no alternative but to request an early date for trial."

Harrigan nudged his glasses farther up his nose. "You've exhausted all other options?"

Rodell took in the Beningsons with a sweep of his arm. "The gravity of the charge here cannot be overlooked, Your Honor. The state cannot ask victims of serious crime to turn the other cheek in the interest of expediency."

"This court makes no such request and never has," Harrigan said sternly.

"It was not my intention to suggest that, Your Honor."

"I would hope not, Mr. Rodell."

"May we approach?" Grantham asked.

Harrigan motioned his assent.

Both lawyers huddled with the judge. Moments later, Harrigan led them into his chambers.

A low buzz rose in the visitors' gallery, which had swelled to near capacity with curious spectators and members of the local press. Danny shifted in his seat and turned to look at Jess. She answered his silent question with a shrug.

Across the aisle, Leo Beningson was talking to a reporter. Jess caught random scraps of the conversation. *We cannot have animals like him roaming the streets. There should be a death penalty for this. As long as he's walking around a free man, no young girl is safe.* The reporter was nodding, taking notes.

Charlie was watching this too. "Let him talk, Jess. Who cares?"

"I do. And so should you. Everyone knows that printing something makes it true. That's Newton's fifth law. The one about conservation of bullshit."

"Sticks and stones," Charlie said. "We need to stand above all this, my love." He raised her hand and kissed it in a grand gesture meant to be observed. If this were a film, there would have been raucous applause, inspirational music swelling in the background. In a film it would have been the time to fade to black and roll the end credits.

That was the fleeting fantasy Jess entertained as the door to Harrigan's chambers opened. If this ended now, today, they could patch the holes and get on with their lives. Danny could get back to school, send out his college applications. They could be a regular family again. Jess could rebuild her sagging practice. She would have strength again for other people's issues. There was still hope for everything to be redeemed.

The attorneys and the judge reentered the courtroom and claimed their respective spots. Grantham's signature grin was intact. Rodell maintained his standard deadpan. Harrigan had the weary guise of someone who had spent forty years mucking through a fetid dump, digging up human detritus, raw evil, hideous debris.

The judge planted his elbows on the bench, so his flowing sleeves drooped like broken bat wings. "New information has just come to the attention of the court that could change the complexion of this matter. I ask that the parties review and reassess their positions in the light of these new facts and prepare to reconvene in, shall we say, one week?" He caught nods of assent from both attorneys. "Fine, then. This court stands adjourned!"

The Beningsons filed out first and stood in the hall conferring with the prosecutor. Grantham led the Magills out and steered them in the opposite direction, toward the conference room. They passed a reporter from the *Stamford Advocate,* talking at a breathless clip on the pay phone. She cupped the receiver so she could not be heard.

Grantham ushered them inside and closed the door. "Sit please. We need to talk."

Jess was bristling with impatience. "What's the new information?"

"Easy, Mrs. Magill. All cases have their ups and downs."

"What happened?" Charlie asked.

"What did Lisa say about me now?" Danny groaned.

"It's not Lisa. Another girl claims you assaulted her after a party late last spring. She claims she was too fearful and ashamed to tell anybody, but when she read about the other charge, she felt she had to come forward."

The color leached from his face. "What girl?"

"Her name is Roseanne Paris. You know her?"

"Barely. She goes to Westhill High."

"The party was in Shippan, on Soundview Avenue at the home of people named Segal. What can you tell me about it?"

Danny's voice was a shiver. "A bunch of us were hanging out at Friendly's, and someone said there was this party going on and we should stop by. When we got there, it was a mob scene. Hundreds of kids. A couple of those idiot West Side boys were drunk and carrying on, trying to pick fights with everybody. The whole thing had the feel of bad things waiting to happen, so we decided to leave after a little while."

Grantham made some notes. "Tell me everything that happened between you and the Paris girl."

"I saw her there and said hello. The music was so loud it was hard to talk to anyone."

"Did you dance with her? Were you seen together? What was the content of your conversation? Did you say anything suggestive to her? Anything at all?"

Danny clutched his skull. "Please. I can't answer everything at once."

Grantham's gaze skittered to his watch. "Here's the drill, Danny. You're going to be charged with that crime. Rodell has agreed to allow you to surrender and avoid the humiliation of a public arrest. We've got ten minutes, then I need to take you in. Hand you over. Before I do, I need to know everything that happened between you and that girl. Did you touch her? Kiss her? Do anything at all out of line?"

"They're putting me in jail again?"

"Standard procedure. We'll have you out on bail by the end of the day. Now stick with me, Danny. Were you out of line in any way with Roseanne Paris?"

"No."

"Were you alone together?"

Something flashed behind the teenager's eyes. "For a little while, we were. Her car door was stuck. She asked me to help her open it. It took maybe five minutes."

Grantham frowned. "Where was this?"

"Right in front of the house, on the street."

The frown deepened as the lawyer consulted his notes. "You said there were hundreds of kids hanging around. Now suddenly, you and this Paris girl were alone in front of the house. It doesn't add up."

"I can't help that. It's the truth."

"Your story has to be consistent and believable," Grantham said. "Nobody is going to buy a fairy tale. Harrigan's not stupid and neither is Rodell. If you come across as a liar, you've got two strikes against you going in."

Slowly, Danny's head came up. Furious defiance was splashed across his face. "What do you want me to say? I threw her down? I threatened her and forced her to have sex with me?"

Grantham looked him hard in the eye. "Is that the way it was?"

"What difference does it make? I am what they think I am. Them and you."

"I asked how it was, Danny," the lawyer persisted. "What happened at the party that night?"

The boy fell silent. The question hung like an icy chill in the air.

TWENTY-FIVE

The conference room at police headquarters had been dressed for the public occasion. An array of books adorned the broad wooden desk where the police commission sat for its monthly policy-making sessions. There was a Bible, several volumes on forensics and the law, a slim work pompously entitled *A Comprehensive Analysis and History of Stamford, Connecticut, and Environs.*

The photos of former police chiefs and antique police department scenes that lined the walls had been polished and precisely aligned. The pungent scent of cleaning solvents rose from the patterned green carpeting. A dozen extra metal-frame black chairs had been added to the forty or so normally provided for interested parties and petitioners to the police commission meetings. Today, the clerical staffers and plainclothes officers who had been conscripted to pack the room occupied the seats. Tucci, who had been nabbed on his way to the men's room, was among them. He sat holding his newspaper and coffee cup, still needing to use the can. He wondered if the articles of the Geneva Convention covered a situation like this. His bowels were more than ready to file the complaint.

Half of Chief Klonsky's harsh, leathery face was lost behind a bouquet of gleaming microphones. A sudden volley of flash pops sent several seasoned hands lurching for hidden guns.

Klonsky waited for a moment of dramatic silence, then cleared his throat. "Based on recent events, we are prepared to launch a comprehensive special initiative to stamp out sex crimes and violence against women in all forms in this community. This is to be a coordinated effort, launched on multiple fronts. The superintendent of schools has agreed to institute appropriate programs at every educational level to teach our children mutual respect and proper boundaries. The mayor has authorized extra police patrols and increased resources to assist victims and prosecute perpetrators. The Voluntary Action Center will contribute public service announcements and distribute public information brochures.

"Personally, I promise to seek out and shut down any enterprise in this city that encourages or tolerates inappropriate sexual behavior or exploitation of women or girls. I ask that every citizen do his or her part to assist us in ensuring the success of this endeavor, which is reflected in our motto:'Be aware, be involved, be safe.' "

Klonsky pointed to the fabric medallion draped beside the replica police shield at the front of the room. Above the motto was a plump bee with a Madonna smile and round eyes like Betty Boop. *Bee aware, bee involved, bee safe.*

That was a real *stinger,* Tucci thought, snickering into his hand, bound to raise a *buzz.*

Around him, several other shills from the force covered their mouths and coughed to hide their laughter.

"At this time, I'd like to open this up to questions from the floor," Klonsky said.

Sally Chandler, a forceful brunette with a Dutchboy do, sprang to her feet. "Is this about the Daniel Magill case, Chief Klonsky?"

"It would be highly inappropriate for me to discuss a case in progress, Ms. Chandler. The charges against Mr. Magill need to be managed through proper legal channels, not in the media. I'm sure you understand."

A lame smile smashed against Klonsky's hard features, then dribbled down his face like a broken egg. Rumor had it that the mayor had been pushing the chief to give the department a more human, community-minded face.

The force had been hit hard by the old chief's departure. Lou Silver, well loved and esteemed, had held the place in a cohesive whole for seventeen years. In short order Klonsky's sledgehammer mentality and hit-and-run management style had trashed department loyalty and morale. Those who could were opting for early retirement or altered careers. Several others had ridden their disaffection and frustration to the low road.

In the past months there had been a measurable uptick in brutality complaints and way too many questionable arrests. Two weeks ago, there was a highly public and very embarrassing incident involving a pack of smashed officers caught partying late one night with a couple of hookers in the LoPresto Funeral Home, clad in nothing but black socks and holstered revolvers.

The widow and three daughters of the late Mr. Alvin Teasdale had happened in on the revelry when they could not sleep and stopped by to sit with their dear departed. They'd found Mr. Teasdale, who had died at eighty-seven after a life of quiet piety, propped in his deluxe-model Eternal Slumber mahogany coffin with a frosted beer mug in his hand and a hot-pink lip imprint on his cheek. A patrolman's hat sat askew on the old man's head. Most horrifying of all, according to his traumatized daughter, Mr. Teasdale appeared to be smiling.

The host of a local radio talk show took the floor. "Exactly who's supposed to pay for this special initiative, Chief Klonsky?"

"The funds will come through normal budgetary channels."

"You mean, more of our tax money will be made available so that your officers can buy ever better brands of hooch and higher-class call girls. Nothing but the best for our boys in blue, I always say."

"I share your frustration and dismay over that unfortunate incident, Mr. Donlon. But I hardly think it's fair or reasonable to indict the entire department for the misguided actions of a few. Those officers have been properly disciplined, and in any event, no tax money was involved."

"It takes tax money to discipline officers, doesn't it?"

"Now you're splitting hairs, Mr. Donlon."

"If splitting hairs means being precise, I'll plead guilty."

Klonsky swatted the air in dismissal. *Bee gone!* "I believe we should concentrate on the anti-assault initiative."

A reporter from *Connecticut* magazine caught the chief's nod. "During your four-year tenure in Detroit, there was a twenty percent increase in the incidence of violent crime and a twenty-seven percent increase in aggravated rape, sexual assault, and domestic violence. Any comment, Chief Klonsky?"

"There are lies, damned lies, and statistics, Mr. Bedell. As a journalist, I would think you would have developed a healthy skepticism about making snap judgments from something as misleading as so-called percentages of change."

Bedell petted his thin brown goatee. "Actually, Chief, I did a comprehensive analysis of your performance in Detroit versus crime statistics for comparable cities during the same time period nationwide. I did the same thing comparing the record during your year as acting chief in Seattle back before Detroit. An increase in violent crimes, especially sex crimes, seems to follow you around."

"Lies, damned lies, and reporters," Klonsky spat. "My record speaks for itself. I won't dignify such nonsense by defending it."

Another hand shot up. It belonged to a paunchy balding man Tucci did not recognize. "My name is Victor Alton, Chief Klonsky. I represent the Briarwood neighborhood association, which happens to be where Daniel Magill lives. We want to know what you plan to do about getting dangerous people like that Magill kid put away. I have two daughters, and I'm afraid to let them leave the house alone. My wife and I are losing time at work, my girls are virtual prisoners in the house, and that boy is free to run around and do whatever he pleases. You think that's right? You call that justice?"

"As I said earlier, this is not the proper venue for dealing with the Magill case or any other matter currently under investigation. Rest assured, Mr. Alton, we're doing everything in our power to bring this matter to an early, satisfactory resolution."

Alton scowled. "I don't rest assured at all. That boy is a menace. If you can't offer us proper protection, we'll find a way to do it ourselves."

"All of us need to keep our heads and stay within the law," Klonsky said. He waited a beat for further questions. "Thank you all for coming. Good day."

Cameras flashed as the chief struck a deliberate pose beside the bee medallion. *Bee-eautiful.*

Tucci led the charge to the rear, eager to complete his thwarted trip to the can. His stomach had not been amused by the unscheduled delay. Several months of stressful days and sleepless nights had taken their toll. Treating his alimentary canal like a garbage disposal had not helped the situation. But he was stopped at the men's room door by a bellowed summons from behind.

"I need to see you in my office, Detective. ASAP."

"Give me five minutes, Chief. Okay?"

Klonsky pointed at the floor. "I'm talking right now, Sergeant. Immediately. Chop chop."

Tucci remembered Sister Marguerite, who had refused to let him leave the room in second grade. He'd had to hand out three black eyes and a bloody nose before the kids stopped calling him Betsy Wetsy. He'd sworn to himself way back then never again. Not for anybody.

"If you need to see me right now, I'll be in here. Can't miss me. Just follow your nose "

Tucci didn't worry much about sinking any lower on the list. As expected, Klonsky was in an even fouler than normal mood when Tucci entered his office. As usual, he was tapping on his desk. Tucci named the tune immediately. "I've Got You Under My Skin."

"Why don't you quit, Detective? Save us both the trouble of keeping up this stupid charade. I don't like you; you don't like me. We agree on that. Fortunately, I'm in charge, so all that matters is the part about me not liking you."

"All I want is to do my job."

"Why don't you do it then?" Klonsky planted his elbows on the desk and propped his square jaw on his hands. "I want to make this simple for you, Tucci. Bring it down to your level, as best I can. I assigned you to this Magill thing because I knew you'd screw it up. And you haven't disappointed me in the least. I've got to hand it to you, Sergeant. I've worked with plenty of losers in my time, major bonzos, but you've given a brand-new meaning to the word inept."

"I've followed every lead, Chief, churned the evidence, interviewed dozens of people. I can't pull rabbits out of an empty hat."

"It's your head that's empty, Tucci. Now why don't you be a good fellow and resign? I'm sure you'd make a wonderful shoe salesman or maybe an Avon lady. Go somewhere, Tucci. Anywhere but here. What do you say?"

"Sorry, Chief. No can do. I'd miss you too much."

Klonsky tipped back his chair and planted his spit-shined shoes on the desk.

"Fine, Detective. We'll do it the hard way. You'll just keep on handing me more and more rope until I have enough to hang you with. Shouldn't take too long with the way you've been going. This fake witness of yours was a fine start."

Tucci's bowels started churning again. "The woman lied. How in hell is that my fault?"

"It's called lousy judgment. Make that no judgment."

"You weren't there, Chief. She was good. Convincing. She came across solid, smart, together. I had no reason to doubt her."

Tucci's self-defense was all the more strident because he knew the chief had a point. His head was so full of mutating viral strains, exotic toxins, and abject terror, he couldn't see or think clearly. He was operating on half a cylinder, maybe less. Making mistakes, no matter how hard he tried to avoid them. "She was good," he said again, dully.

"I bet she was. She's had plenty of practice." Klonsky plucked a note from his pocket, fashioned it into a paper airplane, and sent it in for a landing on Tucci's lap.

The page was a computer-generated record of Dolores Wainscott's past complaints. There were dozens of them against a staggering variety of people, including a retarded five-year-old neighbor child Dolores had accused of stealing a ring and six separate men, including an Orthodox rabbi, against whom she had lodged formal charges of stalking. Other people took aspirin to counter common aches and irritations. Dolores Wainscott took revenge.

"She was convincing," Tucci said again.

Klonsky wove his fingers together and tapped his thumbs. Tucci could not name the tune, but it was something they played at funerals. "Let's put crazy Dolores aside for a moment and move on to something far more serious. I've been making inquiries about your partner, Mike Samuels. No one I've asked has seen him lately, not since the department inquiry into a rather stunning instance of misjudgment of his own. So what's the deal, Tucci? Where is he and where has he been?"

Tucci's mind ran in tight little circles until he found a tiny crack to slip through. "Mule's been keeping away from headquarters as much as he can, because he's having trouble facing people after what happened with that little girl. But he's holding up his end in the field, and he's working with a private shrink to get over it."

"Is that so?" Klonsky was still tapping. "Let me tell you a story, Sergeant. Once upon time there were nine-year-old twin boys. They were absolutely identical in every way, except that one boy was an optimist and the other one was a realist. Now, their parents loved practical jokes, and they were not very nice people. When the boys' birthday came around, the parents walked them out to the backyard and showed them two giant piles of horse manure. 'There are your gifts,' the mother said.

"The realist felt terribly hurt and disappointed, and he started to cry. But the optimist ran right over to that great big pile of manure and started to dig with his bare hands. When the father asked what on earth he was doing, the boy turned with a big smile on his face and said, 'I figure, with all this horseshit, there's got to be a pony in there somewhere.' "

Tucci steeped like a tea bag in the uneasy silence. When he started to squirm, the chief said, "I'm a realist, Sergeant. If there's a pony in that pile of horseshit you're trying to sell me, he'd better be sitting in my office first thing tomorrow morning. He'd better have his mane combed and his tail braided, or I'll have you up on charges of conspiracy to defraud so fast your head will be spinning."

Tucci held his tongue. Whatever he said would only dig him in deeper.

"If you manage somehow to pass go, I'd better see real, solid progress in the Magill case. Harrigan's pushing for an early calendar date. The state's attorney wants the kid tried on both charges as close to back-to-back as we can get them. He's thinking double whammy. Hit them while they're down. The obvious downside is that if we lose trial one, we go into the second in leg irons. Bring me the evidence, Tucci. Bring me the experts. Hang the little scum."

Tucci's parts were rattling, but he tried not to let it show. "I'll do it, Chief. I'll give it everything I've got."

"That's what I'm afraid of, Detective. Exactly."

TWENTY-SIX

How are you holding up, Jess?" Libby asked. "Is there anything I can do?"
"Actually there is. Glad you called. What I need you to do is make me
a couple of years older. What do you say?"

"Oh, honey. I wish I could. I can imagine how tough this must be for you,
for all of you."

Jess's eyes filled. She had not cried this much since infancy, and it was hell
on her looks. Her features were so lumpy and swollen she resembled a depressed
Mrs. Potato Head. "It's the kids I'm worried about mostly. Of course, it's the
hardest on Danny, but Max and Molly are both in a terrible place."

"No they're not, Jessie. They're with you."

"Thanks, Libby. You always know just what to say."

"It's true. The best any parent can do for kids is love them."

"That I do, even when I want to wring their necks."

The doorbell startled her. "Someone's here. I'd better go see who it is."

"Go—maybe it's something good for a change. Maybe it's that prize committee come to drop off your check."

"Sure. I'll tell Ed McMahon you say hello."

The news was nothing nearly as welcome as that. Pearl stood on the porch
in a barber pole sweater set and red slacks. There was something disconcerting
about her appearance, and it took Jess a moment to divine that her mother had
arrived without the cooler. This was almost as strange as seeing her all those
years ago without the towel, dripping naked in her rage, shouting Yiddish
obscenities.

She treated Jess to her famous *punim,* a face foul enough to rot fresh fruit,
then burst inside without a word. Lou stayed in their vintage blue Cadillac on
the driveway. He was slouched in the driver's seat, bearing a look of conster-
nation.

"Where's my little darling?" Pearl shrilled. "Grandma's here, sweetheart. I
came as quickly as I could. Are you all packed?"

Molly trotted down the stairs, toting a red canvas duffel bag. She gave herself over to Pearl's asphyxiating embrace. "I'm ready, Gram."

"Whoa, wait a minute. Ready for what?" Jess asked.

Pearl planted herself in front of the child, forming a pudgy shield. "She's coming to stay with me for a while, Jessie, until things settle down." Over her shoulder, she rasped, "Go, darling. Wait with Papa Lou in the car while I talk to your mother. I'll be out in five minutes."

"Right, Gram. I'll call you, Mom. Okay?"

"No, it's *not* okay. We need to talk about this, Molly, right now."

"Don't make a big thing of this, Jessie. It's all arranged. She can start at Southside Junior High on Monday. They have a wonderful program for smart girls like her, with French and math and science and all that nonsense. Oh, and Molly darling, I spoke to the lady at the gymnastics place, and she'll be delighted to have you come to class. I told her how you do all those twirlygigs and whochamawhatsees, and she said it sounds like you probably belong in her advanced group, but I said I thought the intermediate is plenty. Much better to be a big fish in a little pond. Play it safe. Don't you think?"

"Whatever. Can we go?"

Jess sidestepped her mother and took Molly's bag. "You're not going anywhere until we talk about this, Molly. I want you to come upstairs with me, now."

Pearl tried to wrestle the duffel bag from Jess's grip. "I said she could stay with us, Jessie. Now stop being so stubborn."

Jess surrendered the luggage, but she had no intention of doing the same with her daughter. "Come, Molly. Make yourself at home, Mom. Feel free to help yourself to anything inanimate." Halfway up the stairs, she paused. "Maybe you'd better ask Lou to come inside. This might take a while."

Jess led the child to her bedroom and shut the door. Molly stood with her back to the wall and her small face arranged in a dare. "It doesn't matter what you say, Mom. I've made up my mind. I'm going."

"I'm troubled that you didn't discuss this with me and Dad. What's the problem? Why do you want to go stay with Grandma?" Jess could not imagine anything in the universe awful enough to drive a person to choose to live with Pearl.

"I don't have a problem, Mom. I just want to go."

"Sorry, sweetie. That's not good enough. If you have a legitimate reason, I'll take it under consideration and discuss it with Dad. But I'm not going to allow you to leave just because. We love you. We're your family. This is where you belong."

The child set her jaw and crossed her arms. The outsized sweatshirt draped in generous folds over the pencil-slim jeans. "This is *not* where I belong. I *hate* it here, and I'm *leaving*."

"Then you need to tell me why."

"What do you care? If I go, you'll have more time to spend with your precious baby and Mr. Innocence."

So this was another demand for equal time. A cry for attention. At least, Molly's method hadn't resulted in an orgy of shattered crockery and glass. "I'm sorry if you feel shortchanged, Molly. I know that this business with Danny must be very hard on you. Maybe I haven't been doing such a hot job of listening and watching what you need. I'll try to do better, honey. I hear you."

Molly rolled her eyes. "I don't feel shortchanged, Mom. You just don't get it at all."

"Then explain it to me. You are not going anywhere until you do, Molly. You don't just run away because something doesn't please you. That's not how it works in this house."

The revulsion on her daughter's face tied Jess's intestines in knots. Maybe she should simply let the kid go. Make her life easier.

Danny had been spending more and more of his excessive free time in his room, blasting music so he could not hear or be heard. His friend Emma was the only one capable of coaxing him to talk, but she was up to her sympathetic ears in schoolwork. Max rarely came inside these days except to eat and sleep. Charlie seized every excuse to stay away as well, absorbing himself in his precious work and who knew what else. And Molly had taken on every new commitment she could find: clubs, volunteer work, school projects that kept her at the library until they locked the doors. Often Jess, whose practice had fallen off to near nothing, found herself alone in the sprawling place with Prozac, trying to keep out of her own way.

Jess found it difficult enough to deal with her own superheated emotions. In a sense she was grateful that Charlie and the kids were staging tactical retreats. Maybe letting Molly run off to her grandmother's house was the right answer. At the very least, a couple of weeks with Pearl would put the child in a much more appreciative frame of mind. Jess would seem like a true mother superior by comparison.

"I don't care what you say, Mom. I'm going." Molly wrenched the door open and started toward the hall.

Jess blocked the door. "I'm not saying you can't go, Molly. But there has to be a good reason, and I need to know what it is."

"I don't need your permission."

"Yes you do."

"You don't own me, Mom. Nobody does."

"All I'm asking for is a reason."

The girl's eyes brimmed with tears. "I have to get out of here. Don't you see?"

Jess drew the child to her, and stroked her hair. The trim Parisian hairdo had grown out, so she felt like the old Molly again, a mass of soft, springy curls capping a core of knotty contradictions. Molly was Jess's most challenging child; at least, she always had been until now. Jess understood her daughter least well, found her the most confusing. In certain ways they were so alike that knowing Molly fully would seem like the end of Jess's lifelong independent study course in herself. Other times, the child struck Jess as an alien creature, impossible to know or predict.

When Molly was an infant, Jess had had a morbid fear of crushing her tiny bones. She would bite her lip when she picked the baby up, reminding herself not to hold on too tightly. But now, every instinct told her it would be wrong to let her simply take her secret suffering and go.

Molly's tears soaked the shoulder of Jess's blouse. "Please, Mommy. Please."

"What's wrong, sweetheart? Tell me."

"I can't," she wailed. "I just have to get away."

"I'll make you the following deal. If you still want to go to Gram's in a week or so, maybe you can. But I want to take some time first to talk it over with Dad, figure out what's bothering you and what we can do to fix it."

The child pulled away. "I can't wait a week. I have to go now." Her cries took on a desperate shrill.

"Why, Molly?"

"No, Mom. Please."

"Tell me."

Molly groaned. "I have to get away from Danny. Don't you see?"

Jess grasped her slim shoulders, felt sinew over toothpick bones. "What are you talking about?"

"He did what those girls said."

"No, honey. It's not true."

"Everyone thinks he did. Otherwise, why would that other girl accuse him too?"

That same question had been spinning in Jess's mind for days. "There could be lots of reasons. Fantasies. Emotional illness. Maybe she wants to get her name in the paper, feel important. I don't care what she said. I know Danny and so do you. The court will find him innocent."

"Lisa told the truth, Mom. I know she did."

"You weren't there, Molly. How can you know anything?"

The child unleashed a fearsome wail. "Because he did it to me."

Jess's blood froze, her heart froze, everything. A small eternity passed before she was able to find her voice.

"When did this happen?"

"I was little. Five maybe."

"So Danny was nine." Jess wanted to dismiss this as innocent child's play, but it could be something more. In clinical publications and the popular press, there were frequent accounts of monster children, capable of murder, sex crimes, who knew what, at impossibly tender ages.

"Maxy was an infant." Molly mopped her eyes on her sleeve. "That kid Becky Trainer was sitting for us one night when you and Daddy went out. She was downstairs on the phone practically from the minute she got here, talking to her stupid boyfriend. Danny and I got sick of listening to her, so we went upstairs to watch TV in your room.

"There was nothing on but dumb stuff, boring reruns, so Danny said we should turn the set off and play a game. He told me to sit on his lap. He said we should pretend that we were boyfriend and girlfriend like Becky and Joe and kiss each other good night. He kissed me on the mouth for a long, long time, pressing really hard until my teeth hurt."

Jess's heart threatened to leap out of her chest. "And then what?"

"Danny was wearing boxers. I remember they were some dark color. There was this opening in the front so I could see his—thing. It was sticking up, poking around. And it was all ugly and purple and gross."

Molly flushed and covered her eyes.

Blood was sloshing in Jess's head, raising such a racket she could barely think. She let the words form, then forced them out. "Then what happened, sweetheart?"

Molly's hands dropped and her features scrunched in unpleasant surprise. "Isn't that enough?"

"He didn't hurt you or touch you except for the kiss?"

"No."

"Did Danny ever ask you to play a game like that again?"

"No, but I wouldn't have even if he did. I wouldn't have that time if I wasn't just a dumb little kid."

Jess was rising to the surface, breaking through, able to draw a decent breath. "That was it? You told me everything? You're sure?"

"He made me want to puke, Mom. I'm telling you, it was really disgusting."

"I understand, sweetheart. But it's normal for children to be curious about their bodies, to play games and experiment."

"I never did."

"Actually, you did."

"When?"

"Remember the time the Garbers came over and you and Tommy were upstairs playing and he got Daddy's medical bag out of the linen closet?"

Molly's hand flew to her mouth. "Oh my God, I do remember. We were playing you show me yours and I'll show you mine. Tommy said I looked really bad down there, and I told him he did too. We decided we needed casts like you had that time when you broke your finger, so we used up all of Daddy's tape and bandages. We wrapped up practically our whole bodies, and then I realized I had to go to the bathroom, really really badly, so I had to call you guys to come help me out."

Tears of relieved laughter streamed down Jess's cheeks. "Walt Garber was Daddy's boss at the medical school in those days. I'd arranged this really elegant dinner party to impress him and his wife. You two kids turned out to be very interesting entertainment."

"Ouch. Daddy could have been fired or something."

"No, Molly. You and Tommy were just expressing normal curiosity. Most kids do at some point. It's harmless."

"I guess."

"Do you remember how old you kids were?"

Molly took a long time to answer. "Nine?"

"Exactly."

Her look went sheepish. "What am I supposed to do about Grandma?"

"You can say that you've changed your mind. I'm sure she'll understand."

"Grandma? Are you kidding? She'll be devastated. She'll have one of her infarctions."

"She'll get over it."

"I feel bad. Maybe I should go just for the weekend. At least then she won't have driven all the way up here for nothing."

"Sounds like a good compromise."

"Okay, I'll tell her. Wish me luck."

Jess waited upstairs for ten minutes, long enough for Pearl's ruffled feathers to settle. When she reappeared, Pearl was in the kitchen, bustling about. Molly had gone to the bathroom. Lou sat at the table, still wearing his flannel-lined khaki jacket. The air was heavy with the rich smell of beef gravy. "I ran out in such a hurry I didn't bring a thing, Jessie. But all is not lost. I looked in your freezer, and there were half a dozen packages of brisket. I popped a couple in the microwave, and look. Good as new." She lifted the plate of meat in her fingers and pressed a dripping slice on Jess.

"I don't want any."

"Go on. Take a little taste, Jessie."

The cloying, fatty smell made Jess's gorge rise. "Thanks anyway."

"Come on. It's delicious. Try a bite."

"I do not want any brisket, Mother. Now stop!" The words came out sharper and louder than Jess had intended. Prozac, who had slept through the latest emotional holocaust curled in the rear doorway, cocked an eye. The dog's breathing quickened at the sight of the pot roast, dangling like bait from Pearl's fingers. She bounded to her feet and executed a balletic leap, snatching the meat in one smooth, graceful arc. Back on terra firma, she munched with loud smacking enthusiasm.

Pearl scratched between the floppy ears. "At least someone around here appreciates my cooking."

"Don't start, Mom. Please."

"How do you think it makes me feel to find your freezer full of food I worked so hard to make especially for you, Jessie? If you don't like my pot roast, say so. Tell the truth. I won't be insulted."

Jess was being invited into a bear trap. She chose to decline. "There were leftovers. I didn't want to throw them out, so I froze them. You brisket freezes really well."

"It does, doesn't it? Go on. Try a little bite. What can it hurt?"

"I'm not hungry."

"One bite?" Pearl coaxed. "For me?"

Jess bit.

Pearl waited for her to swallow, then frowned. "I know you're having a lot of aggravation, darling, but you have put on an awful lot of weight."

The brisket lodged like a stone in Jess's esophagus.

"You look beautiful to me, Jess," said Lou. "Just right."

Pearl dismissed his opinion with a sniff. "By the way. Did I tell you, Jessie? We've had some wonderful news for a change. Your nephew Glen was accepted early decision to Tulane."

The food finally shifted so she could speak. "That's nice."

"It's an excellent school. Very competitive. My friend Elaine's granddaughter, Cindy, applied and got rejected, and you should have heard Elaine carrying on all these years about what a genius that girl is. This ought to shut her up but good."

"How nice for you."

Pearl nodded briskly. "Rejected flat out. Not even the waiting list. Serves Elaine right. Meanwhile, you should call Larry and congratulate him."

Jess had not heard from her brother since Danny's arrest. The only time he ever called was when he wanted something, especially to brag. No doubt he would be phoning soon to crow about Glen's college acceptance. Jess could hardly wait.

"It's getting late, Mom. I know how Lou hates to drive after dark."

"Oh my, yes. Come, Lou, Molly. Let's hit the road."

While she sipped her morning coffee, Jess pored over the latest *Journal of the American Psychological Association*. The lead article reported a study of recidivism rates among sex offenders treated by a variety of means. Intensive counseling, including group work with a focus on victim empathy, had proven most effective. Subjects attending group therapy sessions three times a week for one year had a ten percent lower repeat-offense rate than a matched group treated by conventional individual therapy alone. A variety of medications, including highly controversial chemical castration drugs, had shown the least encouraging effects. The researchers concluded that it was simply too difficult to monitor subjects for compliance. If they wanted to restore their twisted urges, it was easy enough to neglect to take the pill.

Reading to the bleak conclusion, Jess shuddered. *Sex offenders remain the most difficult of all criminals to rehabilitate. Even with optimal treatment, recidivism rates of 90 percent obtain.*

Nine out of ten rapists and child molesters would repeat their crimes. They were driven by deep-seated compulsions, often stemming from a fundamental personality flaw or early abuse.

Closing the journal, she had a stern talk with herself. This had nothing to do with Danny. He was not guilty of anything except, perhaps, bad judgment. The kid had trusted the wrong girls, put himself in potentially compromising situations. He was too open, too honest, too ready to help. Or at least, he had been.

Since his arrest, Danny had turned inward. He'd tossed up walls like a city under siege. When his friend Emma called or dropped by, he opened up a bit and let his guard down. Otherwise, he was sullen, silent, a shadowy distortion of himself.

Charlie and Prozac came in from their morning walk. The dog, parched from her exertions, headed straight for the water bowl and lapped noisily. For Charlie, the stroll had aroused different appetites.

"I'd like to shoot those sons of bitches, every one of them. Bloodsucking parasite journalists."

"Don't be shy, honey. Tell me how you really feel about them."

"I caught that Preston character trying to interview Max while he was waiting for the bus. I chased him away, but not before he had the audacity to ask whether Danny had ever talked about the bad things he did to those girls. Max was annoyed with me for interfering. Apparently Preston promised to put him on television, and Max had visions of being the next Bart Simpson."

"I think Bart Simpson is actually the next Max Magill."

Todd Preston was a young local writer who planned to do a true-crime book about Danny's case. Long after the local press had gotten bored with the story, Preston continued to nose around, trying to dig up telling scraps of trash and skeleton bones.

Jess did not share Charlie's outrage. To her, Preston was a persistent but manageable annoyance, like mild ringing in the ears. When Danny was found not guilty, the writer's chance for a book deal would sink to zero. He would have nothing to show for his months of obnoxious effort but empty pockets and egg on his face.

"In a couple of months, we'll be through with him. We'd be through with him by now, if Grantham didn't keep screwing things up."

"Don't start that again, Jessie. Please."

"I didn't start it. He did," she shot back. "If he was doing his job, I'd have no objection to the man."

"He's a good lawyer. Good as any. Your own friend recommended him, for God sakes. Maybe the problem is the case. The man can't be expected to perform miracles."

Jess could see the cliff they were headed for, but she kept plunging straight ahead nonetheless. "What is wrong with getting a second opinion, Charlie? That's all I'm asking."

"It's not necessary, that's what's wrong with it. It's an extra expense we certainly don't need. Plus, it could be damaging. Two girls have accused Danny of rape. Grantham has his hands more than full without us second-guessing him. Give the guy a little credit, Jess. Maybe, just maybe he knows his job better than you do."

"You're the one who insists on getting two or three people in before you let someone fix the washing machine. You got four proposals before you hired that guy to fix the septic system. Since when did you develop all this blind, new-found trust that everyone is competent at his work?"

"Grantham is a professional. He's not some hack plumber or sludge man."

"You went for three opinions when Dr. England recommended the hernia surgery."

Charlie opened the paper with an angry snap and pretended to read. Jess took his cue and let the matter drop. These endless useless arguments were a sorry substitute for the intimacy and affection that used to characterize their private time together.

Jess mourned the loss, though she was hard-pressed to remember what it felt like to rely on Charlie, to agree with him about the important things as they almost always had. Prickly resentments and secrets had replaced their easy closeness.

Lately Jess had asked herself, more than once, if she still loved the man. It was like living through a long power outage. At first you walked around in circles, flipping on dead switches, feeling uneasy and lost. But after a while, you grew accustomed to the stillness and began to view the absence of familiar conveniences as a seductive opportunity. You turned to your own resources, considered appealing options that had not occurred to you in years. A person could get used to almost anything, she supposed, including loneliness and disappointment.

Jess's appointment was at 11:00. She planned to take the 9:48 to Manhattan, which would give her time to walk uptown and clear her head. Charlie would be on the 8:42, headed for a conference on assisted suicide.

In another life they would have gone to the station and ridden in together. At the end of the day, they might have met for dinner or a show. But today, if everything went as planned, Charlie would not even know that she had been in town.

She dressed in a black suit and pumps and carried a briefcase, more as armor than necessity. As the train lurched and jostled toward New York, she made notes to herself, jotting a list of questions. At three hundred and fifty dollars an hour, she did not intend to waste time fishing around for thoughts.

Struggling through the pedestrian crush on Fifth Avenue, Jess was startled to note that the holiday season was already commercially under way. Entire stores had been gift-wrapped, windows festooned with expensive temptations and sparkling lights. Mechanical figures danced to tinkling seasonal tunes. Where had the time gone? Who had stolen the end of summer and half of the fall?

The building was a mammoth spire of smoked glass and steel. A high-speed elevator shot through the center like a rocket off a launch pad. Jess left her knees somewhere between the tenth and twentieth floors. When she emerged on the forty-second, it took several steps before her gelatinous joints firmed up again.

"I'm Jess Magill," she told the striking Hispanic receptionist. "I have an appointment with Sidney Rosenthal."

"Of course, Mrs. Magill. Attorney Rosenthal is expecting you."

Rosenthal's secretary appeared an instant later and ushered Jess to a glass-walled corner office replete with dark, oversized furniture and mammoth ferns in antique Oriental pots. There, yet another young woman, a pixie with close-cropped platinum hair, keen blue eyes, and a comically outsized bosom greeted her. Despite her best intentions, Jess's gaze strayed to the physical curiosity. The woman caught her gaping, and Jess flushed.

"That's okay, Mrs. Magill. I'm used to it. I spent years battling with myself about a reduction, but in the end, I decided against it." Peering down, she smiled fondly. "Actually, they've turned out to be quite useful. People, especially men, tend to underestimate me. I freely admit, I put those misconceptions to full advantage."

Jess admired the honesty and the attitude. Few people were that sensible and secure. She hoped that Attorney Rosenthal had anything near this young woman's insight and presence.

Her wish was answered in a startling way, when the blonde smiled and shook her hand. "Nice meeting you, Mrs. Magill. I'm Sidney Rosenthal. Please, have a seat. Would you care for some tea or coffee?"

Jess was amazed that Charles senior, who held females well below contempt, would have recommended a woman to lead Danny's defense. But she soon found herself forgetting about Rosenthal's gender, even in the face of those two enormous swells of evidence. This lawyer was sharp, smart, competent, commanding, exactly the kind of person Danny needed in his corner.

Gus Grantham was not. Despite his promises to the contrary, he had done nothing at all to impeach Danny's accusers. From everything Jess had observed, his sole focus had been spin and damage control, presenting Danny wrapped in excuses, as if he had something to hide.

Rosenthal had a very different defense philosophy. She would operate on the working assumption that Danny was innocent, and therefore the alleged victims must have had some reason to lie.

"Tell me about the first girl, Lisa Beningson," the attorney said.

"She's been a friend of Danny's since second grade. Probably been to our house about a million times. I was quite fond of her, actually. She's always seemed like a good kid, very thoughtful and polite."

"Always?"

"Yes," Jess said. "I can't honestly remember her ever being anything but sweet and cooperative."

"Would you call that typical?" Rosenthal asked. "I don't have any kids, but I was one, and I can't say that anyone who knew me well as a child would have found me anything close to a perfect angel. How about you?"

Jess thought back to some of the stunts she had pulled as a kid. A particular highlight was the time Pearl was summoned to Camp Piney Woods to fetch Jess home a week early after she was caught drinking the beer her counselor had purchased for hair-setting purposes. "There was plenty of tarnish on my halo."

"Care to speculate on why Lisa Beningson was always so well behaved?"

An image of the girl formed in Jess's mind. The tentative tilt of her head. The protective posture. The skittish uncertainty in her eyes. "My best guess is that she grew up under martial law. Her mother is a mousy, anxious type and the father strikes me as a rigid, humorless man."

Rosenthal scrawled a note on a gray legal pad. "What else do you know about them?"

"Not much."

Jess had met Leo Beningson countless times when he came to pick Lisa up at the house, but she had never had more than a cursory conversation with him. Talk about the weather, polite chitchat. Nothing more. "Sandra's a homebody and something of a hypochondriac from what I've seen. Leo's been in a number of businesses. He does a lot of traveling abroad, mostly to the Far East, and from appearances, seems pretty successful."

Rosenthal jotted more notes. "Anything else? Opinions? Impressions?"

Jess thought of the immaculate house, the pristine yard. They were all a reflection of the man: stiff, formal, forbidding in their shrink-wrapped perfection.

"Sandra always seems on the verge of falling apart. Her husband's the opposite, overcontrolled. Everything with him has to be just so. Sanitized, spotless," she said. "Reminds me of my father-in-law."

The lawyer wrote that down and underlined it twice. "It always strikes me that someone that worried about cleanliness probably has a reason to feel dirty."

"That's one possibility. It could also reflect insecurity, fear. Other things."

"You mean the need for acceptance? A desire to impress?"

Jess smiled. "For a lawyer you make a pretty good psychologist."

"We' re both in the same line, Mrs. Magill, students of human behavior, especially the abnormal kind."

Jess felt an instant connection to Sidney Rosenthal, a strong sense that this woman could help her pull Danny up out of the well.

"What about the other girl?" Rosenthal asked.

"Roseanne Paris lives on the other side of town, goes to a different high school. I barely know anything about her beyond that."

Rosenthal added a few more notes to her list. "Okay, I think I get the picture. Now, let's talk about what, if any, part I might play in helping you and Danny with all this."

"I would love for you to take over Danny's defense. The problem is, my husband wants to stick with counsel we have now. Frankly, I think it's because his father suggested you. Charlie and his dad have agreed to disagree for decades."

She nodded knowingly. "Charles senior is an old, old friend of my father's. They were in service together in Korea, and they've remained buddies. Whenever Senior's in town, they get together once a month or so to catch up and play cards. I discovered at an early age that if I was quiet and unobtrusive enough, the men would forget I was there. I can't tell you all the fascinating things I learned hanging around those games."

As a child, Jess too had been an inveterate eavesdropper. She used to love huddling in the dark at the top of the stairs and listening to Pearl bragging about her during Friday night canasta games. Those were the only compliments Pearl ever threw her way, and Jess was eager to catch every crumb.

"I've been hearing about your husband since I was a little girl," Rosenthal went on. "We've never actually met, but it feels as if I've known him forever. Senior talked about him all the time. His son, the genius."

Jess tapped her ear to clear it. "That's hard to imagine. All Charlie's ever gotten from his father is disapproval, unless you count the disinheritance as a gift."

"It was meant to be exactly that."

"I don't understand," said Jess.

"It's simple. Charles senior blamed his own father for drowning him in family money. Controlling him so he never had the nerve to pursue the career he wanted. You may not know this, but he's a very talented photographer. His dream was to be a photojournalist, but his father wouldn't hear of it. In response, Senior was determined to teach Charlie that he could rely on his own resources."

"Then why didn't he say so? Charlie has always seen his dad as a cold, distant, disapproving man."

"I'm sure that's how Senior's father acted toward him. It's probably how all the Magill men have acted toward their children since the dawn of time. He wouldn't have the first idea of how to treat his son any other way. But believe me, Senior loves Charlie in his own bizarre manner. He cares about you all, and he's brokenhearted about this business with Danny. He's given me a blank check. I'm to help you in any way you wish, as much as you wish, on him. Of course, he would prefer that your husband doesn't find out about his involvement."

Jess could not see a way around that. "What I wish is for you to represent Danny instead of that pompous blowhard. How am I supposed to accomplish that without Charlie finding out that Senior is footing the bill?"

Rosenthal set her notes aside. "Having me take over Danny's defense may be a bad idea for several reasons. I checked out Augustus Grantham's record, and it's a good, solid one. The vast majority of his cases end in favorable plea bargains or acquittals."

"That doesn't make it any more pleasant to deal with," Jess said.

"Maybe so, but Grantham has other advantages. For one thing, he's dealing on his home court. I would have to apply for *pro hac vice,* special permission to practice in Connecticut for the duration of the trial. The petition is routinely granted, but I would still be an interloper, not one of the local boys. Psychologically, that could put me at some disadvantage with the judge, and that kind of thing can make a difference in the outcome of a trial. It's a small risk, but why take it?"

"Then how about having you work with someone who's admitted in Connecticut? Someone other than Gus Grantham, that is."

Rosenthal folded her hands. "Bringing in a new attorney at this point will send a subconscious signal that things have not been going well for Danny. It's like switching horses in midstream, very hard to do neatly."

"What do you propose, then?"

The lawyer scanned her notes. "This firm has excellent research facilities and arrangements with some of the top investigators in the field. With your permission, I'd like to see what we can find out about these girls and their families. Size up the opposition, so to speak."

Jess loved the idea of joining the fight, not lying on the mat as they had been, waiting for the next crushing blow. "That would be wonderful."

"Good then. I'll get on it right away. I'll keep you posted as soon as I hear anything at all. Shouldn't be more than a couple of days."

What a delight that would be. Grantham kept them almost entirely in the dark. "I still don't like the man," Jess said.

Rosenthal smiled knowingly. "Let's focus on getting Danny acquitted. I believe you'll feel much more fondly toward Grantham after that happens."

"Fondly wouldn't begin to cover it."

Sidney Rosenthal handed Jess a business card with her home phone number on the back. "Feel free to call me anytime. I'm glad to answer questions, hold hands, offer my shoulder, whatever you need."

"I'm liable to take you up on that."

"Please do. Senior may be a gruff old goat, but I like him. He's made it perfectly clear that he'll feel much better if I run up a nice big bill on Danny's behalf." Her blue eyes lit with a glint of irony. "Seems like the least I can do."

Jess shook her small hand warmly on the way out. "Thanks. I look forward to hearing from you. Is it okay if I call you Sidney?"

"More than okay. Nice meeting you, Jess. We'll be in touch."

TWENTY-EIGHT

Tucci swiped the razor down Mule's flaccid cheek and across his droopy chin, then paused beneath his nose.

"Go like this," he instructed, demonstrating in the mirror how a normal, unsloshed guy stretched his upper lip over his top teeth so the blade could get at the mustache stubble.

Mule's response was a goofy smile and a burst of drunken sentimentality. "You're really something, Tooch. Like a brother to me. Better even. I love you, buddy. I swear it. You're the best."

"Don't hand me crap like that while I'm holding a lethal weapon, butthead. Just stand up straight and shut your trap, okay?"

Tucci sloshed the blade in the sink, rinsing off a mound of hair-flecked foam. He appraised his handiwork in the steamy glass. Mule was in dire need of a haircut, several good nights' sleep, and a swift kick in the pants. But there was no time for anything but the bare essentials. He had one hour to rid his partner of the beer stink, sober him up, and get him presentable enough to present to Klonsky. On the way downtown, they had to come up with a good, solid cover story, something to ease the chief off the warpath. Otherwise they were both on a collision course with disciplinary action, maybe criminal charges, dismissal for sure.

Tucci eased the razor over the craggy swell of Mule's Adam's apple. Cutting the guy's dumb throat occurred to him. That would put both of them out of this misery.

This was a day for fresh experiences he could do without very nicely. Tucci had never shaved a guy before, except himself. Never held a guy's head while he heaved the evening's excesses into the bowl. Never stood behind some rubber-legged fool and held him under the pits, so he would empty his bladder in the right general direction.

Frannie had offered to get the big jerk in shape, but she had three little kids to dress, feed, and trundle off to day care, so she could get to her private-duty nursing job on time. Tucci hadn't wanted to alarm her, but the last thing she could afford to be right now was out of work. Sooner than he cared to think, she might be called on to keep the wolves away from their door. Mule and Frannie had big debts, three sprouting beanstalks to support. Mule's Bud Ice Lite tab alone had to be astronomical.

His partner's brush smelled of hair oil and pomade. Tucci wet the bristles and attacked Mule's mop, which stuck out in dry clumps like drought-stricken grass.

Mule smiled crookedly at his improved image. "Everybody clean and pretty? Then on with the show! Remember that one, Tooch? It's from the Mickey Mouse Club. Boy, did I ever have a thing for Annette. M-I-C. See you real soon. K-E-Y. Why? Because we like you."

A giant jug of Listerine was sitting on the shelf. Tucci pressed the bottle's mouth to Mule's. "Take a swig and gargle."

The ditty played out in a dramatic swell over the burbling in his throat. "M-O-U-S-Eeeeeeeeee."

"That's enough, you rodent. Put a lid on it and get dressed."

Mule pulled his pants on backward and fumbled over the buttons on his shirt. Finally, he gave up and collapsed on the bed, panting his exhaustion. Tucci had to manipulate his limbs and work him into the clothes like a helpless infant, only this was a big, hairy, ugly, stupid, aggravating baby who smelled like the morning after last night's sour binge.

Tucci shook him. "For Chrissakes, Mule. I told you how important this was. I told you to eat a good dinner and hit the rack early. You promised me you would."

A light snore whistled through Mule's gaping lips.

This whole situation stuck in Tucci's craw. Mule was supposed to be a grown-up, smart enough to avoid shooting himself in the foot like this.

So was Tucci, for that matter. To be absolutely fair, Mule had never asked him to cover up his absence. Tucci had held his nose and jumped in on his own, eyes wide open, brain shut. Somehow, it had seemed like a really good idea at the time. All he'd wanted to do was give Mule a chance to patch himself back together again. Once the department got involved, things would get way harder to unwind. Having that little girl's accidental death on his record was bad enough. An emotional breakdown, even a short, neat one, would mark Mule forever as damaged goods, soft. He would be put on the balmy track, steered toward fringe jobs and early retirement. This was how crossing guards were made, night watchmen, guys who spent their days monitoring hidden cameras in the dressing rooms at Saks, watching size 16 ladies try to stuff their hippo hips into size 6 pants. Mule deserved better than to sink like that over one hideous mistake. He deserved a second chance, or so Tucci had believed.

Maybe someday he'd learn to keep his fat nose out of other people's business.

But not today.

He pulled on Mule's socks and shoes and marched him to the kitchen. Frannie had made the coffee exactly as he instructed, quadruple-strength, pitiless, electric mud. "Drink up, buddy boy. Yum yum."

Choking and sputtering, Samuels downed three mugs of the superheated sludge. Slowly, he started to come alive, snapping and popping like Rice Krispies.

"Christ, Tucci. That stuff tastes like cow flops."

"From only the finest Guernsey, partner. Have some more."

"No more. No way. It goes down like battery acid."

"Bitch, bitch. That sounds more like the Mule I know. Now drink up and get it in gear. It's showtime. We're expected in the chief's office in twenty minutes. I'll brief you on the way."

Tucci had no time to waste words. He filled Mule in on the sketchy essentials. The Magill case was hurtling toward a conclusion. Judge Harrigan and the state's attorney's office were pushing hard for an early trial date. The kid's lawyer had done everything he could to score a delay, but Harrigan refused to budge. That pressed both sides to get their ducks lined up in record time.

"The case looks solid, Mule. At least, Beningson does. The second girl didn't turn up for weeks after the alleged assault, so we have no supporting forensics. It's just her word, and that only has a really good chance of flying if trial number one goes our way. Klonsky claims to want a conviction, but I'm not convinced that's the whole story. I think he'd be just as happy with my head on the platter as Danny Magill's."

Mule was trying to take it all in. Tucci could see how hard the guy was trying. He stretched his eyes, but they kept going soft on him, lids drifting down like the last of the season's dead leaves that rained in slow motion over the road.

"All you need to do is shake your head up and down, Mule. Try to look intelligent. Let me do the talking."

"Let you do talking," droned Mule. "Got it."

Tucci shook his head in disgust. "You got it but good."

He made a pit stop at the Dunkin' Donuts on Summer Street and urged another strong cup of java down Mule's throat.

"Whatever you do, don't tell Klonsky that you've spent the past two months at home, working on your application to the Betty Ford Clinic. I said you've been avoiding headquarters because you were finding it hard to face the guys after—you know."

"You bet I know. I never forget it for one second, Tooch. Everywhere I look I see that little girl crumpling to the floor like a rag doll."

"I want you to forget it for now. Think of Frannie. Think of Nicky, Georgie, and Zach. Everything is riding on this, Mule. For both of us."

"How am I supposed to forget? That kid was not much bigger than Nicky.

But what I saw was an armed dangerous doper. I honestly thought it was over, right then, me or him, so I fired. As soon as the shot flashed, I saw my mistake. But I couldn't take it back. There was so much blood, Tooch. How could so much blood come from such a little girl?"

"Concentrate, Mule. Stick with me."

"Blood everywhere. I can still see it, Tooch. Still hear her mother scream-ing. *My baby, my baby! What have you done?*"

"Tell the shrink, Mule. This is not the time."

They swerved into the lot behind headquarters with a scant two minutes to spare. Tucci fired last-minute instructions as he steered Mule inside and down the hall toward Klonsky's office. "In case he asks, what you've been doing is beating the bushes for witnesses who might be able to nail the Magill kid for suspicious past behavior. Violent outbursts. Unwelcome sexual advances. Evidence of deviant leanings, stuff like that. You can say you've been inter-viewing neighbors, checking out what kind of books the kid has taken out of the library and what videos he rents. Also, you've been quizzing Magill's friends to see what they can tell you about what tickles his pickle, whether he drinks, does drugs. Any mud we can sling at him." As he spoke, Tucci was mindful that several of the items he'd just mentioned should have occurred to him earlier. Of course he should have been looking into what the Magill kid did for amuse-ment, getting evidence that would illustrate the teenager's state of mind and being. How had he neglected all that? Where was his head?

Mule moved stiffly, trying to contain the throbbing brain ache and queasy gut. "I read you, Tooch. Don't worry. I'll be fine."

"Keep it general, even if he pumps you for details. Tell him you're putting it all in a preliminary report. Klonsky loves reports like nobody's business, espe-cially preliminary ones. That's what tickles *his* pickle, working hypotheses, ten-tative conclusions. Ooh, baby. Yes!"

Klonsky materialized in front of them. Tucci couldn't tell how much he might have heard. The chief's normal expression ranged all the way from unpleasant to disagreeable.

"Right on time, gentlemen. Wise move," the chief observed.

He strode inside and claimed his place on the mock-leather throne. A copy of the Magill file sat before him on the desk. As he spoke, he kept running his thumb across the stack of pages. The sharp, grating sound shot up Tucci's spine like a jolt of electricity.

A sneer split Klonsky's leathery face as he looked Mule up and down. "A true pleasure to meet you, Detective Samuels. I always like to see the face behind the pay slip."

Mule grinned. Big mistake. Nothing set Klonsky off faster than other peo-ple's happiness.

"So you find all this amusing, do you, Detective?"

Mule's head whipped around in mute confusion.

"Actually, I'm pretty amused myself," Klonsky said. "You remind me of this lobster I bought at the fish market about ten years ago. Most amazing thing I ever saw. Normally, when you drop those suckers in to cook, they go pretty gently. They might kick around a little, worst case, rattle the pot. But this had to be the smartest lobster the good Lord ever created.

"The water was boiling, and I picked up the lid. I took Mr. Shellfish out of the bag, held him by the tail, and started to lower him in. Damned if he didn't twist up, gather all his strength, and jump out of my hand. He landed on the counter, next to where my ex-wife was making a salad. When I went to pick him up again, she wouldn't let me. 'You can't cook him,' she told me. 'Look. He's smiling.'

"Instead of lobster that night, we had tuna salad on toast. After dinner, she made me drive her over to the Sound, so she could toss that smiling son of a bitch back in the drink. She wouldn't even allow me to return him to the fish market. Fifteen bucks for a lousy tuna sandwich. I call that a bad deal."

The grin hung on Mule's face like a kick-me sign.

"That's the difference between me and my ex-wife, gentlemen. I don't mind cooking smiling things in the least." Klonsky flipped the file pages again and waited for the threat to take root.

When it did, the grin fell off Mule's face, but fast. Poor dope did not know what to make of this. The only chief he had ever worked for had been a bona fide human being.

Klonsky stopped flipping the file and gave it one loud, jarring slap. "You've been assigned to investigate Magill for a couple of months now, Detective. I'd like a comprehensive briefing. Now."

Tucci jumped in. "Everything is falling nicely into place, Chief. We've got the DNA match."

"Not you, Detective. I want to hear from Keystone Cop number two."

"Mule's not much of a talker, Chief. He's a little shy," said Tucci.

"If we're talking brains and talent, so are you. But that never stopped you from shooting off your mouth, and I have every confidence your little friend can speak for himself. You were about to tell me exactly where we are on Magill, Detective Samuels."

Mule shot Tucci a panicky look. "I'm working on a preliminary report, Chief Klonsky. I should have it done in a couple of days. That'll tell you everything you could possibly want to know about the status of the case. Our tentative conclusion, like Tucci said, is that everything is falling right in place. We have the DNA match, all that."

"That's truly amazing," Klonsky said. "I always thought creatures needed some sort of brain before they were able to speak. Enlighten me, Sergeant Tucci. Is your dummy fitted with a tape recorder, or have you learned to throw your voice?"

Tucci cast around for a handhold, a life raft, anything. "Sergeant Samuels happens to be an excellent investigator, Chief. Problem is he's been putting in way too much on this thing. Working it night and day like he always does. I keep telling him, take a day off, Mule. You need the rest, buddy. But he refuses to quit until the job is done. So naturally, he's wiped out. You can see it for yourself, Chief. Guy can hardly talk."

"Pity I can't say the same for you, Detective. Now lock your teeth and close your lips and don't make another sound. If I hear one more word out of you, I'll have you and your mouth up on insubordination charges so fast you'll get whiplash."

Klonsky leaned forward on his desk, edging in for the kill. "Now, Sergeant Samuels. I know this may feel like a pop quiz, but it's not. I want you to think of it as a very *final* examination. You see, what you two consider loyalty to a buddy, the department knows by a variety of other names—conspiracy to defraud, grand larceny, falsifying governmental records, to name a few. You'd better pray that you can convince me that you've been working on this case like Tucci claims you have. Otherwise, it will be my distinct pleasure to toss your sorry butts out the window."

Klonsky opened the file. Tucci's mouth parched. He was afraid to look at Mule, convinced that their terror might somehow combine into one big unmanageable mass. It wouldn't help anything if they broke down, blubbering like scared kids caught with their hands in the cookie jar, even though that's exactly what they were. As long as the chief didn't go into crazy detail, there was still a chance that Mule could bullshit his way out of this mess.

Klonsky squinted at the file. "Question one: According to the lab results, what blood type and detail information do we have about the suspect?"

Tucci strained to hear Mule's reply over the ponderous pounding of his ticker.

"I'm not sure I remember exactly," he stammered. His words rode a cloud of fear and sour stomach juices. Tucci caught a whiff and recoiled.

"What do you think you remember, *inexactly*?"

"I think Magill is a type O-positive secretor," Mule blurted.

Tucci's heart started to beat again, though feebly.

Storm clouds gathered on Klonsky's face. "Good guess."

Mule beamed again. Another big mistake.

"Don't get carried away with yourself, Detective. I know as well as you do that seventy percent of the human male population happens to be that type.

Let's move on to a tougher one, shall we?" He scanned for a moment. "Who is Francis X. O'Sullivan and what does he have to say about Daniel Magill?"

Mule's face twisted up as if he were trying to see inside his own mind. "I think he's someone Tucci interviewed. One of the Magills' neighbors, maybe. Or maybe one of the kid's teachers. There were so many. I can't be sure without checking my notes."

Klonsky locked Mule in the crosshairs of his loaded temper. "You know, Sergeant, I am well aware that people around here don't like me. I'm nothing at all like Chief Silver, and you bozos find that hard to take. Silver was a softy, man of the people, one of the boys. But I have a very different philosophy. I worked hard to rise above inferior trash like you. I'm the boss and you're not, and I like it that way. When I was a kid, my ambition was to grow up and be a stern, arbitrary, inflexible, vindictive son of a bitch, and I believe I have accomplished that. Don't you agree, Samuels?"

Tucci ached to cry out, *Don't move, Mule. Don't blink.* His partner was in quicksand. Anything he did was bound to sink him faster.

"Definitely, sir. You certainly have," said Mule.

Klonsky did not explode, but there was seismic activity. It took a while for Tucci to recognize the chief's silent quiver as a bottled-up laugh that fizzled out as quickly as it began.

"For that display of honesty, you get a bonus question. Answer this one correctly, and I'll give you a passing grade. Foul up, and you get it with both barrels."

Tucci broke out in a rash of sweat. He held his breath. There was nothing else to cling to.

Klonsky leafed through the file one last time. "Tell me, Detective Samuels, what kind of car was the defendant driving at the time of the alleged incident with Lisa Beningson?"

Mule expelled a rush of air. "It was a '65 red Mustang convertible. Cherry condition. Low mileage. Real sweet."

Klonsky cleared his throat. "Part two. What kind of car did Magill have the night of the Roseanne Paris incident?"

Tucci saw Mule's Adam's apple bobble up and down. There was a coin-sized spot of whisker stubble he had missed with the blade. It looked, for all the world, like a target.

"What was he driving?" Klonsky badgered. "Come on, Samuels. You know or you don't. This isn't rocket science."

Mule shot Tucci a sheepish look. "It was a dark green Volvo wagon, 740 turbo. For the life of me, I can't remember whether it was a '90 or a '91. Sorry, Chief."

"You certainly are. But unfortunately, it looks like I'm stuck with you, at least for a while longer. I strongly advise you two numb-nuts to get cracking. And fast. I'm not through with you yet. Not by a long shot."

Tucci held himself in check until they were back in the cruiser. Then, he clapped Mule hard on the back. "Nice going, buddy. How did you happen to pull that off?"

"I told you I've been trying. I must have read that file a dozen times, getting ready to come back on the job."

"So why haven't you?"

Mule's eyes clouded. "Every day I start out telling myself, pull yourself together. Cut the crap. Then this other voice, the louder one, starts nagging at me. What's the point? it says. You'll only screw it up like you did with that poor little girl. Then I think of her lying in that little box, all dressed up like she was going to a party, looking like an angel. And then that louder voice starts up again. You're better off hanging out here, where you can't make trouble for any-one but yourself, it tells me. Take a load off. Cop a cold one. Watch the tube."

"You're back now, Mule. That's the important thing."

"Thanks to you, I am, Tooch. And I've got an idea."

"What's that?"

Mule went coy. "It's a surprise, Tooch. But I bet you're going to love it."

Jess had spent the last ten minutes on the phone with Libby, extolling Sidney Rosenthal's virtues.

"I like the idea of having an investigator on the case, checking out Danny's accusers," Libby observed. "I don't know if I ever told you, Jess, but that's how I got the goods on Alan. I hired a PI who specializes in divorce, a guy who's worked on behalf of several of my clients. Normally, he goes after evidence of adultery, offshore banking accounts, hidden assets. He told me Alan was the first case he ever had where he spent all day every day trailing the subject in and out of department stores. By the end of it, he was hearing cash register bells in his sleep. Dreaming he was suffocating under an avalanche of shopping bags. Nasty business."

Jess sighed. "That's exactly the way I feel about this, Libby. I hate sneaking around behind Charlie's back."

"You have to do what's right for Danny."

"I know. But how can I be sure what that is?"

Through the kitchen window, Jess spied the hazy bloom of Charlie's headlights. The Mustang paused at the roadside mailbox, then crunched onto the drive.

"Speak of the devil, Charlie's home."

"If you want to speak of the devil, stick to Alan. Charlie doesn't qualify."

"Maybe not yet. But he's been working on it."

Hanging up, Jess rehearsed the conversation she and Charlie needed to have. The first trial would start in a couple of weeks. The second would follow soon afterward. It was going to be a long, grueling ordeal. They had to focus on helping Danny through, helping all the kids. Lately, both of them had been self-absorbed, preoccupied, doing a miserable job.

When Charlie called earlier to say he'd be home late from the conference, she had felt more disappointed than annoyed. She was anxious to air the problems, try to get their derailed relationship back on track.

On the phone, he had mumbled something about an important meeting with a colleague, decisions to be made, critical stuff. But Jess could hear light laughter in the background, sloshing ice, clinked glasses. Clearly, this was cocktail time. An opportunity for elbow rubbing and bending. It was highly unlikely that anything more crucial was being decided than whether a given attendee preferred white wine or red.

Lately, Charlie was finding increasingly inventive excuses to avoid coming home. More than once, Jess had considered that he might be having, or attempting to concoct, an affair. Throughout their marriage, she had taken his fidelity for granted. Their sex life had been too good, their easy trust too critical for either of them to engage in anything as foolish, risky, and demeaning as a fling. But now, she weighed with strange detachment the unpleasant possibility that he might be fooling around. She had no strength to deal with the import or consequences if he was. After Danny's case was closed, there would be plenty of time to sweep away the debris and assess what was sound enough between them to salvage.

In truth, Charlie had not missed much by coming home late. These days, they all raced through their so-called family dinners, hoping to escape unscathed. The kids barely responded to Jess's lame attempts to stir a decent batch of talk. *What's new? Nothing. How's school? School.*

There were so many topics they had to tiptoe around, so many loaded areas. Even Max understood that it was easier to circumvent the minefield by saying nothing, eating quickly, keeping his head down and his eyes fixed on his plate.

As soon as they'd finished their cleanup jobs, all three kids had scattered to their rooms. From the jumble of noise, Jess picked out the high-pitched squeal of Max zapping aliens on his Play Station. Molly was chattering nonstop on the phone. Danny was ensconced in his usual stereophonic cocoon. The house throbbed with the primal thump of the bass.

Jess mulled over what she wanted to talk about first. Maybe she would tell him about her visit to Sidney Rosenthal, after all. They had to work together to make the best decisions for Danny, ones that had nothing to do with ancient family divisions or resentments. Surely, Charlie would want Danny to have every advantage.

What was keeping him? Peering out, Jess saw the tire tracks on the driveway. The garage was dark. The porch lights had not been extinguished as the last one in was traditionally bound to do.

Prozac finished scouting the kitchen floor for crumbs and lumbered toward the door. Jess followed her to the foyer and stepped out on the porch. As soon as she did, she caught the strike of Charlie's irate voice from the street. Soon, it tangled with an angry baritone Jess could not identify at first. The words were nipped and swallowed by the howling wind. Jess caught angry snatches. Dueling obscenities. Sharp, accusatory names.

The December cold pierced her thin cotton shirt, raising a crop of goose-flesh. Pearl's phantom nagging filled her head. *What are you trying to do? Get pneumonia?*

Jess trailed Prozac across the shadow-pooled yard, past the dark rippling pond, toward the hedgerow. Soon, the words came into sharper focus. The second voice belonged to Victor Alton, a blowhard bond trader from down the block. Jess had watched him at block parties, belittling his timid wife and shamelessly aggrandizing his ten-year-old daughter, a meek little girl who suffered from severe dyslexia. To hear Alton tell it, the only things separating his Wendy from a Rhodes scholarship were inadequate teachers and age. His eight-year-old, Anita, required no such excuses. She was perfect. She took after him.

Following Prozac's prudent lead, Jess stalled three feet from the hedgerow and listened.

Alton's tone was a strident scold. "People have a right to feel safe in their homes, Magill. Plain and simple."

"Read your Constitution, Victor. There's not a word in the entire document about what people have a right to feel."

"There's plenty in the law about what people have a right *not* to feel. Like that animal of yours ripping their clothes off. Beating them up and—"

"This conversation is over, Victor. I want you to take your unfounded opinions and your idiotic demands and get the hell off my property."

"We're giving you a chance to make a clean, easy move, Magill. Leave like a gentleman. If you don't take advantage, I can't predict what people around here might do."

"I can, Victor. If they're anything like you, they'll behave like ignorant fools."

"Some brain you turn out to be, Magill. You haven't got a clue."

"Go home, Victor. Good night."

"Not before you take these papers."

Charlie snorted. "I'm not taking anything from you, much less that."

"I'm warning you. You're making a big mistake."

Charlie jammed his hands deep in his pockets and strode away. As he reached the stone walk leading to the house, Alton charged after him. He head-butted Charlie, full force, from the rear. Caught off guard, Charlie went down hard. The ground quaked with the harsh concussion.

Jess raced to help him. Prozac stood panting crisply at her side. Charlie lay inert in Alton's wavering shadow. Blood seeped from a ragged gash above his ear.

"I call that one down, four to go," Alton spat. "We'll get rid of you people, one way or another."

Jess knelt beside him. "My God, Charlie. Can you hear me? Are you okay?"

His lids fluttered and he slowly sat, clutching his skull. "Soon as that bastard gets out of my sight, I'll be fine."

"Go home, Victor," Jess demanded. "Deb may choose to put up with you. We don't." She helped Charlie to his feet and clutched his elbow.

Alton held out a rumpled sheaf of pages, rattled them like a sword. "Like I told the nutty professor, I'm not going anywhere until you accept this petition. At least one member of every family in our neighborhood association has signed it. We want you gone, you and that bad seed of yours. We've agreed to chip in and give you a check for fair market value on the house, so you can pack up and move immediately. Play ball, and we'll throw in a couple of thousand extra to cover your expenses. We're not unreasonable people, just decent citizens, trying to protect our own."

Jess gaped in amazement at the mass of pages. There were dozens of them, bunched in his fingers, scrawled with names. There had to be a hundred signatures, minimum. "Everyone signed? I don't believe it."

"See for yourself. " He thrust the stapled sheets at her. By the tepid light of a streetlamp, she scanned the signatures. Some of the names were predictable. Jess would expect no better than this from mean-spirited busybodies like Carla and Mel Levitan or Viv and Micky Belzer, shriveled souls who thrived on other people's misfortune and misery. She was pained to find names of neighbors she had considered friends: Jim and Sylvie Barocas, Walt and Penny Stafford. One of the biggest blows was the spiky hand of old Mr. Willis from down the block. Willy, as he liked to be called, had always been a fan of Danny's, remembered his birthday, asked him over at Christmas to help trim the tree. Danny had responded in kind, especially during the past year as Willy grew increasingly frail. At the first hint of foul weather, he'd checked to see that the Willis walk was shoveled and asked if the old man needed anything from the store. His thoughtfulness had touched Jess. Most kids his age were far too self-involved to concern themselves with the welfare of an elderly neighbor.

Eileen Slattery's name was conspicuously absent, but her husband, John, had signed on the family's behalf. Jess imagined the battle royal *that* must have inspired. After the second charge was filed, many of Danny's supporters had defected. Eileen was one of a handful who'd remained steadfast in her vocal support.

Alton stood his shaky ground. "I'm hoping you're not as thickheaded as your husband, Jess. The simple truth is you're not wanted here. You can see for yourself that's the way it is. We're asking you to leave voluntarily. All of your neighbors are requesting that in a sensible democratic fashion. Now what do you say?"

Jess dropped the petition on the blood-spattered ground and crushed it underfoot. "That's what I say. Now go, Victor. Leave us alone." She took Charlie's hand. "It's cold, honey. Come. Let's go inside."

Alton's threats trailed them up the walk. "We're giving you people a chance to do the reasonable, sensible thing. Remember that, when push comes to shove."

Charlie's hands balled in furious fists. "Ignore him," Jess urged.

"Only decent people are welcome in this neighborhood. Not sicko perverts like that kid of yours."

"I'd like to wring his stupid neck," Charlie rasped.

"He's not worth it. He's not worth anything. He doesn't exist."

They shut the door and left the hateful noise of Alton's voice outside.

Charlie went directly for the liquor cabinet. He poured a double shot of Jack Daniel's, neat, and slugged it back. "Some?" he offered.

"A little dry sherry would be nice."

He poured a modest measure for her and a hefty refill for himself.

"Before you take a liquid leave, there's something I'd like to tell you," she said.

"I've had enough tonight, Jess. More than enough. Can it wait?"

Jess didn't bother to answer. She had seen Charlie like this only a couple of times, both after angry, infuriating encounters with his father. Normally, he wasn't much of a drinker. Under normal circumstances, he preferred to work through problems, talk things out. But from the high color in his cheeks and the glint of fury in his eye, it was clear that no rational problem solving was likely to be accomplished tonight.

Jess poured the remains of her sherry down the sink. Upstairs, she tucked Max in. She called good night to Molly through her door. Danny was on the phone. From his clear, earnest tone, Jess could tell he was talking to Emma.

I keep having these dreams where I'm running as hard and fast as I can but I never get anywhere. And I think the message is, maybe it's time to give up. Say whatever they want me to. It's like knowing that you've lost a match, that there's no way to win, and still, you have to stand there and look as if you're giving it a decent fight. It's stupid, Em. I just don't have the energy to fight this anymore.

He fell silent, listening. Bless Emma, she would not abide self-pity or a concession of defeat. She would haul Danny up from the doldrums and give him a curative boot in the pants. Unfortunately, her therapeutic effect was temporary.

Jess undressed in the dark and burrowed under the covers. Soon, weariness washed over her and she sank into a dense, dreamless sleep.

Suddenly, rough, seeking hands wrenched her awake. There was a crushing weight on her, then a hard nip at the side of her neck.

Her eyes snapped open. "Wait. Stop."

Charlie pressed his need against her thigh. Made passion sounds. He reeked of booze.

She pushed at him, struggling to break free. "No, Charlie. Don't."

"Oh, Jessie. It's been way too long," he slurred. He forced his lips over hers, drilled with his tongue.

His sour bourbon stench made Jess gag. She shut her mouth and snapped her head to the side. "Get off me, Charlie. I don't want this."

"You'll see, sweetheart. It's good for what ails you." His words swirled together. "Shh, now." Charlie fondled her, trying to get her aroused. Working her like some dead engine he could start by sheer determination. She felt numb inside, lost to him, cold.

"Listen to me, Charlie. You're drunk, and you need to sleep it off."

"I know what I need, Jessie. Relax." He shoved his knee between her legs, working them apart. He was on her, pushing himself inside. Breathing low and shallow.

Jess went limp beneath him, sinking in a fetid swell of revulsion. She willed her mind away. Eyes closed, she was lying again on the soft sand beach at La Rochelle. Bathed in soporific sunshine. Lulled by the children's shrieks of pure delight, the gentle lapping of the tides.

Charlie tensed, then cried out and shuddered in release. A moment later, he rolled off of her, sprawled on his back, and sighed.

Jess turned away and drew herself up in a shrimplike curl. She recoiled from his conciliatory touch.

"That was great, Jessie."

She said nothing.

"Come on. No big thing. Let's not make a federal case out of it, okay?"

Jess kept to the answer to herself. *It's not a federal case, Charlie. It's a domestic one.*

Who was this man? What was he? How had she been so blind to him all these years?

Jess thought of what Senior had said when he came to the house. "Charlie?"

He was half submerged in a drunken stupor. "Hmmm?"

"What kind of legal trouble did your father have to bail you out of when you were a kid?"

He groaned and muttered something incoherent.

"Was it something about a girl, Charlie? About sex?"

Charlie smacked his lips and rolled over. She was not going to get any answers from him tonight.

As she tried to find her way back to sleep, another poisonous thought occurred to her. If she could be so wrong about Charlie, who else might she have misjudged? She remembered the nasty woman who had accosted them in court on the day of the arraignment. Her chilling assessment looped through Jess's mind.

Like father like son.

Tucci was expecting a critical call, but every time the phone sounded, it was Mule on the line. This was the third blast from his partner in under an hour.

"For Chrissakes, Mule. What now?"

"I'm just making sure you're there."

"I said I'd be here, and I'm here."

"Stay there. Don't move."

"What about scratching? Is that okay?"

"Just stay and wait. You're going to thank me. You'll see."

"Sure, Mule. Whatever."

Tucci wasn't expecting anything except maybe more bad news. That was the way things had been going lately. Down. "Do me a favor, don't call again."

"I probably won't, Tooch. I'll do my best."

"I mean it. If I pick up this phone one more time and it's you, I may have to rip your throat out."

"Okay, Tooch. I hear you. Just wait."

Tucci hung up and glowered at the phone. Just what he needed, more waiting.

Three days ago, at the latest, they were definitely, positively, without fail going to have the results of Gina's latest blood work back from the infectious disease guys at the CDC.

Now their doc suspected that the samples must have been lost or ruined. When he called the lab, all he got was a runaround. First thing this morning, he was going to try again. He'd promised to let Tucci know as soon as he heard something, one way or the other.

Mule strode into the squad room, sporting a halogen smile. "Ready for your big surprise, Tooch?"

"Ready."

"Close your eyes."

"How about I close yours instead?"

Mule shrugged. He stepped aside and motioned for the mystery guest to enter.

Dr. Lee Chow paused at the squad room door and peered around. His eyes were blown to grotesque proportions by dense, dark-framed glasses. Spotting Tucci, he made for the desk.

"How now, Doc Chow?" Tucci caught his slender hand and shook it with manic enthusiasm. "How's it going? How's the genius business? Haven't seen you in an age."

Chow eyed their pumping hands. "Waste of strength, Detective. Well dry."

Tucci let go. "Sorry, Doc. I just can't tell you how glad I am to see you."

"Glad good," Chow pronounced. "Amount not important."

With his diffident posture and expression of perpetual perplexity, Chow looked anything but the world-renowned forensic scientist he was. His standard garb, on the job or off, was a rumpled lab coat over an equally rumpled white shirt and baggy brown corduroy pants. His dotted bow tie sat askew, like the propeller of a cheap toy plane.

"Doc Chow has agreed to take a look at the Magill case," said Mule proudly. "It occurred to me this was right up his alley."

"I got to hand it to you, Mule," Tucci said.

"I knew you'd be glad." He frowned at his watch. "Listen. I'd better run. I'm supposed to be at the Ferguson Library ten minutes ago. They're letting me check out what the Magill kid checked out. Pretty poetic, huh?"

"Go, Mule. Thanks, kid. You did great."

After Mule left, Chow claimed the chair beside Tucci's desk. He adjusted his bow tie so it lay crooked in the opposite direction.

"Your read on this thing would mean the world, Doc."

"World big place. Maybe hopes too high."

"I don't think so. This is a huge favor. I owe you big."

"Owe nothing. Detective saved Chow's life. If not for you Chow would be singing with angels, flying around heaven. Eating ambrosia," Chow said. "But I'm willing to forgive."

Tucci did not press the point. The scientist was as responsible for saving his hide as Tucci was for pulling Chow out of the flash fire that erupted a decade ago while they were checking out the scene of a major heist in a furniture warehouse on the east side of town. Chow had gotten so absorbed in his work that the flames had spread to trap him before he noticed the fierce, growing blaze. Tucci was downstairs at the time, questioning the floor manager. The heat and choking black smoke drove them outside. From the street, Tucci spied Chow struggling to open an upstairs window that had been glued shut by a century of sloppy paint jobs. Naturally he went back in to help the guy. It had been instinct, not heroics. Plus, they'd both come out okay, so no big deal. The burns on his hand had healed well enough, leaving only a pale, hard scar like fish scales to remember the incident by. Still, Doc Chow considered it grounds for a lifelong obligation. He'd helped Tucci out with tough cases several times since.

Tucci would never understand the rules of Asian honor or quirky genius, and the scientist adhered religiously to both. At the moment, he was glad to reap the fruits of Chow's gratitude. He and Mule needed all the help they could get.

The scientist stared. "Why air around you so heavy, Detective?"

"My kid's been sick. She picked up some mystery bug a couple of months ago. Can't seem to shake it. It's been tough."

"Bug mysteries not my department."

"Too bad."

"Yes, but old professor of mine knows everything about everything about infectious disease, emerging pathogens, all that. Dr. Archer runs big international research project out of London. Best in world. Get sample of daughter's blood, I send to him."

Tucci pressed his hands in praying position. "If only he could help. Oh man, Doc. I'd never forget you for that."

"Dr. Archer is mystery bug's worst nightmare. When your daughter gets well, blame him. Now let's talk about case."

Tucci passed the Beningson file to Chow. "Here's what we've put together so far. This is charge number one out of two. There's a DNA match in this case, but it doesn't count for much. The perp admits to having sex with the girl, but claims it was consensual. She tells a different story."

Chow squinted through puckered lids at the preliminary lab report. "Girl how old?"

"Sixteen and change," Tucci said. "She's just over the line for a statutory rape charge, but that's not what we're looking for in any event. Chief has a real hard-on for this kid. Wants him put away. Us too."

Chow's forehead drew in in worry pleats. "Boy how old?"

"Going on eighteen, but he's no way your ordinary boy. Danny Magill's a cocky athlete, big man on campus. Big-shot family. You know the type. Thinks everything's coming to him. Won't take no for an answer."

The scientist read farther. "Girl know boy?"

"They're schoolmates at Stamford High. Used to be friends. Some friend."

Chow came to the section of the hospital report that detailed Lisa Beningson's injuries. The lurid photographs drew no visible reaction. Given his line of work, the only thing likely to surprise Lee Chow was human decency. "What boy say?"

"Standard rap. She asked for it. It wasn't his fault. He's innocent. They all are. It's amazing, don't you think, Doc? All those jail cells, and every one is filled with an innocent guy."

Chow frowned. "Some are."

"Some, yeah, sure."

"Question is which."

"Not Magill, Doc. Trust me. It's not just a simple date rape case. Poor girl sustained serious injuries, physical and emotional. This is not the kind of thing a kid recovers from so easily. She may never get over it. You should see her. Sweet little thing. Pretty. Good family. Everything going for her, and now this."

Chow sat vague-eyed, tapping his teeth with a pencil eraser to that tune they used to play when contestants were in the booth on *The $64,000 Question*. Tucci had seen this before. The scientist slipped into a sort of trance state when he was flogging a problem. Tucci could almost hear his giant brain firing off cannon shells. Mental mortar rounds. Thought torpedoes. When Chow got through aiming his all at a question, nothing was left but a jewel of an answer surrounded by scorched earth.

Tucci sat picking his cuticles, struggling without success to contain his bristling impatience.

"So what do you think, Doc? Does it look pretty solid to you? Can you spot anything important we might have missed?"

Chow continued to stare at the photographs of the injured girl.

"Doc?"

From the corner of his eye, Tucci caught Chief Klonsky in the rear hall, jawing with a grunt from internal affairs. Normally, the chief kept to his office, preferring that the drones come to him. But once something pried him out of his Naugahyde throne, he liked to spring surprise inspections. With any luck at all, he could uncover something not precisely up to snuff. Make someone crappy.

Panic squeezed Tucci's gut. Mule should not have brought the scientist here. The chief was a control freak. He would not take kindly to their going outside without his prior authorization, especially to consult with an expert of Chow's renown and stature. It wouldn't make any difference that this was not costing the department anything. Tucci had the feeling it was going to cost *him*.

There were two exits from the squad room. If Tucci moved right now, he had a shot at spiriting Chow out unseen.

"We've got to go, Doc."

The scientist sat immobile, unhearing, lost. Klonsky was winding up his discussion with the IA guy. The chief was walking away now, starting toward the rear squad room door.

Klonsky's secretary stepped out of the office with some papers for the chief to sign. That gave Tucci a precious brief reprieve.

"Now, Doc, please."

Chow blinked hard, his magnified lashes flapping like the legs of a frantic tarantula. "Trouble?"

"Could be a big trouble for me if the chief finds you here. We should have checked with him first. Gotten permission."

"Chow say *ciao*, then. I go." The scientist scurried for the door.

"Wait, Doc. When will I hear from you?"

"Fax file. Send blood. Soon as have answers, I call."

"Thanks, Doc. Honest. I can't tell you what this means to me."

The scientist waved away the gratitude. "No thanks yet, Detective. Wait and see if answers are what you want."

Jess poked at her denuded cantaloupe half as she watched Sidney Rosenthal down the last of her blueberry cheesecake. The diet she'd resolved to start was now six hours old, and her stomach was grumbling like an angry labor union, threatening job actions, a general strike, worse. The lawyer had to be a size 4 at most. Except for the balloon breasts, she was tiny.

Rosenthal dabbed her mouth with a paper napkin. "Excuse me for diving in headfirst like that, but I haven't had a chance to eat all day. Now, where were we?"

"You were telling me about Roseanne Paris."

"Of course. Interesting story." She perched half-glasses on her upturned nose and scanned through her notes until she found the relevant section. "She's the oldest of four kids. The mother died of breast cancer a couple of years ago. The father is a dress manufacturer. Thriving business, well-off. Recently, he remarried some aspiring actress from L.A. Apparently, she's drop-dead gorgeous and not all that much older than Roseanne."

Jess winced. "That's got to be tough."

"To say the least. Let's pretend this girl is a patient of yours. What kind of emotional reactions would you expect?"

"Messy ones. Losing a parent at such a young age is a horrible, crushing blow. It can arouse separation anxiety, fear of abandonment, a morbid preoccupation with illness and death, all sorts of things." Jess had learned this the hard way, through devastating firsthand experience.

"What sorts of things?" Rosenthal asked.

"As the oldest, Roseanne was probably promoted in a way to woman of the house when her mother died. Electra's dream. Then, as she's recovering from the worst of her grief and confusion, Daddy throws her over for some young chick with no redeeming features, at least none from the child's perspective. At twenty-something, this actress can hardly serve as a substitute mother figure. Worse, she's a beauty, which is bound to be intimidating to a teenage kid who's struggling to adjust to a new body image and raging hormones on top of everything else. Last, but certainly not least, this new lady in her father's life provides very hard evidence of Daddy's thriving sexuality. No kid feels comfortable having that kind of thing thrown in her face, especially when it seems like a betrayal of her dead mother, especially when the whole issue of the girl's own sexuality is still in a beginning, and very confusing, state."

"Which could lead to . . . ?" prompted Rosenthal.

All the pieces fit perfectly as Jess assessed them from a tidy clinical remove. "To a desperate play for attention for one thing. It wouldn't surprise me if a girl in that situation engaged in some uncharacteristic acting out, especially in the sexual arena."

Rosenthal smiled. "That's exactly what our investigator learned. Roseanne Paris has a rotten reputation. Rosy Roundheels, they call her. School slut."

"Can Grantham use that in Danny's defense? I thought they weren't allowing a woman's past sexual history to be brought up in rape cases anymore."

"He won't be able to use it directly, but it's important foundation. My feeling is we concentrate on getting everything we need to make the Beningson case fall apart. Then, when it comes to Paris, given the lack of any hard evidence and her delay in coming forward plus this, I think it'll be fairly easy to get the prosecutor to listen to reason and drop the charges before he throws away any more of the taxpayers' money."

Jess scraped a transparent sliver of melon from the rind. "How do we get the Beningson case to fall apart?"

"That's still in the works. With Senior's blessing and bankroll, I have three of our best investigators working on it full-time. If there are any bones rattling around the family closet, they'll be found."

"I dearly hope so, Sidney."

The lawyer waved for the check. "I must say, I'm impressed by your insights, Jess. If you ever decide to quit the shrink business and think you might like to try your hand at psychological profiling in defense cases, I'd be happy to have you."

"Speculation is easy. Reality is hard. You wouldn't accuse me of being insightful if you saw what a mess I've managed to make of things at home. Everyone's in terrible shape, the kids, Charlie, me." Her voice broke along with the flimsy dam holding back the tears.

Sidney Rosenthal handed her a paper napkin. "It's a terrible thing you're going through, Jess. Everyone in the family is bound to suffer at a time like this. Why blame yourself?"

"Because it's my job to hold things together for my kids, to be there for them, especially at a time like this, and I haven't been. I can barely breathe half the time, much less do anything useful."

Rosenthal's look was grave. "I find you guilty of being human, Jess Magill. I hereby sentence you to stop being so hard on yourself. Give yourself a break. You're doing the best you can."

"What if it's not good enough?"

"It is, Jess. It has to be. Parents are limited and flawed. That's one of the hardest, most important lessons we need to learn in order to become genuine grown-ups."

"I suppose."

Sidney seized the check as Jess reached for it. "Senior wants me to pick up expenses," she explained. "Why argue?"

They stepped outside the Bull's Head Diner. Sharp sunlight pierced the late-autumn chill. "When do you think you'll have something more on the Beningsons?" Jess asked.

"Soon, I hope," Rosenthal said. "Keep your fingers crossed."

Prozac bounded up to greet Jess as soon as she opened the door. The dog was breathing hard, squeaking as if she needed to be oiled. The normally placid creature looked beleaguered, verging on dismayed.

So was Jess, just back from a vexing day at the office, where her few remaining clients were beginning to show stress fractures. Even Manny Dickler, her long-standing, doggedly loyal patient, was exhibiting signs of strain. *I don't know, Jess. I keep hearing about this business with your boy. My wife keeps saying that you must be really distracted by all that, and maybe I should see someone else.*

Jess ruffled Prozac's scruff. "What, sweetheart? Where is everybody?"

The dog sneezed and rammed the screen, making herself perfectly clear.

"You need to go out? Okay. Let me put my things down, and we're off."

She dropped her purse and briefcase on the kitchen table. A note from Molly drooped from a pie-slice magnet on the refrigerator door. She would be spending the afternoon at Amy's house, maybe having dinner there as well. She was informing Jess, not asking for permission, which she had come to view as beneath her budding dignity. At Molly's age, parents were vestigial organs. Like the appendix, they were best ignored unless they became painful or inflamed and required aggressive intervention.

From the rear yard came the thwack of Max's softball striking the pocket of his mitt. Jess pictured the little boy tossing high shots, staring skyward at the sun and risking instant blindness in utter defiance of one of his grandmother's myriad greatest fears.

Jess couldn't tell whether Danny was home or not. Fed up with the relentless racket from his stereo, Charlie had bought the kid a set of earphones. Now the amplified mother lode of sound was aimed directly at the teenager's fragile ear bones and vulnerable nerve sensors for hours every day. If Pearl's concerns had any validity, Jess could look forward to having one blind child, one deaf, and one destined to suffer some as yet undetermined dire consequences of her inadequate mothering. A hat trick.

Jess clipped on Prozac's leash and led her outside. They crunched through the neglected leaf piles littering the front yard, then circled the pond, picking their way through the barren tendrils trailing from the willow trees. Appraising their reflection on the still surface of the water, Jess weighed how much she and Prozac had in common. They were both middle-aged. Like Jess, the dog had thickened through the middle. These days, both of them were riding somewhat lower in the water, as if they'd taken on too heavy a load.

Prozac dipped her nose to the ground like a dowsing rod and began sniffing her way toward the street. Jess resisted at first, then gave in and heeled obediently at the animal's side. Prozac too had been a victim of situational neglect. Since his run-in with Victor Alton, Charlie had abandoned their routine morning constitutional, letting Prozac out for a solitary romp in the backyard instead.

Jess was no more anxious to deal with their Judas neighbors than Charlie was. But she was not about to let their antipathy hold her prisoner in the house. She would go about what remained of her business. Walk the dog.

Her legs felt stiff and creaky at first. She had not enjoyed a long, brisk hike since their final night in France. They'd had an early flight home out of Charles de Gaulle Airport, which put them back in Paris for the final night of their trip. Charlie's conference host had invited them to dinner at the stunning Restaurant Jules Verne near the peak of the Eiffel Tower. The evening had been perfect— brilliant food, luscious wine, all three kids pop-eyed with the splendor of the place, perched on a gauzy cloud of light atop the world.

Afterward, they had walked and walked, savoring every remaining scrap of the vacation. Charlie had proposed that they play a game called favorites: What was your favorite meal on the trip? Museum? Outing? Hotel room? Funny thing? The most interesting person you met? If you could take home one thing or experience in a bottle, what would it be?

The challenge had silenced them all. Lost in reflection, they'd straggled back toward their hotel, trailing their shadows across the Pont Neuf and over the cobblestone side streets.

Charlie had been first to speak. "If I could take home one thing, it would be visiting that prehistoric cave at Les Eyzies with you kids. I loved observing your curiosity, listening to your questions."

"Remember how I noticed that the cow on the wall didn't have any udders?" Max said proudly.

"That cow was a bull, lame-o," Molly said.

"You're the lame-o, bull brain, " Max shot back.

"I have mine," Jess put in quickly. "It was definitely that dinner we had at the Restaurant Coutanceau, overlooking the sea. I've never seen so many stars, a more beautiful sunset or brighter night. It felt as if the universe was staging a spectacle for our pleasure."

"Plus the *food*," Molly exulted.

"As if you care. You eat like a gerbil," said Danny.

"Yeah, well, you smell like one."

Jess sighed. "I'm going to have to insist that no one be allowed to argue or insult anybody unless they do it in French."

Max frowned. "But I don't know how to say lame-o in French."

"You say, *je t'aime, ma belle soeur*," Jess told him.

His frowned deepened. "That sounds too good for her."

"My favorite was Versailles," Molly said. "I think we should have gardens exactly like that at home."

"Excellent idea. I hereby place you in charge of the project," Charlie said.

She rolled her eyes. "Right, Dad. Have your people call my people, and we'll do lunch."

Max chimed in: "I'd like to take home that beach where they had the ladies with the naked boobies, so I could show it to Jason and Seth. They're never going to believe me when I tell them about it. We don't even have any pictures."

Charlie winked at Jess. "It's inspiring to see that you've focused on something so highbrow and culturally significant, Maximilien."

"They were really, really interesting, especially the old ladies. Remember, Mom? Some of them must have been forty, and they still walked around with their tops off." He frowned in thought. "I don't think any of them would fit in a bottle, though, not even a great *big* bottle."

Danny had spoken last. "Why can't we forget the bottle and stay? I feel so much better here I hate to go back."

At the time, Jess had not given much thought to his comment, but in retrospect it seemed strange. Why had he felt so much better in France? Was it simply being on vacation? Freedom from pressures and obligations? Or had something been troubling him at home? Had there been something wrong inside or around him that Danny preferred not to face? Maybe the kid had been trying to tell them something that night, to warn them that he was headed for some sort of trouble.

Prozac had walked Jess off the cul-de-sac and down the short adjacent block toward Cascade Road, a meandering street that climbed a precipitous hill from their North Stamford neighborhood to nearby New Canaan. Obeying the tug on the leash, Jess turned left and commenced the grueling ascent.

Prozac scampered upward, fur flying, panting hard. Jess scrambled to keep up, giving herself to the rigors of the hike, enjoying the exertion. Her lungs filled with late-fall air tinged with the biting promise of winter.

A flock of birds massed overhead in ragged diamond formation, then dipped and swooped away. An occasional car breezed past, including the Levitans' wagon. Jess pressed into a roadside thicket, hoping Carla wouldn't see her. She breathed relief when the car passed. A mutt jaunted by, pausing to sniff at Prozac. Otherwise, they were alone.

At the crest of the road, Prozac squatted and left her mark, commemorating their conquest of the summit.

Jess's calves were knotted and her back ached. Her feet felt raw inside her flimsy flats. "What do you say, girl? Had enough?"

The dog shot her a baleful look. Both of them would welcome a cold drink and a nice long sprawl.

They scurried down the hill. As they were about to turn onto the cul-de-sac, a car came up behind them. Jess paused, expecting whoever it was to pass, but the vehicle stopped, idling in the road. Gazing over her shoulder, Jess spied the gleaming hood of a black Mercedes. Glare from the sinking sun camouflaged the driver, but she had no doubt it was Dolores Wainscott.

That beast had been stalking Jess ever since she terminated treatment. Several times a week, Dolores would call and hang up. Or, after a prickling silence, she would rasp some nastiness. *So nice to see your perfect little family falling apart, Jess. Couldn't happen to a more deserving soul.* Changing to a new, unlisted number had halted the other anonymous hate calls they'd been getting since Danny was charged. Venomous letters, including a couple of death threats, had replaced those. But Dolores had managed to secure the unpublished number in less than a week. No one would ever accuse that witch of lacking resourcefulness or determination.

Jess quickened her pace and kept walking. The Mercedes crept along behind them, edging closer as they hastened down the dead-end street. Home was in sight when the black car swerved around, cutting them off, and braked to a screeching halt.

"Wait, Jess," called a voice as the driver's door swung open.

Clutching the leash, Jess broke into a run. But before she was able to turn in at the stone walk, a hand clamped her arm. She wrenched free and wheeled around, prepared to face down Dolores Wainscott once and for all, tell the piranha off.

But it was not Dolores.

"What are you doing here?" Jess demanded.

"We need to talk," Sandra Beningson said.

The woman's dazed, distraught appearance aroused no sympathy. All Jess felt was a spark of outrage at the intrusion and the woman's incalculable nerve. "I have nothing to say to you."

"Then just listen. Please. This can't go on any longer. It's hurting everyone. You should see poor Lisa. She can't sleep, can't eat."

"You want it over with, have her drop the charges."

"If it were up to me, she would, Jess. I never wanted this in the first place. I've begged Leo to let it go, but he won't hear of it."

"What am I supposed to do about it?"

"You've always been so wise. So reasonable." Muddy tears trickled down her cheeks. "I'm sure you can see there's only one way out. If Danny would agree to plead guilty, I'm sure I can convince the prosecutor to offer him some kind of a deal. A lesser charge, a lighter sentence. It would be over, Jess. We could all be done with this and get on with our lives."

"What about Danny's life?"

"Danny's strong. He's always been so much stronger than Lisa. I remember once when they were playing in the neighborhood, an older boy named Steph Hartung started picking on them. Steph was twice Danny's size, a mean horrible bully. All the kids were afraid of him, but Danny refused to be intimidated, even when Steph came at him with a bat. If my husband hadn't driven by and put an end to it, who knows what might have happened. Lisa was shaking for hours, but Danny acted as if nothing had happened. He'll bounce back from this, Jess. You'll see."

"Are you honestly suggesting that I should sacrifice my child for yours?"

"He wouldn't have to go to trial. Think of all the grief that would save him. All of us."

"What I think is that you're out of your mind." Prozac had gone to ground and lay snoozing. Jess scratched the dog's ruff to rouse her. "Come on, girl."

"Please, Jess. It's the only way."

"That's where you're wrong."

Tight with fury, Jess led Prozac toward the house. Sandra's entreaties trailed them up the walk. "This way both of them get destroyed, Jess. This way, everyone does. Don't you see?"

Charlie burst into the kitchen, lifted Jess along with the chicken she'd been rinsing at the sink, and spun her around. "Good news, Jessie. Great news!"

"Put me down, Charlie. You'll get a hernia. You'll break your back." Pink-tinged droplets from the bird rained around their feet.

"This is the best! Grantham's office just called to say that the second charge against Danny has been dropped."

"How? That's incredible. What happened?"

"I don't know the details. Grantham's tied up. His secretary said he'd call later and fill us in on the rest. All she knows is that the Paris girl recanted. Little bitch decided to give up the lie. Hallelujah!"

"Oh, Charlie. That's wonderful."

"It's better than wonderful. This is bound to turn the whole case around. Once people hear that Roseanne Paris made up the charge, they have to consider that Lisa Beningson might have done the same thing. Reasonable doubt, Jessie. There it is. For the first time, I really believe Danny has a solid chance to beat this thing."

Jess drew Charlie in a hug, smothering the soggy chicken between them.

Pulling back, he cringed. "If that was dinner, I think we'd better go to plan B."

"I say this calls for a celebration. Let's collect the kids and go out."

"Excellent idea."

The skies were clear when they left home, but during the twenty-minute ride downtown, massive thunderheads tumbled in, shrouding the fading day in darkness. The rain started as a playful mist, but soon intensified, falling in harsh silver sheets. Charlie pulled under the broad green-and-white-striped canopy fronting Iannucci's to let Jess and the kids dash inside.

Compared to the fury of the storm, the restaurant's candlelit interior was a hushed, inviting oasis. They huddled in the red-carpeted vestibule waiting for Sal, the owner, to finish chatting up a table in the rear and seat them. Jess tried in vain to catch his attention as the small, mustachioed man took leave of the first customers and moved on to talk to a large party crammed into a corner banquette.

Charlie raced in, breathless and dripping, from the parking lot. Scanning the half-empty place, he frowned. "What's the holdup?"

"Sal's running for office," said Jess. "You know how he is."

They had been coming to the restaurant since it opened a dozen years ago. At that time, the tiny storefront operation was run single-handedly by Sal and his young bride, Rita. The couple had shared the cooking and serving. Rita had managed the business side, while Sal handled customer service and public relations. As the place gained in popularity, the Iannuccis bought up adjacent stores and added them to the original space, so the restaurant was now a sprawl of artfully appended rectangles and squares. Every few years, Rita swelled with a fresh pregnancy. More often than not, this resulted in two or three additional bouncing Iannucci *bambini*. At last count, they had ten kids and an undetermined number on the way. A staggering collection of mouths to feed. No wonder Sal devoted himself to keeping every customer content.

Charlie went to dry off in the men's room. Jess waved again, but Sal was still too absorbed in dinner diplomacy to notice.

Emerging from the men's room, Charlie puffed his annoyance. "This is getting ridiculous."

"Patience. I'm sure he'll be right here."

The door opened behind them, and a couple hurried in, chased by wind-whipped rain. They crowded into the tiny vestibule behind the Magills.

"God, it's awful out," the woman said.

"Not pretty," Jess agreed. She was rapidly reaching the limits of her own tolerance for being ignored, when the latest arrivals circled them and headed for a table near the blazing gas-driven fireplace in the center of the oversized space. Astonished, Jess watched Sal greet them with his typical beaming enthusiasm. He offered menus, took their drink order, and motioned for a roaming busboy to bring on the olives and bread.

"That's not fair. We were first," Molly said.

"I'm hungry," Max whined.

"I'll take care of this," Charlie said. "Wait here." He made his way through the table maze toward Sal.

Looking up, the owner saw Charlie approaching and hurried to cut him off near the fireplace. Huddled with Charlie, Sal gesticulated grandly. His face was pinched with strain.

"See?" Jess said. "It was only a mix-up."

"Good. Maybe they'll give us free dessert like they did when that waiter spilled the red wine in Daddy's lap on Danny's birthday," Molly said.

Danny shook his head. "Something's wrong. Maybe we should go."

Jess set a hand on his arm. "Don't worry."

Sal's mouth stretched in an unnatural grin as he led Charlie toward the vestibule. "So sorry to keep you waiting, folks. Come." He plucked five menus from the reservation desk and led them toward the bar.

"Wait—can't we sit near the fireplace?" asked Molly.

"Not in there, Sal. We don't want the smoking section," said Jess.

"Nobody's smoking," the owner assured. "You'll see. I have a nice table for you. Very quiet."

Jess cut him off at the entrance to the bar. "What is this, Sal? What's going on?"

He clasped his hands and fixed Jess with a beseeching gaze. "Please, Mrs. Magill. Try to understand. I'm doing the best I can."

"It's about me, isn't it?" Danny said.

"All I want is to keep everybody happy. I've got a business to run. You understand."

"No, he does *not* understand," Charlie said. "And neither do I."

Danny reddened. "Let's go. Please. Everyone's staring."

"This is outrageous," Charlie breathed. "I'm going to sue you, Sal. I'll close your damned doors."

"Stop, Dad. Please. I can't take this," Danny said.

"I'm sorry, Dr. Magill. Whatever I do, someone gets mad. Either way, I lose."

Danny raced outside and stood in the pelting rain, face buried in his hands, oblivious to the drenching downpour.

Molly's chin trembled. Max clung hard to Jess. "What's wrong, Mommy? Aren't we going to eat?"

"Not here, sweetheart."

"But you said we were eating out."

Sal handed the little boy a fistful of bread sticks. Max threw them down with an angry wail. "That's not dinner. I want fried calamari. I want tiramisu."

"We'll stop for a pizza," Charlie said. "Come on. Let's get out of here."

By the time they got home, the storm had played out. Stars preened against the freshly scrubbed night sky. "Sorry that was such a bust," Jess said. "Let's make a reservation somewhere away from Stamford and have that celebration tomorrow night."

"Why don't we wait until the trial is over?" Danny said.

"We can celebrate this now and that later," said Charlie.

"I don't feel much like celebrating anything," Danny said. "Nothing's changed. I'm still accused. Everyone still thinks I'm guilty."

The phone was ringing. Charlie opened the door and Molly charged inside

204 | Judith Kelman

to answer. "It's the lawyer." She sighed. "I'm expecting Amy to call. Please don't hog the phone."

"You talk to him, Jessie," Charlie said.

Jess picked up in the kitchen. "I can't tell you how delighted we are, Mr. Grantham," she said. "It's about time we had some good news."

"This is far from good news, Mrs. Magill. Obviously, you didn't hear the whole story," Grantham said. In grave tones he told her what had caused the Paris girl to recant.

THIRTY-THREE

Bristol Forensics Laboratory operated out of a converted schoolhouse in South Selden, Connecticut. The building was a shabby 1950s red brick Federal-style structure, which still bore the original name, Francis Parkinson White Elementary School. The words "Boys" and "Girls" were still engraved in the concrete over their respective entrances. Rusty swings, a battered slide, a vintage vomit wheel, and a dilapidated jungle gym occupied the abandoned playground in the rear. Prime slots in the parking lot were marked "Principal," "Truant Officer," and "Dean of Boys." Abandoned bicycle racks flanked the entrance, and the circular drive still bore faint traces of the yellow lines set to guide the daily stream of buses and cars.

Despite its prosaic facade, BFL was state-of-the-art. The lab was a private, highly profitable concern, serving wealthy defendants, federal and state investigative agencies, and foreign governments. Operations within the sooty brick and crumbling mortar were kept strictly under wraps. BFL did not tolerate the standard pinhole leaks or easy spreading rumors that besieged more public facilities. They were bent on protecting the delicate secrets they were entrusted to study and unearth.

Dropping the right name got Tucci through the main gate. He parked in a visitor's slot beside the entrance. After identifying himself to a disembodied voice from inside, he was admitted to a locked security bay, manned by a burly, stern-faced guard.

"Purpose of your visit, sir?" asked the man, whose ID described him as Periphery Security Shift 1, Number 2.

"I'm here to see Dr. Lee Chow."

The guard scanned the log of preapproved visitors. "Sorry, sir. I don't see your name on the list."

"That's because it's not there. I tried calling, but I couldn't get through. Your phone system kept bouncing me back to the main menu. Press one if you want to get nowhere. Press two for more frustration. Press three if you'd like to feel like a total ding-a-ling. If you want to waste even more of your time, press four. If you prefer to waste your time in Spanish, press five. If you're stupid enough to think we're going to connect you to an actual person, hang on for the next five hours while we play our collection of the world's most annoying music.' "

"Sorry, sir. I'm afraid you won't be able to see Dr. Chow without an appointment. He sees visitors by appointment only."

Tucci wished he could flash his badge and shield, throw his questionable weight around. But he didn't want news of his visit to leak back to the chief. This bozo seemed like exactly the type who would pick up the phone and rat him out. "We're old friends. Just call and tell him I'm here. Name's Joe Tucci."

The guard's arms girded his massive chest. "I can't disturb the scientists, sir, especially Dr. Chow. Rules."

Tucci feinted at the man's bulging bicep. "Listen, pal. We both know that rules are made to be bent. All I'm asking you to do is call the guy. Blame it on me. Tell him I insisted."

The guard touched his Glock.

Tucci backed up. "Okay, buddy. Lighten up. What's your name, anyway?"

The answer was a dark angry glare.

Tucci squinted at his ID tag. "Can I call you Periphery? Or do you prefer Mr. Day Shift?"

"I'll have to ask you to leave, sir. "

"Look. Give me a break. All you need to do is use that phone over there and call Chow."

The guard reached under the desk and activated a silent alarm. Moments later, three doors burst open and a squadron of musclemen in gray uniforms rushed at Tucci. A dozen hands gripped him, started pushing him around.

"Okay. Easy. I'm a friend of Lee Chow's, for Chrissakes. Chow is not going to be pleased about this. Not one bit." He kept up a running nervous patter as they hauled him out the door with his feet barely grazing the ground. This was a private security squad, goons with guns. Who knew what kind of jungle justice they had been trained to practice?

Meanwhile Tucci had left his own brand-new Glock nine-milly in the glove compartment and come in naked. He hadn't wanted to set off any alarms. His sole purpose was to check in, see how Chow was coming along with the Magill file. "Okay. That's enough. Let go of me."

"We'll see you safely to your car, sir," said Periphery. "We'll escort you to the highway and make sure you are safely on your way."

"I don't need a damned chaperone." He tried to wrench free, but the guards' hold tightened like a Chinese finger puzzle.

A menacing voice growled in his ear, "Relax, Rambo. Be a pity if we had to bust you up."

Tucci went limp and allowed the goons to march him to his car. "Thanks for the escort service, fellows. It's been swell."

They peeled away, except for the nasty number who had whispered in his ear. He was a squat, sallow ape with acne-pitted skin. "I'll see you off, sweetheart," he said. "Get in the car and drive."

The guard pressed his loaded piece to Tucci's temple. "Oops, careful," he said when they hit a bump in the pavement. "You almost made me pull the trigger. Now that would be a terrible shame. I'd have all kinds of paperwork to fill out, and I hate paperwork."

"Yeah, me too."

"You're a cop, aren't you?"

Tucci had never heard of a psychic gorilla. "Actually, I'm a Mary Kay Cosmetics representative. Need anything?"

"You don't have to tell me, I know. Cops have a particular stench, and I can smell it on you." The guard's face warped in a sneer. "Only thing I hate worse than paperwork is smart-ass cops. So happens I come from a long line of them. My old man, his old man. Uncles, cousins, you name it," he said with a nasty snicker.

"It's a funny story, really. Everyone expected me to carry on the family tradition. And I might have. Problem was, my old man liked to cuff me around the head when he got mad. This one time I didn't feel like finishing some slop my old lady made for dinner. Stuff was fit for pigs, so naturally Pop the cop liked it fine. He told me to clean my plate, but I couldn't. Stuff stuck in my craw, made me gag. So my old man got really pissed, madder and madder. 'What kind of cop are you going to make if you can't take orders?' he asked me. What kind of cop? Pretty funny." His laugh was the sharp tick of automatic gunfire.

"Want to hear the punch line? It's really rich. He beat me so bad that time, I lost the vision in one eye. Force wouldn't have me after that. You know what that's called, smart-ass?"

"Felony child abuse?" Tucci offered.

"Wrong. It's called motive. That's why I've got this thing about cops. A shrink would probably call it unconscious hostility, repressed frustration. Real complicated, dangerous psychological stuff like that. Truth is, you never know what a loaded powder keg like me is going to do, when or how I might blow. Could happen anywhere, anytime. So I'd be real careful about those bumps if I were you. Real careful."

Tucci eased off the accelerator and continued at a crawl. Nervous sweat streamed down his face. He cast a longing glance at the glove compartment. His brand-new Glock was a twin to the one nipping at his brow. He wondered if this one was loaded like his, with hollow-points, designed to maximize target damage and avoid harming innocent bystanders. He remembered the department's training film. It showed a perp hit at close range, busting like a tossed pumpkin.

Pulling his attention back to the road, Tucci spied a speed bump dead ahead, too close to avoid. He squeezed the brake, but the wheels and shocks could not absorb the jolt. The car rose and fell, lurching over the speed bump.

The muzzle of the Glock bit harder. The guard's fury rumbled quakelike deep in his chest. "I told you to be careful, ass wipe. I warned you that a loaded piece like mine could go off just like that. One little bump and pow—cop brains all over the dashboard. Blood everywhere. Big frigging mess on my nice clean uniform. Plus all that goddamned paperwork. But did you listen? No."

"Take it easy, buddy. Don't get excited."

"Me? I'm calm as they make them. Easy breezy. Cool as a cuke."

Tucci drew a level breath. If he caught the creep in the solar plexus or the throat, he might have a chance. That was the crucial decision. Did he swing up or out?

There was a sharp metal click. Up, he decided. Tucci swung with the full force of his desperation. He braced for the crack of cartilage or bone. But instead, he felt the hard thwack of pummeled upholstery. The guard had feinted beyond his reach. Creep was doubled over, laughing his dumb butt off as if Tucci's mortal fear was the funniest thing he'd ever seen. Still, he held his grip on the gun. His sights were fixed on Tucci's frontal lobe. His stubby finger looped around the trigger, twitching with mirth.

One tiny tug and Gina would be an orphan. Marie would be left to bear their daughter's illness, and everything else, alone. Tucci had meant to buy more term insurance, maybe a mortgage policy. There were things you could do with pension money, special funds he'd meant to investigate. Last year the department had run a seminar about all that stuff. Tucci had meant to go, but something had come up. Something always did. He couldn't die now, damn it. He wasn't anywhere near ready.

Suddenly, Tucci spotted his salvation bumping toward them. The guard saw it too, and his face blanched.

"How nice," Tucci said. "Looks like I'm going to get what I came for after all."

The guard's larynx bulged as he choked on a dried-up laugh. "Hey, it was just a joke. I was having a little fun with you. No biggie, right?"

"Fun?"

The guard got more and more desperate as they approached a rendezvous. "Come on. I wasn't going to hurt you. You're way smarter than to think I'd really use this peashooter."

Tucci shrugged. "Me smart? Nah. Like you said, I'm nothing but a smartass cop. The kind you hate worse than paperwork."

The guard jiggled around like a kid doing a peepee dance. "Come on, man.

I've got a wife, three kids, a killer mortgage. This lab is the only game in this godforsaken town. You want my family to starve?"

The dark green Cherokee pulled up beside them. Tucci stomped the brake, stalling out the engine.

Dr. Lee Chow rolled down his window. "Detective Tucci? Really you or figment of Chow's imagination?"

"I tried calling, but I couldn't get through. I want to be sure you got what I sent you."

"Hard to get what not sent," Chow observed.

"How's it coming along?"

"Blood sample on way to Dr. Archer. File on desk. Better we talk inside, so I can show what I find." For the first time, the scientist noticed the guard in the car. "Why Stanley with you? Problem?"

"Nope. Stanley insisted on showing me to the road, make sure I didn't get lost or anything. I told him it wasn't necessary, but this guy really goes the extra mile. Don't you, Stanley?"

"Yeah," he stammered. "Exactly."

Chow's eyes narrowed behind his dense, distorting specs. "Follow me back to lab, Detective. We talk there."

Tucci tried to start the car, but all he could raise was a feeble tremor from the moribund battery. He worked the ignition again, then threw up his hands. "Damned thing's dead. You got jumper cables?"

"Raise dead, bad luck. Better you start fresh. Get new battery. Gas station only three miles' walk from here. Stanley want to go extra mile, here's three chances."

"But I'm supposed to be minding the store, Doc. Plus I've got bum feet," the guard whined.

Chow nodded gravely. "Admirable you make sacrifice like this, Stanley. Maybe someday soon be employee of month. Get picture in cafeteria."

"Come on, Doc."

"No, Stanley. You go. Chow stay here. Mind store."

Stanley hauled himself out of the car and trudged off toward the main road, muttering under his nasty breath.

Tucci called after him. "Fill her up and check the oil, will you, Stan old kid? Oh, and give her a wash and vacuum those floor mats for me. I just hate it when they're dusty like that. Only thing worse than dusty floor mats is paperwork. Don't you agree, Stan?"

Chow bit back his amusement as the guard strode away. "Score even now?" he asked Tucci.

"I'd have to say I'm ahead, Doc."

"Ahead good. Two heads better."

With Chow at his side, Tucci was welcomed at the facility like an honored guest. Mr. Day Shift himself buzzed them through the security bay.

Bristol's four principal divisions—Administration, Biology, Chemistry, and Drugs/Toxicology—poised at the ends of the slim angled halls that ran like spokes off the central corridor. The place was spare and spotless. Light bounced off the bright white tile and polished steel fixtures.

"You know how forensic lab works, Detective?"

"Wouldn't mind hearing again, Doc. It's been a while."

"Biology studies crimes against person. Examine hair, fiber, blood, fluids. Like that. Use for murder, sexual assault cases. Chemistry for crimes against property. Look at paint, glass, soil, fire debris, also hair, fibers, and explosives. Cases include robberies, burglaries, hit and run. Drug section gets scales, knives, hypodermic needles. Other things used for smuggling. Interesting technology here. You have minute? I show you."

Tucci was churning to get to the point, but he would not risk insulting the scientist. "I'm yours, Doc."

Chow slid his entry card through an electronic sensor, then pressed his finger to the touch pad. The door to the chemistry section gaped and retracted into the wall, admitting them to a large laboratory, where a dozen scientists and technicians scurried about. Dozens of machines blinked and beeped and spat reams of data. Chow passed among them, patting the devices with affection and introducing them to Tucci by name. "This is scanning electronic microscope. Here new electrophoresis analyzer. Big one over there infrared spectrograph Analyzer, IFSA for short. That one used for thin-layer chromatography. Very handy."

Tucci tried to look alert, despite the tumbleweed swirling in his brain. "I bet, Doc. Don't know how I do without one."

"Come, Detective. My office here."

Chow's name, along with his alphabet soup of earned degrees, was stenciled on the door. Inside, mounds of books and papers crammed every available surface. The scientist moved three tottering stacks of files from a chair near the desk to make room for Tucci. His chair was strewn with newspaper clippings, equipment orders, and departmental memos. He set them on the floor beneath his knee well and sat.

Chow flipped through the Magill file, consulting his marginal notes. "How much detail you want, Detective?"

"Anything. Everything."

"Learned most from injuries on girl. From force and angle can tell that person who delivered these blows was right-handed male with fine finger dexterity. Probably piano player or someone who works a lot on computer."

Tucci nodded. "That fits Magill. Kid's very big on computers from what his teachers told me."

"Assailant well proportioned. Good ratio of muscle mass to frame size. Six feet tall or more. Good athlete. Strong."

Tucci stuck up his thumb. "Danny Magill in a nutshell. He's six two. Tennis champ. Built like an ox. This is great, Doc. Music to my ears."

Chow held up a hand. "No applause yet, please. Maybe music off-key."

"Sure, sorry. Go on."

Chow opened the file to the snapshots depicting Lisa Beningson's injuries. "Notice position of bruise here, Detective. See pattern of capillary damage around ribs. Look here, these four small marks above collarbone." He played a magnifying glass over the area in question. "Imprint made by second knuckle joint of fist."

"I see what you mean, Chow. But what's the point?"

The scientist quoted a paragraph from Lisa Beningson's report of the assault. *Danny climbed on top of me and tore at my clothes. When I told him to stop, he started punching and kicking me.* "Bruises came from someone standing beside victim, Detective. Arm came up, hard blow. Force and angle of injuries inconsistent with situation girl describes."

"So maybe she was confused. Maybe he socked her after she got out of the car, after he was done with her."

Chow scanned another section of the report. "Says here girl's father saw her exit car. Father did not see boy beating girl."

"Then maybe Magill pounded her someplace else, before they got to the Beningson house."

"Not according to girl, Detective. Every time she tells story, same thing. Boy drove straight home, boy forced sex, boy punched and kicked her in car."

"Try this," Tucci urged. "They were kneeling on the seat, in other words upright. Then the injuries could have looked as if they were standing. Isn't that right?"

"In some cars, yes. In '65 Mustang with top up, no way. Not enough space, Detective, especially for boy six foot two. Not enough space for much smaller boy to get leverage necessary to cause injuries like these."

Tucci groaned. "The second case against Magill fell apart. The plaintiff tried to kill herself with an overdose of pills, and the family decided she's not up to the trauma of a trial. They left the state, went into hiding. I need this one, badly, Doc. Are you sure?"

"I am, Detective. So sorry."

"Then it's back to square one. I've got to question the Beningson girl again, interview her father, figure some logical way to patch the holes."

"Perception involved, Detective. Memory, imagination. Mind can play tricks, especially under stress of crime situation," Chow observed. "If only humans not so human."

"You can say that again."

"All not lost. Go back. Ask questions. Maybe this time, get answers you need."

"How am I going to deal with Klonsky?"

"Detective work it out. Chow have faith."

"Sure, Doc. Right. You smell that?"

The scientist sniffed. "Smell what?"

"That burnt stench, Doc. That's my goose cooking."

A s soon as she spotted Sidney Rosenthal's number on the caller-ID, Jess seized the phone.

"You're exactly the person I was hoping to hear from," Jess said. "Tell me you've found some damning evidence against Lisa Beningson. Please."

"Nothing about Lisa, Jess, at least not yet, but the investigator has unearthed some very interesting information about her father," the lawyer said. "Daddy turns out to be a very interesting character indeed."

Beningson's business enterprises had been incorporated in Delaware, a common practice given the favorable tax terms offered in the state, the lawyer told Jess. Lisa's father had partnership interests in several companies, but one, an Asian food import firm called Golden Dragon Provisions, had caught their investigator's practiced eye. The operation appeared to have no logical connection with Beningson's other corporate endeavors, all of which clustered in the transportation and communications sectors.

Beningson was listed as Golden Dragon's president and CEO. The other principal shareholder was a Boston man named Reggie Hanson. Posing as a restaurateur, Rosenthal's investigator had arranged a meeting with Mr. Hanson to find out what he could about the firm.

"According to Hanson, the company is largely a sham," Sidney Rosenthal told Jess. "Leo Beningson bought a failing business and set it up as a cover for the monthly trips he likes to take to Phnom Penh. It seems that authorities there are notoriously tolerant of certain practices that aren't accepted in very many civilized countries."

"Like what?" Jess asked.

"Child prostitution."

That set Jess reeling. "Are you telling me that Leo Beningson has a thing for little girls?"

"If Reggie Hanson is to be believed, he does. But of course, I'm not going to take it on Hanson's word alone. He was happy to talk to our investigator because he and Beningson had a serious falling-out. He claims Beningson reneged on an agreement to pay him a monthly retainer for helping to set up and maintain the legitimate appearance of the business. After a couple of years, Beningson got cocky and decided he didn't need Hanson's help anymore. Business divorces can get even nastier than marital ones, so it is possible that Hanson made up the story out of spite."

"How do we find out whether it's true or not?"

The lawyer chuckled. "If Senior is trying to expiate some guilt he feels by running up a fat legal bill on Danny's behalf, he's getting his wish and then some. Your father-in-law has authorized me to send our best investigator to Cambodia. For a job like this, that has to be Dick Firestone. He makes Sam Spade look suave, but he'll get the job done. It's all set—he's flying out tonight."

"How long do you think it'll be before we hear anything?"

"With Firestone on the case, it shouldn't be long at all. Some PIs take their sweet time circling around and sizing up a situation. This one jumps right in. He's not afraid to get his hands dirty, and from the sound of things, he very likely will."

"Thanks, Sidney. I can't wait to hear what he finds."

With a volley of thumps, Danny carried his friend Ryan down the stairs. He trudged through the foyer and set the boy down gently on the couch. The accident had cost Ryan fifty pounds of bulk from atrophy, but he was still Danny's height and a considerable load. Worse, his was dead weight, awkward and askew.

Jess watched, cringing, from the desk across the room, where she'd spent the last hour chipping away at their unconquerable mountain of bills. Glancing at their monthly statement from Grantham & Greene, she was startled to see that they had run through more than half of their retainer with Danny's lawyer. The charges were breathtaking. A quick question cost the equivalent of groceries for a week. A single pleading ran as high as the family's monthly mortgage, tax, and utility bills combined. As the trial date approached, the legal expenses were mounting with appalling speed, and still, despite Sidney Rosenthal's encouraging input, Danny remained vulnerable to the most negative outcome and severest penalties. Maybe they would have been wiser to use the money to build a wall around their son, cap it with razor wire. Dig a moat for good measure and fill it with aquatic predators. She pictured dozens of Pearl clones in skirted bathing suits, wearing the famous *punim,* her mother's angry face. Even the most determined horrors would turn tail and flee.

Danny was flushed from the exertion of carrying Ryan. His breath came in ragged gasps, but he held his smile steady, determined to act as if his friend presented no burden at all. Gently, he stretched Ryan's arm and positioned his twisted hand on the armrest. "I'll go up and get your chair, bud. Hang with my mom for a minute, okay?"

"Can I help you, honey?" Jess asked.

"Piece of cake, Mom."

Retrieving the chair would take far more than a minute, Jess knew. Danny had insisted on hauling Ryan's motorized wheelchair upstairs, so the teenager would be able to get around on his own. The clunky conveyance with its space-age electronics and twin car batteries weighed at least a hundred and fifty pounds. Easing it up or down one step, much less an entire flight, was a massive effort.

Jess had suggested that it would be much saner and simpler for Danny to visit with Ryan at his house, which had been adapted since the accident to meet his needs. If he wanted to invite Ryan here, it made much more sense to hang out downstairs. With Molly and Max gone to Pearl's for the weekend and Charlie in the city for the day, she could even offer them a guarantee of privacy and relative peace. But Danny insisted on having things with Ryan exactly as they had been before the accident. He was willing to do an extraordinary amount of perilous, unnecessary work to pretend that was possible.

Jess set aside the checkbook and forced a smile. Her heart ached every time she saw Ryan. He had been such a funny, easygoing kid before the accident, so full of life and mischief. Now, everything posed a monstrous, visible struggle. His features warped with the unrelenting battle against gravity and imbalance. His limbs twitched and contorted, powered by a nervous system that ran with the erratic uncertainty of a pinball machine.

"How's it going, Ryan?" Jess asked. "Are they still working you to death down at Easter Seals?" His progress in therapy was one of a very few remaining safe topics. She could no longer talk to him about any of the former pressing concerns: school, college applications, sports, girls. All that had been left in a heap of twisted wreckage, along with his mother's Acura, in the ditch.

"I'm—fine," Ryan said. His words were stretched and distorted like pulled taffy. He gulped a breath and cast his unfocused gaze overhead. "Danny's—not fine. I'm—worried about him."

"That's sweet. Don't worry. He'll be okay."

"Please—listen, Mrs. Magill." He went stiff with emotion. His legs shot out from under him and his head tossed back at an improbable angle. "Don't—know what—he might do. I'm scared."

He had slipped perilously close to the edge of the cushion. Jess rushed to help him. "Can I give you a boost, honey?"

"Thanks."

She stood behind the couch and hoisted him under the arms. She felt the slide of flesh over knots of frozen muscle. A tremor ran beneath it all, as if what remained of the boy lay on an active fault. "Better?"

"Fine. Listen—please." He waited for Jess to take a seat on the chair opposite the couch. "Danny's my—best friend. Good kid but—needs—work."

Jess had to smile. The trademark sense of humor had been dented, not destroyed. "Don't we all?"

"Wasn't—his fault."

"You're right, Ryan. Danny's not to blame if Lisa's screwed up. Or Roseanne. I've told him that. I'll talk to him again."

The doorbell chimed.

"I'll get it. Must be your mom," Jess said.

Faith Harrison stood on the porch clad in a drab green shirtwaist, clutching a brown vinyl purse. She was a shy, skittish person who seemed short despite her considerable height. She started almost every sentence with an implied apology.

"Am I too early?"

"Not at all. Come in."

"I wouldn't want to disturb you, Jess. Is Ryan ready?"

"Just about. Danny's getting his chair." She heard the ponderous thump of Danny's descent, felt the jolt. "Can I get you something? Some tea?"

"I wouldn't want to be any trouble. I'll just get Ryan and be on my way. I can imagine how busy you must be."

Danny bumped down the final step, sat in Ryan's chair, and flipped the switch, engaging the motor. He nudged the joystick, and with a whirring sound, the tanklike vehicle swerved in a drunken wiggle across the room. Seeing Danny in the chair made Ryan laugh with a deep, nasal pull. Jess had to look away. Countless times, she'd considered that an altered blink of fate might have landed her son in his friend's battered condition. But since Danny's arrest, she'd had to wonder which boy's injuries might prove to be the cruelest and most damaging in the end.

"Thanks for coming, Ryan. I hope we'll see you again soon."

"You will. I'm—coming to—the trial."

Faith Harrison gripped the purse like a shield. "I told you, we'll see, sweetheart." She shot Jess a rueful smile. "He's got it in his head that he should come as a show of solidarity. Wants to testify about what a good friend Danny's been. I've tried to explain that he'd only be in the way."

"Stop, Mom!" Ryan groaned. "I'm—going. Don't worry, Dan-o. I'll be—there."

Danny lifted Ryan from the couch and buckled him into the chair. "I know you're there for me, bud. One way or the other."

Ryan raised a splay-fingered hand. "Friends to—"

Danny pressed his palm to Ryan's, their two high fives forming a crooked ten. "—the end," he said. "Come on. I'll help you into the van."

"Wait!" Ryan motioned for Jess to come close. "Closer. It's a—secret." Her ear filled with the rasp of his breath and a few garbled words. Jess struggled to catch what he said. "Knowledge—is—access—then," she heard. *Knowledge is access then?*

Ryan sighed at her quizzical frown. A string of drool stretched from the corner of his mouth.

Danny blotted the stray saliva with his sleeve. "Say good night, Gracie," he instructed.

"Good—night, Gracie," said Ryan. He held Jess in his hopeful sights as he wheeled out the door. Faith Harrison trailed behind, murmuring bonus apologies.

Danny followed Ryan down the walk and maneuvered the chair onto the narrow base of the lift. With practiced moves, he bounded into the van and worked the retractable platform up and inside. He fastened the wheels to metal brackets that had been bolted to the floor. As he slid the side panel shut, he called to Ryan, "Talk to you later, bud."

Faith Harrison executed an artless eight-point turn, and drove away.

As he headed back toward the house, Danny's smile dissolved. He passed Jess like a rootless ghost and made for the stairs.

"Wait, honey, please," she said. "Let's talk."

"Later, okay, Mom? I'm whipped."

"Okay, later."

With deepening concern, she watched him trudge up the stairs. He looked whipped in every sense of the word. He was pale from months of indoor isolation, bleary-eyed from months of fitful, tormented sleep. Jess couldn't remember the last time her normally athletic child had gotten any exercise or enjoyed anything even vaguely resembling fun. His quick infectious smile was a distant memory. Despite his heroic handling of Ryan and the chair, Danny was in lousy, vulnerable condition.

Dr. Rebold's warnings echoed in her mind. Danny was at risk, down on himself, terribly depressed. Weeks ago, he'd told her that he believed he must have done something to deserve all this. Ryan was right. He needed help.

Several times, Jess had lobbied for Danny to get supportive counseling for the duration of this ordeal. But he continued to balk. Forcing him would be futile. Nothing worthwhile could be accomplished against a patient's will.

That didn't mean that Jess couldn't benefit from some wise outside input. She put in a call to Hannah Unger, the brilliant therapist who had talked her through her two-year mandatory training analysis. After they'd finished kicking through the rubble of Jess's ancient ruins and regrets, polishing the gems and discarding the useless artifacts, the two women had become good friends. Like Libby, Hannah had been a close, easy constant in Jess's life.

Then, five years ago after Hannah's husband of forty years died of a sudden heart attack, she'd decided to close her suburban Connecticut practice and move to San Francisco, where her family lived. At first, she and Jess had been diligent about keeping in touch by phone. But gradually, their contacts had fallen off until months might pass before one or the other of them made a catch-up call. Still, no matter how much time elapsed, they fell back at once into easy familiarity. True friendship tracked a steady orbit that could be reentered at any point. There were no vexing schedules to keep, no oppressive obligations.

As she listened to the distant ring, Jess realized that she had not spoken with Hannah since their trip, not since Danny's arrest. There was much to explain.

"Hannah, it's Jess."

"My word. You must be psychic," she said. "I just ran into an old neighbor downtown. She told me what's been happening with Danny. What an awful thing, Jess. How can I help?"

Jess pictured her solid, silver-haired friend. She conjured the square-jawed face etched with seventy years of irony and passionate conviction, the intelligent impish eyes. "Where do I begin?"

"That's easy, my friend. Tell me everything. Begin at the beginning."

Seeking a logical starting point propelled Jess back to their return from France. They had touched down at Kennedy after a cramped, endless flight. Stiff and sore, they'd straggled off the plane. The luggage was delayed, and their bags were among the last to dribble onto the conveyer belt. For a harrowing while, Max was convinced that his beloved teddy bear Killer, who had been packed in a duffel bag by mistake, must have been missing in action.

After boy and bear enjoyed a tearful, talk-show-quality reunion, they made their way to passport control, where the lines snaked back and forth a dozen times through a dizzying maze of roped stanchions. From there, they passed to a second interminable line at customs. By then, most of them were edgy and frustrated. Max had devolved into giddy exhaustion.

The next available inspector, a moon-faced man, beckoned them across the sacred yellow line. Frowning, he riffled through their passports. "Purpose of your visit?" he asked.

"You mean, why'd we go to France?" Max piped up.

"That's right."

"Business and pleasure," Charlie said.

"And bazooms," added Max.

The customs officer cocked his head. "Sorry?"

"Bazooms, busters, teetees." Max giggled madly. He stretched out the front of his T-shirt in illustration. "We saw lots!"

Charlie stifled the child in classic fashion by binding him in a headlock with a hand across the mouth. The nonplussed customs inspector had nodded quickly and waved them through. As soon as they were outside at the taxi stand, Jess observed that Max would be invaluable to smugglers and illegal immigrants. A perfect diversion. Molly seized the idea and suggested that they offer him up, immediately. Cupping her hands in a mock megaphone, she'd announced: *Attention all criminal types and other undesirables. Big-mouth child for sale or rent, cheap.*

Even Max had been moved to laugh. Everyone had except Danny. He'd stepped away and lapsed into a dark, brooding silence.

"It wasn't like him to take Max's nonsense so seriously," Jess told Hannah. "I remember thinking that Danny had changed somehow. All during the trip, there were moments like that, when he would suddenly grow sullen and detached. I chalked it up to the pressures he must be under, worries about senior year, college applications, all that."

"And now you think . . . ?" Hannah asked.

"I'm wondering whether something else might have been going on. His friend Ryan, the boy I told you about who was in the car accident, says that Danny feels guilty, and I think that's true."

"Which leads you where?"

Jess's heart did a drumroll. She had come to the edge of a perilous crevasse. One more step, and she could lose her last solid footing, fall away. She cast around desperately for another way to turn, but she was pressed to face the impossible truth.

Her throat burned. "It leads me to wonder why he feels that way. What if he's done something seriously wrong, Hannah? What if he *is* guilty?"

"That's the question, my dear. What if he is?"

Through her bristling terror, Jess saw the answer clearly. "He's my son, and I love him. No matter what."

"Exactly, Jess. You love him no matter what. The most important thing you can do for Danny is to make sure he knows that."

"I keep telling him."

"Yes, but that doesn't automatically mean he believes you."

"What more can I do?"

"Difficult question. What's clear is where you need to go, not how to get there. Danny needs to feel safe, to have some way to get out whatever he may be carrying around."

"I know that, Hannah. The problem is he refuses to talk to me or anyone."

"You know what they say about Mohammed and the mountain, my dear."

"You're right, of course. Thanks."

"One more thing. Remember, despite your mother's contention to the contrary, things don't always turn out for the worst. There are many reasons besides actual guilt that Danny may consider himself unworthy of good fortune or deserving of blame. All of us harbor personal regrets, feelings that we might have treated someone badly or done something terribly wrong. Shame, inadequacy, a basic sense of imperfection, are part of the human condition, at least as far as so-called normal people are concerned. The only living saints and deities I know require antipsychotic drugs and, often, confinement. They pose a considerable danger to themselves and others, in their blinding perfection if nothing else."

Jess inhaled her friend's wisdom, felt her lungs clear. "In other words, I shouldn't be jumping to any conclusions."

"As hard as that may be, the only reasonable course is the slow, deliberate one, my friend. The only one that's fair to Danny, or any of you."

"Why can't you and Pearl trade places, Hannah, until this trial is over at least. I miss having you nearby."

"I am nearby, Jess. You know that."

"I do."

"Talk to Danny. Don't take no for an answer. See what he has to tell you. We'll figure this out from there."

As Tucci swerved into the Beningson drive, Mule whistled low. "Would you look at that place. You could put my whole house in this one's back pocket."

"Not unless you took it to the cleaners first. Beningson's a neat nut, plus crazy clean."

"And I'm not?" Mule rolled down his window and spat a wad of gum. He flipped down his visor, stared into the vanity mirror, and used the edge of a Visa card to mine for food between his teeth. He examined his find, something green and seedlike, then flicked the mess into the ashtray he'd already anointed with wadded tissues and half-eaten Gummi Bears. He really hated the yellow ones.

"Sure, Mule. You are a regular obsessive-repulsive."

The double doors opened the moment Mule and Tucci hit the walk. Beningson awaited them with his arms folded and a frown on his burnished face. "I hope this won't take long, Sergeant Tucci. We have dinner plans."

"Shouldn't. Like I said on the phone, we just need to ask Lisa a few questions."

"A few questions. A few more questions. How many times must that poor child be forced to relive that terrible night?"

"I told you, Mr. Beningson, we have to clear up a couple of things in your daughter's description of the assault. Otherwise, the case could fall apart."

His shoulders sagged. "All right, I suppose there's no choice."

"This is my partner, Mike Samuels," Tucci said.

"Hello, Detective. Come in. Lisa's in the den." Beningson led them past the string of showcase rooms.

Lisa sat primly on the couch, reading from a leather-bound collection of Jane Austen novels. *Emma, Sense and Sensibility, Northanger Abbey, Mansfield Park.* Clad in a long, prim dress and laced shoes, she looked like an escapee from the book's faded pages. Her hair was bound in a bow at the nape of her delicate neck, and outsized tortoiseshell glasses overwhelmed her fragile features.

"Lisa dear, you remember Detective Tucci. This is Detective Samuels. Sit, gentlemen, please."

Tucci sank into a floral chair that felt like a contoured, orthopedic cloud. A look of foolish delight claimed Mule's mug as he settled on a matching perch nearer the window.

Lisa set the open book facedown in her lap. "What's wrong?"

"We need you to help us clear something up. You said Danny Magill started hitting you in the car."

"He did."

"As I explained to your dad on the phone, there's some confusion about that. A forensic expert analyzed your injuries. He's convinced they couldn't have been inflicted in a confined space like the Mustang."

A thread hung from the book's ancient binding. Lisa tugged at it, unraveling slowly. "That's right. I said he *started* in the car."

"Then what?"

Her eyes skittered behind the giant frames. She glanced at Tucci, then her father, then back at the book, searching for a different thread to pull.

Watching her squirm, Tucci's hopes plunged. If she crumbled, so did the case against Danny Magill.

The girl folded her hands and sat straighter. "Then I managed to get away from him. I opened the door and hurried toward the house. I ran as fast as I could, but my legs felt weak and rubbery. Danny caught up and stopped me before I could make it inside. I had my hand on the door, but he pulled me back. He called me terrible names. Then, he punched me so hard I could barely breathe. I felt something break inside, heard this cracking sound. And still, he kept hitting me, kicking. He was so furious. I've never been more terrified." Tears brimmed in her voice and streamed down her pale, childish face.

Tucci listened raptly to her recitation. On a purely emotional basis, this girl with her wide eyes and Victorian delicacy was irresistible. Big, strapping Danny Magill would come across as a fanged monster by comparison. Left to their own gut-driven devices, any jury would be out knotting the noose by now. Too bad there would be a judge around to keep reminding them about an annoying complication called the law.

He waited until Lisa's tears let up. "That explains most of it. I just have a couple of other questions."

Beningson stared pointedly at his watch. "I told you, we have an appointment, Detective."

"I'll make it as quick as possible." Turning back to Lisa, he said, "What names did Danny Magill call you?"

She stared at her lap.

"I understand it may be hard for you to say such things, especially in front of us, but you're going to be asked in court to repeat exactly what he said."

"Why would they want to hear things like that?"

"Because it will help them decide who's telling the truth."

Lisa gnawed her lower lip. "Slut, he called me. He called me a—whore. How can he say those things about—"

"About?" Tucci prompted.

She met his gaze with a sorrowful shake of her head. "Forget it. I know why. I didn't do what he wanted. I made him mad. He didn't know what he was saying."

"Is that about all, Detective?" Beningson's crocodile-clad foot tapped the rhythm of his impatience on the Oriental rug. Tucci made it out as "I'm in the Mood for Love," but he could have been mistaken.

"I've got one more thing for you, Mr. Beningson. You said you watched from the bedroom window, saw Lisa get out of the car and race toward the house. You didn't mention anything about Danny Magill coming after her, hitting her. You didn't even say you saw Magill. Only his car."

Beningson's foot went still. "That's because I did *not* see him, Detective. Suppose you looked out an upstairs window and there was your daughter with her clothing in disarray, screaming and distraught. Suppose you watched her break from a car and come racing toward the house. What would you do? Stand around and watch or take action?"

Imagining Gina in such a scene tied knots in Tucci's intestines. He was ready to spring off the couch, burst downstairs, and dismember the little scum. It took him a minute to pull himself together and return to reality in the Beningsons' den.

Tucci's neck went hot. He hated like hell being played that way. He didn't know whether he was more furious with Lisa's old man or himself. "What I might do doesn't matter, Mr. Beningson. All that counts is whether your story rings true or not."

Beningson looked ready to argue, then thought better of it. "I threw on a robe and my glasses and hurried downstairs. It took a moment to find the glasses. All told, three, perhaps as much as four minutes passed before I reached the foyer. By then, Lisa was in the house, battered and hysterical. The Magill boy had taken off. Apparently, it doesn't take very long for a crazed animal to strike, do his damage, and run."

Like Lisa, Beningson was articulate, convincing, except—

"So you weren't wearing your glasses when you looked out the window?"

Beningson's foot started tapping again. This time, Tucci heard the tune as a Sousa march, that one about being kind to your web-footed friends. "I only use them for reading."

Mule frowned. "I'm confused."

"Yeah, me too," said Tucci. "If the glasses are only for reading, why did you put them on before you went downstairs?"

Beningson shook his head. "I honestly can't say. A circumstance like that moves one to act instinctively. I have no idea why it seemed necessary to find my eyeglasses. It just did."

"Where was Mrs. Beningson through all this?" Tucci asked.

"Sandra suffers from insomnia. She took a sedative that night. It had her sleeping so soundly she didn't hear a thing."

Tucci nodded. "That's about it for me. How about you, Mule? Anything we haven't covered?"

"Don't think so."

"We won't keep you then. Thanks for your time, Mr. Beningson, Lisa."

Beningson herded them out. As soon as the door smacked behind him, Tucci realized what he had neglected to ask on his last visit. "Wait, Mule." He knocked and waited, but no one appeared. He rang the bell, raising a boisterous chorus of chimes. From inside came the low beat of footfalls. The door opened a crack.

"What is it now, Sergeant?" Beningson asked.

"One more thing. Where exactly is your bedroom?"

"Upstairs."

"Where upstairs? Which windows?"

Beningson puffed his annoyance. "The three center ones, directly above the door. Now if you gentlemen will excuse me."

"Mind if we take a look?"

"Actually, I do. We are terribly late as it is, Detective. If you need anything further, I'm afraid you'll have to wait for a more convenient time."

"It'll only take a minute," Tucci assured.

"I don't have a minute, Detective. Goodbye!"

The door slammed, capping the discussion. Tucci shrugged. "Do you get the feeling that guy doesn't like us, Mule?"

"You never know, Tooch. Maybe he's just shy."

"Yeah, sure. That's probably it."

"Think he could be hiding something?"

"You mean, like he's really a nice guy?"

Peering up, Tucci backed toward the driveway. He calculated the sight lines from the master bedroom. As Beningson had reported, there was a clear view from the driveway. No obstructions.

He adjusted for conditions on the night of the assault. The sky had been mostly clear after an early-evening storm. Security spots were trained on the driveway, the walk, and much of the front and side yards. From a dark interior room, it would have been fairly easy to observe anything happening in those areas.

"Okay, Mule. I guess we can pack it in." Tucci was itching to get home, see how things were going.

"Good deal, Tooch. I was thinking I'd try to round up a poker game tonight. Want to play?"

"With my family I do. What about Frannie?"

"What about her?"

"She's got her hands full all day with those three little Indians of yours, Mule. Why don't you stay home and poke her instead?"

Mule shrugged. "It's an idea."

"Let's hit the road. I need to make a couple of stops."

He left the cruiser running in front of his friend Al's florist shop on High Ridge Road. He bought a dozen of the peach-colored roses Marie loved and an African violet with lavender blooms for Gina. Al threw in a dozen sweetheart roses. "Tell her I said get well, and that's an order."

In the adjacent strip mall, he parked in front of Gina's favorite ice cream place. Tucci wanted to tempt his scrawny girl with some big empty calories.

"What'll it be?" asked the clerk, a ruddy redheaded boy in a white paper hat.

Tucci scanned the list behind the counter, but nothing rang a bell. He couldn't remember the names of the cockamamie flavors his daughter used to drool about. Squirrel nut fudge with banana? Pink chunky chicken?

Before she got sick, he hadn't paid nearly enough attention when his kid talked. Tucci would come home, weary and preoccupied, and only half listen while Gina jabbered on and on, jumping from topic to topic as if her brain were mounted on a pogo stick. Her bristling enthusiasms used to give him a headache. Now, he would give most anything for a headache like that.

"A pint of each," he told the clerk.

"I've got twenty-four flavors," the kid whined. "It's almost closing time."

"Make it quick, or I'll make it half-gallons."

Tucci dropped Mule off at home. As he passed the Italian social club, his Uncle Pasquale stepped out and flagged him down with wide-swirling arms.

"*Mi dispiace.* I've got to get home, Zio," Tucci explained. "I've got a trunk full of ice cream."

Pasquale puffed a frigid breath. "So what's *il problema,* Giuseppe? You're afraid it's going to get cold?"

"No, Uncle. I'm anxious for Gina to have some."

The old man flapped a gnarled hand. "*Vai via,* Giuseppe. Go. I just thought you might like to hear that I have found some interesting *informazione* about your case."

"What?"

"Another time," he huffed. "You want to hear, you'll show an old man a little respect, sit down, have a taste of *vino,* pay *attenzione.* You're too busy with your ice cream, go home."

Tucci sighed. If the old man had uncovered anything really interesting, he'd be crowing his head off about it. Pasquale had always been very, very generous with his words.

"Okay, Zio Pasquale. Another time."

Tucci took the back roads to his house, avoiding the evening crush. As he approached his block, he stopped the car and ventured a silent prayer. Playing invisible hadn't worked. Nothing had. At the risk of being noticed and singled out for even more trouble, he decided it was time to apply directly to the Big Guy.

Please, Lord. Let me walk in and find Gina up and smiling, feeling well. Let that damned germ disappear the way it came.

He cast a wary eye toward the heavens. Everything looked calm enough. He saw no lightning flares or visions to suggest that his plea had pressed any hot celestial buttons. Cautiously, he clenched his lids again, wove his fingers in a ball, and continued.

I'm not going to try to cut any kind of deal with you, Lord. I get that you call the shots one hundred percent, and that's fine with me. Perfetto. *Make my baby well, then send me the bill, whatever you think is fair. No matter what it costs, I'll gladly pay. Everything I've got, everything I'll ever have, a second mortgage on my soul, you name it.*

Tucci opened his eyes and switched the car in gear. He turned the corner, thinking of Gina's smile, Gina's laugh, Gina's motor-mouth eagerness. Then, looking down the block, his heart lurched up and caught in his throat. The house was dark. No one was home.

Jess slipped the seasoned fish fillets into a sizzling frying pan. Heady scents seeped from the stove where rosemary potatoes heated beside a sourdough baguette. The apple tart she'd made earlier was cooling on the kitchen table. Prozac perched beside it, panting with lust.

She was startled by the shrill of the phone.

"Hi, Jess. It's Sidney. I just hung up with our investigator in Phnom Penh. It's seven o'clock tomorrow morning over there, and Firestone spent a highly enlightening night exploring some of the city's low lights. Beningson's partner gave him a very challenging itinerary."

Jess shoved the fillets around, making sure they got equal heat. "What did he find?"

"Seems what Reggie Hanson said is true. For the past couple of years, Beningson has been a regular at an establishment owned and operated by a man named Bin Nol. By day, Nol runs the place as a camera shop and photography studio. After hours, he runs a string of underage girls. Little beauties, I'm told. Beningson's tastes run to the ten-to-twelve set. He's a pederast, Jess. To the trade, creeps like that are known as chicken hawks."

Jess lowered the flame beneath the pan. "Why would this man Nol admit such a thing to your investigator? Even if Cambodian authorities look the other way, it's not the sort of thing most people would brag about to strangers. Plus, why would he tell tales about a good customer?"

"I asked the same questions. Once again, it seems Leo Beningson made an enemy of a former ally. From what Firestone found out, Beningson was a very good client at first. Then, after a few months, he began to rough up the girls. Nol warned Beningson to behave himself, but the beatings got worse and worse. A couple of months ago, the dear man put a ten-year-old in a coma. They still don't know whether or not she's going to make it."

"My God, Sidney. The man's a monster. He must have been the one who beat Lisa."

"It's a good theory, Jess, but that doesn't necessarily follow, especially in the eyes of the law. For one thing, at this point all we have is the secondhand word of a Cambodian criminal who admittedly has an ax to grind. Plus, even if Bin Nol's story proves true, Leo Beningson is not going to trial. If he takes the stand in Danny's case, we get a chance to try to impeach him. But he may elect not to testify at all, especially if he has a lot of dirt under his nails."

Jess puffed her frustration. How could the so-called justice system protect a repulsive creature like Leo Beningson and provide no armor for her son? "Then what was the point in sending your man to Phnom Penh? Sounds as if the whole thing is an exercise in futility."

"It could turn out to be, but we're far from there yet. I'm optimistic that we can find some way to use this in our favor. Let's see how it plays out."

When the phone rang again, Jess wasn't surprised to hear Charlie's voice or one of his routine excuses.

"This meeting is running late, Jessie. I told you how Weltner makes a federal case out of everything. Chances are I won't be able to get away for at least another hour. Don't wait dinner for me."

"Fine."

"I'll try not to be too late."

"Sure. Have a good meeting."

Jess heard the hollowness in his tone, the frosty detachment. She answered with a deliberate coolness of her own. It was well beyond her current energies to confront him with her sorrows and suspicions, and beneath her battered dignity to beg. She wanted the real marriage they used to have, not this clumsy amateur show.

This was how a couple fell apart, she supposed. They took one step in opposing directions, then another, and soon they were too distant to see or recognize one another. First the closeness went, then the open honesty, then the trust. At some point, everything got too damaged to repair. One party or the other had to step back, make a critical assessment of the relationship, and condemn it as a tear-down.

Jess set the matter aside. She looked forward to having a quiet dinner alone with Danny. Maybe she could find a way to pry the kid open as Hannah had urged, get him to vent whenever poisons were festering inside him. He was going to need every scrap of strength for the upcoming trial. They all were.

She turned the fillets and trudged upstairs to Danny's room. She knocked for form. Undoubtedly he had the volume on his stereo set to demolition level and could not hear a thing. After a decent interval, she knocked again, then opened the door.

Spotting her, Danny took off the headset. "What's up?"

"Dinner's ready."

"Thanks anyway, Mom. I'm not hungry."

She frowned. The real Danny had a prodigious appetite. He'd always been one of those kids who ate one meal a day, but it lasted from first thing in the morning until bedtime. Jess used to quip that they should consider replacing his mouth with a vacuum attachment. "Are you feeling all right?"

"I'm fine. I'll have something later." He picked up the headset and moved to put it on.

Jess stood her ground. "If you're not hungry now, I can warm the food up when you are. When do you think? About an hour?"

"Don't wait for me, Mom. Really. I had a bunch of snacks. I don't know if I want dinner at all."

"Why don't you come and sit with me while I eat, then?"

"I'd really rather be alone, if you don't mind."

"I do mind, Danny." Moving mountains was not as simple as Hannah had made it sound. "We need to talk. Would you rather do it now or later?" Having managed three kids and countless recalcitrant patients, Jess knew that most people responded better when presented with a choice, even an artificial one.

"Later."

"Okay, I'll see you downstairs in an hour."

Jess's appetite had vanished. She wrapped the food and put it in the refrigerator. Prozac watched in slack-muzzled astonishment as the series of untouched dishes disappeared into the frigid crypt. After the apple tart followed the rest, the dog lumbered into the pantry, lay beside her kibble sack, and sighed. People behavior was well beyond her comprehension.

Jess passed the time cleaning up the kitchen. She washed the pots and sponged the counters and buffed every spot on the wood plank floor. She alphabetized her cookbooks, then rearranged them by cuisine. After months of unrelenting turmoil, there was precious little remaining mess or dirt.

She considered calling to see how Molly and Max were doing at her mother's, then thought better of it. No matter when she phoned, Pearl would find some reason to deem it a terrible intrusion. Jess's mom had passed the entire week cooking in anticipation of her grandchildren's weekend visit. When she and Lou came to pick the kids up, Pearl had spent a full fifteen minutes reciting the exhaustive, exhausting list of foods she had purchased and prepared: potted chicken, turkey tetrazzini, tuna casserole, sweet-and-sour meatballs, brisket of course. She went on and on, reciting her entire repertoire of culinary affronts.

From the sound of it, Molly and Max would be spending the entire weekend chained to the table, except when they went to bed, at which point Pearl might well continue feeding them in their sleep. Her desire was to turn everyone she could into a human blimp. That way, they were easier to deflate.

Jess eyed the cookbooks. Maybe they would look better in size order. For the third time, she pulled every volume down and dusted the immaculate pages. As she began replacing them, she sensed that she wasn't alone.

Danny had padded in soundlessly and stood watching. "You're busy."

"Not at all. Sit, honey. Can I get you something?"

"No. There's nothing." He perched on the stool beside the breakfast bar and coiled his legs around the uprights. "What do you want to talk about?"

Jess sat beside him and waited for his skittish gaze to light. "Ryan is worried about you."

"So that was the big secret he was whispering to you about?"

"It's no secret. He cares about you. So do I."

Danny shrugged. "What am I supposed to say?"

"Whatever's on your mind, honey. I know all this has been terribly hard on you. You'll feel better if you talk about what you're feeling, get it off your chest."

"There's nothing to say, Mom. The trial starts in a week. It'll go on for as long as it lasts, and then—"

Jess gave him all the space and time he needed to finish the thought. All of them, even the lawyers, had tiptoed around the worst-case possibilities. They'd avoided loaded words like "conviction" and "sentence," favoring a grand show of confidence and optimism. But unspoken words did not cease to exist. Quite the contrary.

His eyes dropped. "Doesn't matter what happens, Mom. I don't care anymore."

"Why is that?"

His shoulders hitched. "I just don't."

"Anyone would be scared, Danny. There's no reason to be ashamed if you are."

"I was at first. I admit that. But no more."

"What do you feel then?"

Another shrug. "Honestly? Nothing. None of it matters, especially *me*."

"That's not so."

Jess cupped his chin. "Listen to me, Danny. I honestly believe this is going to turn out fine, that you'll be found innocent. But I need for you to know that whatever happens, we love you and we're going to be there for you. All of us."

His face went sharp and he pulled away. "Don't give me that, Mom. There's no *us* anymore. The family's trashed."

"No we're not. People get through all sorts of things. You'll see."

"Sure, right."

"Why do you blame yourself? You can tell me, Danny. Whatever it is, it's better to get it out."

"So that's the way it is?"

"What?"

"Everyone thinks I'm guilty. Why should you be different?"

"I don't think that, Danny. That's not what I'm saying at all."

His mouth warped in ugly rebuke. "Can I go now?"

"Please don't. I want you to talk to me."

"I told you, I've got nothing to say. You think talking is the answer to everything, but you're wrong here. It is what it is, Mom. Leave it alone, for God sakes. Leave *me* alone."

With a sinking heart, Jess watched him go. He bounded angrily upstairs and his door slammed with a reverberating fury. "Nice going, Jess," she muttered aloud. "You really made a picture-perfect mess of that."

She searched for mindless ways to pass the time. The ten days until the scheduled start of the trial stretched like a huge, forbidding sea. Once it began, the proceeding could take weeks. How were they going to get through it?

Prozac was sprawled on the pantry floor. Jess stepped over her and began tackling the crowded shelves of provisions. She stacked the canned goods by size and type and arranged the paper goods. They had enough tuna and toilet tissue to sustain them through a major siege. Ditto chocolate chips for making Toll House cookies, one of life's more crucial necessities. There were unopened sacks of dried beans and wild mushrooms and jars of odd herbs and spices with unpronounceable names and no obvious utility. Once upon a time, she had toyed with the idea of making some odd concoction she'd sampled in a restaurant or seen on a cooking show and dutifully gone out to buy these ingredients. She was forever planning to get around to one thing or the other: piano lessons, French class, writing letters, ballroom dancing, arranging their vast jumble of family pictures in albums.

Even as that thought crossed her mind, she spotted a pile of film envelopes beside a five-pound bag of wheat flour. They were still sealed.

At the kitchen table, she opened the first packet. There were Max and Molly on the Champs Élysées. All of them posed in front of the Louvre, tallest in the center, to echo the museum's imposing glass pyramid. Danny sporting a rakish beret and mirrored shades at a sidewalk café.

Jess's eyes stung with bitter regret. She and Charlie had never taken their blessings for granted. They had often talked about how lucky they were, keeping their voices low at Jess's insistence to avoid attracting the evil eye. They had three healthy kids, a good marriage, fun and satisfying work, this rambling, silly, perfect place to live. She would not allow everything they'd built, all they'd had, to be stolen by one twist of a sick kid's mind. She had to find some way to reconnect to the place they'd been mere months ago.

Jess went through the rest of the snapshots, separating the double prints and ordering the pictures chronologically: Paris, Versailles, Chartres, the Loire Valley, the Dordogne, Bordeaux, Brittany. There was Max, dwarfed by endless rows of grapevines at Château Lafite Rothschild. Danny and Charlie in the towering shadow of Mont-Saint-Michel.

The memories pulled at her like a sweet, familiar tune. Yielding to their draw, she felt lighter. Jess was dangerously close to enjoying herself. Maybe the pictures would have a similar effect on Danny.

He did not respond when she called up the stairs. No answer when she knocked at his door. Peering in, she was surprised to find the room enveloped in inky darkness. It was only nine o'clock. Danny, a natural night owl, had not turned in this early since he was two.

Following a time-honored Leffermanian tradition, Jess panicked. Danny must be sick, maybe seriously so. Intense, sustained pressure like this had to be hell on the immune system.

She drew a breath and ordered herself to get a grip. Naturally, he was emotionally spent, weary, seeking refuge in sleep. Lord knew, there were far more destructive and malignant responses to the kind of stress Danny was suffering. Several times since Danny's arrest, Charlie had endeavored to crawl up and disappear in a bourbon bottle. Jess's escapes had run the gamut from comical to frankly bizarre. Her superstitions, or "stupid-stitions," as Max more aptly termed them, kept rearing their ridiculous heads. She read horoscopes, avoided sidewalk cracks, treated mirrors with unwarranted respect. Yesterday, on the way home from the office, she'd found herself drawn like a flamebound moth to a tiny sign above a carpet shop on High Ridge Road.

She'd edged into an undersized spot and squeezed through the meager crack in the door. Despite the deep December chill, her cheeks burned with embarrassment. She glanced around nervously, hoping to sneak inside unseen.

Through the door, she entered a tiny vestibule, redolent of cooked onions and wet wool. A bare bulb, dangling from a noose of twine like a disembodied head, illuminated the steep, narrow staircase. As Jess climbed, the risers wavered and creaked.

Three unmarked doors lined the second-floor hall. The first two she tried were locked. The third yielded when she twisted the knob, and the door squealed open.

Heart racing, Jess turned to leave. But before she could take a step, a plump little girl of five or six appeared, dark ponytail bobbing high on her crown. She popped her thumb from her mouth and offered a gap-toothed grin. "Come in. Make yourself at home. Mommy will be right with you."

"Sounds like she's making dinner. Don't bother her. I'll come back another time," Jess said. She felt suddenly foolish.

"No, don't. Now is good." The child took her hand and tugged Jess into the shabby space. Stuffing spilled from the threadbare arms of a tweed sofa. Mismatched stack tables perched at intervals. A tattered afghan was bunched in front of the muted television set, where a talking head expounded soundlessly on the day's events.

"Sit there," the girl instructed, pressing her toward the couch. "I'll get Madame Elena right now." She pranced out of the room, through a tattered tapestry curtain. "Mommy. Customers. Come quick."

In moments "Madame Elena" appeared, wiping her reddened hands on a cobbler apron. Wisps of dark hair framed a wide, weary face that was an older version of the child's.

The little girl dipped in a practiced bow. "Madame Elena knows all, sees all."

The seer bit back a grin. "Hush now, Lorelei. Go inside with the baby and leave us."

She placed a folding chair opposite the couch and set a stack table between them. "Let me have your hand please."

Despite the noticeable chill in the apartment, heat radiated from the fortune-teller's hands. She examined Jess's palm, tracing several of the lines and contours. "I see trouble with a child, a son, someone with the letter *D* in his name."

Her pronouncement made the hairs rise on Jess's neck. But her inner skeptic warned that Danny's case had been in the local papers. Maybe this woman somehow knew who she was.

But how could she?

Squinting in concentration, Madame Elena continued:"I see a car and water. The two are connected somehow, but the way is unclear."

Jess remembered the rain earlier on the night of Danny's arrest. Wet streets. Puddles on the lawn. Danny said he had slipped on some muck near the school. "What about the trouble? Can you tell me what happens to the boy?"

The fortune-teller traced the pad beneath Jess's thumb. "It's strange. There seem to be two boys in trouble. For one, I see a bright future, clear skies after the storm that is to come. The other is more uncertain. His trouble goes on for some time. I cannot predict the outcome. I believe it depends on forces beyond his control and, therefore, beyond my reckoning."

"You said one boy has a *D* in his name. Is he the one with the bright future?"

Madame Elena pressed a finger to her lips. "Have patience, please. The future cannot be rushed or forced to reveal itself."

Jess wanted to scream. If she had the patience to sit back and see how this played out, she wouldn't be sitting here wasting her time and money, feeling like an utter, unmitigated fool.

The woman's face went limp, and her eyes rolled up so only the whites showed. Jess feared she was having a seizure. Wrenching her hand away, she searched for the phone. "My God!"

"What's wrong?" Madame Elena demanded.

"Nothing. I thought something was the matter with you."

"I go inside where I can see the face of the future. That's how I learn what I do. You have broken the connection. There is no way to retrieve it today. That will be ten dollars."

Thinking back on that foolishness, Jess flushed. She pulled Danny's door shut. Let the kid sleep. It was harmless.

She caught the crunch of Charlie's car on the driveway. The garage door clattered open. He was earlier than she had expected.

In no hurry to see him, Jess dawdled in the hall. Her eyes had accommodated themselves to the stingy light, and she noticed that the family pictures clustered on the wall had been bumped out of alignment. She straightened them and polished the frames with the tail of her blue shirt. A lint speck on the carpet caught her neurotic eye. Sinking to her knees, she plucked it out, then inched toward a second spot down the hall.

Charlie's key clacked in the lock, and he entered in a chill rush of air. "Jessie? Anybody home?" There was the thump of his briefcase hitting the foyer floor. His footsteps, intermingled with Prozac's, faded toward the kitchen.

Jess picked up half a dozen other dirt specks. Approaching the hall bathroom, she noticed a watery wash of light seeping out from under the door. Danny had forgotten to kill the switch.

She stood and turned the knob, but the door wouldn't budge. Thinking it must have swollen with the pumping heat from the radiator, she tried again. Then she noticed the shadow of the dead bolt in the frame. From inside came a barely audible hiss of running water.

Danny was in the shower, not sleeping after all. Typical Jess, she chided herself, getting all worked up over nothing. Maybe her reluctance to face Charlie was equally overblown. Maybe by some miracle they would fall back into their old easy rhythms. Exchange apologies. Kiss and make up.

As she turned toward the stairs, a small sharp cry from the bathroom stopped her cold.

"Danny? What's wrong?"

There was another cry, a tiny terrified whimper.

Jess jiggled the knob. "Open the door, Danny. Let me in."

No answer.

"Charlie, help!"

She tried to muscle the door open, but it would not budge. Charlie bounded up the stairs.

"Hurry," Jess cried. "Something's wrong with Danny."

He slipped off a shoe and used the heel to hammer the long bolts free of the hinges. Jess raced in after him. Her hand flew to her mouth at the sight of Danny slumped in a daze on the floor beside the tub. Blood seeped from a slash that ran up the forearm from his wrist. The ankle-deep water was tinged pink. His Swiss Army knife lay open on the floor, the blade glazed red.

"Danny, no!"

Charlie drew the boy up and sat him on the pot. He stared into the wide blue eyes and checked his pulse. Then he examined the wound. "It's superficial. Get my bag please, Jessie."

She retrieved his medical supplies from the linen closet. Charlie disinfected the wound and pressed the edges together with butterfly adhesives. "Doesn't need sutures." He looked Danny hard in the eye. "No sign of shock. I don't think he lost much blood."

Jess pulled a shaky breath. "I think you should lie down, Danny. Come." She gripped his elbow and guided him toward his room. She felt the quiver of his fear and fragility. It reminded her of walks she'd taken with her father in the dark, final weeks before his death.

"Maybe we should take him to the hospital," Charlie said. "They can keep an eye on him overnight."

"No, Dad. No hospital. Please."

"You need to promise you won't try to hurt yourself again," Jess said. She stalled Charlie's protests with a look. They both knew that the hospital night staff passed the interminable hours of the graveyard shift in a sleepwalk, watching the clock, doing crossword puzzles, with pulp novels and late-night TV. She and Charlie could keep a much better eye on Danny here.

He settled heavily in bed. Jess pulled the covers to his chin. "Need anything?"

"No."

"Try to get some rest then."

Watching him was no guarantee in any event. If Danny was intent on harming himself, he would find a way. But from the nature of the cut and everything Jess knew about suicide attempts, this one had been a classic plea for help.

Danny's eyes drifted shut. Charlie motioned for her to follow him out.

The teenager's forceless voice stopped her at the door. "Mom?"

"Yes, honey."

"Would you mind sitting with me for a minute?"

He hadn't asked for that in a decade. "Not at all."

"Just until I fall asleep, okay? I know it's dumb."

"It's fine."

"See you downstairs," Charlie mouthed.

Jess perched on Danny's desk chair. "Can I ask why?"

He sighed. "I just feel so bad. Mrs. Harrison called tonight and told me that Ryan fell out of his chair and broke his arm. It's a bad break, compound. They have to operate."

"That's too bad."

"He should have been wearing his seat belt. He should have been more careful. He could have killed himself, the stupid jerk."

"I understand that you're upset, Danny, but hurting yourself is certainly not going to help Ryan. That's the last thing he'd want."

"It's not just him. I can't do this, Mom. The trial. All of it. It's too much."

"Hurting yourself is not the answer."

"Then what is?"

"Time," Jess told him. "Soon, all of this will be behind us. Meanwhile, I need you to make that promise. I have to know that I can trust you not to try anything like that again."

"All right, Mom. I promise. No more."

In minutes he drifted off. His breathing settled. Shadows fell across his face, softening the bones and angles, so he looked barely older than Max.

Jess rose with care, anxious not to disturb him. As she did, her eye was drawn to the insistent neon flash of Danny's screensaver, an abstract fireworks display.

As she groped in the dark for the power button on the monitor, her elbow bumped the mouse. With a burst of light, the screensaver vanished, revealing an e-mail that Emma had written from school earlier today. Danny's friend was so swamped with course work that most of their exchanges now occurred on-line.

> *I keep reading the letter you wrote yesterday, and I have to tell you, it makes me really mad. What exactly did you mean by all that* mea culpa *nonsense? What's gotten into you, Magill?*
>
> *Why are you so eager to be the guilty one? Lisa's no vestal virgin and you know it.*
>
> *What gives you the idea that the confessional is a decent hiding place? Anyway, what are you hiding from? In other words, I don't buy what you're selling, Danny, not a word of it.*
>
> *Remember the time I was really miserable about my parents' breakup and you came over and I'd had a few beers from Daddy's precious stash of microbrews for spite? I can't say I remember everything, but I do know I got more than a little friendly. You could have taken advantage of me in a heartbeat. Me and a zillion other girls who've come on to you. But you're always looking out for other people. That's you, Magill, not this other creature you're setting yourself up to be.*
>
> *Send me some sense, Danny. Obviously, you're out of sorts, so I'll send you some of those.*
>
> *Love,*
> *Em*

Emma's letter had been stored in the in-box of Danny's virtual filing cabinet. Without hesitation, Jess clicked the icon marked *mail sent*. This was no time for delicacy or restraint.

She brought up the last note Danny had written to Emma.

> *The hardest thing is dealing with the people who believe in me, Em. I'm not who they think I am. I never have been that model kid who always got it right. In a way all this has been a relief, to be seen for what I really am. Who I am.*
>
> *Years ago I read a story that stuck with me. I can't remember the title, but I'll never forget how it went. The main character was sailing alone in a small boat. A sudden storm came up and he was thrown overboard.*
>
> *He fought for a while, but the currents were too strong and the chill was unbearable. Eventually, his muscles cramped and the cold and exhaustion overwhelmed him. He understood that he was drowning, and rather than keep up the futile fight, he settled into the sea. As soon as he surrendered, the water went warm and calm. It was like a giant cradle, rocking him gently to sleep. I know it sounds sappy, Em. But that guy had such a good end it brought tears to my eyes.*
>
> *I'm ready to settle for that. More than ready. All I need to do is stop fighting. Tell them what they want to hear. What's a jailbird anyway? Here's the riddle: Can a jailbird fly?*

Jess stared at the words until the firework screensaver flared up and consumed them. With a last pained look at her firstborn, she stole out of the room.

Tucci awoke to a rubber-soled stampede and the buzz of voices. An eager herd of white coats crowded into the cramped hospital room Gina shared with three other girls.

A ruddy man with stark white hair led the pack. He looked like an off-season Santa, shed of beard and a few pounds of pork. His industrious elves followed a deferential beat behind, chattering among themselves.

They stopped first at the bed nearest the window, where a girl pale and thin as a Communion wafer stared at a talk show through wide, weary eyes. Alice in Wonderland characters, boldly sketched with candy-colored Magic Markers, festooned her sheets and pillowcases. The March Hare, the Queen of Hearts, a smirking Cheshire Cat. From Alice's mouth trailed a thought balloon filled with words that summed up this place and situation perfectly. *Curiouser and Curiouser.* She had replaced the standard thermal blanket with a leopard-print duvet. Huge stuffed animals and clumps of Mylar balloons left almost no room for the girl.

Tucci's back was in knots from the three nights he'd spent folded in a nasty plastic chair. He was fuzzy-eyed and heartsick and in a generally wretched mood.

Santa scanned the first girl's chart. "Good morning, Cynthia."

"Morning."

Her gaze stayed riveted on the morning show's meteorologist. He was a balding human weather balloon who could barely contain his excitement at the prospect of the season's first snow. *Flurries,* he said gleefully. *Some accumulation likely. Possibly an inch!*

"How are *we* today?" asked the doc with exorbitant cheer.

The kid's response was a tepid sigh.

Saint Dick talked to his drones as if the girl did not exist. "This is Cynthia's seventh admission to the hospital since her family moved from Wisconsin a year ago. Based on observation alone, would anyone care to take a stab at a diagnosis?"

"Anorexia nervosa," intoned a female intern whose massive rear end, swaddled in the lab coat, was suitable for screening feature films. "Severe."

The girl pulled herself away from the meteorologist's tips on snow shoveling long enough to set the woman straight. "I bet I eat more calories than you do."

"Actually, I'm a very small eater," the intern bristled.

"Yeah, sure," the girl muttered.

"Cynthia does consume a striking amount of food and two to three nutrient shakes a day," said the chief doc. "Given that added piece of information, would anyone else care to venture a guess?"

"Cystic fibrosis?" pronounced a Sikh Indian resident with a turban and beard. The genetic condition caused respiratory problems and progressive lung damage that left its young victims starved for air. Weight loss to the point of emaciation was a common side effect.

Something about all this delighted Dr. Claus. The ruddy face split in a giant grin. "Excellent, Dr. Singh. Cynthia has a particularly pernicious case. She has outlived almost everyone's expectations. At this point, her only reasonable hope is a lung transplant, and she's far from strong enough to survive the procedure. Our current intervention strategy is largely palliative. Any questions?"

Tucci had plenty, starting with where this jerk had gone for his insensitivity training. Poor Cynthia lay staring at the tube, pretending that the predicted snow flurries were far more interesting than the death sentence still reverberating in the room.

The head of rounds moved toward Gina, who was still out cold from the sleeping pill the nurse had pushed her into taking late last night.

"Good morning, Gina," said the jolly old head of the pack. Turning to his followers, he said, "Here we have a seventeen-year-old female, admitted through emergency three days ago. She presents with multiple sequellae of an infectious process of unknown origin, commencing in early June. Anyone care to take a crack at this?"

Tucci wanted to crack him but good. He bolted up and pressed into the huddle. "Look, the kid doesn't feel well. She needs her sleep. Be a good guy and leave her alone. Okay?"

Santa squinted at the chart, then returned it to the holder at the foot of the bed. "Morning rounds are an integral part of hospital routine, sir. I'm sure you understand."

"I don't actually."

Gina's eyes shot open. "Daddy? What's going on?"

"Nothing, baby. Go back to sleep." Tucci stroked her hollow cheek. "I'm asking you nicely. Get the hell away from my daughter, *please.*"

"Visiting hours are one to eight p.m. You are not even authorized to be here, Mr. Tucci. You are the one who needs to leave."

"I don't need your damned authorization to stay with my own kid. Now back off!"

"I'll have to insist that you lower your voice and calm down, Mr. Tucci. I cannot have you upsetting the patients."

"I wouldn't think of it. That's *your* job."

"I think it's best if I speak with this gentleman alone," he told his ugly docklings. "Dr. Sterbakov, please take over and continue with the overdose in 542. I'll catch up with you in a few moments." After his entourage shuffled out, Santa's face flamed with outrage. "I have no intention of standing here and taking this abuse."

"Good with me. Stand someplace else."

Tucci straightened Gina's covers and smoothed back a stray wisp of hair. Her forehead felt warm, and he wondered if she was brewing a fresh fever.

"You are here in violation of the rules, Mr. Tucci. Please leave at once."

Tucci eyed him wearily. "Look. The last thing I need from you is a hard time. All I'm trying to do is take care of my kid."

"That happens to be *our* job at the moment. If things are not proceeding as well as they might, perhaps your interference has something to do with it."

Tucci's temper blew. "Don't try to pin your screwups on me. You guys haven't got a clue. Whatever you do, she gets worse."

"Obviously, you're distraught."

"Great diagnosis. Brilliant. My kid is sick, so I don't feel like dancing. Now tell me something I don't know."

"If you cannot control yourself, I'll have no choice but to refuse you further access to this institution."

Tucci blew out the trapped steam. "I don't need this crap. Really I don't."

Gina was coming awake again. "Morning, Daddy," she said with a squeaky yawn.

"Morning, baby. Sleep okay?"

"I was really zonked."

Dr. Claus kept sputtering, threatening. "I'm asking you to leave, Mr. Tucci. Right now, or else."

"And I'm telling you, no."

"This is unacceptable."

"I agree. Now please, be a good guy and leave us alone."

The doc strode to Gina's bedside phone and set a hand on the receiver. "If you won't leave peacefully, I'll have you ejected."

"I'm staying with my girl."

"We'll see about that." He lifted the receiver.

Tucci leaned across the bed and slammed it down. Marie had gone home to get some sleep and a shower. She wouldn't be back for another hour or two. He wasn't about to leave Gina alone in this horror house.

Backing off, he tempered his tone. "Look. I'm sorry I got upset. Let's bury the hatchet and forget it, okay? You can bring your students in. I'll keep quiet."

The doc crossed the room and picked up Cynthia's line. "Get me security."

"Don't do that!" Tucci howled. This was far worse than getting bounced from Lee Chow's lab. Plus, this time, the scientist would not appear like a knight in a rumpled lab coat to save his sorry hide.

"This is Dr. McManus. I need someone immediately in 426 east."

"Come on, pal. Be reasonable."

"You wouldn't know what that was, Mr. Tucci."

"Excuse me?" came a voice. A burly man with a walrus mustache stood in the doorway.

"It's fine. Nothing's wrong. No big deal. Just a simple misunderstanding," Tucci said. He fixed his pleading gaze on McManus. "Have a heart, Doc. Please. Give me another chance. I don't want to leave my kid alone."

McManus gaped at the burly stranger. A high shrill escaped him. "My word. Look who's here." He crossed to the door and gripped the man's hand warmly. "I can't tell you how delighted I am to see you. Come in, come in."

The stranger fixed Tucci with a quizzical look "Mr. Tucci?"

Tucci backed away. "I was wrong, I admit it. I got a little emotional. It won't happen again."

"I'm afraid you've lost me. My name is Sebastian Archer. I am a friend of Lee Chow's."

"You're the bug guy?"

His smile bloomed behind the mustache. "That's one way to put it."

The white-haired doc was fizzing over. "Dr. Archer, I can't tell you what a privilege this is. I've been reading your books and papers for years. Name's Rusty McManus. I'm an internist specializing in pathology. I can't believe I'm actually meeting you in the flesh."

"A pleasure, to be sure." The scientist turned to Tucci. "Lee Chow thinks the world of you, Detective. When he heard that I was scheduled to be in the area for a meeting, he asked me to stop by and explain my theories about your daughter's illness. I called your house, and your wife said I could find you here. Which of these charming young ladies is Gina?"

Tucci made the introductions.

As Dr. Archer chatted with Gina, two guards rushed into the room. "Got here soon as we could, Dr. McManus," said one. "What's the trouble?"

"Nothing at all," McManus said. "Just a small misunderstanding."

"You sure?"

"Positive. Sorry to bring you up here for nothing."

After they left, McManus fixed his adoring gaze on Archer once again.

"Forgive the interruption. Now, if you gentlemen will follow me, I'll find a nice, quiet spot where we can hear your impressions of young Gina's case, Dr. Archer."

"Most kind of you, Dr. McManus," Archer said. "But we would not wish to take up any more of your valuable time."

"Not at all. There's nothing in the world I'd rather do than hear what you have to say."

"Actually, I prefer to discuss this with Mr. Tucci alone. Of course, I will include a summary report and my detailed recommendations in Gina's record."

The smile froze on McManus's florid face. "I'm sure it would be helpful for me to hear what you have to say directly, Dr. Archer. That way I can better coordinate the girl's treatment."

"Actually, I have arranged for Dr. Claxton to oversee Gina's treatment for the duration of her stay."

"Claxton doesn't care for patients. He runs the place."

"Precisely the reason I've asked him to take this on," said Archer. "Dr. Claxton has optimal access to the hospital's central lines of communications. He can most efficiently disseminate information about the case to relevant in-house staff and me. Of course, we hate to sacrifice your excellent management skills, but alas, on balance, it seems prudent and necessary to do so."

"You're taking me off the case?"

Archer pursed his lips. "I wouldn't put it that way at all. This is merely a question of efficiency. Now, if you will kindly show us to a room where we can confer in private, I shall be certain to apprise Dr. Claxton of your exemplary professionalism and cooperation."

"Very well," McManus said tightly. "I'll find you a space."

Tucci stifled a laugh. *Maybe soon be employee of month. Get picture in cafeteria.*

McManus installed them in the staff lounge beside the nursing station. During the harried start of the morning shift, the space was deserted.

Archer waited until McManus was well down the hall. "This is a somewhat delicate situation, Detective Tucci. For your daughter's sake, it would be imprudent of us to overlook hospital politics and the sensitivities of the staff. As you no doubt observed, I took what pains I could to avoid disaffecting Dr. McManus any more than was absolutely essential. I believe the treatment course I plan to propose will proceed far more smoothly if we avoid unnecessary divisiveness and acrimony."

Tucci braced for whatever fresh tortures Archer was about to suggest. What hadn't Gina been through already? Hanging by the toes? Spikes under the fingernails? A marathon of Lawrence Welk music? "What treatment?"

"I shall get to that in a moment. First, allow me to offer a bit of background. I have reviewed your daughter's illness from its inception. At first glance, it seemed an enigma. Despite our excellent facilities, my staff was unable to isolate any pathogen or toxin that could account for the staggering range of symptoms the girl has suffered. In fact, nothing in our collective experience has come close to behaving in like fashion."

Archer drew a pad from his briefcase and began listing from memory the nightmarish problems that had stricken Gina since she first took sick in June: digestive disorders, kidney failure, liver toxicity, personality changes, anemia, hallucinations. The list went on and on.

Tucci's head drooped from the weight of it. "Poor kid has had every *itis* and *emia* in the book. Every *ologist* you can imagine has had a crack at her. I don't know how she stands it, Doc. Honest I don't."

"I quite agree with you. Your daughter has shown remarkable fortitude and forbearance. At this point, my firm recommendation is that we cease all treatment at once."

Tucci blinked. "I don't understand."

"I believe that Gina has been a victim of a condition I have come to call yogurt syndrome. Years ago, a patient was referred to me who presented with a similar lengthy, debilitating, intractable illness. Her problem had commenced months earlier with a common yeast infection secondary to antibiotic administration. In addition to a standard medication protocol, the physician suggested that this patient consume yogurt to restore the normal microbial balance in her system.

"Her condition steadily deteriorated. They tried increasingly aggressive therapies, but none proved effective. New, more virulent symptoms kept cropping up. Plus, the original yeast problem kept recurring and getting worse.

"Everyone was baffled by the pernicious course of her affliction. Exhaustive tests shed no light on the problem. They presumed she might be suffering from a new immunodeficiency disease.

"When the case was referred to me for review, I was similarly at a loss. Then, a young researcher on my staff observed that this patient's symptoms had worsened after each new therapy commenced. The symptoms she experienced were rare but not necessarily unconnected to the medication protocols. My assistant hypothesized that she might be hypersensitive to all treatments, including something as seemingly benign as consuming yogurt. Skeptical though I was, I recommended that all treatment be terminated. At that point, the patient's condition was grave, and we kept her under close observation. That night she was terribly ill, but by morning, her symptoms had vanished."

Tucci thought of all the chemicals that had been pumped into Gina's veins, the bitter medicines they had forced her to swallow. "You're saying all this has been caused by the cure?"

"I can't be certain until we cease all medications, but on close analysis, I did detect a pattern wherein two to three days after each new regimen was commenced, Gina developed a new set of symptoms. Logically, every one of them might have been a rare and therefore unexpected side effect."

"Jeez, Doc. What are we sitting around for? I'll go pack Gina up and get her the hell out of here before those dirtbags do her any more harm."

"I don't recommend moving her, Detective. Gina needs to be under medical supervision, especially as we wean her from the medications. I've arranged to have her transferred to a private room, where she will be more comfortable and we can maintain precautions against incidental infection. Dr. Claxton has the means to reach me night or day for the next several days, by which time I believe we shall have our answer. If you are in agreement, I can assure you that your daughter will not have so much as her pillow fluffed without my prior approval."

"You bet, Doc. I'm in total agreement. You're going to turn this around for Gina, I can feel it in my bones."

"I am cautiously optimistic, Mr. Tucci. Let's hope all of our bones are correct."

The journal reprint lay between them on the kitchen table. "I don't owe you an explanation, Jessie," Charlie said angrily. "You're the one who should be explaining why you opened my mail, why you think it's okay to snoop around like that."

"I told you, when I saw that it was from the American Psychological Association, I thought it was for me. I wasn't snooping, Charlie, and I'm not now. I would simply like to understand why you sent for this particular article."

Since they found Danny in the bathroom with his arm cut, a knot of pain had formed behind Jess's eyes. The ache intensified as she reread the title of the piece: "Familial patterns of deviant sexual behavior, a longitudinal study."

Charlie threw up his hands. "I'm a curious person, Jessie. I read all kinds of things. Now can we drop this stupidity?"

Max strode in. "What's going on?"

"You're supposed to knock when the door is shut, Max," Jess said.

The little boy turned around and knocked. "Are you having a family meeting?"

"Just the executive and finance committee," Charlie said. "Now, please excuse us."

"Sounds boring," Max pronounced. "What's that you're reading?"

Charlie swiped the reprint out of sight. "It's nothing. Grown-up stuff."

"I like grown-up stuff. Can't I see?"

"Sure you can," Charlie said. "In about twelve years. Now take a hike."

Jess waited until the child grumped out of the room. "Does this have anything to do with what happened between us the other night?"

His exasperation grew. "I was drunk for God sakes, Jessie. We're man and wife. I'd hardly call that deviant sexual behavior."

"Maybe not, but having been on the receiving end, I can tell you it was no Doris Day movie."

"I'm sorry if you weren't in the mood. I'm sorry if you felt that I was pushing you."

"It was so unlike you, Charlie. You've changed so. I honestly feel as if I'm living with a stranger. Plus, everything's suddenly such a big secret."

"Such as?"

She didn't want to say, but the issues demanded release. "Where you've been. What you've been doing. Do you honestly expect me to believe that you need to put in so many evenings at the Institute?"

"What right do you have to talk about openness and honesty? Do *you* honestly expect *me* to believe that all those secret conversations you've been having are recipe exchanges with Libby?" he shot back.

"What you talking about?"

"I noticed a strange New York number on the caller-ID. After the third or fourth time, I was curious enough to try it. When were you going to get around to telling me that you've been using my father's lawyer behind my back?"

Jess drew a breath and got her bearings. "I planned to tell you a hundred times, but something always came up, mostly some sudden emergency meeting at the Institute. How can I tell you anything when you're never around?"

"It was wrong to keep that secret. Don't turn it around and try to blame it on me."

"It's not a matter of blame, it's about getting Danny all the help we can. It so happens your father was right. Sidney Rosenthal's firm has terrific resources. Her investigators have turned up damning information about Leo Beningson. Seems Mr. Righteous has an appetite for child prostitutes. He goes to Cambodia as often as once a month to satisfy the urge. He used to patronize one particular brothel, but he's not welcome there anymore. Apparently he beat one of the pleasure girls into a coma."

"So Beningson is scum. What difference does it make? He's not the one who stands accused."

"No, but the whole case against Danny hangs on Lisa's credibility. Destroy that and everything falls apart."

"Exactly my point. Have Rosenthal's investigators found out anything about Lisa?"

"No, but this could eliminate Leo Beningson as a corroborating witness."

"They don't need him if the jury believes Lisa. All you've accomplished by this is to give my old man one more thing to lord over me. Don't you understand?"

"No, I don't. I don't understand you at all. How can you be worried about saving face with Senior when Danny's entire future is on the line?"

"I'm not worried about saving face. I just don't see the point of giving that old bastard more ammunition and the power to misuse it with. And I don't appreciate your sneaking around behind my back. Talk about keeping secrets."

"You're right. I should have told you. But I did what I thought was right for Danny."

His face twisted in revulsion. "So unselfish. If only all of us could be as perfect and wonderful as you."

The words struck her like sharp stones. She glanced at the journal article, then at her husband's cruel, unyielding sneer. It was time to get everything on the table. "Tell me, Charlie. Is there somebody else?"

He stared at her for a long time before answering. "If you need to know, there is."

The room swam with dizzy currents. "Who?"

"Me."

"What's that supposed to mean?"

"I've been staying away because it's too hard to be here. Everyone's so touchy and volatile I can't stand to be around it. I'm trying to get through this as best I can."

His face, his words, all of it had the ring of truth. "The kids need you here. They miss you. So do I."

Charlie pressed her hand to his cheek. "I'm sorry, Jessie. I know I've been doing a lousy job."

"Who isn't?"

He tipped his head toward the journal article. "I saw a reference to this piece when I was mucking around on-line. I sent for it because I wanted to know whether it's my fault, whether I might be responsible for this business with Danny."

"How could you possibly be responsible?"

He took her hand. "Remember the trouble my father mentioned my having when I was about Danny's age?"

"I do."

"One night, when I was in my last year of high school, a friend had half a dozen of us over when his parents weren't home. We got snockered on his father's single-malt Scotch, and we decided it would be a terrific idea to call up the ugliest girl in our class and invite her to a little party. Her name was Estelle Fink. She was a tall, gawky thing with a big hooked nose and no chin.

"Estelle was never invited anyplace, so she was thrilled. She didn't ask any questions, just agreed to come over right away. When she showed up, my friend Butch Aspen pretended he had a big crush on her. He kept plying her with compliments and vodka-spiked lemonade. Somehow, we all managed to keep from laughing out loud as that poor girl got drunker and drunker.

"After a while, Butch took her into the back room. When he was done with her, he had us come in and take turns. We thought that was fair game back then, get a girl drunk and take advantage of her. We were shocked when her parents threatened to bring charges against us. Shocked and furious and scared out of our minds."

"What happened?"

"Senior and the other fathers chipped in to make the problem go away. They paid for Estelle to go to private school for the rest of senior year, then college. They funded the plastic surgery she wanted. They bought her father a pickup truck. That was his price."

Jess shivered, thinking of the girl. "They couldn't make it go away for her."

"I know, Jessie. Believe me, I think about it more than you can imagine. I've kept track of Estelle for all these years. She got an engineering degree, then an MBA. At last count, she was working as a securities analyst, doing extraordinarily well. She's married with four kids, and everyone seems to be okay—at least they were when I checked them out last about a year ago. I had myself convinced that the incident was finally over and forgotten, that it could be put to rest. Then this happens with Danny, and I'm forced to consider that it may never be over. Whatever craziness allowed me to participate in abusing that girl might be passed on from generation to generation." He stared at Jess through frightened, pleading eyes. "What if it *is* genetic, Jessie? What if I passed on some twisted legacy to Danny?"

"I read that study months ago. The findings were inconclusive. But it doesn't matter, Charlie. The simple fact is I've known you for twenty years and Danny for almost eighteen. You may be an unpleasant, pushy drunk, but you're no sexual deviant and neither is he."

"What about the other night?"

"It wasn't romance, Charlie. But I'd hardly call it a rape."

His face fell. "I don't know anything anymore. I've spent the last twenty years trying to figure out what's right and what's wrong and how to act on the conclusion in some rational way. And all I've managed to do is get more and more confused."

Jess could relate. Twenty years ago, she had been dead certain about practically everything. Like Molly, she had seen the world as a series of simple absolutes. Her father was a dear loving man. Pearl was a hideous monster. School was a sorry fact of life made tolerable only because of the opportunity it presented to meet cute boys. The central importance of religion was buying new outfits for the High Holidays. God was fine, taken in small discretionary doses like an over-the-counter medication.

Since then, the pile of questions had grown until it far outstripped her supply of answers. The more she knew, the less she understood.

Jess snuggled onto Charlie's lap and melted in his familiar embrace. "Why don't we work on it together? Maybe we can figure something out."

Klonsky stood blocking the squad room door. "You're late, Detective." Tucci checked his watch. "Two minutes."

He had lingered at the hospital as long as he dared, enthralled by the miraculous sight of Gina with an actual appetite. A day and a half after treatment was stopped, she was like a new kid. She'd downed two pieces of buttered toast with strawberry jam, most of the scrambled eggs. Watching her drain that little plastic cup of orange juice was beyond words. Tucci still choked up just thinking about it.

"Two *minutes* is not what I'm talking about," Klonsky said. "Try two *months*. Jury selection in the Magill trial starts in four days, and I'm still waiting, very impatiently I might add, for the evidence you were supposed to bring me."

"I've been working on it nonstop, Chief."

Frown lines dented Klonsky's luggage-quality complexion. "Let me ask you something, Sergeant. Do I ask too much? Do you think I'm a big, unreasonable bully?"

Tucci kept it to a noncommittal shrug.

"The correct answer is yes. That's exactly what I am—a big, demanding perfectionist and a giant pain in the ass. That's what I need to be. And you know why?"

Tucci raised his shoulders again. Let them drop.

"Because I take my work very seriously, that's why. Because ultimately, the buck stops right here. I'm responsible for how this city functions. When my officers get the job done, everyone can relax, feel confident, sleep a little more soundly. When my people dick around and fail to make a case, people don't feel safe, which reflects badly on me, and on all of us. And that's what you've been doing, Tucci, dicking around."

Mule and Patsy were at their desks, mugging behind Klonsky's back. Patsy rolled her eyes. Mule stood and swiveled his hips like a beer-bellied hula girl. Tucci did his level best to ignore them.

"This case happens not to fall into a nice neat package, Chief. Sometimes they don't," he said.

"I don't buy that. Figure out how to make it fit, Detective. Walk the walk."

Mule strutted like John Travolta in *Saturday Night Fever.* Patsy, in her bumwear, vamped like Marilyn Monroe.

"By this time tomorrow, I had better have something solid to hand to the prosecutor." He pointed over his shoulder at Mule. "Take your monkey and go get it, Detective. No holds barred. Whatever it takes. Go get me what I need."

"By tomorrow. Got you, Chief," Tucci said. "Come on, Mule. Let's hit it. We've got that guy to see."

Mule frowned in perplexity, but he went along. "Sure, Tooch. Right."

Tucci dragged his feet until Klonsky disappeared into his office. Then he changed course and hurried down the rear hall to human resources. "Wait out here, Mule. I need to get a little pension information."

"Why?"

"I've got no time to explain. Just wait."

"Okay. But as a friend I have to tell you, you're not making a whole lot of sense."

Five minutes later, he emerged with a slip of paper and a triumphant grin. "Got it," he said.

"What?" Mule asked as he followed Tucci out to the lot.

"Keys to the kingdom. Secret of life." He handed Mule the paper. "See for yourself."

Mule's eyes bugged. "If you don't mind my saying, I think you're running two bricks shy of a load."

"Must be why I feel so light."

Tucci swerved out and gunned the cruiser. He shot through a yellow light and headed north on High Ridge Road. At Vine Road, he hung a right. By his calculations, they were moments from glory.

Mule stomped the imaginary brake on the floor of the shotgun seat. "Whoa, easy. Where are we going in such a hot hurry?"

"We're going to see a man about a horse's ass."

"I don't get it. I don't get you. How come you're in such a good mood all of a sudden?"

Veering right again, Tucci set an avuncular hand on his partner's shoulder. "For one thing, Gina's feeling better. Starting to act like her old self."

"That's great news, Tooch. What finally worked?"

"Nothing."

Mule scratched his head. "But I thought you said she's better."

"I'll explain later. Here we are."

He pulled to a screeching halt beside the blinking light at the entrance to the Turn of River Middle School. With minutes to go before the late bell, the street was clotted with yellow buses, harried parents ferrying carpools, and edgy kids on foot. Horns blared. Idling engines spawned a haze of acrid exhaust. Spiky voices pierced the morning chill.

Tucci pulled onto the grass and circled the line of cars, drawing a chorus of strident honks. Spotting his mark, he angled off the road and left the cruiser idling. Dodging a minivan and a pack of gum-cracking girls, he crossed to the epicenter of the traffic crush.

Will Huppert blew his whistle. "Hey. Watch yourself," he shouted at a scrawny punk who loped mindlessly through the line of cars.

The kid withdrew a hand from the pocket of his tent-sized jeans and popped Hup the bird. "Watch that, you old fart."

Huppert bared his teeth and growled.

Tucci caught the rumble low in Huppert's chest as he clapped him on the back. "Will Huppert? Is that really you?"

"More or less. Mostly less. What brings you to puberty hell?"

"That's what *I* was about to ask. What's a nice fellow like you doing in a place like this?"

From across the street came a taunting voice. "Hey, Mr. Crossing Guard. Look. I've got something for you."

As Huppert watched, the punk turned and flashed his round, pink rear. He rushed inside, where he was swallowed by the swirling crush of kids. A loud assemblage lagged behind, cheering.

"I think he was just trying to butter the old man up," one girl howled. "Butter, get it?"

A boy turned and wiggled his hips at Hup. "Bet that made his day. Bet he's a big time butt man."

Several of the kids took up the taunt. "Butt man. Butt man."

Huppert's face went hot. He continued directing the traffic stream with his hands fisted.

"I got to hand it to you, Hup. That bunch makes Klonsky look like a walk in the park."

Butt man, butt man. Butt-er up the butt man.

Huppert's jaw twitched. Strangled fury pulsed from his throat. The guy looked locked and loaded, ready to blow.

The explosion was aborted by the scream of the late bell. The mocking monsters forgot about Huppert and charged inside. The last of the carpools disgorged their loads and breezed away. The air went still.

Huppert turned his anger on Tucci and Mule. "What the hell did you clowns come here for? The last thing I need is a goddamned audience."

Tucci ticked his tongue. "Looks like we've caught him in a bad mood, Mule."

Maybe we should just forget about talking to Hup directly. I guess you're right, makes more sense to go ahead and take the whole thing up with internal affairs."

"What whole thing?" Huppert said.

"It's just that I'd hate to cost the guy his pension. Seems like a shame." Tucci sucked a breath and let it out in a frosty plume. He loved mornings like this, when your kid was showing signs of health and the air was celery crisp. For the first time in months, he felt almost human.

"What are you talking about, Tucci?" Huppert demanded. "I'm in no mood for games."

"How about a cup of coffee? You in the mood for that?"

"Okay, fine. I'm through here in five minutes."

Tucci drove to the Country Diner on High Ridge Road. Gina's renewed appetite had spurred his. Seated in a corner booth, he ordered bacon and fried eggs with hash browns and a short stack of pancakes on the side. Following his inspiration, Mule asked for a Belgian waffle with extra whipped cream and sausages. Huppert wanted his coffee black and strong, that was all.

After the waitress left, Hup leaned in. "What do you want from me, Tucci? Spit it out."

"Three things." He held up a trio of fingers and peeled them down in turn. "First, I want to know why you were canned, and don't give me that early retirement crap, I got the real word. Two, what statement did Magill make to you on the night of his arrest? And three, will you help me nail Klonsky, or would *you* rather be it? Up to you."

"Who told you I was canned?"

"Can't reveal my sources, Hup. I've got relatives from Sicily. You understand."

Huppert stared at his coffee, trying to read the steam. "Why the hell should I tell you? It's not as if things can get any worse."

"Doesn't look that way," said Mule. "I used to think the worst job in the world was that guy with the shovel who follows the circus elephants around, or maybe the attendants who sit in the ladies' rooms at fancy restaurants. But jeez, Hup."

"You're right. It's the pits. And I blame Klonsky for every minute I have to be with those walking pimple factories. Why should I suffer? I may have crossed the line a little, but he trampled it."

"I'm all ears," said Tucci.

Huppert started with the night of Danny Magill's arrest. He had caught the call from dispatch in the middle of a gin game. He was holding a losing hand. Going down hard. Looking back, he should have viewed that as a premonition.

From the moment he entered the alleged perpetrator's house, he'd had a bad feeling about the case. The Magill kid had a slick, slippery feel, and his parents gave off a stink of privileged entitlement that reminded Huppert of the Storrows, whose twin boys had beaten a sex assault rap three years back.

"That case cost me big, Tooch."

Huppert had been a laughingstock then too. But in addition to face, he had lost the three critical R's: rank, reputation, and raises. "I remember," Tucci said.

All that aside, the intake process had shaken the kid, and the interrogation had proceeded far better than he'd hoped, Huppert recalled. He drew the kid in, set him up. Danny Magill had his head in the noose and was ready to kick away the stool when Huppert got word that a hotshot attorney was on the case. Someone was on the way with bail money. It was down to the wire.

"I couldn't let that kid walk. He had guilt written all over him. So, I turned the screws a little."

"What screws?" Tucci asked.

"I told the kid a fairy tale, that's all. You know the one about the bodies in the Dumpsters?"

"I do," Tucci said.

"Which version? Whole or dismembered?" Mule wanted to know.

Huppert slugged back the rest of his coffee. "Dismembered of course. Works way better. No dental records, no prints. I told him it was teenage girls. Same MO as the Beningson situation, only these victims had been offed after the rape."

Mule was nodding eagerly. "So you said if he didn't confess to Beningson, he would probably get nailed for the unidentified Dumpster bodies."

"Kid folded like a cheap tent. Started bawling and telling me how sorry he was. I got it on tape, got him to sign a confession, for Chrissakes."

Tucci nibbled the last of his toast. "So what went wrong?"

"Klonsky happened to review that night's security tape, hoping to catch someone screwing off. Later, I found out that's his favorite hobby—scalp collecting. Anyhow, the video camera happened to be making a random sweep through the interrogation room when I was telling the Dumpster story. Klonsky went ballistic. He said I threatened the entire case, that the prosecutor might drop the charges if he found out I'd squeezed the kid that way. I tried to explain why I had to speed things up. I tried to make him understand about Storrow and how things work around here. But he refused to even hear me out. Son of a bitch bounced me, just like that." He snapped his fingers. "Told me to clean out my desk and get the hell out. No notice. Nothing. Twenty-two years on the damned job, and I don't even get a chance to tell my side."

"Now you do," Tucci said. "Where's the tape, Hup? Where's the confession? How come none of that turned up in the Magill file?"

"Because Klonsky wanted them to disappear. He tossed them at me when I was on the way out. Said I should take care of them."

Tucci's pulse raced into overdrive. "You still have them?"

"Honestly don't know. I threw out half the stuff from the office and tossed the rest in a box. I haven't had the stomach to look at it since." Huppert's lips pressed in a rueful smile. "I never thought I'd say this, but I miss being a cop."

"Laugh a minute," Tucci said.

"Compared to teenybop patrol it is. How are things at headquarters? How's the Magill case?"

"This box you tossed your stuff in, where is it now?" Tucci asked.

"Where we keep all the junk, in the garage."

Tucci tossed a fat pile of singles on the check. "Let's go check it out, Hup. When we see what you've got, I'll have a way better idea of how things are going with Magill."

FORTY

Jess jolted awake, heart thwacking. Worries thundered through her mind in a torrent, as if the retaining wall around her neuroses had collapsed. What if Danny was convicted? What if the harshest sentence was imposed?

She could not bear to look behind that dark, forbidding unknown. Instead, she forced herself to focus on Danny's defense. Had they missed anything? Was there anyone useful they had failed to contact?

The display on her bedside clock read 1:11. She hadn't fallen asleep until after midnight. One hour did not constitute a decent night's sleep by anyone's definition, and that was about all she had been getting of late. The next several weeks were going to be extra tough. She would not be much use to Danny or anyone else as a jelly-legged zombie.

Turning onto her side, she molded her body against Charlie's back. When that had no effect, she flung an arm across his chest and cleared her throat loudly. "Honey? Are you up?"

He was not.

Jess tried harder, nudging him with knees, elbows, then more tantalizing parts, but he was in some dead zone of the land of Nod where there was no transmission. The customer she was trying to reach was unavailable. Too bad.

She slipped out of bed and padded downstairs, pausing to check on the children. Everyone was out cold, including the house. At night, the thermostat set back automatically to sixty-two degrees. A howling December wind pierced the creaky beams and joists. Ribs of frost like prison bars striped the windows. Everything conspired to remind her of the upcoming trial. Not that there was any way to forget.

Jess put the kettle on and steeped a cup of Sleepytime tea. When the whistle sounded, Prozac cocked an eye, then lumbered up on rickety legs and reported for duty. Any shift was fine with the dog, as long as it involved refreshments.

Jess stroked behind Prozac's ears and fed her a biscuit. As she chewed, the dog's eyelids drooped with ecstasy, and she moaned deep in her chest like a phone sex operator. Finished, she cocked her head and gazed at Jess provocatively. Anything for another biscuit. *Anything.*

Jess relented. Prozac downed the treat with striking speed, then shimmied with a thrill of pure pleasure. The sight spurred a memory. There was something she had forgotten after all. The call she made confirmed that this was the perfect time to resolve that particular oversight.

Groping in the dark, she pulled on jeans, a sweater, and low brown boots. She propped a note of explanation on her pillow. Charlie did not stir when she kissed him on the cheek. Jess inhaled his warmth and the infectious peace of his slack-jawed unconsciousness. "I'm so scared, Charlie. Scared and lost," she whispered. "If you honestly believe all this is going to turn out all right, say nothing."

Silence.

Jess stole out of the house and into the gusty, forbidding night. Her headlights blazed through the dark, silent neighborhood. As she passed the houses of their sleeping enemies, she wished them sudden enlightenment and guilty dreams.

High Ridge Road was deserted. Dark shops lined the strip malls. Devoid of cars, the lots resembled sprawling seas of frost-capped ink. Hillocks of muddy snow framed the meandering roadway. Traffic signals winked like jittery, jaundiced eyes.

At Bull's Head, she turned right onto Washington Boulevard. An ambulance, sirens squalling, sped from behind and passed. A car full of raucous kids barreled by in the opposite direction. Closer to town, lights blazed in a scatter of apartments and offices. Otherwise, all the sane folks were tucked into bed.

She passed under the Metro North railroad bridge, then traversed a weave of streets into a strikingly ugly commercial district. There was a wholesale plumbing-supply house, a car wash, a pizza place, a string of auto body shops, a mattress warehouse, a long-defunct branch of the motor vehicle bureau.

The address she sought was down a meandering side street. The entrance could only be accessed through a dim back alley. Jess parked on the street and hurried along the littered concrete path squeezed between the crumbling brick wall of a warehouse and a chain-link fence capped by razor wire. She was spooked by eerie night sounds, shifting shadows, a sharp inhuman cry. Her skin erupted in an electric rash of fear.

Her instinct was to bolt, but she forced herself to move on, rushing stiffly toward the alley's end. Turning out, she warmed to the reassuring shine of lights, sultry jazz strains, a beckoning neon sign.

Her relief evaporated when an enormous tattooed bald man in a black studded jacket and an obvious foul mood challenged her at the entrance. An oversized gold tooth shone through his belligerent scowl.

"What do you want, lady?"

"To go inside."

"This is a private club. Invitation only."

Through the glass storefront, Jess saw a scatter of patrons at small round tables. A couple swayed in place on the dance floor like trees in a heavy wind. A statuesque blonde strutted across the stage on Tina Turner legs with a microphone plugged in her mouth.

"I have one. Wait." Fishing through her cluttered purse, Jess found the card. "Here's my invitation."

The bouncer looked it over. "Natch. Who else? Anytime someone like you shows up, guaranteed that bird is behind it." He flapped his ham-sized hand. "Go on in."

"Where can I find her?"

"Try the dressing room."

As Jess entered the smoky space, the blonde onstage launched a booming rendition of "A Foggy Day in London Town." With the microphone buried millimeters from her tonsils and the half-dozen giant speakers planted around the room, the sound was loud enough to loosen the fillings in Jess's teeth.

Several doors fanned from the central space. Jess flagged down a cocktail waitress in a plunging peasant blouse and thigh-high skirt and asked the way to the dressing room, but the woman could not hear the question through the din. Jess pantomimed applying makeup, combing her hair, slipping a costume over her head. Zipping up. Finally, the waitress's face lit with comprehension. She pointed to a narrow door behind the bar.

Jess knocked, then poked her head in tentatively. "Excuse me," she called. "Anyone here?"

"Come in, come in, whoever you are. Join the party. More the merrier," trilled a voice.

The long, narrow space was soundproofed against the music booming from the stage. Along one wall ran a line of mirrors framed by frosted vanity lights. Several performers perched on studded red velvet chairs at skirted tables overflowing with makeup, garish costume jewelry, and extravagant wigs on featureless fabric skulls. Coatracks packed with sequined gowns, tulle skirts, bustiers, gossamer chiffon wisps, and feather boas ran the length of the opposite wall. Tottering spike-heeled shoes in a rainbow of eye-popping hues lined the floor underneath. Clearly, the club had cornered the market on Lurex, hot-pink velvet, low-end rhinestones, candy-colored Dynel hair, and stays.

"How can we help you, sugar?" asked a honey-skinned drag queen in a mermaid dress.

"I'm looking for Aquaria."

"If you want find a big star like that, you got to look up, honey. Take the stairs right over there. It's third to the left, then straight on till morning."

Jess mounted the narrow metal flight to a dingy smoke-scented hall. As she approached the third door on the left, she heard the loud, churning gargle of a toilet flush. The door burst open and Aquaria strode forth in a flash of silver and darting fish. Spotting Jess, she held up a long-nailed finger. "I'd give it a minute if I were you, sweetheart. That or a gas mask. If pretty is as pretty does, I'm in deep doo-doo, so to speak."

"I don't need the rest room. I came to see you."

"And you will, darling. You just go downstairs, get yourself a long, cool one, and old Aquaria will be on in ten minutes flat. I've got a big surprise planned for tonight. All two of my loyal fans are going to love it."

"It's about my son. You met him at the police station a few months ago. You said you could tell me something about him. Remember?"

She frowned in thought, then pursed her hot-pink lips. "Of course. Now I do. How's that child doing?"

"Could be better."

She ticked her tongue. "Come with me, sweetheart. Let me tell you what I know. I don't have a whole lot of time."

Aquaria led Jess to a small room at the end of the hall. The walls were bare, the furnishings Spartan: a swaybacked army cot, two wooden folding chairs, and a card table. Beside the slim, grimy window was a squat refrigerator and a hot plate.

"Welcome to my world, honey. Home sweet home. It isn't much, but then, neither am I. Have a seat. Can I get you anything? This place has all the conveniences, hot and cold running cockroaches, indoor slumming, you name it."

"Nothing thanks." Jess sat on one of the folding chairs.

Aquaria dipped into the fridge and plucked out a Diet Coke, then drew up a chair beside Jess. "Manager simply hates it when I'm late, so let me cut right to the chase. I was in and out for some nonsense on the night of your boy's arrest. Can't even remember the charge, there have been so many. Typically it's some made-up thing like conspiracy to felicitation, mopery with intent to gawk, gobbledygook like that. Cops raid this place, three, four times a year, just because. Gets to be part of the routine.

"But that time I remember, because of your boy. We spent some time together in the holding cell while he was waiting to be processed. They do that sometimes, lock you up to cool your heels. They figure it will shake you up, make you more cooperative, eager to talk. Works too, especially with a boy like yours. He started talking right away, soon as they locked us in."

"What did he tell you?" Jess asked.

Aquaria tossed back her head and poured a stream of fizzy liquid down her throat. "He told me he knew something like this was going to happen. He said he had it coming because of something bad he did."

"What?"

"Wouldn't say. I tried to coax it out of him, but he just hung his cute little head and said he couldn't talk about it. They only left him with me for a couple of minutes, so I didn't have much chance to push."

She downed the rest of the can, crushed it in a manicured hand, and belched. "Excuse me, honey. Can't ever go on without my Diet Coke and a nice big round of burps. Sets me right up for some reason. Don't know why.

"What I *do* know is that your boy needs to get shed of whatever sack of stones he's carrying. Otherwise, take my word, he will find some way to shoot himself in the foot, make sure that he winds up convicted. Maybe worse. I know boys like that. I used to be one."

An angelfish flicked its tail and darted around the right-hand bowl. A striped little fish on the left perched near the glass and stared.

"How can I help him if I don't know what's wrong?"

"Wish I knew, honey."

"Did he tell you anything else? Anything more specific?"

Aquaria's dark eyes, behind the dense false lashes, went vague. "Let me take your number and think on it. Meanwhile, I better run. Come with me. I'll put you in a front-row seat."

"I should probably go."

The drag queen pouted. "One little number can't hurt. Won't you please stay? It'd mean the world to me. You'll about double my audience."

As soon as Jess settled in her ringside seat, the announcer appeared. "And now, ladies and gentlemen, for your entertainment pleasure, the Purple Passion is proud to present one singular sensation. The one and only—Aquaria!"

She entered to a drumroll and the blinding sweep of spots. Lifting the mike from its stand, she strode to the center of the stage. With a meaningful look at Jess, she said, "This first number is dedicated to a young man and what happened to him a year ago. That's *one year*." Her brow peaked.

Jess answered with a nod. *Message received.*

Aquaria flashed a neon smile, took up the mike again, and started to sing. *Oh, Danny boy, the pipes, the pipes are calling . . .*

When Jess stole back into the house, Prozac, yawning broadly, trotted out to greet her in the hall. Confirming that it was only Jess and not, say, pizza delivery, the dog turned tail and headed back to her favorite sleeping spot in the pantry.

Charlie did not stir when Jess crawled beneath the covers. She lay awake, staring at the darkness, trying to make sense of what Aquaria had said. What happened a year ago?

She scrolled back past Danny's arrest, before their trip to France, through the largely uneventful spring, through the mild winter, to December a year ago. The holiday season had been unremarkable. As usual, they had celebrated Hanukkah with Pearl and Lou and paid their ritual Christmas visit to Senior and Charlie's mom at the country club. Aside from that and their annual pilgrimage to Rockefeller Center and FAO Schwartz, they had all been content to hang around, visit with friends, relax. Everyone had been healthy and in a place of relative calm.

A year ago?

For the life of her, she couldn't think of anything guilt-provoking that Danny might have done. No wild parties, no heirloom damage, no bad grades. No adolescent acting out, not even one little case of fratricide.

Nothing bad had happened a year ago. Jess was certain of that. Danny had been with them virtually all the time.

At the time Jess had not thought to question that. But looking back, Danny's behavior struck her as strange. What had turned their sociable, active son into a homebody?

That had not been the only change in Danny. He had always been a good, thoughtful kid, but sometime last year, he'd developed a major interest in helping out elderly neighbors like old Willy Willis. Still, Jess could not think of any occurrence at around that time that might logically account for the change.

A year ago.

The puzzle was making her head ache. Jess pressed against Charlie and closed her eyes. The solution came to her as she was drifting off.

A year from when?

Danny had spoken to Aquaria on the night of his arrest. A year before *that,* almost to the day, Ryan's car had swerved off the road and landed in the ditch beside the reservoir. Could that be it? Could Danny somehow feel responsible for Ryan's accident?

Jess turned that notion over and over, but she could not make the pieces fit. Danny had not left home on the night his friend was hurt. She remembered it vividly. He had eaten dinner, then gone up to his room to study for a history test. How could he possibly have had anything to do with the wreck?

Ryan's words came back to her. *Knowledge is access then.* What in the world was that supposed to mean?

She was slipping beneath a wave of sleep. Sinking. Jess struggled against it. There had to be some way to find the answer.

A larger, more powerful rush washed over her. But before she drifted away, the solution came to her. So simple and obvious. All she'd needed to do was open her eyes.

Charlie stopped under the broad canopy fronting the hospital entrance. "We're due to see the lawyers in an hour, Danny. You need to meet us back here in forty minutes, tops."

"Actually, I thought we'd all go in and say hello," Jess said.

"Won't that be too much for Ryan? So many people?" Charlie asked.

"With all the time he's spent in hospitals, I bet he's happy for any distraction," said Jess.

"Mom's right. You should come," Danny urged. He pressed against the rear seat, like a fearful child seeking refuge in his mother's skirts.

Jess had noticed his increasing reluctance to go anywhere in public alone. Not that she could blame him. Months of rude looks and nasty comments had left her skittish too. With the trial coming up, local press interest in the case had escalated. So had the hate mail and verbal assaults. Yesterday in the supermarket, a stranger had assailed Jess in the produce aisle. *I was raped once myself. Never got over it,* she said. *You should keep that kid of yours locked up.*

"Look, Dad. There's a spot opening up. Go for it."

Jess braced against the lashing wind as they crossed the crowded lot. Her nose ran and her eyes sprang with tears as if the bitter temperatures had triggered an emergency sprinkler system. Through the automatic doors, they were blasted by radiant heat. Her face flamed, and her few remaining brain cells toppled in a swoon.

The plump, pewter-haired woman at the information desk smiled at the mention of Ryan's name. "So you're here to see my little buddy. Such a sweetheart that one is. Keeps his chin up, no matter what. It's room 420, east wing. Take the elevator right around the corner."

With a wink, she waved them through with the one remaining visitor's pass in Ryan's folder. "Give him a nice big hug for me. Tell him Margie says hello."

As they stepped off the elevator on four, sharp antiseptic scents and mechanical noises assailed Jess. Bleeping monitors, the pig squeal of alarms. Someone cried in harsh pulses of pain. A phone shrilled. Over the intercom came the chilling summons, *Code blue.*

Jess loathed hospitals. Since her father took sick, she'd come to view them as centers of cruel decline and death. Lethal mistakes lurked everywhere. These places were filled with unthinkable sights, sounds, and sufferings, not to mention Pearl-quality cuisine. After each child was born, she had checked out as soon as she was able to make her shaky way to the car. Her favorite part of any hospital, hands down, was the exit.

Ryan's parents were leaving as they arrived. Mr. Harrison answered their greetings with a look of befuddlement. Faith Harrison smiled apologetically and gripped her purse like a nursing infant.

"Oh my. I wish we could stay and visit with you, but Harold has an appointment with his internist."

"That's fine," Charlie said.

"No. I feel terrible, really," she said.

Ryan was in the bed nearer the door. A plaster sleeve encased his left arm. The privacy curtain was drawn, reducing his roommate to a pair of oversized feet and a play of images on the wall-mounted TV.

Danny clapped a high five against his friend's uninjured hand. "How's it hanging?"

Ryan rapped on the cast. "What can—I tell you, bud? I'm—a klutz."

"How many times have I told you, no tightrope walking without a net."

"Who's Annette?"

The laugh faded quickly.

In the silence, Jess turned to Danny. "I'd love a cup of coffee, honey. Mind going to the cafeteria for me?"

"I'll go," Charlie offered. "What can I get for you, guys? Snack? Something to drink? Cute nurse?"

"Make that—one cute, one gorgeous," Ryan said.

"I'll see what they have that's nice and fresh," Charlie said.

Ryan's laugh was a strangled snort. "Fresh is—fine with me."

"Sounds like too much for one person to carry," Jess said. "Why don't both of you go?"

She waited until they had reached the end of the hall and turned toward the elevators. "You're a good friend to Danny," she told Ryan.

Ryan beamed. "He's—the best."

"That day at our house, you were trying to tell me something. A secret, you said."

His lips pressed in a crooked seam. "Don't—remember."

This was exactly what she had feared. Ryan's mental circuits were in sorry disarray. He suffered random word loss and sudden lapses of memory, as if some angry operator had scrambled the switchboard plugs in his brain.

"You told me you were worried about him. You said Danny was a good kid, but needed work. Remember?"

His forehead wrinkled with the effort to find the thought. "Must be—getting old—like my dad."

Like shy children, reticent memories needed to be gently, carefully coaxed. In her practice Jess did this all the time. Months, sometimes years passed in treatment before a buried chunk of insight broke free and rose to the surface. Prodding too hard or too soon might drive the painful recollections deeper. "Take your time, honey. Think back to that day when Danny was up getting your chair and you told me you were worried about him. Remember?"

He chewed his lip, then dipped his chin. "That chair—is so heavy. I—told him—it was dumb."

"That's right. Danny was doing a lot of dumb things. You told me he was blaming himself for something he didn't do. I thought it must have something to do with Lisa, but you said no. When your mom showed up, you tried to whisper what it was, but I didn't quite get it."

His look went blank again.

"Try to remember, Ryan. If not Lisa, what was Danny feeling guilty about?"

Excitement tossed his head askew. "Accident. Not Lisa—accident. I—remember now."

Not Lisa, accident. *Knowledge is access then.*

"I don't understand. Why would Danny feel responsible for your accident?"

Ryan's chest heaved. "Don't—know. He won't—tell."

A noise from the hall caught her ear. Tracking it, Jess saw Charlie locked in heated conversation with a stocky, dark-haired man whose vaguely familiar form she couldn't place. Danny pressed against the corridor wall, trying to disappear in the shadows.

What now?

"Excuse me, Ryan. I'll be right back."

As she approached, their angry words came clear. "Can't you let it go? That's ancient history," Charlie said.

"No, *you* are, Magill," snarled the man. "Nothing will give me greater pleasure than to see that kid of yours where he belongs. It's about time you people learned that you can't just keep on taking whatever you want. Big shot or no, sooner or later, the bill comes due."

A plump old woman in a somber black dress appeared in the doorway of the nearest room. *"Che cosa fai, Giuseppe? Basta!"*

"Leave me alone, Mama. I'm doing what I have to do."

"Lui non e male, Giuseppe. Lascialo solo."

"How can you defend him? Don't you remember the crap he used to pull?"

The old woman crossed herself, then tugged him by the hand. *"Non in ospedale, mio figlio. Sta zitto."*

Angrily, he shook her off. "I don't care if it's a hospital, and I'm not going to be quiet. Now go inside with Gina and Marie, Mama. Leave me alone."

She exhaled on a whistled shrill. *"Stupidissimo."*

"Well put, Mrs. Tucci," Charlie said as the door closed behind her. "Too bad you didn't inherit your mother's good sense, Joe."

Jess recognized the name Joe Tucci as one of the detectives who had been assigned to investigate Danny's case. She turned to Danny. "Ryan's waiting for you, honey. You should go."

The teenager thrust his hands deep in his pockets and retreated to Ryan's room.

"You know him, Charlie?" Jess asked incredulously.

"Hardly. We went to school together a billion years ago. That's about it."

"You forgot the part about how you and your jackass friends used to drive my old lady crazy, just for fun," Tucci said. "That was your idea of a good time, wasn't it, Magill? Taking advantage of defenseless old ladies and poor trusting girls. Looks like that kid of yours is a regular chip off the old block."

Charlie lunged and grabbed the collar of the cop's dark blue shirt. With blinding speed, Tucci whipped out a pistol and pressed it to Charlie's throat. "Assaulting an officer of the law? Shame, shame. You want to join your kid in big trouble? Happy to oblige."

"Daddy, stop!"

Tucci turned to the voice. A pale girl in a long pink nightgown stood in the doorway. Her dark eyes shone from the gaunt face like twin moons. Patches of scalp showed through her wispy hair. Still, she held an air of quiet authority.

"Go back inside and close the door, baby. This has nothing to do with you."

"Yes it does. Please stop. Listen to me, Daddy. I'm begging you."

Tucci backed off and holstered his gun beneath the baseball jacket. "There. It's away. Now go back to bed, sweetheart, please."

"Only if you come with me."

"Okay. You win." He scowled at Charlie. "But *you* don't, Magill. Not you or that kid of yours. Not if I have anything to say about it." Turning away, he made for his daughter's room.

Charlie's voice trailed him. "You're right, Joe. I was a stupid kid, and I did plenty of things I regret. Giving your mother a hard time is certainly one of them. She knows I'm sorry for that."

Tucci turned back with a sneer. "Her knowing doesn't erase the fact that you tortured that poor woman for years."

"Maybe you're right. Maybe I can't fix anything. But whatever gripe you have is with me, not my son. If you need to take it out on someone, let it be me."

Tucci sniffed. "Your kid got into this mess all by himself. I had nothing to do with it."

"Now you do."

"I call that a lucky coincidence."

Charlie tipped his head toward the girl's room. "I'm sorry your daughter is sick. No matter what I might think of you, I can't imagine wishing harm on your kid."

"I told you, Magill. I didn't cause this. I didn't wish it on your kid. I'm just doing my job."

"Be fair, that's all I'm asking. Don't let what you think of me color the way you treat Danny's case."

"I've always been fair," Tucci said. "A regular Solomon."

"Always? That's not how I remember it. You screwed up just as much as I did. Spread just as much misery."

"What's your point?"

"Kids make mistakes. They shouldn't have to carry them for the rest of their lives. Their kids shouldn't have to pay. Somewhere, sometime, you have to let it go."

FORTY-TWO

Gus Grantham paced the room, snorting whenever Sidney Rosenthal had the audacity to speak. When he deigned to address his visiting colleague, he spoke to her breasts, making it clear that he considered anything north of them a hood ornament. Grantham acted like a sneering seventh-grader in a thousand-dollar suit. Dennis the Menace, Attorney-at-Law.

Sidney Rosenthal refused to be provoked. She held her unwavering focus on the case. Faced with her obvious poise and intelligence, Charlie's resistance eroded. Much to Grantham's dismay, the lawyer from New York took easy command of the meeting.

She updated them on the progress of the investigation in Phnom Penh. "Bin Nol has agreed to appear as a rebuttal witness against Leo Beningson should it become necessary, but only if we can arrange a grant of blanket immunity."

"The state's attorney is just about to grant immunity to a kiddie pimp. That would really set him up for reelection." Grantham chuckled.

"Of course, I understand that such a request might be denied, Mr. Grantham. It's also possible that Bin Nol's testimony may prove unnecessary. All I'm asking at this time is that you feel the situation out. Test our options."

Grantham poked his inflated chest. "I'm not about to put my hard-earned reputation on the line, Ms. Rosenthal. Asking such a thing would make me look like an idiot."

Jess ached to suggest that he didn't need any help in that department, but she resisted. Sidney was doing fine on her own.

"My office will be glad to make that request on Danny's behalf if you prefer," Rosenthal said.

"Your office doesn't represent him. I do."

"Given that, I can't imagine that you would be unwilling to request a grant of immunity for a potentially valuable witness."

Grantham's cheeks flamed. "Since when is a gook pimp a valuable witness?"

"Since he can undermine a potentially damaging witness on the other side," Rosenthal said evenly. "One whose behavior happens to be equally reprehensible."

"If I listened to you, I'd have all of us laughed out of court. Except for Danny, of course. He'd be laughed into twenty years in maximum without parole."

Jess was thankful that Grantham's assistant was prepping Danny for trial in an office down the hall. The lawyer's dire predictions were the last thing he needed to hear.

"You misunderstand me, Mr. Grantham," said Sidney Rosenthal. "I was not suggesting that you barrel in like a circus clown and make a spectacle of yourself. I presumed that you might be able to test the waters informally."

"I could, but I don't choose to. Hear me, Counselor, it's a fool's mission, and I'm nobody's fool."

Rosenthal frowned. "I do hear you. In fact, I think you may be right."

The last thing Grantham expected was a reasonable response. He gawked as if she had just sprung a third giant breast.

"I'm inclined to suggest an alternate course. Actually, it's something I've been considering since this information first came to light."

Grantham rolled his eyes. "Imagine that. Another bright idea."

"A different tactic, yes. Unfortunately, there's a certain element of risk involved. Allow me to explain."

They all listened as she detailed her plan. Halfway through, Grantham took a seat. His look went serious. He did not say a word.

M ule trailed a reluctant step behind as Tucci strode toward Klonsky's office. "You sure about this, Tooch?"

"Positive."

"Maybe it's not such a good idea."

"Trust me, Mule. This is going to be fun."

The chief was on the phone, reaming out some poor soul by remote. "One week, doofus. You heard me. That's seven days, to save you the trouble of having to look it up."

He hung up and smirked at Tucci. "This must be National Incompetence Day. Otherwise, why would you people be having a parade?"

Tucci chuckled. "No matter what else people may say about you, Chief, no one would ever accuse you of having a sense of humor."

Mule sat bolt upright in a straitjacket of fear. "He's kidding. You're kidding, right, Tooch?"

"If only you had something upstairs to back up that smart mouth of yours, Detective."

Tucci tossed the tape and signed statement on the desk. "How's that for backup?"

"Don't tell me you've bought actual evidence. I don't know if the old ticker could take a shock like that."

"Oh, you'll take it okay, Klonsky. In the ear."

"Hold it right there." The chief's eyes drew in in lizard slits. "Did I hear you right, you lump of slime? Are you threatening me?"

"Let's say I'm contributing to your education."

"I can't tell you how much I'm enjoying this. Watching a jackass like you string himself up is one of the true pleasures of the job." Klonsky waved Mule off. "I'd lean back if I were you, Sergeant Samuels. This is liable to be messy." He laced his hands behind his ropy neck and planted his spit-shined shoes on the desk. "Continue, please, Detective Tucci. You were about to educate me in some way."

"That happens to be a taped confession and signed statement made by Danny

Magill on the night of his arrest. I know that you fired Will Huppert and ordered him to bury this evidence. That's felony obstruction, for starters, Klonsky. I'm surprised a great big important smart guy like you doesn't know a thing like that. Or maybe you just forgot."

Klonsky chuckled. "Tucci, Tucci. If you weren't so adorable, I honestly think I'd be just the least bit miffed."

"I don't get you."

"No. You *don't* get me, and you never will." He threw the tape and statement in Tucci's lap. "Get out of my office. Take your garbage with you, him and those."

"Fine. I'll take it right down the hall to internal affairs."

"Do that. Talk to Dave Eddy. He has the rest of the incident report on Huppert. Might as well keep the whole thing together, including these copies."

"Copies?" Iced fear filled Tucci's veins. His testicles shrank like freeze-dried peas, then skittered into hiding near his throat. "You reported this?"

"Only to internal affairs and the prosecutor's office." He tapped his teeth to the rhythm of "The Party's Over." "Does that about cover it, Sergeant? Or have I forgotten someone?"

"Huppert knew?"

"He did indeed. He elected to submit his resignation rather than go through a long, unpleasant disciplinary process. For once, he made the wise choice."

"Huppert lied," he said dully. "Why would he lie?"

"Oh my, there must be lots of excellent reasons. Why don't you ask him? I'm sure a forthright soul like the sergeant will be happy to explain. No doubt he's reformed completely since he became a crossing guard. As everyone knows, there's much more valor in their noble ranks."

Tucci set his Glock on Klonsky's desk. He followed with his shield and department ID.

Klonsky's eyes stretched in mock surprise. "What's this?"

"I'll clear my desk and be out of here in an hour. All I ask is that you leave Samuels alone. He had nothing to do with this."

"Didn't your mother teach you anything, Tucci? You don't leave your junk lying around in somebody else's space. Now take your things like a good boy and go back where you belong. You've got work to do. Jury selection in Magill starts in two days. Chop chop."

"You're not firing me?"

"Why would I do a thing like that when I can make your life much more miserable right here? You've got five years, four months, two weeks, and twelve days to go until you qualify for a full pension. I plan to make that feel like a very, very long time indeed."

"It already does."

Klonsky's laugh rang with honest delight. "Go, children. I'd like to be alone for a while to savor the prospects."

Brooding clouds slumped in the glum pewter sky. Perfect match for Tucci's mood. "Let's call it a day, Mule. I've had it."

"Sure, Tooch. Whatever you say. I'm really sorry about what happened with Huppert. That sucks. I mean, Klonsky didn't like you before, but now you're really at the top of his list."

"I get that."

"I don't envy you one bit, buddy. When he says miserable, I bet he really means it."

Tucci slipped into the cruiser. "One thing about you, Mule. You really know how to cheer a guy up."

"All I want is to help out, any way I can."

"The best thing you can do right now is put a lid on and keep it there. Can you do that?"

"I'll try."

"Try hard."

"I told you, I'll do anything for you, Tooch. No matter what kind of deep trouble you're in, no matter who's out to get you, I'm there for you, pal. You can count on me no matter how rough things get."

"Try harder, Mule. Shut your trap."

Mule obliged, and on the silent drive, Tucci had plenty of time for regrets. From the start, he had made a colossal mess of this case. He'd allowed that phony informant to take him for a ride. He'd failed to close open issues and track all the logical leads. His entire approach had been sloppy and haphazard. Worse, when things didn't fit, he'd tried to force them, like a kid breaking the edges off puzzle pieces rather than working them patiently into place. Instead of digging in any systematic way, he'd hacked at random as if he could find what he needed by blind force of will. Since his rookie year, he could not think of a single case he had handled with such stunning incompetence.

He would have liked to lay the blame on some external force, like Gina's illness. But the real cloud over his judgment had been good old revenge.

Running into Charlie Magill at the hospital had cued him to the size of his rank feelings. Telling him off had given Tucci a moment's satisfaction. But as soon as he returned to Gina's room, he'd paid a hefty price for the fleeting pleasure.

His mama had lit into him for carrying on like that in a place where sick people needed their rest. Charlie Magill might have been a foolish, troubled teenager, but as a man, he had reformed, she told him. Many years ago, he'd shown up at the deli to apologize and express his shame. Of course, she'd forgiven him.

After that, he would come in two, sometimes three times a week to buy a sandwich for his lunch or something to bring home to his family, or to pick up a tray he'd ordered to take to some meeting at his work. He was always a perfect gentleman, she said, *sempre molto gentile.*

As soon as Tucci's mother set down the bludgeon, Gina had picked it up. She had known Danny Magill since seventh grade. He was a great kid, nice to everyone, smart and thoughtful. She refused to believe that he was guilty of sexual assault or hurting Lisa Beningson in any way.

Lisa had a crush on Danny, Gina said, though Danny was not the type to take advantage. He and Lisa had been friends, no more. If anyone had tried to escalate the relationship, it must have been Lisa.

Someone should force Lisa to take a lie detector test, she said. Danny too, because the results were bound to prove him innocent. Marie and his mama had rushed to take Gina's side. Hadn't he been blinded by his grudge against the boy's father? Could he really be fair or objective about Danny Magill?

And then, Gina had flattened him with the words that still reverberated in his mind. *I used to think you were the fairest, most honest person I knew, Daddy. But you don't care about the truth at all. What happened to you?*

Tucci hadn't bothered to defend himself. They were right. So was Klonsky. He had messed this thing up royally, beginning to end. An ancient grudge had directed his actions.

He dropped Mule off, then headed up Virgil Street. Two blocks later, he swerved in a U-turn and parked in front of the Italian social club.

Approaching dinnertime, the room was nearly empty. A scatter of men on barstools watched a soccer game on the large screen TV. Two grizzled *paesani* hunched over a chessboard. Uncle Pasquale occupied his regular table in the rear, sipping *vino* and arguing politics.

His brow shot up when he spotted Tucci. "To what do we owe this *onore?* Imagine a busy *uomo importante* like you coming to our foolish little place."

Tucci was willing to wear the kick-me sign, whatever it took. "I want to hear what you have to tell me, Uncle. If you're not too busy, that is. You are the important man. The honor is mine."

Pasquale exchanged meaningful glances with his friends. Tucci's subservience would be valuable currency for weeks to come: Pasquale's views would hold extra weight. His glass would be filled more fully from the jug of home brew in the center of the table.

"I suppose I can find a few minutes. *Mi dispiace,*" he told the men. "I must go now. The boy needs my advice."

Tucci led him out to the cruiser, where they would not be overheard.

"So finally, you have the time for an old man, Giuseppe," the old man huffed.

"You wait much longer, I could be *morto.* Then you would have to ask your questions of my bones."

"I'm sorry, Uncle. You're right. Please forgive me."

Pasquale studied Tucci's face for signs of real remorse. "Suddenly you need my *consiglio*? How come?"

"The case goes to trial in two days. If you have something I should know, please tell me now."

The old man eyed him harshly. "I tell you for justice only. If not for that, I let you learn the *lezione* the hard way."

"I have learned. Believe me."

"Okay then, but you'd better listen good."

"You got it. Let me warm up the car, so you'll be comfortable." Tucci started the engine and nudged up the thermostat.

Pasquale relaxed in the enveloping heat. The anger on his face melted away. "Some men at the club were talking about this case of yours, so naturally, my ears went sharp. One of them, a man named Salvatore who is the son of an *amico* from my village, said he knows the father of the girl who brought the charge. He works for this man, as a *giardiniere, capisci*?"

"He's the Beningsons' gardener. Yes, I understand."

"Salvatore said this man Beningson is *molto strano.* Not *normale,* if you know what I mean."

"Not normal how?"

"In the way he looks at his daughter, like she is a bowl of *gelato,* and he has not eaten in days. I told him he is not behind the man's eyes, that it is wrong to say such a thing. But Salvatore told me it was not only in the looks that the man showed his strangeness."

Pasquale pulled out a handkerchief and pressed it to his lips. A cough racked his bony frame.

"Are you okay, Uncle?"

He waved the question off. "Are you listening or talking foolishness, Giuseppe? I thought you wanted to hear what I have to say."

Tucci's penance was not yet paid in full. "I am listening to every word. What did Beningson do besides look at his daughter strangely?"

"One day, the girl was reading on a chair in the backyard. She was wearing a *costume da bagno.*"

"A bathing suit," Tucci offered.

"*Sì,* a bathing suit, a small one in two parts like the young girls wear. But innocent. This is a little girl, Salvatore says, with the body of a child. Still the father was watching her from a chair across the pool with that hungry look on his face. He did not realize that Salvatore could see him as he trimmed the hedge near the house. To that man, a worker does not exist. He is a *niente,* nothing, a machine. So the father put his hand on himself down there under the towel, and he, you know, *ha fato abuso.*"

"Abused himself? He whacked off, you mean?"

Pasquale's face registered shock. "Such a thing to say. *Maleducato.*"

"Sorry if it's rude, Zio. But I need to know."

"Yes, that's what he did." He spat into the handkerchief. "What kind of a man looks at his *figlia* in such a way? What kind of a man does such a thing?"

That was Tucci's question exactly: What kind of a man?

Pearl tugged the red-striped hat down hard over Max's ears, then looped the matching scarf around his neck.

"There you are, darling. Are you warm enough?"

"I'm boiling, Grandma. I feel like soup."

"You'll be thankful. You'll see. It's freezing out."

"We're only going to the car," Max whined.

"The last thing you need is to catch a chill, God forbid. It's colder than Romania out there. Now zip up. All the way. That's a good boy." She stretched the hood of his jacket over the hat and scarf. His arms lifted involuntarily like the levers on a corkscrew.

Molly skipped downstairs toting her red canvas duffel and a backpack. "All set, Gram. Let's go."

"You have everything, darling? A nice heavy sweater? Snow boots? They're talking snow."

"You don't let us go out in the snow anyway."

"You have to take bad weather seriously. I just read about a woman who was driving to the supermarket for a few things and got caught in a blizzard. They found her three days later, frozen like a flounder."

"I have everything, Gram. I have so much stuff I could go to the North Pole for a year."

"Perfect."

Jess hugged the plump cocoon containing Max and bent over the hill of luggage to kiss Molly. "You guys have fun. See you in a week."

"We're going to have a wonderful time," Pearl declared. "The refrigerator is full to bursting. I cooked all your favorites, children. Wait till you see."

"Call when you get there," Jess said.

"Tell Danny I said to have a good trial," said Max.

"I will."

Jess watched Lou back the Cadillac out of the drive. Pearl's mouth worked in frantic rounds. She was probably warning Lou not to hit the tree or the mailbox, warning him to go slowly and watch out for traffic. She raved on, probably warning him that children play in the neighborhood and could come darting out after a ball at any time, warning him to watch out for unleashed animals, warning him that she was warning him. Leaving nothing to chance.

After they left, Jess drove to the whale-shaped Presbyterian church to pick up Danny. He stepped out as she pulled to the curb. Before he reached the car, Jess slid over to the passenger seat. "I'm beat. You drive, honey. Okay?"

"I'd rather not."

"Why?"

"I just don't feel like it."

Jess held her ground. "I'll drive if you tell me why you don't feel like it, Danny. It's time to talk about that."

Danny stood in the cold, spewing visible plumes of exasperation. "Come on, Mom. Don't give me a hard time. It's no big deal."

"In the past few months, you've gotten more and more reluctant to get behind the wheel, Danny. There has to be a reason, and I'd like to hear what it is."

"All right, I'll drive the damned car if it's so important to you." He flung his books in the back seat, adjusted the mirrors, and slipped the Volvo in gear. At the end of the long looping drive, he stopped and stared at the scatter of oncoming traffic on Bedford Street. Few cars rode the right lane and he had ample opportunity to ease into the flow of cars, but he made no move to do so.

Spying a long break between cars, Jess urged, "You can go now, Danny."

He shoved the door open and burst out. A scream caught in Jess's throat as he raced across the four traffic lanes, heedless of the speeding cars.

Brakes screeched. Horns blared. An incensed motorist rolled down his window and shrieked, "What are you, nuts?"

Somehow, Danny reached the other side unhurt. He ran down the street and into the rear lot of a shopping mall.

There was no way Jess could catch up to him on foot. Bedford Street ran one way in the wrong direction. She wove through the traffic, turned left on High Ridge, then left again at Bull's Head.

Passing the strip mall, Jess spotted Danny near the service entrance to the Tara Hotel. "Stop!"

He took a few halting steps, then crumpled to the grass beside the driveway. By the time Jess reached him, he was sobbing in deep, anguished bursts. She drew him up and guided him toward the car.

"What's wrong, Danny? Tell me, please."

Slowly, his tears subsided. He stared out the window. His breath fogged the glass.

Jess saw no choice. She had to force the issue open, lance it like a boil and let the poison out. "I know you blame yourself for Ryan's accident, honey. I just don't understand why."

"Because it was my fault," he cried. "Because none of it would have happened if not for me."

"You were home the night he got hurt. I remember that. How could you be responsible?"

"Ryan called and asked me to take him out to get a pizza. He'd been up the whole night before, studying for his physics exam, and he was really exhausted. I was so sick of hearing him carry on about that stupid test. For weeks, it was all I heard from him. Mr. Bolitow was a crummy teacher. The work was impossible. No matter how hard he studied, he didn't get any of it. He was going to flunk. Then he'd never get into a decent school, and his life would be over."

"I never knew he was such a worrier," Jess said.

"He was about school. He'd always get himself worked up over some subject or other. One year it was French, another time history. He'd worry himself sick before every test, and then after it was over, he'd swear he had failed. Of course, after all the carrying on, he'd get an A. Never failed. It got old. I didn't want to hear it anymore."

"That sounds reasonable."

Danny rolled his eyes. "Why do you always have to be so damned understanding?"

The lash of his anger stung. "I'm trying to listen to you, Danny."

"But you're not listening. You're doing exactly what Grandma does. I tell you I did something wrong, and you say I didn't. It's like I don't exist."

Something shifted deep inside Jess, admitting a harsh ray of light. By its unrelenting glare, she was forced to face the troubling truth. Her reassurance had been well intended, but Danny had received it as an affront. In his view she was holding out a slice of stringy, unpalatable pot roast and forcing him to eat. All the time, he was hungry for something else or nothing at all. "I'm sorry, honey. Go on please."

"It wasn't reasonable. I lied to Ryan. I told him you needed me to baby-sit. His parents were away, and the kid wanted a stupid pizza, and I refused to help him out. He said he was too tired to drive, and I told him that was ridiculous. I said he should stop being such a whiny little wuss. So because of me, he went out and fell asleep behind the wheel."

Jess looked Danny hard in the eye and chose her words carefully. This was about truth, not reassurance. "Hear me, Danny. You are not responsible for that. Ryan chose to go out for that pizza. He could have eaten something at home. He could have called to have a pizza delivered, for God sakes. It was his decision to get in the car even though he knew he was too tired to drive. I can understand if you feel bad about lying to him or refusing to do him a favor, but none of that caused the accident. How can you take that on yourself?"

The tears flowed again. "You don't understand because you've never done anything like that, Mom. If you'd ever hurt anyone really, really badly, you'd get how I feel."

A bitter lump lodged in her throat. "But I have."

"You're only saying that."

"No. It's real." She swallowed hard. Jess had never talked about this, to anyone. She had held it in a dark, airless crypt where it had been causing guilt and pain for years.

"I was about your age when my father got sick. Suddenly, he was tired all the time, feeling lousy. He wasn't the kind to complain, but even as a kid, I could see there was something wrong with him, and it scared me to death. I suppose I couldn't face the possibility that he had a serious illness, so I looked for something innocent to blame. There was a lot of talk at the time about smoking and how it was bad for you, so I started nagging my dad to give up cigarettes. I was positive that would make him feel better, and we could all go on with things the way they were.

"My mother wanted him to go to the doctor, but he refused. He said I was right, that he was feeling bad because of the cigarettes. So he stopped smoking for a day or two, and he did feel better. His color improved, and he had more energy. Then, when he started smoking again, he blamed the cigarettes for everything that bothered him. He got weaker and weaker, but he refused to take it seriously. No matter how my mother nagged him to see a doctor, he refused to listen.

"Months later, he passed out at work. An ambulance took him to the hospital. They performed emergency surgery, but the cancer was too advanced. Three months later, he was gone.

"I blamed myself for giving him bad advice. I still blame myself. I can't help but think that if not for me, he might still be alive. You would have loved my father, Danny. He was such a dear sweet man and you never even got to meet him. I blame myself for that too."

"You didn't know. You were just a kid." He frowned in thought. "It was different with Ryan."

"I think it's exactly the same. You think you should have known what was going to happen and found a way to stop it. You carry that with you, and it eats you up inside. Try to let it go, honey. Let's both try to do that."

The Last Supper," Danny pronounced as he slumped in his chair.
Jess passed out plates laden with comfort foods—roast chicken, mashed potatoes, corn bread—but no one was comforted in the least.

"Let's try to look on the bright side. The sooner the trial starts, the sooner we'll be done with it," Jess said.

"That's the problem, Mom," Danny said. "I'll be done with."

"I didn't mean that. Try to be optimistic, honey. You've heard the lawyers. The prosecution case is far from solid."

"That doesn't exactly make me leap with confidence."

"Maybe we shouldn't talk about the trial at all," Charlie suggested.

They made a few abortive attempts at conversation, but most of the meal passed without a word. The only breach in the silence was the irritating clink of cutlery. Swallows and sighs.

When they ferried the dishes to the sink, Jess was appalled to see that it was only seven o'clock. How were they going to get through the rest of this interminable evening? She had cleaned and straightened the house beyond all reason. Even her purse was devoid of clutter. The situation was dire.

When the doorbell rang, she hoped for some miraculous distraction. And sure enough, there was Libby Amory, red-nosed from the biting cold, bearing a gargantuan grocery bag.

"Libby, hi. I'm so glad to see you. Come in."

"Can't. A miracle has happened and I've got an actual date. I just came to drop off the emergency kit I've developed for times of particular stress. Guaranteed to get you through the night."

"You're an angel. What is it?"

"You'll see. I've got to run. I'm in court tomorrow. I'll check in with you every chance I get."

"Thanks."

Jess emptied the bag on the kitchen counter. There was a giant sack of cheddar cheese popcorn, two jars of dry roasted nuts, a bag of snack-sized Snickers, a six-pack of Smutty Nose pale ale, a six-pack of Classic Coke, and three Monty Python tapes from the video store. "Bless that woman," Jess said. "I think we're saved."

They decided to watch *Monty Python and the Holy Grail* first, Danny's favorite. Soon they were all doubled over, laughing. They got lost in the brilliant British farce, carried away with the coconut-clacking knights, absorbed in the absurd adventure.

Halfway through the movie, Charlie sniffed. "You must have left the stove on, Jessie. I smell something burning."

"I'll go see."

Danny went for the remote. "Want me to stop it?"

"Don't bother. I'll be back in a second."

The scorched scent was stronger in the kitchen. Jess checked the burner and oven controls, but everything was off.

Prozac ambled in with her muzzle raised, nose twitching.

Jess opened the oven door. No smoke billowed forth. She saw no charred matter on the heater coils to account for the acrid smell.

The dog sniffed toward the foyer and started whimpering.

"What's wrong, girl?"

As Jess trailed Prozac into the hall, her heart seized. The front lawn was a fiery sea. Flames leaped beyond the frosted-glass panels.

Pulsing heat penetrated the door. Wind-whipped blazing spikes strained toward the house. Jess found her voice. "Come here, Charlie. Quick!"

Charlie raced in and opened the door. He shielded his face against the glaring blaze. "Call the fire department, Danny. Hurry!"

Jess followed Charlie outside and circled the mass of flames. He grabbed the hose and twisted the faucet. He aimed the nozzle at the fire, but nothing happened. "Damn it! The water's turned off."

Charlie ran to the basement. Jess held the nozzle, braced for the soaking burst. But instead, fine pins sprayed from the hose at useless intervals.

"I called. They're on the way," Danny said.

Charlie filled a bucket from the garage and started dousing the fire. Jess grabbed a plastic pail and Danny took the watering can. The flames outpaced their frantic efforts, but it was better to do something. The blaze was threatening the house. Tongues of flame licked the clapboard.

Where were the fire engines?

A terrible thought occurred to Jess as she hurled another pailful at the blaze. With a sizzling rush, a tiny swath went out, only to be quickly reignited by the wind-churned conflagration. *What if they didn't come? What if they heard the name Magill and decided to let the fire rage on unimpeded?* Charlie was wetting down the side of the house, but it was only a matter of time before the old clapboard caught. They had minimal insurance. Full coverage was too expensive, they'd decided. They could lose everything.

At last came the distant swell of sirens. In a dizzying swirl of lights, two engine companies and a rescue truck turned onto the cul-de-sac and pulled up to the house. A dozen men in helmets and turnout coats swarmed out. They hitched their hose to a hydrant down the block. Soon, a giant rush of water assailed the blaze. "Get back, folks. Watch yourself," called one.

Jess, Charlie, Danny, and Prozac huddled shivering in the street, watching until the flames played out and only a scorched band remained.

"That should do it," said one of firefighters.

"Thanks," Charlie told him.

Another man approached. "Name's Morgan. I'm the inspector. Any idea what started this?"

Jess shrugged. "Could it be an underground oil tank, a gas line, something like that?"

"Out of the blue in this cold? Doubtful."

Danny stood near the sodden remains of the blaze. "Jesus," he said. "My God."

"What is it?" Charlie asked.

Danny clutched his ribs as if he'd been punched.

Jess and Charlie moved closer to see what was wrong. Several of the firefighters followed. One played his flashlight over the singed ground. A word had been etched in broad shaky letters: PIG.

Kneeling, the inspector traced a finger over the charred ground and held it to his nose. "Lighter fluid. Seems someone tried to send you a message the hard way."

There was a flash near the hedgerow. Wheeling quickly, Jess spotted a young blond man with a camera. "That's it, Mrs. Magill. Smile pretty now. Hey, Danny. Turn around. Say cheese."

"Get out of here!" Charlie demanded.

Another flash. "Nice face, mister. Thanks. It'll go great with the story."

Charlie ran at him, and he dashed away, chuckling in delight. From ten yards back came another light burst, then another.

"Looks like you people are going to have your fifteen minutes," the reporter taunted from beyond the hedge. "Might as well enjoy it."

FORTY-SIX

When Tucci entered the lab, Lee Chow peered up from the printout he'd been studying at his desk. His magnified eyes registered amusement.

"Knew you'd be back, Detective," the scientist said. "You left something important behind last time here."

"What was that?"

"Questions not asked."

"I don't get it, Doc. If you saw I was missing something, why didn't you open my eyes?"

Chow wiped his glasses with the tail of his lab coat. "Could only make you look, not see. Horse to water same thing."

Tucci took in the cluttered office and the scientist's foolish, rumpled look. Here was the seat and voice of wisdom. Anyone who put major stock in appearances should get a load of this.

"You're not going to make it easy on me, are you, Doc?"

"You pitch, Chow catch. Very easy."

It wasn't easy for Tucci at all. He had to use the muscle between his ears, which had gone flabby with distraction and disuse. He rescued the Magill file from the paper blizzard on Chow's desk. Reviewing the forensic section, he beat his head against the problem. What hadn't he covered? What questions hadn't he asked? Was there a cure for charley horse of the brain? "How about a hint, Doc?"

Chow pointed at a picture of Lisa Beningson's injured ribs. "Find question and answer at end of rainbow."

In the photo, the girl was naked except for a couple of strategically placed black stripes. A couple of livid blotches stained her skin. Hours after the alleged attack, the photos showed purple and rose-colored bruises, turquoise and greenish areas. Others were faded to olive drab and pale yellow. Tucci could see the gruesome rainbow. But what did it mean?

"Looks like Gina's arm after they poked her a zillion times. She was a mess like this. Fresh bruises every day. Damned rainbow of bruises." Suddenly, his wheels spun into place like the tumblers of a lock. "My God, Doc. I see what you mean."

Chow grinned. "Now have answer, Detective. Question all that's left."

"What question?"

"Most important one. What do now?"

"There's only one thing I can do, Doc," said Tucci. "Try to make my kid proud of me again."

Jess awakened to the shrill of the phone. It was only six a.m. by the bedside clock, and this was her third wake-up call. This time, a reporter from CNN wanted a statement. She had already heard from the *Hartford Courant* and cable channel 12. "Tell me, Mrs. Magill, how does it feel to be reviled by the community?"

"Why ask me? You're a reporter. Surely you know how it feels to be reviled." She hung up in a fury, then threw off the covers and tossed on her robe.

"Where you going, Jessie?" Charlie yawned.

"Downstairs to sputter and fume. Get some sleep for both of us."

She turned off the ringer on the bedside phone and padded downstairs. Peering outside, she eyed the enormous legend scorched on the front lawn. By the grainy light of dawn, it looked even uglier. She couldn't wait to turn the ground and make it disappear. Hopefully, the soil was not too frozen.

Jess brewed a pot of French-roast. As she poured a cup, the phone rang again. Libby's number registered on the caller-ID.

"Sorry to call so early, but I just heard about the fire, Jess. Are you okay?"

"We're shaken, but thankfully no one was hurt. Where did you hear, Lib? Is it all over the news?"

"I'm afraid so. I saw it on *Good Morning America*. It's a top story. 'Return of the vigilante. Is jungle justice the answer?' There's no end to the public appetite for sheer, unadulterated garbage, I'm afraid."

Jess groaned. "More attention is exactly what we don't need. Poor Danny."

"Remember what I told you, kiddo. The public has a very short attention span. This too shall pass. Meanwhile, try to keep your chin up."

"I'm afraid it's pretty much hanging on the floor. But thanks, Lib. You've been so terrific. I don't know what we'd do without you."

As soon as she set the receiver down, the phone trilled again. The caller-ID registered some unknown New York number, so she let the machine pick up. As Jess had feared, it was another reporter, this time from the *Post*. They had no trouble latching onto unlisted numbers and unwilling subjects, no qualms about trampling someone's privacy or twisting a painful blade. *Tell me, Mrs. Smith, how do you feel about your baby being hit by a train and splattered like an overripe tomato?*

Jess took her coffee to the den and perched on the arm of the couch. Working the remote, she flipped through the channels. It was a quarter past the hour, time for headline updates. On CBS, the lead story was about the devastating crash of an American Airlines Boeing 727 at La Guardia. The plane had over-run the landing strip and broken up in the water. Hundreds were feared dead.

There was a cereal commercial, another thirty-second spot for stain-lifting laundry soap. When the announcer came back on, Jess's blood froze. *Frightened Citizens Fight Back,* read the headline. The picture behind him was a blowup of their house, their scorched lawn, the word etched in the grass: PIG.

The clear editorial slant was in favor of the trespassing vandals who had lit the match. Outraged, Jess pressed the channel button until she came to another report of the incident. The story was the same. Decent people were taking mat-ters into their own hands, protecting their threatened women and children. Who could blame them?

Somehow, while he sat on the couch, watching Monty Python and drink-ing a Coke, Danny had become the symbol of lurking evil in suburban America.

The story was the same on the next report she came to, and the next. Only one colorless commentator on a local cable show bothered to mention that they had been the victims of this particular crime. No matter what public passions Danny's alleged actions might have aroused, people had no right to take the law into their own hands. Still, the announcer said in grim summary, anyone could understand the urge to do so.

The next time the phone rang, Gus Grantham's number flashed on the dig-ital display. The attorney was already in the office.

"I wanted to let you know that everything is under control, Jess," he said brightly. "Even as we speak, I'm preparing a motion for a postponement and change of venue. Actually, all this hullabaloo could turn out to be a blessing in disguise."

"If it is, it's an exceptionally good disguise, Gus."

"Trust me. I'll see you in court at ten sharp. Meanwhile, if anyone tries to get a statement from you, duck."

The next call was from her mother. Pearl always awakened early and flipped on the radio to catch the news and weather. Anticipating the enormity of her mother's hysteria, Jess cringed. Bless Pearl. Whatever happened happened to her.

Reluctantly, Jess picked up the phone. She braced for the worst, but what came was beyond her bleakest imagining.

"Jessie dear. I'm so sorry to bother you, especially with the trial and all, but I thought you'd want to know."

"What is it, Lou? Are the kids all right?"

"They're fine. And your mother is going to be fine too, dear. Try not to worry. The doctors say it might be nothing at all."

"What's going on, Lou? For the love of God, tell me what happened."

In his halting, diffident way, her stepfather explained that Pearl had awakened at two in the morning with chest pains. After all her false infarction threats, Lou had not taken her seriously at first. But the pain had gotten worse and started radiating into her arm.

Despite her mighty objections, Lou had insisted that she go to the hospital. He'd called 911, and the medics had arrived in moments. Their next-door neighbor had come in to stay with the children while he followed the ambulance to the emergency room at South Nassau. The resident there had noticed certain irregularities in Pearl's EKG, Lou said, but her heart rhythms might have been that way for ages. Anyway, the blood tests had been negative, which was very good news.

"Even if she did have a little heart attack, it didn't cause any permanent damage," Lou said. "The cardiologist is coming in first thing this morning to look at all the tests, and he'll decide whether she can come home or needs further treatment."

"What kind of treatment?"

"They may want to do one of those balloon things. But that's only if the tests show her arteries are blocked. Pearl is beside herself, as you can imagine. She was carrying on something awful. She has things to do. Her grandkids are visiting. But I told her, be reasonable. These people are just trying to make sure everything checks out. I told her I'd take care of the little ones until they were ready to let her go. Everything is under control. I'm only calling because I was afraid you might phone here and get the story from one of the children. Now please, Jessie, you just go about your business and don't give us another thought. We'll be absolutely fine."

"You don't need Molly and Max on your hands at a time like this. I don't have time to come for them before we go to court, but you can call a car service to bring them home. Molly can keep an eye on Max here until we get back later today. I think that's the best idea."

"Nonsense. They're no bother at all. You concentrate on what you need to do there and don't worry about us."

"You shouldn't be alone with all this, Lou. What about Larry? Can't you get him to come and help out?"

"Your brother and Irene are in Cancún. Listen to me. Everything is under control. Your mother has plenty of fight left in her yet. Trust me."

Jess was on overload. Out of hands and choices. "Promise you'll call as soon as you know something."

"I will. Of course."

"If I don't hear from you by the time we have to leave, I'll call from the court-house." She couldn't have him call on her portable phone. There was no signal in the building.

"Fine, Jessie."

"Oh, and Lou, whatever you do, don't let Pearl get anywhere near the news."

Mobile news vans and curious onlookers lined the cul-de-sac. As they rolled out of the driveway, Charlie leaned on the horn, scattering the mike-wielding reporters.

"Hey, stop. Can't we get a statement?" hollered one.

"Wait. Tell us, Magill. What do you think your chances are? What's your defense?"

Another mass of reporters assailed them on the street outside the courthouse. Huddled together, they ran the gauntlet of snide comments and rude demands.

"What is it, Magill? You think every girl wants you? You think no means yes?"

"Smile for the camera, Magill. Give us some beefcake. Thatta boy."

Finally, they made it to the courthouse door, but the media mob pressed in on them relentlessly. Danny looked shell-shocked. Jess was brewing a murderous rage: "Let us go! Leave us alone! Get away from him!" Still, they came at the poor kid like ravenous vultures, swooping in from unexpected angles, pecking mercilessly.

"Please, can't you get these characters away from us," Charlie asked the guard, who by now knew them well.

"Sure can, Dr. Magill. Wait just a minute." He called for backup on his walkie-talkie. "Next time, tell your lawyer to have you brought around to the rear. That'll make it much easier on everyone."

Two cops quickly appeared. They escorted the Magills upstairs to Harrigan's courtroom and muscled them through the queue of hopeful spectators. Among them, Jess spotted several neighbors: Mel and Carla Levitan, Victor Alton, John Slattery. She saw her phobic patient Manny Dickler, who had braved his fear of heights and elevators to reach the courtroom. Several of Danny's classmates had skipped school to attend. They greeted him with whistles and applause. "Go, Big Mac!" one kid yelled, as if this was fourth down in some crucial game and Danny was bearing down on the goal.

Their arrival in the courtroom raised a strident buzz. As they made their way to the seats that had been reserved for them, Jess spotted Sidney Rosenthal behind the defense table. Charlie's parents occupied side seats on the right. As Jess was trying to catch their attention, someone whispered her name from behind. The voice sent an icy jolt up her spine. Dolores Wainscott.

"So lovely to see you get exactly what's coming to you, Jessica dear," Dolores rasped. "I warned you, *chérie*. Too bad you didn't take me seriously."

Jess pretended not to hear. She slipped into the row beside Charlie and clenched her hands to still their trembling. Grantham greeted Danny with elaborate enthusiasm. The lawyer postured for the half-dozen artists hunched over giant sketch pads in the second row. He took care to tip his head at an advantageous angle and suck in his gut.

In contrast, Prosecutor Rodell kept the lowest possible profile. He scrawled notes on a legal pad, studied the file.

The bailiff, a wizened man with jug ears, stepped to the front of the room. "Oyez, oyez. All those having business before this court draw nigh. The Honorable Harold Harrigan presiding. All rise."

Harrigan took the bench. He peered at Grantham over his silver-framed specs. "I've reviewed your pleadings, Mr. Grantham. At this point, the court will hear arguments regarding defendant's motion for a change of venue in this matter. Counselor, you may proceed."

Grantham buttoned the jacket of his double-breasted, quadruple-digit suit. He smiled at the gallery, then commenced his impassioned plea. "My client has a constitutional right to a fair trial by an unbiased jury of his peers, Your Honor. Based on recent events, including the heinous attack last night on his home and family, I believe it is patently clear that such an impartial panel cannot be mustered in this community." He gestured grandly in Danny's direction. "This young man has already been tried and convicted in the local press. He has been convicted, sentenced, and subjected to cruel and unusual punishments by neighbors who consider themselves above and beyond the law. An atmosphere of vigilantism prevails here. I challenge Your Honor to find twelve good citizens in this city who have not already solidified premature, unfounded judgments in this case."

Harrigan smacked his gavel on the bench. "I accept your challenge, Counselor. Clear the gallery, bailiff, please. Bring in the first of the jury pool and let's proceed with the voir dire."

"If it please the court, I have not finished my oral arguments in this matter," Grantham railed.

"I believe you have," Harrigan said. "Motion denied."

"Objection."

"Overruled."

"Exception."

"So noted. Now let us proceed."

After the spectators filed out, two dozen people straggled in through a door at the front of the courtroom.

Harrigan posed several general questions to the group. "Do any of you know the defendant personally? Have any of you been the victim of a violent crime? Raise your hand if anyone in your family has ever been the victim of a sex crime, whether reported or not. Are any of you employed in law enforcement or related to anyone who is? Thank you, numbers four, six, and eleven. You are dismissed."

Grantham and the prosecutor interviewed the remaining candidates. Each excused several people for cause and exercised some of their limited peremptory challenges. Rodell eliminated several young, single men, who might be expected to sympathize with the accused. In conference with his jury consultant, a willowy redheaded woman from New Haven, Grantham culled three people, two women and a man, whose responses suggested that they might be biased toward the prosecution. From the first pool, only three jurors were empaneled. The others left with the judge's thanks. Most looked relieved. According to Harrigan, Danny's trial could be expected to run as long as six weeks. Despite the frank and sometimes graphic sexual evidence that Harrigan had also promised, six weeks would constitute a major disruption in most lives.

As Libby had warned, the wheels of justice ground at an excruciating pace. Jess felt as if she were being crushed beneath them, one molecule at a time. All she could see of Danny was the back of his head. She could not assess how he was holding up, what this was doing to him.

Jess's worries veered back and forth between Danny and her mother. Countless times, she had fantasized about a Pearl-free existence. But faced with the real prospect, her insides squeezed in a searing lump of pain. Her mother could not die. She must not. No matter how perverse Pearl could be, maybe because of that, Jess was nowhere near ready to let her go.

The moment Judge Harrigan called a recess, Jess hurried out to the pay phone. On the way, she ignored the loitering reporters, the court groupies, the comments. All but one.

"That animal of yours is not going to get away with this, Jess," Victor Alton said. "He's a pig, that kid. You all are."

PIG.

Jess approached him and sniffed. "You stink of smoke, Victor. Smoke and lighter fluid. I'm sure the prosecutor will find that fascinating."

"Don't give me that crap. You were warned to get the hell away. I warned you myself. You should have listened."

"Yes, you did warn me, Victor, and in front of all these nice people." Jess turned to the Levitans, who stood behind Alton. "You heard him, didn't you, Carla and Mel?"

Carla scowled. "What did you have to open your big mouth for, Victor? What's wrong with you?"

"Talk about a big mouth."

Jess left them bickering and went to the phone. The call rang through to Pearl's hospital room, but no one answered. Checking the number Lou had given her, she tried again. Nothing.

Jess dialed the main number and asked for patient information. "Pearl Lefferman please."

"I'm sorry. We have no patient by that name."

"She must have been discharged, then. Can you tell me when?"

"One moment please. I'll check." Soon the voice came back on the line. "Sorry, ma'am. We have no record of a Pearl Lefferman being discharged."

"Can you check again please? It's L-e-f-f-e-r-m-a-n."

"That's what I looked under—sorry."

Jess's mind was racing in desperate circles. If Pearl wasn't registered as a patient and she hadn't checked out, where could she be? "Are you sure?"

"Positive. This is South Nassau Community Hospital. Maybe you have the wrong place."

"No, I'm sure it's right." Lou had given her the hospital's main number and the number of Pearl's room. There was no mistake.

She tried to stay rational and calm. Maybe there was a clerical error. That had to be it. Pearl had checked out and some computer had failed to register the fact. Simple. Whole lives could be eradicated by an errant keystroke. This was one of modern technology's more profound contributions to the human condition.

When she dialed the house, Max picked up.

"Hi, Maxy. Is Grandma home?"

"Nope. She was being a severe pain so Grandpa Lou took her to the hospital."

Jess heard Molly in the background. "She wasn't *being* a pain. She *had* a pain, lame-o."

"That's what I said," Max huffed.

"Let me speak to Grandpa Lou," Jess said.

"He's not here. Someone called from the hospital, and he had to go in a big hurry. He looked really, really scared."

Molly's voice shrilled in the background. "What are you doing, bean-brain? Don't tell her that." There was a scuffle in the background, and Molly came on the line. "Don't listen to him, Mom. He doesn't know anything."

Jess went ice calm. Thankfully, Pearl had made her wishes clear. She wanted to be buried in a plain pine box in the blue dress she'd had made for Glen's bar mitzvah.

"Who called Grandpa, Molly?" she asked.

"He didn't say."

"Did he say what happened at the hospital?"

"No."

"What did he say before he left?"

"Nothing, Mom. Just that he'd be back soon."

Jess was numb. Everything had to go according to her mother's wishes. They would have a graveside service at New Mount Carmel. Rabbi Klein would officiate. The deed to the plot was in the vault at Rockville Centre Savings. Jess had a duplicate key.

"He told me to keep an eye on Max and not to worry," Molly said. "I'm sure everything is fine, Mom. How's it going there?"

"Okay." Someone would have to track Larry down in Cancún. They could get emergency tickets home through the Red Cross. Pearl would want the funeral to take place quickly, tomorrow if possible, according to Jewish tradition.

Molly kept trying to reassure her. "You know Grandpa. He always looks scared. I'm sure everything's okay. Honest. Hang on a minute, Mom. I'm getting another call."

Jess's throat burned. Every child ached for her mother's love and acceptance. Every child longed for a chance to say a proper goodbye. She wanted to face Pearl, to see the fearsome *punim* one more time. She would get out all the unspoken things, even if Pearl refused to listen.

The connection came alive again. "That was Grandpa, Mom. He said to tell you they're on the way home."

"*They?*"

"Grandma's fine. It was gas, the doctor said."

"Gas," Jess repeated dully.

Molly giggled. "Grandpa Lou said she passed the longest blast of wind in recorded history, and then she felt much better. He said he was going to call the people from the Guinness book and get her written up. Grandma must be ready to kill him."

"If the Guinness book prints her name, she'll get over it."

Harrigan had called a ten-minute recess. The time was up. "Tell Grandma I'm glad she's all right. Very glad. Call you later, sweetie. Take care."

Jury selection stretched over five interminable days. Now, the eight men, four women, and three alternates took their places in the rectangular pen at the front of the courtroom.

Gus Grantham had declared this an excellent panel, though Jess found no evidence to back his enthusiasm. The jurors looked in varying degrees disheveled, distracted, and bored. The youngest man's eyes had the webbed look of limited intelligence, and the oldest, a seventy-five-year-old retired letter carrier, had needed to produce a doctor's note at the judge's request, declaring him mentally fit to serve. One of the women held a wad of chewing gum in her rouged cheek and cracked it loudly. Two of the men wore ratty jeans, and one sported a hunter's vest and baggy blue corduroys.

This bunch held Danny's future in their dubious hands. That thought was enough to snap the cable on Jess's hopes and send them plummeting. She tried to squeeze some comfort from Sidney Rosenthal's assessment that the case against Danny was weak.

Lisa Beningson was unlikely to make a strong witness. An intimidating bully like Grantham would probably level the girl on cross-examination. Of course, he'd have to avoid brute tactics that could turn the jury against Danny.

An independent forensic analysis arranged by Rosenthal's office had cast encouraging doubt on Lisa's version of the assault. There was no evidence of forcible penetration to indicate that she had resisted the sexual encounter. Danny had sustained no defense wounds. As Grantham had pointed out, his hands had not been swollen or bruised, as they would have been had he inflicted a serious beating. The scratches on his knee and forehead proved to be from a fall on muddy ground, exactly as he had asserted.

Reasonable doubt, Grantham said again and again. They had it in spades.

The only wild card was Leo Beningson. Grantham doubted that Lisa's father would have the audacity to take the stand. Sidney Rosenthal was inclined to agree, though not with nearly the certainty Jess would have wished.

Whatever else he might be, Leo Beningson was an articulate, convincing man. His impassioned account of Lisa's emotional and physical appearance on the night of the alleged assault could be devastating. She was Daddy's little girl. The light of his life. As Beningson would surely paint it, Danny was the strapping sex-crazed beast who had defiled his pure, innocent little flower. Hearing him was bound to put that ragtag bunch in the jury box in a tar-and-feather frame of mind.

If Beningson did testify, they would have to resort to Sidney Rosenthal's plan for damage control. It was a last resort and the outcome was far from certain. Worse, if it failed, the consequences could be devastating.

But that wasn't going to happen. Jess kept telling herself that. It wasn't going to happen.

The prosecutor droned through an opening statement filled with legal blather. Several of the jurors' eyes glazed with boredom. For what seemed the first time all day, Jess exhaled.

After Rodell finished, Grantham approached the jury box. Here, his outsized confidence and presence had a positive effect. The jurors sat straighter, eyes wide.

"The evidence will show that the real victim in this case is the defendant, Danny Magill. This young man has spent all of his life doing the right thing. You will hear from his teachers and neighbors and friends what an extraordinary person he is—a gifted student, an exceptional athlete, a caring, giving friend. They will tell you that Danny Magill is a selfless, gentle soul who would never hurt anyone.

"On the night in question, Danny Magill picked up his friend Ryan Harrison to take him to an orientation session at the high school. Now, normally, one boy driving another one to a school function is no big thing, but Ryan is not an ordinary boy, and neither is Danny Magill. You see, eighteen months ago, a devastating car accident left Ryan brain-damaged and partially paralyzed. Ryan uses a wheelchair. He needs to be lifted in and out of a car. He needs help when he has to use the rest room. His mother told me how tough it's been on Ryan since the accident. Most of his former friends have drifted away. Most teenagers are too self-absorbed to deal with the needs of a boy like Ryan, but not Danny Magill. Danny has stuck by his friend all along. He sat at Ryan's bedside in the hospital. He encouraged that boy to keep fighting. Danny Magill is always there for a friend. Any friend."

He propped his hands on the jury box and swung his head in a rueful arc. "You know how they say no good deed goes unpunished?"

The jurors exchanged smiles and knowing glances. Then they tuned their rapt attention back to Grantham.

"That is certainly the case here," the lawyer said. "Lisa Beningson was a friend of Danny Magill's, though with a friend like that, you certainly don't need enemies.

"The evidence will show that on the night of the alleged assault, Lisa asked Danny for a ride home. She said she wanted to talk to him. Danny was never one to refuse a favor, so he agreed. He dropped Ryan off across town and then drove directly to Lisa's house. By Lisa's own account, he stopped the car on the Beningsons' driveway, right below her parents' bedroom window, directly in the bright light from the security spots. This is hardly what one would expect from someone planning a sexual assault.

"Because, you see, that was the last thing on Danny Magill's mind when he did Lisa Beningson a favor and drove her home. The evidence will show that it was Lisa, not Danny, who initiated the sexual encounter. In fact, Danny was shocked by her advances and his initial instinct was to resist."

Grantham held up his hand. "Now, I can imagine what you must be thinking. Boys will be boys. All of them have one thing on their mind and one thing only. If Lisa came on to him, he must at least have gone along willingly. But the evidence will show that Danny Magill is no ordinary boy.

"Is he a saint? No. Actually, Danny Magill stands guilty of one thing, and this we will stipulate. On the night in question, Danny exercised unfortunate judgment. He chose to go along rather than hurt Lisa Beningson's feelings. He did not want to reject Lisa, even though he had no romantic or sexual interest in her at all. Danny considered Lisa a friend, and friendship means the world to him. That's the sad, simple truth. Danny Magill sits before you today because he cares about people, because he does not choose to hurt anyone's feelings. I urge you to listen to the evidence in this case and find Danny Magill not guilty. Thank you."

Charlie squeezed Jess's hand. It was all she could do to keep from applauding. One of the jurors did just that, drawing a swift stern rebuke from the judge. All her objections to Grantham evaporated. The man was worth every ounce of his obnoxious, overbearing weight in gold.

Harrigan squinted over his glasses at the prosecutor. "We have about two hours until we adjourn for the week, Counselor. If that will give you enough time on direct for your first witness, I'll ask you to proceed. Otherwise, I'm inclined to recess now."

Rodell stood. "Two hours should be more than enough, Your Honor."

"Fine. We'll take a ten-minute break, then reconvene."

During the recess, Grantham enjoyed a feast of compliments. Danny caught Jess's eye and shot her a tentative smile.

She winked back. This was better than she could have imagined. Better than she'd dared to hope.

Resuming the bench, Harrigan dipped his head at the prosecutor. "You may call your first witness, Mr. Rodell."

The prosecutor's scalp shone as he rose. "The state calls Leo Beningson."

Danny leaned over and whispered frantically to Grantham. Jess swallowed a groan of despair.

Beningson took the stand, stated his name and address, and swore on a shabby Bible to tell the truth. Rodell led him through the standard preliminaries.

"What is your profession, Mr. Beningson?"

"I have interests in several businesses worldwide. I suppose you could call me an entrepreneur."

"You travel extensively?"

"For business, yes. I do."

Jess and Charlie exchanged a look. His "business" in Cambodia was their ace in the hole. The question was whether they would have the chance to use it.

Rodell went on: "And yet, I understand you find time in your busy schedule to support a number of local charities."

"I feel I have a responsibility to help people less fortunate than myself."

At the prosecutor's insistence, Beningson described his extensive catalogue of good works. He did so with convincing reluctance and humility.

Rodell shifted to Beningson's family life. "You have a wife and one daughter. Is that correct?"

Beningson's voice broke. "Yes. Lisa is our only child."

Rodell paused for maximum effect. "I know this is difficult, Mr. Beningson. But I need you to tell us in your own words what you witnessed on the night in question."

Beningson spoke in a grim, compelling tone. He told of awakening in the night to his daughter's screams. He recounted every horrific detail in bold, graphic strokes. Harrigan gaveled down every one of Grantham's vigorous objections, dismissing them so quickly they failed to break the rhythm or impact of Beningson's account.

"How would you describe Lisa when you raced downstairs?"

"She was terribly upset, frightened and hurt. Her clothes were torn."

"What did Lisa say, Mr. Beningson?"

"She was weeping uncontrollably, barely coherent. Once I calmed her to the point where she could speak, I'll never forget what she said. 'Danny raped me, Daddy. Why, Daddy? Why?'"

By the end of it, Jess could barely breathe. The faces in the jury box said it all. They were up to their necks and sinking fast.

As soon as he entered Klonsky's office, Tucci knew that something was very wrong. The chief looked happy to see him. The smile was enough to make a man weak in the knees.

"Come in, Sergeant. Take a load off. Have a seat."

"I need to talk to you, Chief. It's about Magill."

"First, I need to talk to you about that very same subject."

Tucci braced for the blow.

Klonsky's smile held. "I've always believed in admitting when I'm wrong, Detective. And in this case, I was wrong about you. I just had a call from the prosecutor's office, and they tell me things couldn't be better. They're confident they'll win this one in a cakewalk. So congratulations, Sergeant Tucci. Consider yourself out of the hot seat and in my good graces. You get a star and a happy face, my highest rewards."

Tucci wished he could whip out his Glock and shoot himself. It would be much less painful. "You're not going to like this, Chief."

"What?"

"The case is a loser. You need to tell the prosecutor to drop the charges."

Klonsky's smile dropped like a rock. "What the hell are you talking about?"

Tucci told the chief what he'd heard from his Uncle Pasquale: Beningson had the hots for his daughter. As if that wasn't damning enough, Lee Chow had noticed old bruises in addition to the fresh ones Lisa had sustained in the alleged attack. Someone had beaten her long before she got in that car with Danny Magill. Her father was the logical candidate.

"My guess is, Leo Beningson somehow found out that Lisa and Danny had sex. In a jealous rage, he whipped the kid, and not for the first time. Naturally, she's terrified of the old bastard. So she tells him that Danny forced himself on her. Beningson picks up on that, and the rest is history."

Klonsky took up a pen and started drumming it on his desk. There was no mistaking the tune. It was "Taps."

The chief let Tucci squirm. A slow smirk bloomed on his leathery face. "Let me get this straight, Detective. Part of this brilliant deduction of yours comes from a senile old wino that speaks halting English and claims to be a retired spy. Part comes from your unauthorized consultation with a forensic scientist who happened to observe that Lisa fell down or whatever before the assault, and the rest springs directly from your fertile imagination. Am I missing anything?"

"I'm telling you, Chief, it smells bad."

"The only bad smell I get around here is you. Now hear me, and hear me good. This absurd theory of yours had better go no further than this room. If you compromise the Magill case, I will nail your insubordinate butt so fast you won't know what hit you. But it'll be me, Detective. You can bank on that."

"The case is going south, Chief. I'm telling you."

"No, *I'm* telling *you*. I'm the boss. I give the orders. You get to carry them out. Now get out of my office and stay there, Tucci. And keep your dumb trap shut."

Charlie paused at the Beningson driveway. After Bin Nol and Sidney Rosenthal got out, he pulled to the curb and killed the engine.

Jess's heart was hammering. Her shallow breaths marked misty circles on the windowpane. Everything was riding on what amounted to a bluff. Sidney Rosenthal would confront Leo Beningson about his nefarious activities in Phnom Penh. When he denied it, as he no doubt would, she would produce the Cambodian. Bin Nol had agreed to remain out of sight at the side of the house, awaiting his cue. He was as eager as the rest of them to take Leo Beningson down. His hatred of the man, coupled with a twenty-thousand-dollar payment from Senior, had put Nol firmly in Danny's camp.

Hopefully, the threat of exposure would induce Beningson to recant. But the real risk remained that Lisa's father might report the incident to the prose-cutor, express righteous outrage, and proceed to cross-examination Monday morning. If that happened, Sidney Rosenthal could be charged with witness tampering. Danny's defense could bear the taint. The risk was huge, but they could not see a reasonable way around it.

Jess shuddered with the cold. The sight of the Beningsons' house, festooned with Christmas lights, did nothing to warm her. Fifteen minutes passed, an excruciating second at a time.

Finally, Rosenthal and Bin Nol returned to the car.

"How did he react? What did he say? Tell me everything," Jess urged.

"He was shocked at first," said the lawyer. "Then of course, he tried to deny everything. As soon as he climbed on his high horse, I signaled Nol. When Beningson saw him, he went so pale I thought he might do us all a big favor and have a stroke, but no such luck. He collected himself sooner than I would have liked, and then he did the oddest thing. He shook Nol's hand and asked after his family. He offered us refreshments, which we refused. Then he smiled, thanked us for stopping by, and showed us the door. The man was positively pleasant."

"Sounds as if he dissociated," Jess said.

"Meaning . . . ?" the lawyer asked.

"It's something we see in multiple personalities and schizophrenics. But under extreme stress, it can happen to anyone. It's total unconscious denial. He couldn't deal with the situation, so he closed it off."

"How long might such a thing last?" Rosenthal asked.

"Impossible to say. It could be moments, or it could be permanent. Depends on how sick Beningson is. How sick and how desperate."

Rosenthal spewed a noisy breath. "This is the last thing I expected."

"It's the last thing any of us expected," Charlie said. "What now?"

"Now we wait for Monday," said the lawyer. "And I suppose it couldn't hurt to pray."

As if the interminable wait weren't bad enough, they had to do it under siege. The reporters lingered in front of the house like a stubborn, debilitating flu. Venturing outside, even to get the mail, meant an involuntary photo op and a hail of questions. On Sunday night, Charlie had stepped out the back door to dispose of a bundle of trash and found one of the two-legged rats rooting around in their garbage.

"I hope you didn't catch anything," he'd said with a straight, somber face. "I do experiments with lethal toxins. Some of the nastier waste was in there. If you feel at all sick in any way, you'd better get right to the hospital. Not that there's anything much they can do."

When he related the story to Jess, she fell in love with him all over again.

On Monday morning, Jess lurched awake as if someone had shot off a starter pistol in her head. Her heart was racing; and she fought to quell a rising tide of bile. She tried to put on a confident face for Danny's sake, but it felt lame and unconvincing, like a cheap paper Halloween mask.

Everything went wrong. Danny was fully dressed and ready to knot his tie when he noticed the broken button at his shirt collar. Jess ripped two pairs of brand-new pantyhose. She was so absorbed in trying to find a wearable pair among the sea of used ones rolled in her drawer that she forgot about the corn muffins warming in the oven. After the fire on the lawn, they were all doubly spooked by the burnt smell and billowing smoke.

As they prepared to leave, Prozac reminded them with a chuffed reproach that she had not yet completed her morning toilette. Jess let her out and waited impatiently while the dog circled the yard, seeking inspiration. On this, of all mornings, she was stricken with performance anxiety.

After that issue was resolved, Charlie fumed around the house for ten minutes, smacking drawers and cupboard doors, trying to track the car keys. Once he found them, in the ignition of all places, the Volvo refused to start. They had no choice but to take Charlie's Mustang, despite the extra, unwanted attention it had drawn since being described in countless articles about the case.

"Maybe all these glitches mean good luck," Charlie offered.

"Sure, Dad," Danny said. "Burnt muffins are bound to be the rabbits' feet of the new millennium."

They chattered nervous nonsense all the way to the courthouse. Charlie pulled in behind the building and they were admitted through a service bay, as they had been since the second day of jury selection. A guard conducted the required security check, tracing each of them in turn with the wand of a portable metal detector.

"Can't be too careful," he said as he passed the metal loop over Jess's torso. "Murder victim's husband went berserk in a courtroom in Cleveland last week and shot the judge. Missed his heart by inches."

The detector squealed. The guard stood back and waited while Jess emptied her pockets of stray change and keys.

"Plenty bloody though," the guard said. "Real mess."

As they entered the packed courtroom, Jess spotted several regulars: Victor Alton, Carla Levitan, John Slattery, Dolores Wainscott. The Beningsons were notably absent. Masking tape spanned their customary seats.

Danny took his place beside Grantham at the defense table. Sidney Rosenthal, who had shuffled her schedule to be here, approached as soon as Jess and Charlie took their places in the third row.

"Any news?" Jess asked.

The lawyer looked worried. "Nothing yet. Rodell is in talking to the judge, but Grantham says he has Harrigan's assurance that it's unrelated to the case."

Jess checked her watch. The morning session would start any minute. "What happens if Leo Beningson doesn't show up?"

"Harrigan would issue a bench warrant. Everything would be put on hold until the cops tracked him down."

The bailiff posed before the bench. "Oyez, oyez—"

"I'd better go. Hang in there." Rosenthal hurried to her seat.

The judge folded his hands. "I understand that your witness is not present, Mr. Rodell. What's the problem?"

"I don't know, Your Honor. My attempts to reach Mr. Beningson have been unsuccessful. I'm sure he's on the way."

"I certainly hope so."

Harrigan huddled with his clerk, flipping through files and signing documents. The noise level in the gallery climbed to a buzz saw of impatience. The judge hammered his gavel.

"Order!"

Through the hush came a rapid strike of footsteps. The Beningsons entered along with a dark-haired young stranger.

Harrigan nodded at the prosecutor. "You may call your witness to the stand, Mr. Rodell."

The young man set a proprietary hand on Leo Beningson's forearm. "If it please the court. My name is Peter Buettner. I'm here as counsel to the Beningsons. At this time, I request the opportunity to speak with Your Honor privately."

The name stirred a ripple of excitement. Buettner had been connected with a number of recent high-profile cases, including the murder of a studio head by an actress he'd rejected for a role and a lurid rape case involving a popular senator's son.

"The court is anxious to proceed, Counselor."

"It's a matter of considerable urgency, Your Honor. And it bears directly on my client's continued testimony."

"Very well. You may approach."

They conferred for several moments at the bench. Harrigan's expression went dark. "At this time, I'm going to call a brief recess."

The judge, black robes billowing, led Buettner to his chambers. The clerk ushered the jury out to wait in the lounge.

Ten minutes later, Harrigan's clerk summoned the prosecutor and Leo Beningson into the judge's chambers.

"This is unacceptable!" Grantham railed to the clerk. "The court has no right to keep the defense in the dark."

The clerk shrugged and left the room with a stack of pleadings. Grantham paced before the bench, muttering angrily.

Jess envisioned the doom hurtling toward them like a runaway train. There was no way to stop what they had set in motion. If the Beningson ploy failed, it could prove a huge advantage for the prosecution. Surely, it would prejudice the judge against Danny. Even if they managed to counteract Leo Beningson's damaging testimony, some dangerous wreckage would remain.

"What could they possibly be talking about for so long, Charlie? I feel like I'm going to explode," she rasped.

He set his jaw. "We're about to find out."

Harrigan returned to the bench and waited until the last of the jurors were seated. "New information has come to light that could change the entire complexion of this matter," said the judge.

The gallery erupted with a buzz of speculation.

Harrigan thumped the gavel furiously. "Order! I'll have order, or I'll clear this courtroom now." Silence settled slowly like a sail deprived of wind. The judge continued his rebuke. "I'll remind you that this is a court of law, not a sporting event. Anyone incapable of treating these proceedings with the proper respect and dignity will be ejected from the courtroom. The witness may resume the stand."

Beningson strode to the witness box.

"I'll remind you that you're still under oath, Mr. Beningson," said the judge.

"I understand, Your Honor."

Rodell stood. "You testified that you awoke and observed the defendant's car in your driveway on the night of August twenty-eighth of this year, Mr. Beningson. Is that correct?"

"It is."

"Please tell the court what transpired following that initial observation?"

Grantham shot from his seat in a fury. "Objection! The state has already covered that ground, Your Honor."

"I'll allow it. Proceed, Mr. Rodell."

Beningson shifted in the witness chair. "My daughter got out of the car. As I said, she appeared distraught. Naturally, seeing her like that upset me as well. I hurried downstairs to see what was wrong.

"Lisa was shaken and disheveled, her clothes in disarray. She was so hysterical she could barely speak. I saw that she was hurt, and I'm afraid I came to an understandable but erroneous conclusion."

"And what was that?" Rodell prompted.

"I assumed that Danny Magill had forced himself on Lisa, sexually that is, and injured her. When I suggested as much, my daughter concurred. At that point, of course I insisted on pressing charges."

"Have you now come to regret that action?"

"I have, sir," Beningson intoned.

"And why is that?"

Jess glanced at Lisa, who sat stone-faced across the aisle.

"Yesterday, my daughter told me that she could no longer allow the charges against Danny Magill to stand. She admitted that their sexual encounter had been consensual. She said she'd gone along with my misperception because she was fearful that otherwise I would be furious with her. Once the lie was set in motion, she didn't know how to withdraw it."

"I take it that Lisa is prepared to confirm your testimony?"

"She is, Your Honor."

"You may step down then. Call Lisa Beningson to the stand."

Trembling visibly, Lisa took her father's place in the witness box.

Harrigan echoed her vow. "The truth, the whole truth, and nothing but the truth. Do you understand the meaning of those words, Miss Beningson?"

"I do."

"Speak up, please. Are you now saying that the defendant stands falsely accused?"

"I am."

Harrigan's brow tensed in disapproval. "Did Daniel Magill assault you in any way?"

"No." Tears pooled in her eyes. "I wanted to be with Danny that night. It was my idea. When my father woke up and saw me with my clothes all messed up, I didn't know what to do. He was so mad I was afraid to do anything but agree with him. Next thing I knew, he was calling the police. I tried to stop him, but I couldn't. Please, forgive me, Danny," she cried. "I'm so sorry."

Harrigan faced her gravely. "How do you account for the bodily injuries you sustained that night, Miss Beningson? The court has seen documented evidence of those injuries, including photographs taken at the hospital hours after the alleged assault."

Lisa pulled a ragged breath. "I saw my father looking out from his bedroom window. I was sure he would know what happened if he saw me. He's always been able to tell what I'm thinking, what I've done. I was desperate to get into the house and hide somewhere, anywhere, so I ran as hard as I could. I lost my balance and tripped on the porch stairs. I fell on my fist, so it looked as if I'd been punched. Everyone thought that."

Harrigan's look was stern. "Did anyone coerce you to make this statement?"

"No."

"You have testified of your own free will?"

"I have."

"And this is the truth, the whole truth, as you know it, Miss Beningson? Under penalty of perjury, you are now testifying to the facts?"

"I am."

Harrigan dismissed her and addressed the prosecutor. "Mr. Rodell?"

"Your Honor, the state moves at this time for an immediate dismissal of all charges in the State versus Daniel Magill."

"In the interest of justice, the state's request is granted." The judge thumped his gavel once. "Case dismissed." He turned to Danny. "The court regrets the ordeal you have been put through. Good luck to you, young man. You're free to go."

FIFTY-THREE

Tucci had cleared his desk, collected the necessary forms, and said his farewells. The time had come to put his head on the block and wait for the blade to drop.

Klonsky had it sharpened and ready to go. "What is it this time, Sergeant? Wait. Let me guess. You want me to hire your goombah uncle to head a special Dementia Division? Terrific idea. The uniforms can be bulletproof bibs and Depends."

"I can't sit back and let the Magill kid take a fall he doesn't deserve, Chief. Orders aside, I'm going to turn over what I know."

"Really? May I ask who you plan to grace with your enlightenment, Detective?"

Tucci had twisted over the answer to that all weekend. "Whoever it takes. The family. Magill's lawyers. The press, if it comes to that."

The chief leaned back on his faux-leather throne. "Let me tell you a story, Sergeant. Once upon a time a wise old goat and a foolish younger goat were standing on a hill. Down below, the fog cleared and they saw a valley strewn with lots and lots of delectable garbage. The young goat got really excited and he said, 'Let's run down there and eat a tin can.' But the old goat said, 'I have a much better idea. Let's walk down slowly and eat as much as we want.' Do you catch my drift, Sergeant?"

"Frankly, no."

Klonsky snickered. "Didn't think you would. The moral of the story is that patience pays." He tossed a new file across the desk. "This is a nice normal, uncomplicated liquor store heist. Now, I want you to pack up your righteous indignation and get on it."

Tucci stared at the file in amazement. He didn't get this at all. He was supposed to be unemployed at this point, out on his insubordinate ear. For that, he'd been prepared. All weekend he'd agonized over his options. In the end he'd decided that the only reasonable choice was to follow his conscience off the cliff. A kid had precious little if she couldn't respect her parents. A parent had nothing at all to offer if he couldn't respect himself.

"What is it now, Tucci?"

"I was just wondering when you were planning to drop the other shoe."

Klonsky shook his head. "You know what your biggest problem is, Sergeant? Want to guess?"

"Stubbornness? Indigestion? Flat feet? Hay fever? You? I don't know, Chief. So many choices."

"Your biggest problem is that you don't keep up. If you listened to the news, you'd know that the Beningson girl recanted. The case against Danny Magill has been dropped. The prosecutor made a deal—Lisa Beningson's testimony in exchange for a guarantee that he wouldn't bring perjury charges against the father. The Beningsons are bound to make a public apology, and the girl gets a smack on the wrist. A couple of years suspended. Community service. The end."

"Sounds like a rotten deal for the Magills."

"Could be worse. The kid gets off. They get their good name back. What more could they expect?"

"Maybe some sweet revenge. Who knows? Anyway, doesn't matter that the case is closed. I'm still going to give them what I've got."

"No you're not. You are not going to cause this department embarrassment, and you are not going to encourage an expensive lawsuit. The case is finished and you're going to let it stay that way. Next up, you're going to learn how to listen, Tucci. If I have to punch more holes in that head of yours, you're going to learn."

Tucci set down his Glock and his shield, this time for good. "School's out, Chief. If *you'd* been listening, you would have heard the bell."

"I don't get you, Detective."

"Didn't think you would. Oh and by the way, that's Mr. Tucci from now on."

Leaving headquarters, he felt lighter somehow. This wasn't for him anymore. The more he thought about it, the more he warmed to the plan he and Marie had concocted late last night.

Gina was on the mend. His mama was not. In the past few years since Tucci's father died, her health had deteriorated. She contracted diabetes; her arthritis was worse. She needed more help in the store, the family kind. Marie could run her catering operation out of the kitchen. Tucci could help out between cases. He'd always wanted to try his hand as a private eye, concentrate on the digging part, leave the politics alone. If things went well, maybe Mule would join him in a couple of years.

The sun broke through a bank of low wispy clouds. The temperature had climbed to a record-breaking sixty-five. The day was dangerously close to perfect.

On the ride home, Jess kept turning to look at Danny. Yes, he was real. This was real. She had never felt so utterly lost and found, so high and low, so outraged and furious and relieved.

Clearly, Charlie felt it too. His features sagged with the weight of events. She could not remember the last time he had driven the Mustang with such extravagant care.

Yes, she could. It was on the crisp November morning when they brought Max home from the hospital as a newborn. This moment had the same air of frightening fragility. Leo Beningson had cracked. In fear for his precious reputation, he had induced Lisa to recant. The case was closed.

But was it really?

They were all enraged at the stunning injustice. As soon as they were able to extricate Danny from the congratulatory crush, Grantham had spirited them to a conference room. He'd explained that a deal had been struck. Leo Beningson would not be charged with perjury. Lisa would plead to filing a false report, a misdemeanor that carried a thousand-dollar fine and a maximum one-year term, which the prosecutor had agreed to suspend.

Just when she thought they were through with the nasty surprises, yet another one had slapped them in the face.

Jess was mostly relieved to find that the only surprise awaiting them at home was her parents' Cadillac. As soon as they opened the door, Max and Molly rushed Danny like a rock star. Pearl caught him next.

"You see, Jessie? I told you it was nonsense. Sometimes I wonder why you're so stubborn."

"Maybe she takes after her mother," Lou suggested.

Pearl vaporized her husband with a flash of the killer *punim*. Lou got visibly smaller. It was amazing. "Come now. You must be starved. I brought tons of food. Wait until you see."

Jess held back the groan. The last thing she felt like right now was Pearl's *boeuf à la merde*. "Why don't we save it for later, Mom? I thought we could go out for lunch and celebrate."

Pearl's look went sharp. "Fine. If that's what you want, I won't be insulted in the least."

No, she would be insulted *completely.* "Fine, Mom. Forget it. Since you went to all that trouble, we may as well eat here," Jess said.

"Excellent idea," said Pearl.

Prozac agreed. The dog dredged herself up from her nap and trotted into the kitchen. She shadowed Pearl, panting eagerly, as the old woman started to heap the table with towering platters of vegetables, potatoes, and meats. Humans might be a general nuisance, but they did have the grace to overindulge in food with pleasing regularity.

Jess went up to shed her court suit and pull on her favorite ratty sweats. As she passed through the foyer again, the doorbell rang. Maybe it was Libby or some other well-wisher. Any number of extra mouths would be welcome. Surely they had enough food should half the town decide to stop by.

She was startled to find Charlie's old nemesis, Detective Joe Tucci, standing on the porch. Panic gripped her by the throat. "What's wrong?"

He handed her a large manila envelope. "It's a bogus confession someone squeezed from Danny on the night he was arrested. That, and a tape. I figure it's yours. Could come in handy if you decide to sue or anything."

The thought had occurred to her, but she had dismissed it. The joy of retribution could not begin to offset the agony of keeping this ugly episode alive. What they needed most of all was to try to forget. "Thanks."

"I've got a kid in Danny's class. Her name's Gina." He pointed over his shoulder at the car, where a girl sat waiting. "She's a big fan of your boy. Please tell him Gina Tucci says hi, that she's glad things turned out okay."

"Maybe she'd like to come in and tell him herself."

Tucci shook his head. "She's been sick. That's why you saw me at the hospital. I've got to get her home to rest."

"Sure. I'll tell Danny. Thanks again."

Jess stuck the envelope out of sight beneath the couch and went back to the kitchen. Pearl had everyone's cheeks stuffed like nut-gathering squirrels.

"I thought of a French name for Grandpa," Max reported between bites. "We can call him Grandpa Louvres."

Lou ran an affectionate hand across Max's new-mown head. "Very good. That's a perfect name for an old museum like me."

"Listen to the baby. How adorable. What French name have you figured out for me, darling?"

Max hitched his scrawny shoulders. "I can't think of one, Grandma. Nothing goes with 'Pearl.'"

Her smile dissolved.

"That's because you're an original," Charlie offered, valiantly risking his safety to spirit his child out of harm's way.

That satisfied Pearl, though only for the moment. Then she realized to her horror that Jess had nothing on her plate. She dipped a serving fork into the stew pot and fished out a dripping slice of brisket.

Jess backed away. "Thanks anyway, Mom. I'm not hungry."

"Of course you are."

"No, Mom. I'm not. I'm pretty wound up right now. I'll eat later."

Pearl went coy. "Come on now. Have a little bite. What could it hurt?"

Jess's retreat was blocked by the kitchen cabinets. A cabinet knob poked her in the back like an accusing finger. She looked at her mother, that plump, ferocious little woman, and she saw no choice. And she bit.

As she did, it occurred to her that she did have a choice. She could be a damaged child, or she could let that go and accept Pearl for what she was and would always be. Stunningly flawed. Infuriating. The only mother she had.

"Isn't it delicious? Tell the truth," Pearl said.

Jess nodded in grudging agreement. In truth it tasted pretty good. Pearl must have changed her ancient recipe.

Danny had slipped into one of his brooding silences.

"Are you okay?" Jess asked.

"I don't know what I am. How can Lisa do this to me, put all of us through months of hell, then walk away like that?"

"She gets to live with herself. A life sentence," Charlie offered.

Danny considered that, then shrugged it off. No matter how harsh that might be, it didn't seem to cover the question. "Mind if I go upstairs? I promised Ryan and Em I'd call and tell them how things went."

"Of course, honey. Go," Jess said.

He hesitated. "Everything feels so weird. It's as if someone shot me to the dark side of the moon. Then, just as I'm getting used to that, I'm thrown back here. Everything looks familiar, but it doesn't feel that way. It's so confusing. What am I supposed to do now? What do I do about school, college applications, all that? How do I start to put my life back together?"

"Call your friends. Hang around. Give yourself time to get used to it," Charlie said.

"We all need that," Jess agreed.

Molly frowned. "It feels weird to me too. But I'm glad for you, Dan-boy."

"Did you really go to the moon?" Max asked. "Was it scary?"

"Of course he didn't really go to the moon. You are such a bean-brain, Max," said Molly.

"Takes one to know one."

Pearl started loading empty Tupperware into the cooler. "If you children will excuse us, I think we'd better hit the road. Jessie's exhausted."

"No I'm not, Mom."

"Of course you are. Look at you."

"I'm fine."

Pearl flapped a hand. "You don't know what you are."

Jess walked them out to the car. "Thanks for helping with the kids."

"A mother doesn't need thanks, Jessie. Don't be silly."

"Thanks anyway."

Molly had gone up to do homework. Max was out skipping pebbles on the pond. Soon it would be frozen over, firm and smooth enough to skate on. Jess could picture them gliding in slow lazy loops, coming in flame-cheeked and breathless to hot cocoa and a cozy fire.

Jess had always loved winter and summer best, seasons of well-defined extremes. Despite their virtues, spring and fall struck her as times of unsettling uncertainty, neither here nor there.

She tried to see past this endless day to the next step, but she could not dredge up the strength to pull everything into clear focus. What Charlie had suggested to Danny applied to them all. They had to hang around and get used to things, try to restore what had been, reconnect what had been broken, find their way again.

Charlie was sprawled on the couch in his study, half asleep. Jess curled up beside him and closed her eyes. A crushing wave of weariness washed over her. It had been a long, difficult fall. Her mother was right for once. She was exhausted.